PRAISE FOR THE NOVELS OF
THE BLACK DAGGER BROTHERHOOD

Lover Unbound
*Winner of the Romantic Times 2007 Reviewers' Choice Award
for Best Vampire Romance*

"The newest in Ward's ferociously popular Black Dagger Brotherhood series bears all the marks of a polished storyteller at home in her world. . . . This fix will give Brotherhood addicts a powerful rush." —*Publishers Weekly*

"Loss, sacrifice, and darkness continue to be major themes as one of Ward's most damaged heroes gets his story. Sex and violence make this tale of emotional redemption unusually graphic and powerful. Ward pulls no punches and delivers an extraordinary paranormal drama." —*Romantic Times* (Top Pick, 4½ stars)

Lover Revealed

"[T]hese erotic paranormals are well worth it, and frighteningly addictive. . . . It all works to great, page-turning effect. . . . In just two years, the . . . series [has] earned Ward an Anne Rice–style following, deservedly so." —*Publishers Weekly*

"It's tough to keep raising the bar in a series, but the phenomenal Ward manages to do just that! . . . The world of the Black Dagger Brotherhood continues to grow and become more layered, ramping up the tension, risk and passion. . . . Awesome stuff." —*Romantic Times* (Top Pick, 4½ stars)

continued . . .

Lover Awakened

Winner of the Romantic Times *2006 Reviewers' Choice Award
for Best Vampire Romance*

"Best new series I've read in years! Tautly written, wickedly sexy, and just plain fun."   —Lisa Gardner, *New York Times* bestselling author of *Hide*

"*Lover Awakened* is utterly absorbing and deliciously erotic. I found myself turning pages faster and faster—and then I wished I hadn't, because there was no more to read! The Brotherhood is the hottest collection of studs in romance, and I can't wait for the next one!"
          —Angela Knight, *USA Today* bestselling author of *Master of Dragons*

"Ward pulls no punches in this dark, dangerous, and at times tragic series. Waiting for successive installments is getting harder and harder."
          —*Romantic Times* (Top Pick, 4½ stars)

Lover Eternal

"Ward wields a commanding voice perfect for the genre, and readers new to the world of the Black Dagger Brotherhood should hold on tight for an intriguing, adrenaline-pumping ride featuring a race of warrior vampires who fill enemies with terror and women with desire. Like any good thrill ride, the pace changes with a tender story of survival and hope and leaves readers begging for more. Fans of L. A. Banks, Laurell K. Hamilton, and Sherrilyn Kenyon will add Ward to their must-read list."   —*Booklist*

"[An] extremely intense and emotionally powerful tale. . . . Ward's paranormal world is, among other things, colorful, dangerous, and richly conceived. . . . Intricate plots and believable characters."   —*Romantic Times* (Top Pick, 4½ stars)

Dark Lover

"It's not easy to find a new twist on the vampire myth, but Ward succeeds beautifully. This dark and compelling world is filled with enticing romance as well as perilous adventure. With myriad possibilities to choose from, the Black Dagger Brotherhood series promises tons of thrills and chills."

—*Romantic Times* (Top Pick, 4½ stars)

"A dynamite new vampire series—delicious, erotic, and thrilling! J. R. Ward has created a wonderful cast of characters, with a sexy, tormented, to-die-for hero. . . . A fabulous treat for romance readers!"

—Nicole Jordan, *New York Times* bestselling author of *Touch Me with Fire*

"J. R. Ward has a great style of writing, and she shines. . . . You will lose yourself in this world; it is different, creative, dark, violent, and flat-out amazing."

—All About Romance

"An awesome, instantly addictive debut novel. It's a midnight whirlwind of dangerous characters and mesmerizing erotic romance. The Black Dagger Brotherhood owns me now. Dark fantasy lovers, you just got served."

—Lynn Viehl, author of *Twilight Fall*

THE
BLACK
DAGGER

BROTHERHOOD

An Insider's Guide

J. R. WARD

NAL
NEW AMERICAN LIBRARY

New American Library
Published by New American Library, a division of Penguin Group (USA) Inc.,
375 Hudson Street, New York, New York 10014, USA
Penguin Group (Canada), 90 Eglinton Avenue East, Suite 700, Toronto,
Ontario M4P 2Y3, Canada (a division of Pearson Penguin Canada Inc.)
Penguin Books Ltd., 80 Strand, London WC2R 0RL, England
Penguin Ireland, 25 St. Stephen's Green, Dublin 2, Ireland (a division of Penguin Books Ltd.)
Penguin Group (Australia), 250 Camberwell Road, Camberwell, Victoria 3124,
Australia (a division of Pearson Australia Group Pty. Ltd.)
Penguin Books India Pvt. Ltd., 11 Community Centre, Panchsheel Park, New Delhi – 110 017, India
Penguin Group (NZ), 67 Apollo Drive, Rosedale, North Shore 0632,
New Zealand (a division of Pearson New Zealand Ltd.)
Penguin Books (South Africa) (Pty.) Ltd., 24 Sturdee Avenue,
Rosebank, Johannesburg 2196, South Africa

Penguin Books Ltd., Registered Offices: 80 Strand, London WC2R 0RL, England

First published by New American Library, a division of Penguin Group (USA) Inc.

First Printing, October 2008
10 9 8 7 6 5 4 3 2 1

 REGISTERED TRADEMARK—MARCA REGISTRADA

LIBRARY OF CONGRESS CATALOGING-IN-PUBLICATION DATA
Ward, J. R. (Jessica Bird)
The Black Dagger Brotherhood : an insider's guide / J. R. Ward.
p. cm.
ISBN 978-0-451-22500-9
1. Ward, J. R. (Jessica Bird). Black dagger brotherhood. 2. Ward, J. R. (Jessica Bird)—
Authorship. 3. Fantasy fiction—Authorship. I. Title.
PS3623.A73227B55 2008
813'.6—dc22   2008023931

Set in Goudy Old Style
Designed by Patrice Sheridan

Printed in the United States of America

To the Brothers

ACKNOWLEDGMENTS

WITH THANKS TO:

Kara Cesare, without whom this whole BDB thing couldn't possibly have gone as far as it has. You are the champion and the cheerleader and the chess master of everything I do—and I'll stop the gushing there, otherwise this book will be longer than even Phury's.

Everyone at New American Library, especially:
Claire Zion, Kara Welsh, and Leslie Gelbman, Craig Burke and Jodi Rosoff, Lindsay Nouis, the great Anthony, and the wonderful Rachel Granfield, who deals so graciously with my twenty-pound manuscripts.

Steve Axelrod, who's the captain of my ship.

Monstrous thanks to The Incomparable Suzanne Brockmann (I'm getting her a sash with that on it and a sparkly crown), Christine Feehan (whose obelisk I'm building as we speak) and her amazing family (Domini, Manda, Denise, and Brian), Sue Grafton, aka Mother Sue, Linda Francis Lee, Lisa Gardner, and *all* my other writer friends.

Once again a huge thank-you to the best dental teams in the world: Scott A. Norton, DMD, MSD, and Kelly Eichler, along with Kim and Rebecca and Crystal; and David B. Fox, DMD, and Vickie Stein.

D.L.B., who's the best metal-studded, ass-kicking baby boy in the whole world. xxx mummy N.T.M., whose idea this whole *Insider's Guide* was and who did so much work on it—and whose kind nature is bested only by his patience and his sense of humor.

Dr. Jessica Andersen—my CP and confidante and sparring partner.
LeElla Scott—you have too many nicknames at this point to list.
So I'll just go with the most important one: Bestie.
And Kaylie's momma—who's still my Idol.

As always to Mom, Boat, and the Boo.

CONTENTS

THE
BLACK
DAGGER
BROTHERHOOD
An Insider's Guide

Father Mine

ONE

"So, Bella looks good."

At the counter of the Brotherhood's kitchen, Zsadist picked up a knife, squeezed a head of romaine lettuce together, and started drawing the blade through at one-inch intervals. "Yeah, she does."

He liked Doc Jane. Hell, he owed her. But he had to remind himself of his manners: It would be damn tacky to bite the head off a female who was not only your brother's *shellan*, but who had saved the love of your life from bleeding out on the birth table.

"She's recovered beautifully in the last two months." Doc Jane watched him from the table across the way, her *Marcus Welby, M.D.*, bag beside her ghostly hand. "And Nalla's thriving. Man, vampire young progress so much faster than human babies. Cognitively, it's like she's nine months old."

"They're doing great." He kept slicing, moving his hand down and through, down and through. On the far side of the blade, the leaves sprang free in curly green ribbons like they were clapping at having been liberated.

"And how are you doing with the whole dad thing—"

"Fuck!"

Dropping the knife, he cursed and brought up the hand that had been on the lettuce. The cut was deep, down to the bone, and his blood was red as it welled up and dripped off his skin.

Doc Jane came over to him. "Okay, let's get you to the sink."

To her credit, she didn't touch him on the arm or try to lead him with a push on his shoulder blade; she just loomed and pointed the way to Kohler-land.

He still didn't like anyone but Bella putting their hands on his body, al-though he had made some progress. Now, if the contact was unexpected, his first move wasn't going for a concealed weapon and capping whoever had let their palms do the walking.

When they were in front of the sink, Doc Jane cranked the thing's throttle over and fired it back so that there was a warm rush landing in the deep porcelain belly.

"Under," she said.

He extended his arm and put his thumb into the hot water. The slice burned like a bitch, but he didn't wince. "Let me guess. Bella asked you to come talk to me just now."

"Nope." When he shot her a look, the good doctor shook her head. "I exam-ined her and the baby. That was it."

"Well, good. Because I'm fine."

"Had a feeling you'd say that." Doc Jane crossed her arms over her chest and regarded him with a stare that made him want to build a brick wall between the two of them. Whether in a solid state or translucent as she was at the moment, it didn't matter. When you got eyeballed by the female like this, it was as if you'd been sandblasted. No wonder she and V got along.

"She did mention you won't feed from her."

Z shrugged. "Nalla needs what her body can provide more than I do."

"It's not an either-or situation, though. Bella's young and healthy and she has great eating habits. And you've let her feed."

"Of course. Anything for her. Her and her baby."

There was a long silence. Then, "Maybe you want to talk to Mary?"

"About what." He shut the water off and shook his palm out over the sink. "Just because I'm respectful of the demands on my *shellan*, you think I need a shrink? What the hell?"

He snapped a paper towel free from the roll mounted under the cabinets and dried his hand.

"Who's the salad for, Z?" the doctor asked.

"What?"

"The salad. Who's it for?"

He pulled out the trash bin and pitched the towel inside. "Bella. It's for Bella. Look, no offense, but—"

"And when's the last time you ate?"

He put his hands up, all "Stop! In the Name of Love." "Enough. I know you mean well, but I'm a short fuse, and the last thing any of us needs is Vishous com-ing after me because I snapped at you. I get your point—"

"Look at your hand."

He glanced down. Blood was running from the pad of his thumb onto his wrist and his forearm. If he hadn't had a short-sleeved T-shirt on, the shit would have been pooling at his elbow. Instead, it was trickling onto the terra-cotta tile.

Doc Jane's voice was annoyingly level, her logic offensively sound. "You are in a dangerous line of work where you rely on your body to do things that keep you from getting killed. You don't want to talk to Mary? Fine. But you need to make some concessions physically. That cut should have closed by now. It hasn't, and I'm willing to bet it bleeds for the next hour or so." She shook her head. "Here's my deal. Wrath's appointed me as the Brotherhood's personal physician. You screw around with eating and feeding and sleeping such that it impairs your performance, I will bench your ass."

Z stared at the glossy red droplets seeping up from the wound. The river of them went straight over the inch-wide black slave band that had been tattooed on his wrist nearly two hundred years ago. He had one on his other arm and another around his neck.

Reaching forward, he peeled off another section of paper towel. The blood wiped off just fine, but there was no getting rid of what his sick bitch Mistress had marked him with. The ink was imbedded in his tissue, put there to show that he was property to be used, not an individual to live.

For no good reason, he thought of Nalla's infant skin, so incredibly smooth and completely unmarred. Everyone remarked on how soft it was. Bella. All his brothers. All the *shellans* of the house. It was one of the first things they commented on when they held her. That and how she was like a down pillow, she was so huggable.

"Have you ever tried to get those removed?" Doc Jane said softly.

"They can't be removed," he said briskly, dropping his hand. "The ink has salt in it. It's permanent."

"But have you ever tried? There are lasers now that—"

"I'd better go take care of this cut so I can finish here." He grabbed another paper towel. "I'll need some gauze and tape—"

"I have that in my bag." She turned to go over to the table. "I have everything—"

"No, thanks, I'll take care of it myself."

Doc Jane stared up at him, her eyes clear. "I don't care if you're independent. But stupidity I won't stand for. We clear? That bench has your name on it."

If she'd been one of his brothers, he would have bared his fangs and hissed at her. But he couldn't do that to Doc Jane, and not just because she was a female. Thing was, there was nothing to push back at with her. She was just objective medical opinion.

"We clear?" she prompted, utterly unimpressed by how fierce he had to be looking.

"Yeah. I hear you."

"Good."

"He has these nightmares. . . . God, the nightmares."

Bella leaned down and stuffed the dirty diaper into the bin. On the way back up, she snagged another Huggies from under the dressing table and brought out the talc and the baby wipes. Palming Nalla's ankles, she hipped up her daughter's little butt, did a fast-and-dash sweep with the cloth, sprinkled some powder, then slid the fresh diaper into place.

From across the nursery, Phury's voice was low. "Nightmares about being a blood slave?"

"Has to be it." She put Nalla's clean bottom down and taped up the sides of the Huggies. "Because he won't talk to me about it."

"Has he been eating? Feeding?"

Bella shook her head as she did up the snaps on Nalla's onesie. The thing was pastel pink and had a white skull and crossbones appliquéd on it. "Not much on the food and no on feeding. It's like . . . I don't know, the day she was born, he seemed so amazed and engaged and happy. But then some kind of switch was triggered and he just closed up. It's almost as bad as it was in the beginning." She stared down at Nalla, who was patting at the pattern on her little chest. "I'm sorry I asked you to come down here. . . . I just don't know what else to do."

"I'm glad you did. I'm always there for you both, you know that."

Cradling Nalla on her shoulder, she turned around. Phury was leaning against the creamy wall of the nursery, his huge body breaking up the pattern of hand-painted bunnies and squirrels and fawns.

"I don't want to put you in an awkward position. Or take you away from Cormia unnecessarily."

"You haven't." He shook his head, his multicolored hair gleaming. "If I'm quiet, it's because I'm trying to think of what the best thing to do is. Talking with him isn't always the solution."

"True. But I'm running out of both ideas and patience." Bella went over and sat in the rocker, repositioning the young in her arms.

Nalla's brilliant yellow eyes stared up out of her angelic little face, and recognition was in her stare. She knew exactly who was with her . . . and who wasn't. The awareness had come in the last week or so. And changed everything.

"He won't hold her, Phury. He won't even pick her up."

"Are you serious?"

Bella's tears made her daughter's face wavy. "Damn it, when is this post-partum depression going to lift? I well up at almost nothing."

"Wait, not even once? He hasn't gotten her out of the crib or—"

"He won't touch her. Crap, will you hand me a frickin' tissue." When the Kleenex box got in range, she snapped one free and pressed it to her eyes. "I'm such a mess. All I can think about is Nalla going through her whole life wondering why her father doesn't love her." She cursed softly as more tears came. "Okay, this is ridiculous."

"It's not ridiculous," he said. "It's really not."

Phury knelt down, keeping the tissues front and center. Absurdly, Bella noticed that the box had the picture of an alley of leafy trees with a lovely dirt road stretching off into the distance. On either side, flowering bushes with magenta blooms made the maples look like they were wearing tulle ballet skirts.

She imagined walking down the dirt road . . . to a place that was far better than where she was now.

She took another tissue. "The thing is, I grew up without a father, but at least I had Rehvenge. I can't imagine what it would be like to have a dad who was alive but dead to you." With a little cooing sound, Nalla yawned wide and snuffled, rubbing her face with the back of her fist. "Look at her. She's so innocent. And she responds to love so well . . . I mean . . . Oh, for God's sake, I'm going to buy stock in Kleenex."

With a disgusted noise she flipped another tissue free. To avoid looking at Phury as she blotted, she let her eyes wander around the cheery room that had been a walk-in closet before the birth. Now it was all about the young, all about family, with the pine rocker Fritz had hand-made, and the matching dressing table, and the crib that was still festooned with multicolored bows.

When her stare landed on the low-slung bookcase with all its big, flat books, she felt even worse. She and the other Brothers were the ones who read to Nalla, who settled the young on a lap and unfolded shiny covers and spoke rhyming words.

It was never her father, even though Z had learned to read almost a year ago.

"He doesn't refer to her as his daughter. It's my daughter. To him, she's mine, not ours."

Phury made a disgusted sound. "FYI, I'm trying to resist the urge to pound him out right now."

"It's not his fault. I mean, after all he went through . . . I should have expected this, I guess." She cleared her throat. "I mean, this whole pregnancy thing wasn't planned, and I wonder . . . maybe he resents me and regrets her?"

"You're his miracle. You know you are."

She took more tissues and shook her head. "But it's not just me anymore. And I won't raise her here if he can't come to terms with the two of us. . . . I will leave him."

"Whoa, I think that's a little premature—"

"She's beginning to recognize folks, Phury. She's starting to understand she's being shut out. And he's had three months to get used to the idea. Over time, he's gotten worse, not better."

As Phury cursed, she lifted her eyes to the brilliant yellow stare of her *hellren's* twin. God, that citrine color was what shone out of her daughter's face as well, so there was no looking at Nalla without thinking of her father. And yet . . .

"Seriously," she said, "what's this all going to be like a year from now? There is nothing more lonely than sleeping next to someone you're missing as if they were gone. Or having that as a father."

Nalla reached up with her fat hand and grabbed onto one of the tissues.

"I didn't know you were here."

Bella's eyes shot to the doorway. Zsadist was standing in it, a tray in his hands bearing salad and a pitcher of lemonade. There was a white bandage on his left hand and a whole lot of don't-ask on his face.

Looming there, on the verge of the nursery, he was exactly as she had fallen in love and mated him: a gigantic male with a skull trim and a scar down his face and slave bands at his wrists and neck and nipple rings that showed through his tight black T-shirt.

She thought of him the first time she'd seen him, punching a bag down in the training center's gym. He'd been viciously fast on his feet, his fists flying faster than her eye could track, the bag being driven back from the beating. And then, without even a pause, he'd unsheathed a black dagger from his chest holster and stabbed the thing he'd been pounding, ripping the blade through the bag's leather flesh, the stuffing falling free like the internal organs of a *lesser*.

She'd come to learn that the fierce fighter wasn't all there was to him. Those hands of his had great kindness in them as well. And that ruined face with its distorted upper lip had smiled and looked at her with love.

"I came down to see Wrath," Phury said, getting to his feet.

Z's eyes flicked to the Kleenex box his twin held, then went to the wad of tissues in Bella's hand. "Did you."

As he came in and put the tray down on the bureau where Nalla's clothes were kept, he didn't look at his daughter. She, however, knew he was in the room. The young turned her face in his direction, her unfocused eyes pleading, her chubby little arms reaching for him.

Z stepped back out into the hall. "Have a good meeting. I'm going out hunting."

"I'll walk you to the door," Phury said.

"No time. Later." Z's eyes met Bella's for a moment. "I love you."

Bella hugged Nalla closer to her heart. "I love you, too. Be safe."

He nodded once and then he was gone.

TWO

As Zsadist came awake in a panic, he tried to calm his breathing and figure out where he was, but his eyes weren't much help. Everything was dark . . . he was enveloped in a dense, cold blackness that, no matter how hard he strained his vision, he couldn't see through. He could have been in a bedroom, out in a field . . . in a cell.

He'd come out of sleep like this many, many times. For a hundred years as a blood slave, he'd woken up in a panicked blindness and wondered what was going to be done to him and by whom. After he was free? Nightmares caused him to do the same thing.

In both cases it was such bullshit. When he'd been the Mistress's property, worrying about the who and the what and the when hadn't helped him. The abuse was inevitable whether he was faceup or facedown on the bedding platform: He was used until she and her studs were sated; then he was left to lie degraded and leaking, alone in his prison.

And now, with the bad dreams? Waking up in the same terror he'd been in as a slave just validated the past horrors his subconscious insisted on burping up.

At least . . . he thought he was dreaming.

True panic hit him as he wondered which dark owned him. Was it the dark of the cell? Or the dark of his bedroom with Bella? He didn't know. Both looked the same when there were no visual clues to decipher and only the sound of his pounding heart in his ears.

Solution? He'd try to move his arms and legs. If they were unchained, if they were not shackled, it was just a case of being caught in his mind's choke hold once again, the past reaching out through the graveyard dirt of his memories and grabbing him with bony hands. As long as he could shift his arms and legs through clean sheets, he was okay.

Right. Move his arms and legs.

His arms. His legs. Needed to move.

Move.

Oh, God . . . damn you, move.

His limbs didn't budge, and in the paralysis of his body the clawed truth ripped through him. He was in the damp darkness of the Mistress's cell, chained on his back, thick iron cuffs keeping him on the bedding platform. She and her lovers would be coming for him again, and they would do to him whatever they wanted, staining his skin, soiling the inside of him.

He moaned, the pathetic sound vibrating up from his chest and breaching his mouth like it was relieved to be free of him. Bella was the dream. He lived in the nightmare.

Bella was the dream. . . .

The footsteps approached from the hidden stairwell that ran down from the Mistress's bedroom, the sound echoing, getting louder. And there were more than one set on the stone steps.

With an animal's horror, his muscles grabbed and pulled against his skeleton, fighting desperately to get loose from the dirty binding of flesh that was about to be fondled and invaded and used. Sweat broke out on his face, and his stomach seized, bile marshaling an assault up his esophagus to the base of his tongue—

Someone was crying.

No . . . wailing.

A young's cry sounded out from the far corner of the cell.

His fight stalled while he wondered what an infant was doing in this place. The Mistress had no offspring, nor had she been pregnant during the years he had been owned by her—

No . . . wait . . . he had brought the young here. It was his young who cried—and the Mistress was going to find the infant. She was going to find the infant and . . . Oh, God.

This was his fault. He had brought the young here.

Get the young out. Get the young—

Z curled his fists and punched his elbows into the bedding platform, heaving with every ounce of strength he had. The power came from more than his body; it was born of his will. With a massive surge, he . . .

. . . got absolutely nowhere. The shackles cut through his wrists and his ankles down to his bones, slicing through his skin so that blood mixed with his cold sweat.

As the door opened, the young was crying and he couldn't save her. The Mistress was going to—

Light poured over him, rocketing him into true consciousness.

He was off his mated bed like he'd been bootlicked by a Chevy, landing in a fighting stance with fists up at his chest, shoulders drawn in steel knots, thighs ready to spring.

Bella slowly eased back from the lamp she'd turned on, as if she didn't want to spook him.

He looked around the bedroom. There was, as usual, no one to fight, but he'd woken everyone up. In the corner, Nalla was in her crib crying, and he'd scared the ever-loving shit out of his *shellan*. Again.

There was no Mistress. None of her consorts. No cell or chains stretching him out on a bedding platform.

No young in his cell with him.

Bella slipped out of bed and went over to the crib, scooping up a red-faced and screaming Nalla. The daughter, however, would have nothing of the comfort offered. The young held its little chubby arms straight out for Zsadist, wailing for its father, tears streaming.

Bella waited for a moment, as if she were hoping this time would be different and he would go over and take the child into his arms and comfort the infant who so clearly wanted him.

Z backed away until his shoulder blades hit the far wall, tucking his arms around his chest.

Bella turned and whispered to her darling one as she went into the adjoining nursery. The door muffled the daughter's whimpering as it slid shut.

Z let himself slide down until his ass hit the floor. "Fuck."

He rubbed his skull trim back and forth, then let both hands hang off his knees. After a moment, he realized he was sitting as he had back in the cell, his back against the corner facing the door, his knees up, his naked body shivering.

He looked at the slave bands around his wrists. The black was so dense in his skin, so solid, it was like the iron cuffs he'd once worn.

After God only knew how long, the door to the nursery slid open and Bella came back with the young. Nalla was asleep again, but as Bella laid her out in the crib, it was with care, as if a bomb were about to go off at any moment.

"I'm sorry," he said softly, rubbing his wrists.

Bella put on a dressing gown and went to the door that led out into the hall. With her hand on the knob, she looked back at him, her eyes remote. "I can't say this is okay anymore."

"I'm really sorry about the dreams—"

"I'm talking about Nalla. I can't say that your shunning her is all right . . . that I understand, that it's going to get better and I'll be patient. The fact is, she is your child as well as mine, and it kills me to see you pulling away from her. I know what you went through, and I don't want to be callous, but . . . everything's different for me now. I need to think in terms of what's good for her, and having a father who won't even touch her? That's not it."

Z flexed open both his hands and stared at his palms, trying to imagine picking the young up.

The slave bands seemed huge to him. Huge . . . and contagious.

The word wasn't *won't*, he thought. It was *can't*.

The thing was if he did comfort Nalla and play with her and read to her, it would mean she had him for a father, and his legacy was nothing you wanted to saddle a young with. Bella's born daughter deserved better than that.

"I need you to decide what you want to do," Bella said. "If you can't be her father, I'm leaving you. I know that sounds harsh, but . . . I have to think of what's best for her. I love you and I will always love you, but it's not about me anymore."

For a moment, he didn't think he'd heard right. Leaving him?

Bella stepped out into the hall of statues. "I'm going to go grab something to eat. Don't worry about her—I'll be right back."

She closed the door behind her without a sound.

When night fell about two hours later, the way that door had shut so quietly was still banging around Z's head.

Standing in front of his closet full of black shirts and leathers and shitkickers, he sought his inner intentions, chasing them around the maze of his emotions.

Sure, he wanted to overcome the head fuck with his daughter. Of course he did.

It was just insurmountable: What had been done to him might have been in the past, but all he had to do was look at his wrists to see that he was still dirtied by it all—and he didn't want that kind of shit anywhere near Nalla. He'd had the same problem with Bella in the beginning of their relationship, and had managed to get over it with his *shellan*, but the implications were more grave with the young: Z was the corporeal embodiment of the kind of cruelty that existed in the world. He didn't want his daughter to know that such depths of depravity existed, much less expose her to their aftereffects.

Fuck.

What the hell was he going to do when she got to be old enough to look up into his face and ask him why he was scarred and how he'd gotten that way? What would he do when she wanted to know why he had black bands on his skin? What was her uncle Phury going to reply when she asked him why he was missing a leg?

Z dragged on a shirt and a pair of leathers, then pulled on his chest holster of daggers and opened the gun closet. As he took out a pair of SIG Sauer forties, he checked them quickly. He used to palm nines—shit, he used to fight with nothing but his bare hands. Ever since Bella had come into his life, however, he'd been more careful.

And this, of course, was the other part of his brain twist. He killed for a living. That was his job. Nalla was going to have to grow up worrying about him every night. How could she not? Bella did.

He shut the gun closet and relocked it, then tucked the muzzles into his hip holster, checked his daggers, and pulled on his leather jacket.

He glanced over to the crib where Nalla was still sleeping.

Guns. Blades. Throwing stars. Christ, the infant needed to be surrounded by rattles and plush teddy bears.

Bottom line was, he wasn't cut out to be a father. Never had been. Biology, however, had jacked him into the role, and now they were all chained to his past: As much as he couldn't imagine living without Bella, there was no fathoming how he could be the dad Nalla deserved.

With a frown, he pictured Nalla's coming-out party, something all females of the *glymera* had one year after their transitions. The daughter always had the first dance with her father, and he saw Nalla dressed in a flowing red gown, her multi-colored hair up, rubies at her throat . . . and himself with his fucked-up face and his slave bands peeking out of the cuffs of his tuxedo.

Great. Helluva picture.

Cursing, Z went to the bathroom, where Bella was getting ready for the evening. He was going to tell her that he was heading out on a follow-up from the night before and that as soon as he was finished, he'd come home and they would talk. As he looked around the corner, though, he stopped dead.

In the mist that lingered from her shower, Bella was drying off her body. Her hair was wrapped in a towel, her long neck exposed, her creamy shoulders working this way and that as she made quick work with the terry cloth across her back. Her breasts swayed, catching his eyes, hardening him.

Fuck him, but as he watched her, all he could think about was sex. God, she was beautiful. He'd liked her rounded by the pregnancy, and he liked her as she was now, too. She'd thinned out quickly after Nalla's birth, her stomach as tight as it had been before, her hips regaining their lean contours. Her breasts were bigger, though, the nipples a deeper pink, the swells heavier.

His cock punched into his leathers, a criminal wanting out of jail.

As he rearranged himself, he realized he and Bella hadn't been together since well before the birth. The pregnancy had been difficult, and afterward Bella had needed time to heal and had been rightfully consumed with taking care of her infant.

He missed her. Wanted her. Thought she was still the most spectacularly erotic female on the face of the planet.

Bella dropped her robe on the counter, faced the mirror, and stared at herself. With a grimace, she leaned forward and prodded at her cheekbones, her jawline, under her chin. Straightening, she frowned and turned to the side, sucking in her stomach.

He cleared his throat to get her attention. "I'm about to go out now."

At the sound of his voice, Bella scrambled to get her robe. Pulling it on quickly, she tied the sash and dragged the lapels in close to her throat. "I didn't know you were there."

"Well . . ." His erection deflated. "I am."

"Are you leaving?" she said as she unwrapped her hair.

She hadn't even heard his words, he thought. "Yeah, I'm about to go out now. I'm going to be reachable, though, as always—"

"We'll be fine." She bent over and started rubbing her hair dry, the towel's flapping loud to his ear.

Even though she was only ten feet away, he couldn't reach her. Couldn't ask her why she hid herself from him. Was too afraid of what the answer might be.

"Have a good evening," he said roughly. He waited a moment, praying that she would look up at him, smile at him a little, give him a kiss on his way out into the war.

"You, too." She flipped her hair up and reached for the hair dryer. "Be safe."

"I will."

Bella flicked on the hair dryer and picked up her brush to look busy as Z turned and walked out. When she was sure he had to be gone, she stopped the pretense, turning off the dryer and letting it fall to the marble counter.

Her heart ached so badly, she was sick to her stomach, and as she stared at her reflection, she wanted to throw something at the glass.

The two of them hadn't been together, as in *been* together, since . . . God, it must have been four or five months ago, before she'd started spotting.

He didn't think of her sexually anymore. Not since Nalla had come. It was as if the birth had turned off that part of their relationship for him. When he touched her now, it was as a brother would—gently, with compassion.

Never with passion.

At first, she'd thought it was maybe because she wasn't as thin as she'd been, but in the last four weeks her body had bounced back.

At least, she thought it had. Maybe she was fooling herself?

Loosening the robe, she parted the two halves, turned to the side, and measured her stomach. Back when her father had been around, back when she'd been growing up, the importance of females in the *glymera* being thin had been drilled into her, and even after his death all those years ago, those stern warnings about being fat stuck with her.

Bella wound herself back up, tying the sash tight.

Yes, she wanted Nalla to have her father, and that was the primary concern. But she missed her *hellren*. The pregnancy had happened so quickly that they hadn't had the chance to enjoy a lovebird period where they just reveled in each other's company.

As she picked up the dryer and flicked on the switch again, she tried not to count the number of days since he'd last reached for her as a male would. It had been so long since he'd fished through the sheets with his big, warm hands and woken her up with lips on the back of her neck and a hard arousal pressing into her hip.

She hadn't reached for him, either, true. But she wasn't taking for granted the kind of reception she'd receive. The last thing she needed now was to be turned down because he wasn't attracted to her anymore. She was already an emotional wreck as a mother, thank you very much. Failure on the female front was too much to handle.

When her hair was dry, she gave it a quick brush and then went out to check on Nalla. Standing over the crib, looking at their daughter, she couldn't believe things had come down to ultimatums. She'd always known that Z would have continuing issues after what he'd been put through, but it had never dawned on her that they couldn't bridge his past.

Their love had seemed like it would be enough to get them through everything.

Maybe it wasn't.

THREE

The house was set back from the dirt road and crowded by overgrown bushes and shaggy trees with brown leaves. The design of the thing was a hodgepodge of various architectural styles, with the only unifying element being that they'd all been repro'd badly: It had a roof like a Cape Cod, but was on one story like a ranch; it had pillars on the front porch like a colonial, but was sided in plastic like a trailer; it was set up on its lot like a castle and yet had the nobility of a busted trash bin.

Oh, and it was painted green. Like, Jolly Green Giant green.

Twenty years ago the place had probably been built by a city guy with bad taste looking to start life over as a gentleman farmer. Now everything about it was run down, except for one thing: The door was made out of shiny, fresh-as-a-daisy stainless steel and reinforced like something you'd find in a psych hospital or a jail.

And the windows were boarded up with rows of two-by-sixes.

Z crouched behind the rotted shell of what had been a '92 Trans Am and waited for the clouds above to pull together and cover the moon so he could move in. Across the weedy lawn and gravel driveway, Rhage was behind an oak.

Which was really the only tree big enough to hide the mofo.

The Brotherhood had found the site the night before by stroke of luck. Z had been downtown patrolling the needle park under Caldwell's bridges when he'd caught a pair of thugs dumping a body into the Hudson River. The disposal had been quick and professional: Nondescript sedan drove up, two guys in black hoodies got out and went to the trunk, body was head-and-footed, remains were tossed into the current.

Splish-splash, taking a bath.

Z had been downstream by about ten yards, so when the dead guy floated by, he saw from its grimacing mouth that it was a human male. Normally this would have been cause for doing absolutely nothing at all. If some man had been *God-father*'d, that was not his biz.

But the wind changed directions and brought him a whiff of something cotton-candy sweet.

There were only two things Z knew of that smelled like that and walked upright: old ladies and his race's enemy. Considering it was unlikely that Betty White and Bea Arthur were under those hoods channeling their inner Tony Soprano, that meant there were two *lessers* up ahead. So the sitch was very much on Z's list of things to do.

With perfect timing, the pair of slayers got into an argument. While they went nose-to-nose and did a couple punch-shoves, Z dematerialized to the pylon nearest the sedan. The license plate on the Impala junker read 818 NPA, and there didn't appear to be any other passenger of either the stiff or the quick variety.

In the blink of an eye, he dematerialized again, this time to the roof of the warehouse that flanked the bridge. From his crow's-eye view, he waited with his phone to his ear and a line open to Qhuinn, bracing himself against the rush of wind coming up the building's ass.

Lessers didn't ordinarily kill humans. It was a waste of time, for one thing, because it didn't gain you points with the Omega, and a lot of hassle if you got caught, for another. That being said, if some guy saw something he shouldn't have, the slayers wouldn't hesitate to cash-and-carry him to his royal reward.

When the Impala finally came out from under the bridge, it took a right and headed away from downtown. Z spoke into his phone, and a moment later a black Hummer emerged right where the Impala had come out.

Qhuinn and John Matthew had been taking the night off with Blay at Zero-Sum, but those boys were always ready for action. As soon as Z had called, the three raced for Qhuinn's brand-new wheels, which had been parked a block and a half away.

At Z's direction, the boys floored it to catch up with the sedan. While they closed in, Z kept an eye on the *lessers*, dematerializing from building top to building top as their POS made its way down the river's edge. Thank fuck the slayers didn't highway it or they might have gotten away.

Qhuinn had skills behind the wheel and once his Hummer was tailing the SUV reliably, Z stopped his Spidey shit and let the boys do the work. About ten miles later, Rhage took over from them in his GTO just to mix it up and reduce the chance the *lessers* would catch on that they were being tracked.

Just before dawn, Rhage had followed them to this place, but it had been too close to daylight to do any kind of infiltration.

Tonight was follow-up. Big time.

And what do you know, the Impala was sitting pretty in the driveway.

As the clouds finally got their act together, Z gave the nod to Hollywood, and the two of them dematerialized to either side of the front door. A quick listen revealed arguing, the voices the same ones Z had heard by the Hudson the night before. Evidently the pair of slayers were still oil-and-watering it.

Three, two . . . one—

Rhage kicked the door to the house open, bootlicking the bitch so hard his shitkicker left a dent in the metal panel.

The two *lessers* in the hall swung around, and Z didn't give them a chance to respond. Leading with his SIG's muzzle, he popped both right in the chest, the bullets sending the pair pinwheeling backward.

Rhage went on dagger duty, leaping forward, stabbing first one and then the other. As the flashes of white light and the sharp sounds faded, the brother leaped to his feet and froze like a boulder.

Neither Z nor Rhage moved. Using their senses, they sifted through the house's silence, searching for anything that suggested further inhabitation.

The moan that bubbled up into all the quiet came from the back, and Z walked swiftly toward the sound, muzzle first. In the kitchen the cellar door was open, and he dematerialized to the left of it. A quick head jab and he took a look-see down the stairs. A bald lightbulb hung from a red-and-black wire at the bottom, but the pool of light showed nothing but stained floorboards.

Z willed the light off down below and Rhage provided cover from upstairs as Z bypassed the rickety steps and dematerialized into the darkness.

On the lower level he smelled fresh blood and heard the staccato click of rattling teeth from the left.

He willed the cellar light back on . . . and lost his breath.

A male civilian vampire was tied by the arms and legs to a table. He was naked and covered with bruises, and instead of looking at Z, he squeezed his eyes shut, as if he couldn't bear to know what was coming at him.

For a moment Z couldn't move. It was his own nightmare in living color, and reality blurred such that he wasn't sure whether he was the one tied down or the guy who was coming to the rescue.

"Z?" Rhage said from above. " Anything there?"

Z snapped to attention and cleared his throat. "I'm on it."

As he approached the civilian, he said softly in the Old Language, *"Be of ease."*

The vampire's eyes flipped open and his head jerked up on his spine. There was a look of disbelief, then astonishment.

"Be of ease." Z double-checked the corners of the basement, his eyesight

penetrating the shadows, seeking signs of a security system. All he saw was a lot of concrete walls and wooden flooring, along with old piping and wiring snaking around the ceiling. No electric eyes or sparkling new power supplies.

They were alone and unsupervised, but God only knew for how long. "Rhage, still clear?" he shouted up the stairwell.

"Clear!"

"One civilian." Z assessed the male's body. He'd been beaten, and though he didn't seem to have any open wounds, there was no telling whether he could dematerialize. "Call the boys in case we need transport."

"Already have."

Z took a step forward—

The floor broke apart beneath his feet, splintering right out from under him.

As gravity grabbed him hard with greedy hands and he went into a free fall, all he could think about was Bella. Depending on what lay at the bottom, this could be—

He landed on something that shattered on impact, shards of whatever it was slicing at his leathers and his hands before bouncing up to cut into his face and neck. He kept hold of his gun because he'd been trained to, and because the jolt of pain tightened him up from head to foot.

It took some deep breathing before he could reboot his brain and try to assess any damage.

As he sat up slowly, the chiming sound of bits of glass falling to a stone floor echoed around him. In the circle of light that fell from the cellar above, he saw that he was sitting in the midst of a brilliant shimmer of crystals. . . .

He'd fallen on a chandelier the size of a bed.

And his left boot was facing backward.

"Fuck. Me."

His broken lower leg started to pound with pain, making him think that if only he hadn't looked at the damn thing, maybe he would have kept on not feeling it.

Rhage's face popped over the rim of the ragged hole above. "You okay?"

"Free the civilian."

"Are you all right?"

"Leg's shot."

"How shot?"

"Well, I'm looking at the heel of my shitkicker and the front of my knee at the same time. And there's a high probability I'm going to throw up." He swallowed hard, trying to convince his gag reflex to pipe down. "Get the civilian loose and then we'll see about getting me out of here. Oh, and stick to the rows of nails on the floor. Clearly the boards are weak."

Rhage nodded, then disappeared. As massive footsteps above caused drifts of dust to powder down, Z went into his jacket and took out a Maglite. The thing was about the size of a finger but could throw a beam as strong as the headlight on a car.

As he panned the thing around, his leg problem bothered him a little less. "What . . . the hell?"

It was like being in an Egyptian tomb. The forty-by-forty-foot room was stocked with objects that gleamed, from oil paintings in gilt frames to silver candelabra to bejeweled statuary to whole mounds of sterling flatware. And across the way there were stacked boxes that probably contained jewelry, as well as a lineup of fifteen or so metal briefcases that must have had money in them.

This was a looting repository, filled with what had been taken during the raids this past summer. All of this shit had belonged to the *glymera*—he even recognized the faces in some of the portraits.

Lot of value down here. And what do you know. Over to the right, close to the packed dirt floor, a red light started blinking. His fall had triggered the alarm system.

Rhage's head popped back into view. "Civilian is free, but unable to dematerialize. Qhuinn's less than a half mile away. What the fuck are you on?"

"A chandelier, and that's not the half of it. Listen, we're going to have company. This place is wired and I tripped it."

"There a staircase to you?"

Z wiped the pain sweat off his brow, the shit cold and greasy on the back of his bleeding hand. As he moved the flashlight around, he shook his head. "Can't see one, but they had to have gotten the loot in here somehow, and sure as hell it wasn't through that floor."

Rhage's head flipped up and the brother frowned. The sound of him unsheathing his dagger was a metal-on-metal gasp of anticipation. "That's either Qhuinn or a slayer. Drag yourself out of the light while I sort this."

Hollywood disappeared from the hole in the floor, his footsteps now whisper quiet.

Z holstered his gun because he had to, and cleared some of the crystal fragments out of the way. Palming his ass off the ground, he braced his good foot and spidered away into the darkness, heading for the security beacon. After backing his ass right up to the damn thing, as it was the only break he could find in the piles of art and silver, he settled against the wall.

When upstairs stayed way too quiet, he knew it wasn't Qhuinn and the boys. And yet there wasn't any fighting.

And then shit went from bad to worse.

The "wall" he was leaning against slid away and he fell flat on his back . . . at the feet of a pair of white-haired, pissed-off *lessers*.

FOUR

here were many great things about being a mom.

Holding your young in your arms and rocking them to sleep was definitely one of them. So was folding their little clothes. And feeding them. And watching them look up at you in happiness and wonder when they first came awake.

Bella repositioned herself in the nursery's rocker, tucked the blanket under her daughter's chin, and gave Nalla's cheek a little stroke.

A not-so-hot corollary to momdom, however, was that the whole female-intuition thing was totally heightened.

Sitting in the safety of the Brotherhood's mansion, Bella knew there was something wrong. Even though she was safe and sound, and in a nursery that was right out of an article entitled "The Perfect Family Lives Here," it was as if there were a draft going through the room that smelled like dead skunk. And Nalla had picked up on the vibe as well. The young was preternaturally quiet and tense, her yellow eyes focused on some middle ground as if she were waiting for a big noise to go off.

Of course, the problem with intuition, whether tied to the mother thing or not, was that it was a story with no words and no time line. Although it got you prepared for bad news, there were no nouns or verbs to go with the anxiety, no time/date stamp, either. So as you sat with the ambient dread clamped on the back of your neck like a cold, wet cloth, your mind got to rationalizing because that was the best anyone could do. Maybe it was just First Meal not sitting well. Maybe it was just free floating anxiety.

Maybe . . .

Hell, maybe what was churning in her gut wasn't intuition at all. Maybe it was because she'd reached a decision that didn't sit well.

Yeah, that was more likely the case. After having stewed and hoped and worried and tried to think her way out of the problems with Z, she had to be realistic. She'd confronted him . . . and there had been no real response from him.

Not *I want you two to stay*. Not even *I'll work on it*.

All she'd gotten from him was that he was going out to fight.

Which was a reply of sorts, wasn't it.

Looking around the nursery, she cataloged what she would have to pack up . . . not much, just an overnight bag for Nalla and a duffle for herself. She could get another diaper pail and crib and changing table set up easily enough—

Where would she go?

The easiest solution was one of her brother's houses. Rehvenge had a number of them, and all she'd have to do was ask. Man, how ironic was that? After having fought to get away from him, now she was contemplating going back.

Not contemplating. Deciding.

Bella leaned to the side, took her cell phone out of the pocket of her jeans, and hit Rehv's number.

After two rings a deep, familiar voice answered, "Bella?"

There was a roar of music and people talking in the background, the various sounds like a crowd competing for space.

"Hi."

"Hello? Bella? Hold on, let me get into my office." After a long, noisy pause, the din was cut off sharply. "Hey, how are you and your little miracle doing?"

"I need a place to stay."

Total silence. Then her brother said, "Would that be for three or for two?"

"Two."

Another long pause. "Do I need to kill that fool bastard?"

The cold, vicious tone scared her a little, reminding her that her beloved brother was not a male you wanted to screw with. "God, no."

"Talk, sister mine. Tell me what's going on."

Death was a black parcel that came in a lot of different shapes and weights and sizes. Still, it was the kind of thing that when it hit your front doorstep, you knew the sender without checking the return address or even opening the thing up.

You just knew.

As Z back-flatted into the path of those two *lessers*, he knew that his FedEx-tinction package had arrived, and the only thing that went through his mind was that he wasn't ready to take delivery.

Course, it wasn't the kind of thing you could refuse to sign for.

Above him, cast in a dim glow from some kind of light, the *lessers* froze as if he were the last thing they expected to see. Then they took out their guns.

Z didn't have a last word; he had a last image, one that totally eclipsed the double-barreled action that was at point-blank range of his head. In his mind he saw Bella and Nalla together in that rocker back in the nursery. It was not a picture from the night before when there had been Kleenexes and red-rimmed eyes and his twin looking grave. It was from a couple of weeks ago, when Bella had been staring down at the young in her arms with such tenderness and love. As if she'd sensed him in the doorway, she'd lifted her eyes, and for a moment the love that was in her face had wrapped around him as well.

The two gunshots rang out, and the weirdest thing was that the only pain he felt was the sting of the sound in his ears.

Two flopping *thunchs* followed, echoing around the stolen riches.

Z lifted his head. Qhuinn and Rhage were standing right behind where the *lessers* had been, their guns just lowering. Blay and John Matthew were with them, their guns drawn as well.

"You okay?" Rhage asked.

No. That would be one big fat hairy fuck-no. "Yeah. Yeah, I'm tight."

"Blay, back into the tunnel with me," Rhage said. "John and Qhuinn, you stay with him."

Z let his head fall back and listened as two sets of shitkickers headed off in the distance. In the eerie silence that followed, a wave of nausea rolled over him and every inch of him started to shake, his hands flapping like flags in a brisk wind as he brought them up to feel his face.

John's hand touched his arm and he jumped. "I'm okay . . . I'm okay. . . ."

John signed, *We're going to get you out of here.*

"How—" He cleared his throat. "How do I know this is happening?"

I'm sorry? How do you know . . . ?

Zsadist's fingers skipped along his forehead as he tried to prod where the slayers had aimed their guns. "How do I know this is real? And not a . . . How do I know I didn't just die?"

John glanced over his shoulder at Qhuinn like he had no idea how to respond and was looking for backup. Then he pounded on his own chest with a solid thumping. *I know I'm here.*

Qhuinn leaned down and did the same, a heavy bass sound rising from his chest. "Me, too."

Zsadist let his head fall back again, his body scrambling in its own skin so badly his feet tap-danced on the hard-packed floor. "I don't know . . . if this is real . . . oh, shit . . ."

John stared at him as if measuring his increasing agitation and trying to figure out what the hell to do.

Abruptly the guy reached down to Z's broken leg and gave his turned-around shitkicker a quick tug.

Z shot upright and barked, "Mother*fucker*!"

But it was good. The pain acted like a great broom sweep of his brain, clearing out the web of delusions and replacing them with a focused, pounding clarity. He was very much alive. He really was.

Right on the heels of that realization he thought of Bella. And Nalla.

He had to reach them.

Z shifted to the side to get his phone, but his vision went furry from what was doing with his leg. "Shit. Can you get me my cell? In my back pocket?"

John carefully rolled him over, took out the RAZR, and handed it to him.

"So you don't think there's any working this out?" Rehv said.

Bella shook her head in answer to her brother's question, then remembered he couldn't see her. "No, I don't think so. At least not in the short term."

"Shit. Well, I'm always here for you, you know that. You want to stay with *mahmen*?"

"No. I mean, I'm happy to have her come visit during the night, but I need my own space."

"Because you're hoping he comes after you."

"He's not going to. This time is different. Nalla . . . has made everything different."

The young snuffled and burrowed in closer to her favorite nook between upper arm and breast. Bella propped the cell phone against her shoulder and stroked the downy-soft hair that was growing in. The waves, when they grew out, were going to be multicolored, with blondes and reds and browns mixed together, just as her father's would be if he didn't trim it so tightly.

As Rehv laughed awkwardly, she said, "What?"

"After all these years fighting to keep you on my property, now I don't want you leaving the Brotherhood mansion. For real, nothing is safer than that compound . . . but I do have a house on the Hudson River that's tight. It's next to a friend of mine's, and it's nothing fancy, but there's a tunnel linkup between them. She'll keep you safe."

After he gave her the address, Bella murmured, "Thank you. I'm going to pack a few things up and have Fritz take me there in an hour."

"I'll get the fridge stocked for you right now."

The phone made a beeping noise as a text came through. "Thank you."

"Have you told him?"

"Z knows it's coming. And no, I'm not going to keep him from seeing Nalla if he wants, but he's going to have to choose to come and see her."

"What about you?"

"I love him . . . but this has been really hard on me."

They ended the call shortly thereafter, and as Bella took the phone away from her ear, she saw that a text had come through from Zsadist:

I'M SO SORRY. I LOVE YOU. PLEASE FORGIVE ME—
CAN'T LIVE WITHOUT YOU.

She bit her lip and blinked hard. And texted back.

FIVE

Z stared at the screen of his phone, praying for a response from Bella. He would have called, but his voice was so shaky he didn't want to alarm her. Plus getting into a huge emotional thing wasn't a great idea, considering he had a broken leg on *lesser* real estate.

Rhage and Blay came back through the tunnel.

". . . is why they didn't come into the house," Rhage was saying. "The entrance to this storage unit is through the shed out back. They were checking on the security system first, clearly less concerned that the house had been infiltrated."

Z cleared his throat and warbled, "The alarm is still blinking. If it doesn't get shut off, more will—"

Rhage leveled his gun at the red light, pulled the trigger, and dusted the thing. "Maybe that'll work."

"You are such a techie, Hollywood," Z muttered. "Right up there with Bill Gates."

"Whatever. We need to get you and the civilian out—"

Z's phone vibrated and he opened the text from Bella, holding his breath. After he read it twice, he shut his eyes hard and clipped the phone shut. Oh, God . . . *no.*

Propping his upper body off the dirt floor, he made a lurch to get on his feet. The shot of agony that ran up his leg helped to distract him from the sight of all the blood that had pooled underneath him.

"What the . . ."

". . . fuck are . . ."

". . . you doing . . ."

John signed what the other three were saying: *What are you doing?*

"I need to get home." Dematerializing wasn't an option because of his leg—which was making him want to throw up as it flopped around. "I need to—"

Hollywood shoved his perfectly beautiful face right in Z's grille. "Will you just relax? You're in shock—"

Z grabbed the male's upper arm and squeezed to shut the brother up. He spoke softly, and when he was done, Rhage could only blink.

After a moment Hollywood said quietly, "Here's the issue, though. You have a compound fracture, my brother. I promise we'll get you back, but we need to take you to a doctor. Dead is not where you want to be, feel me?"

As a wave of light-headedness came swooping in from out of nowhere, Z had a feeling his brother had a point. But fuck it. "Home. I want—."

His body collapsed. Just folded on him like a house of cards.

Rhage caught his weight and turned to the boys. "You two, carry him out of the tunnel. Move it. I'll cover."

Zsadist grunted as he changed hands and was hauled off like a deer carcass found in the middle of a road. The pain was a stunner, making his heart palpitate and his skin shiver, but it was good. He need the physical manifestation of the emotion trapped in the center of his chest.

The tunnel was about fifty yards in length and tall enough so that only a hobbit could have any headroom—so the trip out was about as much fun as being born. Qhuinn and John were cranked over, scrambling to hold on to him while hauling ass, two grown-ups in a kid-scaled model. As Z's body jangled and his fucked-up foot rang like a bell, the only thing that kept him conscious was the text from Bella:

I'M SORRY. I LOVE YOU, BUT SHE AND I HAVE TO GO. I'LL GIVE YOU
THE ADDRESS WHEN WE'RE SETTLED LATER TONIGHT.

Outside the air was cool, and Z dragged the shit into his lungs in hopes of calming his stomach. He was taken directly to the Hummer and settled in the back, along with the civilian who had passed out cold. John, Blay, and Qhuinn piled in, and then there was a stretch of hurry-up-and-wait.

Finally Rhage bolted from the house, flashed three fingers and a fist, and dove into the shotgun seat. While the brother started texting on his phone, Qhuinn hit the gas and once again proved he had half a brain: The guy had been smart enough to back in so he had a straight shot down the driveway, and he took the way out with a vengeance.

Rhage looked at his watch as they bumped along. "Four . . . three . . . two . . ."

The house behind them exploded into a fireball, the aftershocks sending waves of buffering energy through the air—

Just as a minivan full of the enemy pulled into the end of the driveway, blocking the way onto Route 9.

Bella double-checked the two L.L. Bean bags and was pretty sure she had everything she needed for the short term. In the one with the green handles she had some clothes for herself, along with her cell phone charger, her toothbrush, and two thousand dollars in cash. The blue-handled one had Nalla's clothes, bottles and diapers, along with wet wipes, rash cream, blankies, a teddy bear, and *Oh, the Places You'll Go!* by Dr. Seuss.

The title of Nalla's favorite book was a shitkicker on a night like tonight. It really was.

When there was a knock on the nursery door, Bella called out, "Come in."

Mary, Rhage's *shellan*, popped her head in. Her face was tight, her gray eyes grim even before she looked down at the bags.

"Rhage texted me. Z's been injured. I know you're going to leave, and the why is none of my business, but you might consider waiting. From what Rhage said, Z is desperately going to need to feed."

Bella slowly straightened. "How . . . how badly injured? What—"

"I don't have any more details other than that they'll be home as soon as they can."

Oh . . . God. It was the news she had always dreaded. Z injured out in the field.

"What's their ETA?"

"Rhage didn't say. I know they have to drop off an injured civilian at Havers's new clinic, but that's on the way. I'm not sure whether Z's getting treated here or there."

Bella shut her eyes. Zsadist had sent her that text while injured. He'd been reaching out to her when he was in pain . . . and she'd slapped him back with the fact that she was abandoning him to his demons.

"What have I done," she said softly.

"I'm sorry?" Mary asked.

Bella shook her head as much at herself as in response to the female.

Going over to the crib, she looked at their daughter. Nalla was sleeping with the hard, dense exhaustion of the young, her little chest pumping up and down with purpose, her pink hands curled into fists, her brows bunched together as if she were concentrating on growing.

"Will you stay with her?" Bella asked.

"Absolutely."

"There's milk in the fridge over there."
"I'll be right here. I won't go anywhere."

Back in the driveway of the Jolly Green Giant house in the sticks, Z felt the heavy-duty lurch of Qhuinn slamming on the Hummer's brakes. The SUV held steady as the laws of physics gripped its mass hard, putting an end to its acceleration just before the vehicle crushed the frontal lobe of the minivan in its path.

Gun muzzles came out of the windows of the Lessening Society's soccer-mom special like the bitch was a stagecoach, and bullets went ape shit, pinging the Hummer's reinforced-steel body and ricocheting off its inch-thick Plexiglas windows.

"Second night out with my ride," Qhuinn spat. "And these fuckers are Swiss-cheesing me? Hell, no. Hold on."

Qhuinn threw them into reverse, jumped the SUV back fifteen feet, then punched the engine into first gear and nailed his foot to the floor. Wrenching the wheel to the left, he dodged around the Town & Country, chunks of earth clumping up and clapping against both cars.

As they bounced around like a boat in bad weather, Rhage reached into his jacket and took out a hand grenade. Opening his bulletproof window just far enough, he popped the pin with his teeth and tossed the fist-size explosive out. By the grace of God the damn thing tripped off the minivan's roof and rolled under the vehicle.

The three *lessers* leaped out of that fucker like the thing was on fire.

And ten seconds later it was, its flames lighting up the night.

Fuuuuuck, if Z thought the trip through the tunnel had been bad on his leg, it was nothing compared to the bump-and-shatter act it took to get away from those slayers. By the time the Hummer burst out onto Route 9 after having clipped at least one of the *lessers* on its hood, Zsadist was on the verge of blacking out.

"Shit, he's going into shock."

Z realized with little interest that Rhage had turned around and was looking at him, not at the civilian.

"Am not," he mumbled as his eyes rolled back in his head. "Just taking a little break."

Rhage's spectacular Bahama-blue stare narrowed. "Compound. Fracture. Motherfucker. You're bleeding out as we speak."

Z lifted his eyes to Qhuinn's in the rearview mirror. "Sorry 'bout the carpet."

The male shook his head. "Not to worry. You, I will abso trash my ride for."

Rhage put his hand on Z's neck. "Damn it, you're white as snow and about as warm. You're going to have to get treated at the clinic."

"Home."

In a low voice Rhage said, "I texted Mary not to let her go, okay? Bella's still going to be there no matter how long it takes us to get back to the mansion. She's not leaving you before you get home."

A whole lot of resounding quiet settled in the Hummer, like everyone was busy pretending they didn't hear any of Rhage's newsflash.

Z opened his mouth to argue.

But fainted dead away before he could marshal any more objections.

SIX

ella paced around the PT room in the training center, orbiting the examination table on shaky legs. She stopped regularly to check the clock.

Where were they? What else had gone wrong? It had been over an hour. . . .

Oh, God, please let Zsadist be alive. Please let them bring him back alive.

Pacing, more pacing. Eventually she paused at the head of the gurney and looked down its length. Putting her hand on its padded top, she found herself thinking of when she had been on the thing as a patient. Three months ago. For Nalla's birth.

God, what a nightmare that had been.

And God, what a nightmare this was . . . waiting for her *hellren* to be rolled in injured, bleeding, in pain. And that was the best-case scenario. The worst case was a body with a sheet over it, something she couldn't even contemplate.

To keep herself from going crazy, she thought about the birth, about that moment when both her and Z's lives had changed forever. Like a lot of dramatic things, the big event had been anticipated, but when it arrived had nonetheless been a shock. She'd been in her ninth month out of the usual eighteen and it had been a Monday night.

Helluva way to start the workweek.

She'd had a craving for chili, and Fritz had indulged her, whipping up a batch that was spicy as a blowtorch. When the beloved butler had brought the steaming bowl to her, though, she'd abruptly been unable to stomach the smell or the sight of it. Nauseous and sweaty, she'd gone to take a cool shower, and as she'd lumbered into the bathroom, she'd wondered how in the hell she could fit another seven months of the young getting larger in her belly.

Nalla, evidently, had taken the random thought to heart. For the first time in weeks she moved strongly—and, with a sharp kick, broke her water.

Bella had lifted her robe and looked down at the wetness, wondering for a moment whether she'd lost control of her bladder. Then light had dawned. Although she'd followed Doc Jane's advice and avoided reading the vampire version of *What to Expect When You're Expecting,* she had enough background to know that once your water breaks, the bus has left the station.

Ten minutes later she'd been flat on this gurney, with Doc Jane moving quickly, but thoroughly, through an exam. The conclusion was that Bella's body didn't seem ready to get with the program, but Nalla had to be taken out. Pitocin, which was used frequently to induce labor in human women, was administered, and shortly thereafter Bella learned that there was a difference between pain and labor.

Pain got your attention. Labor got *all* your attention.

Zsadist had been out in the field, and when he'd arrived he was so frantic that what little hair was left from his skull trim was standing straight up. As soon as he got through the door, he'd ditched his weapons, the pile growing to the size of a love seat, and rushed to stand at her side.

She'd never seen him so scared. Not even when he woke up from his dreams of that sadistic Mistress he'd had. His eyes had been black, not from anger but from fear, and his lips drawn so tightly they were a pair of white slashes.

Having him there had helped her get through the pain. And she'd needed him. Doc Jane had advised against an epidural, as vampires could experience alarming decreases in blood pressure with them. So there had been no buffering at all.

And no time to move her to Havers's clinic. Once the Pitocin had fired up her body, the labor had progressed too fast for her to be taken anywhere—although it wouldn't have mattered because dawn was near. Which meant there was no way to get the race's physician to the training center, either.

Bella came back to the present, smoothing her hand over the thin pillow that rested on the gurney. She could remember holding on to Z's hand hard enough to break his bones as she'd strained until her teeth hurt and she felt as if she were getting ripped in half.

And then her vitals had crashed.

"Bella?"

She wheeled around. Wrath was in the PT room's doorway, the king's huge body filling the jambs. With his hip-length black hair and his wraparound sunglasses and his black leathers, he seemed in his silent arrival like a modern-day version of the Grim Reaper.

"Oh, please, no," she said, gripping onto the gurney. "Please—"

"No, it's okay. He's okay." Wrath came forward and took her arm, holding her up. "He's been stabilized."

"Stabilized?"

"He has a compound fracture of his lower leg and it's caused some bleeding."

Some being massive, no doubt. "Where is he?"

"He's coming home from Havers's right now. I figured you'd be worried, so I wanted to let you know."

"Thank you. Thank you . . ." Even with the problems they'd been having lately, the idea of losing her *hellren* was catastrophic.

"Whoa, easy, there." The king wrapped her in his huge arms and held her gently. "Let the shakes go through you. You'll breathe more that way, believe it or not."

She did as he suggested, loosening the rigid control she'd clamped onto her muscles. Her body shimmied from shoulder to calf and she relied on the king's strength to keep standing. He was right, though. Even as she trembled, she was able to take a deep breath or two.

When she'd become more stable, she pulled back. As she caught sight of the gurney she frowned and had to start walking around again.

"Wrath, may I ask you something?"

"Absolutely."

She had to pace a little more before she could frame the question properly. "If Beth had a baby, would you love the child as much as you love her?"

The king looked surprised. "Ah . . ."

"I'm sorry," she said, shaking her head. "That's none of my business—"

"No, it's not that. I'm trying to figure out the answer." He reached up and lifted the sunglasses from his brilliant, pale green eyes. Though they were unfocused, his stare nonetheless was utterly arresting. "Here's the thing . . . and I believe this is true for all bonded males. Your *shellan* is the beating heart in your chest. More than that, even. She's your body and your skin and your mind . . . everything you ever were and ever will be. So a male can never feel more for anyone than he does his mate. It's just not possible—and I think there's some evolution at work. The deeper you love, the more you protect, and keeping your female alive at all costs means she can care for whatever young she has. That being said, of course you love your children. I think of Darius with Beth . . . I mean, he was desperate for her to be safe. And Tohr with John . . . and . . . yeah, I mean, you feel deeply for them, sure."

It was logical, but not much of a relief, considering Zsadist wouldn't even pick Nalla up—

The double doors of the PT room bounced open as Z was wheeled in. He was dressed in a hospital johnny, probably because his clothes had had to be cut off him at Havers's clinic, and there was no color in his face at all. Both his hands were bandaged, and there was a cast on his lower leg.

He was out cold.

She rushed to his side and took his hand. "Zsadist? *Zsadist?*"

Sometimes IVs and pills weren't always the best course of treatment for the injured. Sometimes all you needed was the touch of the one you loved and the sound of their voice and the knowledge that you were home, and that was enough to drag you back from the brink.

Z opened his eyes. The sapphire blue stare he met brought a tangle of tears to his lashes. Bella was leaning over him, her thick mahogany hair trailing off one shoulder, her classically boned face drawn in lines of worry.

"Hi," he said, because it was the best he could do.

He'd refused any pain meds at the clinic, because the sluggish effect they had always reminded him of the way he'd been drugged at the hands of the Mistress— so he'd been fully conscious as his leg had been opened up and pinned back together by Doc Jane. Well, he'd been with it for part of the time, at any rate. He'd passed out for a while. Upshot was, he felt like death. No doubt looked like it, as well. And there was just too much to say.

"Hi." Bella smoothed her hand over his skull trim. "Hi . . ."

"Hi . . ." Before he broke down and made an ass of himself, he glanced around her to see who else was in the PT suite. Wrath was talking to Rhage in the corner next to the whirlpool bath, and Qhuinn, John, and Blay were standing in front of the banks of steel-and-glass cabinetry.

Witnesses. Shit. He needed to pull it together.

As he blinked hard, the details of the room came into clear focus, and he thought of the last time he'd been in it.

The birth.

"Shhh . . ." Bella murmured, clearly mistaking the reason for his wince. "Just close your eyes and relax."

He did as he was told, because he was back on the brink, and not because of how badly his leg and his hands were hurting.

God, that night when Nalla had been born . . . when he'd nearly lost his *shellan* . . .

Z squeezed his lids shut, not wanting to relive the past . . . or look too closely at the present. He was in danger of losing Bella. Again.

"I love you . . ." he whispered. "Please don't leave me."

"I'm right here."

Yeah, but for how long.

The panic he felt now took him back to the night of the birth . . . he'd been out in the field with Vishous, investigating a civilian abduction downtown. When the call had come from Doc Jane, he'd dumped V like a bad habit and dematerized to the mansion's courtyard, plowing through the foyer and into the tunnel. Everyone, *shellans* and *doggens* and Wrath alike, had gotten the hell out of his way to avoid becoming bowling pins.

Down in the training center, in this very room, he'd found Bella stretched out on the gurney he now lay upon. He'd come in right in the middle of a contraction and had had to watch as Bella's body became locked into place as if a giant hand were crushing her around the middle. When the pain eased off she'd taken a deep inhale, then looked at him and offered him a weak smile. As she reached out for him, he'd peeled his weapons off, dropping them on the linoleum.

"Hands," Doc Jane barked. "You wash your hands before you come over here."

He'd nodded and gone directly to the deep bucket sinks with the foot pedals. He'd worked a lather all the way up his arms until his skin glowed Barbie pink then he'd dried with a blue surgical cloth and rushed to Bella's side.

Their palms had just made contact when the next contraction came roaring through. Bella had squeezed his hand until it was crushed in her grip, but he didn't care. Holding her stare as she'd strained, he would have done anything to take the pain from her . . . and at that moment he would have cheerfully cut his own balls off. He couldn't believe he'd put her through that kind of suffering.

It got worse. The labor was like a locomotive gathering speed, and its tracks were all over Bella's body. Harder, longer, faster. Harder, longer, faster. He didn't know how she could stand it. And then she couldn't.

She'd crashed, all her vital signs dropping—heart rate, blood pressure, everything going into the shitter. He'd known how serious it was by how fast Doc Jane had moved. He remembered the drugs going into the IV, and Vishous coming forward with . . . shit, surgical tools and a fetal incubator.

Doc Jane snapped on a fresh pair of latex gloves, looking first at Bella, then at him. "We're going to have to go in and get the baby, okay? She's in distress as well."

Nodding. He'd done some nodding at that point on both his and Bella's parts. The Betadine had been a rusty orange as V had rubbed it all over Bella's swollen abdomen.

"Is she going to be okay?" Bella mumbled desperately. "Is our young going to be—"

Doc Jane had leaned down. "Look at me."

The two females had locked eyes. "I'm going to do everything I can to get both of you through this. I want you to calm yourself, that's your job. Calm yourself and let me do what I'm best at it. Deep breath now."

Zsadist had taken one along with his *shellan* . . . and then he'd watched as Bella's eyelids suddenly flared and her stare focused on the ceiling with an odd fixation. Before he could ask her what she was looking at, she'd closed her eyes.

He'd had a moment of terror that he would never see them open again.

Then she'd said, "Just make sure the young is okay."

He'd gone cold at that point, utterly cold, because it was clear Bella didn't think she was coming out of it alive. And the only thing she cared about was the young.

"Please stay with me," he'd groaned as the incision was made.

Bella hadn't heard him. She'd drifted away from consciousness, sure as if she were on a boat that had left its mooring and floated off over calm waters.

Nalla had been born at six twenty-four a.m.

"Is it alive?" he'd asked.

Though it shamed him to admit it now, the only reason he'd wanted to know was because God forbid Bella had to come around and learn that her daughter had been stillborn.

While Doc Jane stitched up Bella, Vishous had worked fast with a suction balloon over the young's mouth and nose, then he'd fired up a tiny IV and done something with the hands and feet. Fast. He'd been as fast as his *shellan* at that point.

"*Is she alive?*"

"Zsadist?"

His eyes popped open and he came back to the present.

"Do you need more painkillers?" Bella asked. "You look as if you're in agony."

"I can't believe she lived. She was so small."

As the words came out of Zsadist's mouth, Bella was confused, but only for a split second. The birth . . . he was thinking about the birth.

She stroked the fine, short hair on his head, trying to ease him in some small way. "Yes . . . yes, she was."

His yellow eyes shifted to the other folks in the room and his voice got quiet. "Can I be honest?"

Oh, shit, she thought. "Yes, please."

"The only reason I cared whether she was alive was because I didn't want you to be told she wasn't. She was the only thing you were worried about . . . and I couldn't bear for you to lose her."

Bella frowned. "You mean at the end?"

"Yes . . . you said you just wanted to make sure she was okay. Those were your last words."

Bella reached out and put her palm on his cheek. "I thought I was dying and I didn't want you to be left all alone. I . . . I saw the light of the Fade. It was all around me, bathing me. I was worried about you . . . about what would happen if I weren't living."

His face blanched even further, proving that there was a color paler than white on the spectrum. "I thought that's what had been happening. Oh . . . God, I can't believe how close it was."

Doc Jane came up to the gurney. "Sorry to interrupt. I just want to do a quick check on his vitals?"

"Of course."

As Bella watched the doctor make fast work of the examination, she thought of the way those ghostly hands had helped her daughter come into the world.

"Good," Doc Jane said, linking her stethoscope around her neck. "This is good. He's stabilized and should be able to get up and move around in another hour or so."

"Thank you," Bella murmured as Z did the same.

"My pleasure. Believe me. Now, how about the rest of us take off and let you two have some time alone."

The crowd dispersed amid offers of help and food and anything else that might be needed. As Wrath went over to the door, he paused and looked at Bella.

Her grip tightened on Z's shoulder as the king bowed his head a little and then shut the door.

She cleared her throat. "May I get you something to—"

"We need to talk."

"It can wait—"

"Until you leave here?" Z shook his head. "No. It has to be now."

Bella pulled a rolling stool over and sat down, stroking his forearm because she couldn't hold his bandaged hands. "I'm scared. If we don't . . . can't bridge this gap . . ."

"Me too."

As their words hung in the quiet of the tiled, clinical room, Bella remembered waking up from the C-section that day of the birth. Zsadist's eyes had been the first thing she'd seen. He'd been in agony as he'd stared down at her, but slowly his pain had lifted, revealing disbelief and then hope.

"Show her the young," Z had called out sharply. "Quickly."

Vishous had rolled the fetal incubator over, and Bella had gotten her first look at their daughter. Dragging with her the IV line that was in her arm, she'd put her fingertips on the Plexiglas shell. The instant her touch fell upon the clear shield, the young had turned her head.

Bella had looked at Zsadist. "Can we call her Nalla?"

His eyes had watered. "Yes. Absolutely. Anything you want."

He had kissed her and given her his vein and been everything you could want in an attentive, caring mate.

Coming back to the present she shook her head. "You seemed so happy. Right after the birth. You were rejoicing with the others. You were there for the ribboning of her crib . . . You went to Phury and you sang to him. . . . "

"Because you were alive and you didn't have to suffer the loss of your young. My worst fears hadn't come to pass." Zsadist lifted one of his hands as if he wanted to rub his eyes, but he frowned, clearly realizing he couldn't because of the bandages. "I was happy for you."

"But after you fed me, you sat by the incubator and reached out to her. You even smiled as she looked your way. There was love in your face, not just relief. What changed?" As he hesitated, she said, "I'm willing to give you more time if that's what it takes, but I can't be shut out of the process. What happened?"

Z stared up at the cage of medical lighting hanging above him and there was a long silence, one so long that Bella thought maybe they'd hit an insurmountable wall.

But then a single fat tear had formed at the corner of his left eye. "She's in the dream with me."

The words were so soft, Bella had to make sure she'd heard him right. "I'm sorry?"

"The dream I have of still being with the Mistress. Nalla . . . she's in the cell. I can hear her crying as the Mistress comes for me. I strain at the shackles to get free . . . so I can protect her . . . get her out . . . stop what's going to happen. But I can't move. The Mistress is going to find the young." His haunted eyes shifted over. "The Mistress is going to find her, and it's my fault Nalla's in the cell."

"Oh . . . my love . . . oh, Z." Bella stood up and draped herself carefully over his upper body, hugging him lightly. "Oh . . . God . . . and you're afraid the Mistress will kill her—"

"No." Z cleared his throat once. And again. And again. His chest started to pump up and down. "She's going to . . . make Nalla watch . . . what they do to me. Nalla has to watch. . . ."

Zsadist struggled to keep his emotions in, then lost the fight, weeping in the hard, powerful bursts of a male. "She's going to have . . . to watch her . . . father get . . ."

All Bella could do was hold on tight and wet his hospital gown with her own tears. She'd known whatever it was was bad. But she'd had no idea how bad.

"Oh, my love," she said, as his arms came around her and his head lifted so that his face was buried in her hair. "Oh, my darling love . . ."

SEVEN

It was about five the following afternoon when Zsadist finally woke up properly. It was good to be in his own bed. It was not so great having a cast on his lower leg.

Rolling over, he opened his eyes and looked at Bella. She was awake and staring back at him.

"How are you feeling?" she asked.

"Okay." Physically speaking, at least. The rest of him, his mind and his emotions, were open to question.

"Would you like something to eat?"

"Yeah. In a little bit." What he really wanted was to just lie around and stare into his *shellan*'s eyes for a while.

Bella eased over onto her back and looked up to the ceiling.

"I'm glad we talked," he said. As much as he hated the past, he'd do anything to keep her from leaving, and if that meant conversation, he'd blabber on until his voice box bit it.

"Me too."

He frowned, feeling the distance. "What's on your mind?"

After a moment she said softly, "Do you still want me?"

He actually had to shake himself. She couldn't possibly be asking . . . "*Good Lord*, of course I want you as my *shellan*. The idea of you leaving is just—"

"Sexually, I mean."

He blinked, thinking about the hardcore arousal he'd gotten the night before—just from watching her towel off. "How could I not?"

She turned her head to him. "You don't feed and you haven't reached for me . . . well, I haven't either, but I mean—"

"Nalla needs you most right now."

"But you do, too . . . at least for my vein." She nodded down his body. "Would your leg have broken if you'd been fed properly? Probably not."

"I don't know. I fell through a floor . . . onto glass."

"Glass?"

"A chandelier."

"God . . ."

There was a long silence, and he wondered what she wanted him to do. Was she opening the door to . . . ?

At even the prospect of sex, his body woke up sure as if it were a gong she'd banged with one hell of an over-the-shoulder shot.

Except Bella stayed where she was. And he stayed where he was.

As silence stretched, he thought about how close to the edge of no return they were. If they didn't take steps to reconnect . . .

He reached through the sheets, took her hand, and brought it forward to his body.

"I want you," he said as he placed it on his erection. At the contact, he let out a groan and rolled his hips, pushing himself into her palm. "Oh . . . man . . . I've missed you."

The fact that Bella seemed surprised shamed him and made him think about her in the bathroom with that towel. When she'd stopped and looked at herself in the mirror, she'd been inspecting her body, he realized now—looking for flaws that weren't there. And she'd covered herself when she'd seen him not because she didn't want to attract his attention, but because she was sure she didn't have it anymore.

He moved her hand up and down on his shaft. "I'm desperate to touch you again. All over."

She came closer to him, moving through the sheets. "You are?"

"How could I not be? You're the most perfect female I've ever seen."

"Even after—"

He shot forward and pressed his lips to hers. "Especially after." He pulled back so she could read his eyes. "You are just as beautiful as the first time I saw you in the gym all those nights and days ago. You stopped my heart then—just froze it in my chest. And you stop it now."

She blinked quickly, and he kissed her tears away. "Bella . . . if I had known, I would have said something . . . done something. I just assumed you knew that nothing had changed for me."

"Since Nalla's come around, everything is different. The rhythm of my nights and days. My body. You and me. So I just assumed—"

"Feel me," he groaned, arching into her. "Feel me and know—Oh, God."

She felt him, all right. Wrapped both her hands around him and stroked him up and down, riding his hard length.

"Is this good for you?" she whispered.

All he could do was nod and moan. With her gripping him like that, surrounding him with her palms, working him, his brain had pretty much shorted out. "Bella . . ." He reached for her with his bandaged hands, then stopped. "Damn gauze—"

"I'll take it off for you." She pressed her lips to his. "And then you can put your hands wherever you like—"

"*Fuck.*"

He came. Right then and there. But instead of feeling let down, Bella just laughed in the deep, throaty way of a female who knows she's about to get sex from her male.

He recognized the sound. Loved it. Missed it. Needed to hear—

From across the room Nalla let out a warm-up wail that quickly escalated into a full-blown, carrier jet–launching, I-need-my-*mahmen*-NOW cry.

Bella felt Z's erection deflate and was well aware it wasn't because he'd just had a release. He was capable of going four or five orgasms at a clip—and that was on an average night, not after a dry spell of months and months.

"I'm so sorry," she said, looking over her shoulder at the crib, feeling torn as to which one she tended to.

Zsadist took her face in his bandaged palms and turned her to him. "Go take care of the young. I'll be fine."

There was absolutely no censure in his eyes or his tone. But then, there never had been. He'd never been resentful of Nalla; if anything he'd been too self-sacrificing.

"I'll just be—"

"Take your time."

She got off the bed and went to the crib. Nalla reached her little hands out and calmed some—especially as she was picked up.

Right. Wet diaper and hungry.

"I won't be long."

"Not to worry." Z lay back against the black satin sheets, his scarred face no longer pulled in hungry lines, his body still, not straining.

She hoped it was because the orgasm had relaxed him. Feared it was because he didn't think she'd be back anytime soon.

Bella nipped into the nursery, executed a fast diaper swap, then went to the rocker and gave Nalla what she needed. As she held her young and rocked, she realized how true it was that having a baby changed everything.

Including the concept of time.

What she'd meant to be a quick fifteen-minute feeding turned into a two-hour fuss, throw-up, fuss, feed, throw-up, burp, cry, diaper-change, fuss, feed marathon.

When Nalla finally settled, Bella let her head fall back against the rocker in a familiar state of exhaustion and satisfaction.

The mother business was amazing, transformative, and a little addictive—and she could now understand how females got way overfocused on their off-spring. You were fed by taking care of and doing right by them. You were also all-powerful as The Mother. Anything she said went when it came to Nalla.

Thing was, though, she missed being Z's *shellan*. Missed waking up with him moving on top of her, hot and hungry. Missed the feel of his fangs going deep into her throat. Missed the way that scarred face of his looked after they'd made love, all flushed and soft and full of reverence and love.

The fact that he was so hard with everyone else, even his Brothers, made his sweetness with her even more special. Always had.

God, that dream of his. She wasn't willing to say it changed everything be-tween them, but it changed enough so that she wouldn't leave him now. What she wasn't sure of was what came next. Z required more help than she could pro-vide him. He needed professional intervention, not just loving support from his mate.

Maybe there was a way Mary could step in. She had a counseling background and had been the one to teach him to read and write. There was no way he would talk to a stranger, but Mary . . .

Ah, hell, there was no way he'd talk to Rhage's *shellan* about the ins and outs of his past. The experiences were too horrific and the pain went too deep. Plus he hated getting emotional in front of anybody.

Bella got up and put Nalla in the smaller crib in the nursery—on the off chance Zsadist was still in bed, naked and in the mood.

He wasn't. He was in the bathroom, and going by the whirring sound and the spray of water, he was trimming his hair in the shower. On the bedside table there was a pair of scissors and the bandages that had been on his hands, and all she could think of was that she wished she had done it for him. No doubt he'd waited and waited and waited for her, and then given up, not just about the sex but about the help. He must have struggled to get the scissors to work with just the top half of his fingers showing . . . but given what time it was, he either stripped off the gauze himself or had no shower before he went out to fight.

Bella sat on the bed and found herself arranging the split in her robe so that when she crossed her legs they'd stay covered. This was a familiar ritual, she real-ized, her waiting for him outside of the bath. When Z finished showering and emerged in a towel, they would talk about nothing at all while he dressed in his closet. Then after he went down for First Meal, she would bathe and dress with equal privacy.

God, she felt small. Small compared to the problems they had and the demands of their daughter and the fact that she wanted a lover for a *hellren*, not a polite roommate.

The knock on the door made her jump. "Hello?"

"It's Doc Jane."

"Come on in."

The doctor poked her head around the door. "Hey, is himself around? I thought I'd remove his bandages—Okay, clearly you two have covered that part."

As the doctor jumped to the wrong conclusion, Bella kept her mouth shut. "He should be out of the bathroom soon. Can his cast come off?"

"I believe so. Why don't you tell him to meet me down in the PT suite when he's ready? I'm working on the medical facility expansion, so I'll just be puttering around with my tool belt."

"Will do."

There was a long moment with just the buzzing razor and the shower running in the background.

Doc Jane frowned. "Are you okay, Bella?"

Forcing a smile, she put both hands up in ward-off mode. "I'm perfectly healthy. I don't need another examination. Ever."

"That I believe." Jane smiled, then glanced at the bathroom's doorway. "Listen . . . maybe you should go wash his back, if you know what I mean."

"I'll wait."

Another silence. "May I make a suggestion that is completely intrusive?"

"Hard to imagine you can be more intrusive than you already have," Bella said with a wink.

"I'm serious."

"All right."

"Keep Nalla's main crib in the nursery and leave the door mostly closed as she sleeps in there. Get a baby monitor so you can hear her." Doc Jane swept her eyes around. "This is the room you and your husband share . . . you need to be something more than mommy, and he needs you to himself for a little bit each day. Nalla will be fine and it's important she get used to sleeping on her own."

Bella looked at the crib. The idea of moving it out was oddly and irrationally terrifying. As if she were throwing their daughter to the wolves. Except if she wanted more than a roommate, they needed the kind of space that had nothing to do with square footage.

"That might be a good idea."

"I've worked with a lot of people who have had babies. Doctors like to procreate. What can I say. After the first one comes along, there's always an adjustment period. It doesn't mean there's anything wrong with the marriage, it just means that new boundaries have to be established."

"Thank you . . . really, I appreciate it."

Doc Jane nodded. "I'm always here if you need me."

When the door shut, Bella went over to the crib and smoothed the multicolored satin ribbons that hung from its rails. As the cool lengths slid through her fingers, she thought of the pledging ceremony and all the love that had been shared. Nalla would always be adored in this house, cared for, protected.

She had a moment of panic as she released the brakes and started rolling the infant's bed toward the nursery—but she was going to get over that. Had to. And she would buy a baby monitor right away.

She parked the crib next to the one that was there, the one Nalla never slept as well in. Even now the young's forehead was crinkled, and she was pinwheeling her arms and legs, a sure sign she was going to wake up soon.

"Shhh, *mahmen's* got you." Bella lifted the young up and put her down in her preferred place. The young snuffled and positively cooed as she snuggled into herself and put her little hand through the slats, grabbing onto Wrath and Beth's red-and-black bow.

This was promising. Deep breathing and a full belly meant a nice long sleep.

At least Nalla didn't feel as though she'd been kicked to the curb.

Bella went back into the bedroom. The bath was quiet, and as she put her head through the doorway, she saw the fine humidity left in the air from the shower and caught the lingering scent of cedar shampoo.

He was gone.

"You moved the crib?"

She turned around. Z was standing in the double doors of his closet, his bootcut leathers on and his black shirt hanging from his hand. His chest, with its marking of the Brotherhood and its nipple rings, gleamed in the light thrown over his shoulders.

Bella glanced over to where Nalla had always slept. "Well, this is . . . you know, our space. And, ah, she's fine in the other room."

"You sure you're going to be okay with this?"

If it meant she could be with him as his *shellan?* "Nalla will be fine. She's just next door if she needs me, and she's started to sleep through big hunks of the day so . . . yes, I feel all right about it."

"You're . . . sure?"

Bella looked up at him. "Yes. Absolutely sure—"

Z threw down his shirt, dematerialized right at her, and took her down on the bed, all but tackling her. His bonding scent went crazy as his mouth ground into hers and his hard, heavy weight pushed her down into the mattress. His hands were rough with her nightgown, ripping it as he wrenched the two sides apart. As her breasts were bared, he growled deep and low.

"Oh, yes . . ." she moaned, frantic as he was.

She shoved her hands between their hips and broke a nail flipping his fly open and unzipping it—

Z let out another animal sound as his erection popped out into her hand. Rearing back, he nearly shredded his leathers trying to get them down his legs and off the cast. After struggling, he left them around his knees with a "Fuck it."

He leaped back on her, finished tearing apart her nightgown, and split her thighs wide. Except then he paused, a worried look threatening to overtake the passion in his face. He opened his mouth, clearly about to ask her if she was okay with—

"Shut up and get inside of me," she barked, grabbing the back of his neck and pulling him down to her lips.

He roared and punched into her core, the penetration a bomb that went off in her body, sparks shooting through her, igniting her blood. She gripped his ass hard as his hips jackhammered until he followed where she was, coming in a massive, full-torso contraction.

The instant it passed he threw his head back, bared his fangs, and hissed like a great cat. Arching back into the pillow, she put her face to the side, giving him her throat so that he—

As Zsadist struck hard and deep, she orgasmed again, and while he drew on her vein the sex pounded on. He was even better than she'd remembered, his muscles and bones churning on top of her, his skin so smooth, his bonding scent blanketing her in that special dark spice.

When he finished feeding and orgasmed for . . . God only knew how many times he'd come . . . his body stilled and he lapped at her throat to close the bite wound. The lingering, luscious strokes of his tongue made her want him again, and as if he read her mind, he rolled over onto his back and took her with him, keeping them joined.

"Do me," he demanded, his wild yellow eyes locking on her full breasts.

She cupped herself where his stare was fixated and pinched her own nipples as she rode him nice and slow. His moans and the way his hands tightened on her knees made her feel more beautiful than any words he could have spoken.

"God . . . I've missed you," he said.

"Me too." Dropping her hands to his shoulders, she leaned into him and swung her hips more freely.

"Oh, fuck, Bella—take my vein—"

The invitation was accepted before he finished issuing it and she was no more gentle than he had been. His taste was spectacular, and more intense than it had been. Ever since the birth, when she'd fed it had been . . . courteous. But this was raw, a champagne cocktail of power and sex, not just nutrition.

"I love you," he sighed as she took from him.

They made love four more times.

Once more on the bed.

Twice on the floor halfway to the bathroom.

Once again in the shower.

Afterward they wrapped themselves in thick white towels and climbed back into bed.

Zsadist tucked her into his side and kissed her forehead. "Is the whole issue as to whether I'm still attracted to you settled?"

She laughed, trailing her hand over the pads of his pecs and down onto his six-pack. She swore she could feel his muscles strengthening under her palm, his body drawing on what he'd gotten from his feeding. The fact that she was making him strong made her proud . . . but more than that, it made her feel connected to him.

The Scribe Virgin had been a smart one when she'd created a race that needed to feed from itself.

"Well? Has it?" Z rolled over on top of her, his scarred face breaking into an I-am-the-man smile. "Or do I need to prove it again?"

She ran her hands up his heavy arms. "No, I think we're— Z!"

"What?" he drawled as he nestled his way in between her legs again. "I'm sorry. I can't help it. I'm still hungry." He put his mouth to hers as gentle as a breath. "Mmmm . . ."

His lips went down to her neck and he gave his bite mark a little nuzzle, as if he were saying thank-you.

"Mmm . . . mine," he growled.

So slow, so soft . . . his mouth went down farther, to her breast. He paused at the nipple.

"Are they sensitive?" he asked, rubbing the tip of his nose over her crest, then licking her.

"Yes . . ." She shivered as he blew a stream of air over where his tongue had been.

"They look it. All red and pouty and pretty." He was ever so careful with her breasts, caressing them with his hands and kissing them lightly.

When he moved down to her stomach she started to get hot and restless again, and he smiled up at her. "Have you missed my kisses, darling mate? The ones I like to give you between your thighs?"

"Yes," she choked out while anticipation shivered through her. Given the erotic little grin on his face and the evil cast to his yellow stare, he was once again a male with plans and a wide-open schedule.

He rose up on his knees. "Open your legs for me. I like to watch you— Oh . . . shit . . . *yeah.*" He rubbed at his mouth like he was warming the thing up. "That's what I'm talking about."

His shoulders bunched up hard as he leaned down and made like a cat to a bowl of milk—while she made like an *ehros*, giving herself up to him and his warm wet mouth.

"I want to go slowly," he murmured against her core as she groaned his name. "I don't want to finish my treat too quickly."

That wasn't going to be a problem, she thought. For him, she was a pool with no bottom . . .

His tongue slipped inside of her, in a hot penetration, then went back to its sweet, dragging strokes. Looking down her body, she saw him staring up at her with glowing citrine eyes . . . and as if he'd waited for her gaze to meet his, he flicked the top of her sex back and forth.

Watching his pink flesh work hers threw her over the edge again.

"*Zsadist* . . ." she groaned, palming his head and pushing her hips up.

There was nothing more delicious than being between your *shellan*'s legs.

It wasn't just the taste; it was the sounds and the scents and the way she looked at you with her head cocked to the side and her rosy lips open so she could breathe. It was the soft, welling center of everything that made her female against your mouth and the trust she had in letting you get this close. It was everything private and sensual and special. . . .

And the kind of thing you could do forever.

As his *shellan* let out the most incredible moan and started to orgasm, Zsadist moved up her body and put himself inside so he could feel the contractions along his shaft.

He put his mouth to her ear as he came into her. "You are *everything* to me."

When they rested together afterward, he stared down her full breasts to her abdomen and thought of how amazing her body was compared to his. Her curves and feminine strength had created a whole new person, had provided the protective place for the alchemy of them coming together and making life.

The two of them.

"Nalla . . ." he whispered. "Nalla has . . ."

He felt her tense up. "Has what?"

"Nalla has my eyes. Doesn't she."

His *shellan*'s voice became soft and careful, like she didn't want to spook him. "Yes, she does."

Z put his hand on Bella's stomach and rubbed circles over the taut skin, as she had done so many times while pregnant. He was ashamed of himself now . . . ashamed that he hadn't touched her belly once. He'd been so worried about the birth that the looming roundness had seemed like a threat to both their lives, not something to rejoice in.

"I'm sorry," he said abruptly.

"What for?"

"You've had to do all this on your own, haven't you. Not just these last three months, but before. When you were pregnant."

"You were always there for me—"

"But not for Nalla, and she was a part of you. Is a part of you."

Bella propped her head up. "She's a part of you, too."

He thought of the wide, bright yellow eyes of the young. "Sometimes I think she might look a little like me as well."

"She looks almost identical to you. She has your chin and your eyebrows. And her hair . . ." Bella's voice started to get excited, as if she had wanted to talk with him about all the ins and outs of the young's makeup for a while. "Her hair is going to be exactly like yours and Phury's. And have you seen her hands? Her forefingers are longer than her ring fingers, just like yours."

"Really?" Man, what kind of father was he that he didn't know all this.

Well, that was easy. He hadn't been any sort of father at all.

Bella extended her hand. "Let's shower, and then come with me. Let me introduce you to your daughter."

Z took a deep breath. Then nodded.

"I'd like that," he said.

EIGHT

As Zsadist breached the doorway of the nursery, he actually double-checked to make sure his shirt was properly tucked into his leathers.

Man, he loved the smell of the room. Lemon-scented innocence was what he called it in his mind. Sweet like a flower, but not cloying. Clean.

Bella squeezed his hand and led him over to the crib. Surrounded by satin bows that were bigger than she was, Nalla was curled up on her side, her arms and legs tucked in tight, her eyes shut hard as if she were working really, really, really diligently at being asleep.

The instant Z looked over the lip of the crib, she stirred. Made a little noise. In her sleep her hand reached out, not toward her mother, but to him.

"What does she want?" he asked like an idiot.

"She wants you to touch her." When he didn't move, Bella murmured, "She does this in her sleep . . . she seems to know who's around and she likes a little pat."

To his *shellan*'s absolute credit, she didn't force him to do anything.

But Nalla wasn't happy. Her little hand and arm strained for him.

Z wiped his palm on the front of his shirt, then rubbed it up and down a couple of times on his hip. As he reached forward, his fingers trembled.

Nalla made the connection. His daughter took his thumb and held it with such strength he felt a spear of pure, undiluted pride shoot through his chest.

"She's strong," he pronounced, his approval positively dripping off the words.

Bella made a little noise beside him.

"Nalla?" he whispered as he bent down. His daughter pursed her little lips and held on even stronger.

"I can't believe that grip of hers." He let his forefinger brush lightly on his daughter's wrist. "Soft . . . oh, my God, she's so soft—"

Nalla's eyes flipped open. And as he looked into a stare the exact golden color of his own, his heart stopped. "Hi . . ."

Nalla blinked and waved his finger and transformed him: Everything stopped as she moved not just his hand, but his heart.

"You're like your *mahmen*," he whispered. "You make the world go away for me. . . ."

Nalla kept wagging his hand and let out a coo.

"I can't believe her grip. . . ." He glanced up at Bella. "She's so—"

Tears were streaming down Bella's face, and her arms were locked around her chest as if she were trying not to shatter apart.

His heart moved again, but for a different reason.

"Come here, *nalla*," he said, reaching out to his *shellan*, tucking her in against him with his free hand. "Come here to your male."

Bella buried her face into his chest and her palm found his.

As Z stood there, with a hold on both his daughter and his mate, he felt eight thousand feet tall, and faster than his Carrera and stronger than an army.

His chest swelled with renewed purpose. They were both his, these two. His and his alone, and he had to take care of them. One was his heart and the other a piece of himself, and they completed him by filling voids he didn't know he had.

Nalla looked up at her parents and the most adorable sound came out of her button mouth, a kind of, *Well, isn't this lovely, the way things have sorted out.*

But then his daughter reached up with her other hand . . . and touched the slave band on his wrist.

Z stiffened. He couldn't help it.

"She doesn't know what they are," Bella said softly.

He took a hard breath. "She will. Someday she will know exactly what they are."

Before Z went down to see Doc Jane, he spent more time with his ladies. He ordered some food for Bella, and while it was being prepared he watched for the first time as his daughter was fed. Nalla zonked right out afterward, which was perfect timing, as Fritz arrived with the food. Z fed his *shellan* from his own hand, taking special satisfaction in choosing the very best parts of the chicken breast and the homemade rolls and the broccoli spears for her.

When the plate was clean and the wineglass empty, he wiped Bella's mouth with a damask napkin as her lids fluttered down. Tucking her in, he kissed her, picked up the tray and his right shitkicker, and stepped out.

As he closed the door quietly and heard the knob click, a glow of contentment bathed him. His females were fed and sleeping and safe. He'd done his job well.

Job? Try mission in life.

He glanced toward the nursery door and wondered whether, as a male, you bonded with your children or not. He'd always heard it was only with your *shellan* . . . but he was starting to have some serious protective instincts over Nalla. And he hadn't even picked her up yet. Give him two weeks of getting familiar with her? He was liable to become an H-bomb if anything threatened her.

Was that what being a father was like? He didn't know. None of his brothers had young and there was no one else he could think of to ask.

Heading for the stairs, he limped down the hall of statues, boot, cast, boot, cast, boot, cast. . . . and he looked at his wrists as he went along.

Downstairs he took the dishes into the kitchen and thanked Fritz, then went into the tunnel that led to the training center. If Doc Jane had given up waiting on him, he was going to cut the cast off himself.

Stepping out through the closet in the office, he heard the high whining sound of a table saw and followed the scream to the gym. On the way he was looking forward to seeing how Jane's new clinic was coming along. The three treatment bays, which were being constructed out of one of the facility's audience halls, were designed to function as either surgical suites or patient bays, and the equipment was going to be state of the art. Doc Jane was investing in a CAT scan, digital X-ray imaging, and ultrasound technology, along with an electronic medical records system and a host of hi-tech surgical tools. With a supply room worthy of a fully functioning emergency department, the goal was to circumvent the Brotherhood's use of Havers's clinic.

Which was safer for everybody. The Brotherhood's compound was surrounded by *mhis*, thanks to V, but the same couldn't be said for where Havers practiced— as had been proven when the clinic was sacked over the summer. Considering that the Brothers could be tailed at any time, it was smart to keep as many things having to do with them in-house.

Z cracked one of the gym's metal doors open and paused. Yeah, whoa. Doc Jane evidently had some serious *Extreme Home Makeover* in her.

Last night, when Z had been rolled in, everything had been as it always was. Now, less than twenty-four hours later, a six-foot-by-twelve-foot hole had been busted out of the cinder-block wall across the way. The opening exposed the audience hall that was going to be converted, and right in front of the chasm, V's mate was taking a two-by-four and feeding it into a table saw, her hands solid, the rest of her ghostly transparent.

When she caught sight of Z, she finished with the board and turned the machine off. "Hey!" she called out as the din faded. "You ready to have that cast removed?"

"Yeah. And clearly you're good with a saw."

"You better believe it." She grinned and gestured toward the hole. "So, you like my interior decorating?"

"You don't fool around."

"Masonry hammers rock, what can I say?"

"I'm ready for the next board," V hollered from the lecture hall.

"It's ready."

V came out wearing a tool belt hung with a hammer and several chisels. As he went over to his female, he said, "Hey, Z, how's your leg?"

"Gonna be better once Doc Jane takes this deadweight off." Z nodded across the way. "Man, you guys are going to town."

"Yeah, we should be able to take care of the framing tonight."

Doc Jane handed her male the board and gave him a quick kiss, her face becoming solid as contact was made. "I'll be right back. Just going to take off his cast."

"Don't rush." V nodded at Zsadist. "You look tight. I'm glad."

"Your female's a miracle worker."

"That she is."

"Okay, enough with the ego stroking, boys." She smiled and kissed her mate again. "Come on, Z. Let's do it."

As she turned away, V's eyes followed her body . . . which no doubt meant that as soon as Zsadist was out of their hair, the new clinic wasn't the only thing that was going to get worked on.

When Doc Jane and Z got to the PT suite, he went over and hopped up onto the gurney. "Thought maybe you'd want to use that table saw on me."

"Nah. You already have one person in your bloodline missing a leg. Two would be overkill." Her smile was gentle. "Any pain?"

"Nope."

She rolled over a portable X-ray machine. "Put your leg up—perfect. Thanks."

As she came back at him with a lead drape, he took it from her and settled it over himself.

"Can I ask you something?" he said.

"Yup. Let me get this done first, though." She arranged the eye of the machine and took a picture, a short, humming burst rising up into the room. After checking a computer screen across the way, she said, "On your side, please."

He rolled over and she moved his leg around. After another quick hum and a check of the monitor, she said, "Okay, you can sit up. Leg looks great, so I'm just going to get rid of this outstanding plaster job I did."

She handed him a blanket and turned her back as he shucked his leathers. Then she brought over a stainless-steel saw and carefully went to work on his cast.

"So what's your question?" she said over the buzzing as she worked.

Z rubbed the slave band on his left wrist, then extended his arm toward her. "Do you really think I could get these taken off?"

Jane paused with the saw still running, no doubt collecting her thoughts not only from a medical standpoint but a personal one. She made a noise, a little *huh*, and quickly finished shucking the cast.

"You want to clean your leg up?" she asked, bringing over a damp washcloth.

"Yeah. Thanks."

After he made quick work with the tidy business, she gave him something to dry off with.

"Mind if I take a closer look at the skin?" she said, nodding to his wrist. When he shook his head, she bent over his arm.

"Laser removal of tattoos in humans is quite common. I don't have the technology here, but with your help, I have an idea how we could give it a shot. And who could do it for you."

He stared down at the black band and thought of his daughter's little hand on that dense black ink.

"I think . . . yeah, I think I want to try."

When Bella woke up and stretched in her mated bed, she felt like she'd been on vacation for a month. Her body was refreshed and strong . . . as well as sore in all the right places. And in spite of her earlier shower, Z's scent remained all over her, and wasn't that just perfect.

Going by the clock on the bedside table, she'd been out like a light for about two hours, so she got up, put on her robe, and brushed her teeth, thinking a check on Nalla and maybe a snack was a good thing. She was on her way into the nursery when Z came through the door.

She couldn't help beaming at him. "Your cast is off."

"Mmm-hmmm . . . come here, female." He walked over to her, wrapped his arms around her, and bent her backward so she had to grab onto his arms to stay upright. He kissed her long and slow, rubbing his lower body and his huge erection into the juncture of her thighs.

"I missed you," he purred against her throat.

"You just had me only two hour—"

His tongue in her mouth silenced her, as did his hands, which ended up on her butt. He carried her over to one of the windowsills, propped her up on the molding, unzipped himself, and—

"Oh . . . God," she groaned with a smile.

Now this . . . this was the male she knew and loved. Always hungry for her.

Always wanting to be close. As he started to move slowly inside of her, she remembered back in the beginning, after he'd finally opened himself up to her. She'd been surprised by how much he wanted to be cozied against her, whether it was during meals or when they were hanging with the Brothers or during the day when they slept. It was as if he'd been making up for centuries of not having warm, nurturing contact.

Bella wrapped her arms around his neck and put her cheek to his ear, the baby-soft brush of his skull trim caressing her face as he moved.

"I'm going to . . . need your help," he said as he surged forward and slid back.

"Anything . . . just don't stop. . . ."

"Wouldn't . . . dream . . . of it—" The rest of what he said was lost as the sex took control. "Oh, God . . . Bella!"

After they were finished, her male pulled back a little, his citrine eyes sparkling like champagne. "By the way . . . hi. I forgot to say that when I walked in."

"Oh, I think you greeted me just fine, thank you very much." She kissed his mouth. "Now . . . help?"

"Let's get you tidied up," he drawled, the light in that yellow stare of his telling her that the cleaning might well lead to more messiness.

Which it certainly did.

When they were both satiated and she'd had yet a third shower, she wrapped herself up in her robe and started toweling her hair. "Now, what do you need my help with?"

Z propped himself against the marble counter next to the sinks, rubbed his palm over his skull trim, and got dead serious.

Bella stopped what she was doing. As he stayed quiet, she backed up and sat down on the edge of the Jacuzzi to give him some space. She waited, hands clenching and releasing in her lap.

For some reason, as he sat there collecting his thoughts, she realized that they had done a lot in this bathroom. It was here that she'd found him throwing up after he'd aroused her for the very first time at that party. And then . . . after he'd rescued her from the lessers, he'd bathed her in this tub. And in the shower across the way she'd fed from him for the first time.

She thought of that rough period in their lives, her just out of her abduction, him struggling with his attraction to her. Glancing over to the right, she recalled finding him on the tile beneath an ice-cold spray, scrubbing at his wrists, believing himself unclean and unable to feed her.

He'd shown a lot of courage. Getting over what had been done to him enough to trust her had taken a lot of courage.

Bella's eyes went back to him, and when she realized he was staring at his wrists, she said, "You're going to try to get them removed, aren't you."

His mouth twitched into a half smile, the side distorted by the tail of his facial scar lifting. "You know me so well."

"How will you get it done?" When he finished telling her, she nodded. "Excellent plan. And I'll go with you."

He looked up at her. "Good. Thank you. I don't think I could do it without you."

She stood up and went over to him. "You're not going to have to worry about that."

NINE

Dr. Thomas Wolcott Franklin III had the second-best office in the St. Francis Hospital complex.

When it came to quality administrative real estate, the pecking order was determined by your revenues, and as chief of dermatology, T.W. was behind only one other department head.

Of course, the fact that his department was such a good earner was because he'd "sold out," as some of the academic stalwarts maintained. Under his leadership, dermatology not only handled lesions and cancers and burns in addition to chronic skin conditions such as psoriasis, eczema, and acne, but there was a whole subdivision that did only cosmetic procedures.

Face-lifts. Brow-lifts. Breast enhancements. Lipo. Botox. Restylane. A hundred other improvements. The health care model was private-practice service delivered in an academic setting, and wealthy clients loved the concept. The bulk of them came up from the Big Apple—at first making the trip for the anonymity of getting first-class treatment out of the tight-knit plastics community in Manhattan, but then, perversely, for the status. Getting "work" done in Caldwell was the chic thing to do, and, courtesy of the trend, only the chief of surgery, Manny Manello, had a better office view.

Well, Manello's private bathroom also had marble in the shower, not just on the counters and walls, but really, who was counting.

T.W. liked his view. Liked his office. Loved his work.

Which was a good thing, as his days started at seven and ended at—he checked his watch—nearly seven.

Tonight, though, he should have already been gone by now. T.W. had a standing racquetball game every Monday night at seven p.m. at the Caldwell Country Club . . . so he was a little confused as to why he'd agreed to see a patient now. Somehow he'd said yes and had his secretary find a replacement for him on the courts, but he couldn't for the life of him remember the whys or whos of it all.

He took his printed schedule out of the breast pocket of his white coat and shook his head. Right next to seven o'clock was the name B. *Nalla* and the words *laser cosmetics*. Man, he had no recollection how the appointment had been made or who it was or who'd given the referral . . . but nothing got onto that grid of hours without his permission.

So it must be someone important. Or the patient of someone important.

Clearly he was working too hard.

T.W. logged on to the electronic medical records system and ran a search, again, for B. Nalla. Closest match was Belinda Nalda. Typo? Could be. But his assistant had left at six, and it seemed rude to interrupt her while she was having dinner with her family with just a what-the-hell-is-this?

He stood up, checked his tie and buttoned his white coat, then picked up some work to review while he waited downstairs for B. Nalla or Nalda to show.

As he headed out of the department's top-floor stretch of offices and treatment areas, he thought about the difference between up here and down in the private clinic. Night and day. Here the decor was done in hospital non-chic: low-napped dark carpet, cream walls, lots of plain cream doors. The prints that were hung had spare stainless-steel frames, and the plants were few and far between.

Downstairs? Top-tier spa land with concierge services delivered in the kind of luxury the very rich expected: the treatment rooms had HD flat-screen TVs, DVDs, couches, chairs, tiny Sub-Zero refrigerators with rare fruit juices, food that could be ordered from restaurants, and wireless Internet for laptops. The clinic even had a reciprocal agreement with Caldwell's Stillwell Hotel, the five-star grande dame of lodging in all of upstate New York, so that patients could rest overnight after receiving care.

Over-the-top? Yes. And was there a surcharge? Absolutely. But the reality was, reimbursements from the federal government were down, insurers were denying medically necessary procedures left and right, and T.W. needed funds to fulfill his mission.

Catering to the rich was the way to do it.

Thing was, T.W. had two rules for his doctors and nurses. One, offer the best damn care on the planet with a compassionate hand. And two, never turn a patient away. Ever. Especially the burn victims.

No matter how expensive or how long the course of treatment for a burn was, he never said no. Especially to the children.

If he was seen as a sellout to commercial demand? Fine. No problem. He didn't make a big deal about what he did on the free-care side of things, and if his colleagues in other cities wanted to portray him as a money-grubber, he'd take the hit.

When he got to the elevators, he reached out with his left hand, the one that was scarred, the one that was missing a pinkie and had mottled skin, and pressed the button for down.

He was going to do whatever he had to to make sure folks got the help they needed. Someone had done it for him, and it had made all the difference in his life.

Down on the first floor he hung a right and walked along a stretch of corridor until he came to the mahogany-paneled entrance of the cosmetics clinic. In discreet lettering that was frosted into the glass were his name and the names of seven of his colleagues. There was no mention of what kind of medicine was practiced inside.

Patients had told him they loved the exclusive, members-only-club vibe.

Using a pass card, he let himself in. The reception room was dim, and not because the lighting had been turned off after main business hours were through: Bright lights were not becoming on people of a certain age, either pre- or post-operatively, and besides, the calming, soothing atmosphere was part of the spa environment they were trying to create. The floor was tiled in soft sandstone, the walls were a comforting deep red, and a fountain made from cream and white and tan rocks twinkled in the center of the area.

"Marcia?" he called out, pronouncing the name MAR-*see-uh*, in the European fashion.

"'Allo, Dr. Franklin," came a smooth voice from the back where the office was.

When Marcia came around the corner, T.W. put his left hand in his pocket. As usual, she looked right out of *Vogue* with her coiffed black hair and her tailored black suit.

"Your patient is not here yet," she said with a serene smile. "But I have the second lasering bay set up for you."

Marcia was a perfectly touched up forty-year-old who was married to one of the plastics guys and was, as far as T.W. knew, the only woman on the planet except for Ava Gardner who could wear bloodred lipstick and still look classy. Her wardrobe was by Chanel, and she'd been hired and was paid well to be a walking testimonial to the outstanding work performed by the staff.

And the fact that she had an aristocratic French accent was a bonus. Particularly with the nouveau riche types.

"Thanks," T.W. said. "Hopefully the patient will be here soon and you can go."

"So you do not need an assistant, no?"

This was the other great thing about Marcia: She was not just decorative; she was useful, a fully trained nurse who was always happy to assist.

"I appreciate the offer, but just send the patient back and I'll take care of everything."

"Even the registering?"

He smiled. "I'm sure you want to get home to Phillippe."

"Ah, *oui*. It is our anniversary."

He winked at her. "Heard something about that."

Her cheeks reddened a little, which was one of the charming things about her. She might be classy but she was real, too. "My husband, he says I am to meet him at the front door. He says he has a surprise for his wife."

"I know what it is. You're going to love it." But what woman wouldn't like a pair of flashers from Harry Winston?

Marcia brought her hand up to her mouth, hiding her smile and her sudden flusters. "He is too good to me."

T.W. felt a momentary pang, wondering when the last time was that he'd bought something frivolous and fancy for his wife. It had been . . . well, he'd gotten her a Volvo last year.

Wow.

"You deserve it," he said roughly, thinking for some reason about the number of nights his wife ate alone. "So please go home and celebrate."

"I will, Doctor. *Merci mille fois*." Marcia bowed and went over to the receiving desk—which was really nothing more than an antique table with a phone hidden in the side drawer and a laptop you accessed by flipping open a mahogany panel. "I shall just sign out of the system and wait to welcome your patient."

"Have a great night."

As T.W. turned away and left her to her glow, he took his ruined hand back out of his pocket. He always hid it from her, part of the leftover from having been a teenager with the damn thing. It was so ridiculous. He was happily married and not even attracted to Marcia, so it shouldn't have mattered at all. Scars, though, left wounds on the inside of you, and as with skin that didn't heal right, you still felt the rough spots from time to time.

The three lasers in the clinic's facility were used to treat spider veins in legs, port-wine-stain birthmarks, and red dermal imperfections, as well as provide resurfacing treatments for the face, and the removal of the guiding tattoo marks of cancer patients who'd received radiation.

B. Nalla might need any one of those things done—but if he were a betting man, he would go with cosmetic resurfacing. Just seemed to fit . . . after hours, in the downstairs clinic, with a mysterious name. No doubt another one of the very wealthy, with a paralytic need for confidentiality.

Still, you had to respect your cash cows.

Going into the second laser suite, which he preferred for no good reason, he took a seat behind the mahogany desk and logged on to the computer, reviewing the patients who were coming in the morning and then focusing on the dermatology fellows' reports he'd brought with him.

As the minutes ticked by, he started to get annoyed at these rich people and their demands and their self-important view of their place in the world. Sure . . . some of them were fine, and all of them helped support his efforts, but man, sometimes he wanted to choke the entitlement right out of them—

A six-foot-tall woman appeared in the doorway of the exam room, and he froze solid. What she was wearing was simple, just a crisp white button-down shirt tucked into a pair of ultraslim blue jeans, but she had Christian Louboutin's red-soled stillies on her feet and Prada hanging off her shoulder.

She was exactly his kind of private clientele, and not just because she was wearing about three grand's worth of accessories. She was . . . indescribably beautiful, with deep brown hair and sapphire eyes and a face that was the sort of thing other women asked to be surgically altered to resemble.

T.W. slowly stood up, shoving his left hand deep into his pocket. "Belinda? Belinda Nalda?"

Unlike a lot of women of her class, which was clearly stratospheric, she didn't waltz in like she owned the place. She took just one step past the doorway.

"Actually, it's Bella." Her voice made his eyes want to roll back into his head. Deep, husky . . . but kind.

"I, ah . . ." T.W. cleared his throat. "I'm Dr. Franklin."

He extended his good hand and she took it. As they shook he knew he was staring, and not in a professional way, but he couldn't help himself. He'd seen a lot of beautiful women in his day, but nothing like her. It was almost as if she were from another planet.

"Please . . . please come and have a seat." He indicated the silk-covered club chair next to the desk. "We'll get your history and—"

"I'm not the one being treated. My *hell*—husband is." She took a deep breath and looked over her shoulder. "Darling?"

T.W. scrambled back and hit the wall so hard the framed watercolor next to him bounced. His first thought as he looked at what walked in was that maybe he should get closer to the phone so he could call security.

The man had a scarred face and serial-killer black eyes, and as he came in, he filled the entire room: He was big enough and broad enough to classify as a heavy-weight boxer, or maybe two of them put together, but Christ, that was the least of your problems as he stared at you. He was dead inside. Absolutely without affect. Which made him capable of anything.

And T.W. could have sworn the temperature of the room actually went down as the man came to stand next to his wife.

The woman spoke calmly and quietly. "We're here to see if his tattoos can be removed."

T.W. swallowed and told himself to get a grip. Okay, maybe this thug was just your garden-variety punk-rock star. T.W.'s own taste in music ran more toward jazz, so there was no reason he'd recognize this guy in the leathers and the black turtleneck and the gauge in his ear, but it could explain things. Including why the wife was model gorgeous. Most singers had beautiful women, didn't they?

Yeah . . . the only problem with that theory was the black stare. That was no manufactured, commercially viable, hard-ass front. There was real violence in there. True depravity.

"Doctor?" the woman said. "Is there going to be a problem?"

He swallowed again, wishing he hadn't told Marcia to go. Then again, women and children and all that. Probably safer for her not to be here.

"Doctor?"

He just kept looking at the guy—who made no move other than breathing.

Hell, if the big bastard wanted to, he could have busted up the place twelve times over by now. Instead? He was just standing there.

And standing there.

And . . . standing there.

Eventually, T.W. cleared his throat and decided that if there was going to be trouble, it would have happened already. "No, there's no problem. I'm going to sit down. Now."

He planted it in the desk's chair and bent to the side, pulling open a refrigerated drawer that had a variety of sparkling waters in it. "May I offer you anything to drink?"

When they both said no, he cracked open a Perrier with lemon and downed half of it like it was Scotch.

"Right. I'll need to take a medical history."

The wife took a seat and the husband loomed over her, eyes locked on T.W. Odd, though. They were holding hands and T.W. got the impression that the wife was the husband's tether in some way.

Calling on his training, he took out his Waterman pen and asked the usual questions. The wife did the answering: No known allergies. No surgical procedures. No health problems.

"Ah . . . where are the tattoos?" Please, God, let them not be below the waist.

"On his wrists and his neck." She looked up at her husband, her eyes luminous. "Show him, darling."

The man reached to one side and pulled up his sleeve. T.W. frowned, medical curiosity taking over. The black band was incredibly dense, and though he wasn't an expert on tattooing by a long shot, he could safely say he'd never seen such deep coloration before.

"That is very dark," he said, leaning in. Something told him not to touch the man unless he had to, and he followed the instinct, keeping his hands to himself. "That is very, very dark."

They were almost like shackles, he thought.

T.W. eased back into the chair. "I'm not sure whether you're a good candidate for laser removal. The ink appears to be so dense that at a minimum it's going to require multiple sessions to make even a dent in the pigmentation."

"Will you try, though?" the wife asked. "Please?"

T.W.'s eyebrows popped. *Please* was not a word in the vocabulary of most of the patients down here. And her tone was equally foreign to the locale, its quiet desperation more what you would find in families of patients treated upstairs—those with medical issues that affected their lives, not just their crow's-feet and laugh lines.

"I can try," he said, well aware that if she used that tone on him again, she could get him to eat his own legs just to please her.

He looked at the husband. "Would you remove your shirt and get up on the table?"

The wife squeezed the big hand in hers. "It's okay."

The husband's hollow-cheeked, hard-jawed face turned to her, and he seemed to draw tangible strength from her eyes. After a moment he went over to the table, got his huge body up on the thing, and removed his turtleneck.

T.W. left his chair and walked around—

He froze. The man's back was covered with scars. Scars . . . that looked like they had been left by whips.

In his entire medical career he had seen nothing even resembling this—and knew it must have been left by some kind of torture.

"My tats, Doc," the husband said in a nasty tone. "You're supposed to be eyeballing my tats, thank you very much."

As T.W. blinked, the husband shook his head. "This isn't going to work—"

The wife rushed forward. "No, it will. It—"

"Let's find someone else."

T.W. came around to face the man, blocking the way to the door. And then he deliberately took his left hand out of his pocket. That black stare dipped down and fixated on the mottled skin and the ruined pinkie.

The patient looked up in surprise; then his eyes narrowed like he was wondering how far up the burn went.

"All the way to my shoulder and down my back," T.W. said. "House fire when I was ten. Got trapped in my room. I was conscious while I was burned . . . the entire time. Spent eight weeks in the hospital afterward. Have had seventeen surgeries."

There was a beat of silence, as if the husband were running through the implications in his head: *If you were conscious, you'd have smelled the flesh cook and felt every lick of pain. And the hospital time . . . the surgeries . . .*

Abruptly the man's whole body eased up, the tension flowing out of him as if a valve had been released.

T.W. had seen it happen time and time again with his burn patients. If your doctor knew what it was like to be where you were, not because they had been taught about it at medical school but because they had lived it, you felt safer with them: The two of you were members of the same exclusive hard-core club.

"So can you do anything for these things, Doc?" the man asked, laying his forearms out on his thighs.

"Is it okay to touch you?"

The man's scarred lip lifted slightly, as if he'd just given T.W. another point in the good category. "Yup."

T.W. deliberately used both his hands on the patient's wrists so the guy could have plenty of time to look at the scars of his doctor and relax even more.

When he was through, he stepped back.

"Well, I'm not sure how this is going to go, but let's give it a shot—" T.W. looked up and stopped. The man's irises . . . were yellow now. Not black anymore.

"Don't you worry 'bout my eyes, Doc."

From out of nowhere, the idea that everything was fine with what he'd seen flooded into his brain. Right. No. Big. Deal. "Where was I . . . Oh, yes. Well, let's give the laser a shot." He turned to the wife. "Perhaps you'd like to pull up a chair and hold his hand? I think he'll feel more comfortable that way. I'm going to start on one wrist and we'll see how it goes."

"Do I have to lie down?" the patient said darkly. "'Cause I don't think . . . yeah, I might not be cool with that."

"Not at all. You can stay sitting up, even when we do the neck, and for that part I'll get you a mirror so you can watch me. At all times I'll tell you exactly what I'm doing, what you're likely to feel, and we can always stop. You just say the word and it's over. This is your body. You are in control. Okay?"

There was a moment of silence as both of them stared at him. And then the wife said in a broken tone, "You, Dr. Franklin, are a total peach."

The patient had an incredible pain tolerance, T.W. thought an hour later as he tapped the floor toggle and the laser snapped out yet another thin red beam onto the inked skin of that thick wrist. An *incredible* pain tolerance. Each zap was like getting hit with a rubber band, which was not a big deal if it was done only once or twice. But after a couple of minutes of those strikes, most patients needed to rest. This guy? Never flinched, not even once. So T.W. just kept going and going. . . .

Of course, with his nipples pierced as they were and his gauge and all his scars, he'd obviously been intimately familiar with agony, both by choice and without it.

Unfortunately his tattoos were utterly resistant to the laser.

T.W. let out his breath on a curse and shook his right hand, which was getting tired.

"It's okay, Doc," the patient said softly. "You gave it your best shot."

"I just don't understand." He whipped off his eye protection and glanced over at the machine. For a moment he wondered whether the thing was working properly. But he'd seen the laser. "There's no change in coloration at all."

"Doc, for real, it's cool." The patient took off his goggles and smiled a little. "I appreciate your taking this as seriously as you have."

"Goddamn it." T.W. sat back on his stool and glared at the ink.

From out of nowhere words jumped out of his mouth, even though they were arguably unprofessional. "You didn't volunteer for those, did you."

The wife fidgeted as if she were worried about the answer. But the husband just shook his head. "No, Doc. I didn't."

"God*damn* it." He crossed his arms and refiled through his encyclopedic knowledge of the human skin. "I just don't understand why . . . and I'm trying to think of other options. I don't think a chemical removal would be any more efficacious. I mean, you took everything that laser could give you."

The husband ran his curiously elegant fingers over his wrist. "Could we cut them out?"

The wife shook her head. "I don't think that's a good idea."

"She's right," T.W. murmured. He leaned forward and prodded at the dermis. "You have excellent elasticity, but then again, as you're in your mid-twenties, that's expected. I mean, it would have to be done in strips and the skin stitched closed. You'd get scarring. And I wouldn't recommend it around the neck. Too many risks with the arteries."

"What if scarring wasn't a problem?"

He wasn't going to touch that question. Scarring was obviously an issue, given the man's back. "I couldn't recommend it."

There was a long silence while he continued to think things over and they gave him space. When he got to the end of all the options, he just stared at the two of them. The gorgeous wife was seated next to the scary-looking husband, one hand on his free arm, the other on his mutilated back, stroking.

It was obvious that his scars didn't affect his worth in her eyes. He was whole and beautiful to her in spite of the condition of his skin.

T.W. thought of his own wife. Who was just like that.

"Out of ideas, Doc?" the husband asked.

"I am so sorry." He shifted his eyes around, hating how helpless he felt. As a doctor he was trained to *do* something. As a human with a heart, he *needed* to do something. "I am so very sorry."

The husband smiled that little smile of his again. "You treat a lot of people with burns, don't you."

"It's my specialty. Kids, mostly. You know, because of . . ."

"Yeah, I know. Betcha you're good to them."

"How could I not be?"

The patient leaned forward and put his huge hand on T.W.'s shoulder. "We're going to take off now, Doc. But my *shellan's* going to leave the payment on the desk over there."

T.W. glanced at the wife, who was bent over a checkbook, then shook his head. "Why don't we just call it even. This really didn't help you."

"Nah, we took your time. We'll pay."

T.W. cursed under his breath a couple of times. Then just spat out, "*Damn* it."

"Doc? Look at me now?"

T.W. glanced up at the guy. Man, that yellow stare was positively hypnotic. "Wow. You have incredible eyes."

The patient smiled more widely, flashing teeth that were . . . not normal. "Thank you, Doc. Now listen up. You're probably going to have dreams about this, and I want you to remember I left here tight, 'kay?"

T.W. frowned. "Why would I dream—"

"Just remember, I'm okay with what happened. Knowing you, that's what's going to bother you most."

"I still don't understand why I would h—"

T.W. blinked and looked around the examination room. He was sitting on the little rolling stool he used when he treated patients, and there was a chair pulled over next to the patient table, and he had his eye protection in his hand . . . except there was no one in the room but him.

Odd. He could have sworn he was just talking to the most amazing—

As a headache came on he rubbed his temples and became suddenly exhausted . . . exhausted and curiously depressed, as if he'd failed at something that had been important to him.

.And worried. Worried about a m—

The headache got worse, and with a groan he stood up and went over to the desk. There was an envelope on it, a plain creamy envelope with flowing cursive script that read, *In gratitude to T.W. Franklin, M.D., to be applied at his direction in favor of his department's good works.*

He turned it over, ripped open the flap, and took out a check.

His jaw hit the floor.

One hundred thousand dollars. Made out to the Department of Dermatology, St. Francis Hospital.

The name of the person listed was Fritz Perlmutter, and there was no address at the upper left, just a discreet notation: *Caldwell National Bank, Private Client Group*.

One hundred thousand dollars.

An image of a scarred husband and a gorgeous wife flickered in his mind, then was buried by his headache.

T.W. took the check and slipped it inside his shirt pocket, then shut down the laser machine and the computer and made his way to the back clinic exit, turning lights off as he went.

On his way home he found himself thinking of his wife, of the way she'd been when she'd first seen him after the fire all those decades ago. She'd been eleven and had come to visit him with her parents. He'd been absolutely mortified when she'd walked through the door because he'd already had a crush on her at that point, and there he'd been, stuck in a hospital bed, one side of him covered with bandages.

She'd smiled at him and taken his good hand and told him no matter what his arm looked like, she still wanted to be his friend.

She'd meant it. And then, proved it over and over again.

Even liked him as more than a friend.

Sometimes, T.W. thought, the fact that the one you cared about didn't care how you looked was the best healing there was.

As he drove along, he passed by a jewelry store that was locked up tight for the night, and then a florist and then an antique shop that he knew his wife liked to browse in.

She'd given him three children. Nearly twenty years of marriage. And space to work this career of his.

He'd given her a lot of lonely nights. Dinners with just the kids. Vacations that were limited to a day or two tacked onto dermatology conferences.

And a Volvo.

It took T.W. twenty minutes to get to a Hannaford that was open all night, and he jogged into the supermarket even though there was no closing time to worry about.

The flower section was to the left, just as he walked in through the automatic doors. As he saw the roses and the chrysanthemums and the lilies, he thought about backing up his Lexus and filling the trunk with bouquets. And the backseat.

In the end though, he chose one single flower, and he held it carefully between his thumb and forefinger all the way home.

He parked in the garage, but didn't go in through the kitchen. Instead he went to the front door and rang the bell.

His wife's familiar, lovely face peeked out of the long, thin windows that framed their colonial's entryway. She looked confused as she opened the door.

"Did you forget your—"

T.W. held the flower out in his burned hand.

It was a lowly little daisy. Exactly the kind she'd brought to him once a week in the hospital. For two months straight.

"I don't say thank-you enough," T.W. murmured. "Or I love you. Or that I still think you're as beautiful as the day I married you."

His wife's hand trembled as she took the flower. "T.W. . . . are you okay?"

"God . . . the fact that you have to ask that just because I bring you a flower . . ." He shook his head and hugged her into his arms, holding her tight. "I'm sorry."

Their teenage daughter walked by them and rolled her eyes before heading up the stairs. "Get a room."

T.W. pulled back and tucked his wife's salt-and-pepper hair back behind her ears. "I think we should take her advice, what do you say? And by the way, we're going somewhere for our anniversary—and not to a conference."

His wife smiled and then outright beamed. "What has gotten into you?"

"I saw this patient and his wife tonight. . . ." He winced and rubbed his temple. "I mean . . . what was I saying?"

"How about dinner?" his wife said, fitting herself into his side. "And then we'll see about that room?"

T.W. leaned into his wife as he shut the door. As they went down the hall to the kitchen together, he kissed her. "That sounds perfect. Just perfect."

TEN

Back at the Brotherhood's mansion, Z stood at one of the windows in his and Bella's bedroom and looked down over the terrace and the back gardens. His wrist burned from where the laser had been applied, but the pain wasn't bad.

"I'm not surprised by the whole thing," he said. "Well, other than the fact that I liked the doc."

Bella came up behind him and put her arms around his waist. "He was a good guy, wasn't he."

As they stood together, there was a whole lot of what-now floating around the room. Unfortunately he didn't have any answers. He'd kind of banked on the bands being removed, like that would somehow make everything better.

Although it wasn't as if there weren't still scars on his face.

From the nursery Nalla let out a burble and then a hiccup. A cry was next.

"I just fed her and changed her," Bella said, pulling away. "I'm not sure what this is about—"

"Let me go to her," he said in a tight voice. "Let me see if I can . . ."

Bella's eyebrows lifted, but then she nodded. "Okay. I'll stay here."

"I won't drop her. I promise."

"I know you won't. Just make sure you support her head."

"Right. Got it."

Z felt like he was going unarmed into a field of *lessers* when he walked into the nursery.

As if sensing him, Nalla let out a whiffle.

"It's your father. Dad. Papa." What would she call him?

He went over and peered down at his daughter. She was dressed in a Red Sox onesie, no doubt a gift from V and/or Butch, and her lower lip was quivering like it wanted to leap off the tip of her chin but was afraid of the drop.

"Why are you crying, little one?" he said softly.

When she lifted her arms up to him, he checked the doorway. Bella wasn't in it, and he was glad. He didn't want anyone seeing how awkward he was as he reached into the crib and . . .

Nalla fit between his hands perfectly, her butt in one of his palms, her head cradled in the other. As he straightened and brought her up, she was surprisingly sturdy and warm and—

She grabbed onto his turtleneck and pulled into him, demanding close-ness . . . and obliging her seemed shockingly easy. As he held her against his chest, she settled immediately, turning herself flush into his body.

Having her in his arms was so natural. And so was heading for the rocker and sitting down and using one of his feet to make them go back and forth.

Staring at her lashes and her plump little cheeks and her death grip on his turtleneck, he realized just how much she needed him—and not just to protect her. She needed him to love her, too.

"Looks like you are getting along," Bella said quietly from the doorway.

He glanced up. "She seems to like me."

"How could she not?"

Looking back down at his daughter, he said after a while, "It would have been great to get them removed. The tats. But she'd still ask about my face."

"She's going to love you anyway. She already does."

He ran his forefinger over Nalla's arm, stroking her as she snuggled even deeper against his heart and played patty-cake on the back of his free hand.

From out of nowhere, he said, "You didn't talk to me much about your abduction."

"I . . . ah, I didn't want to upset you."

"Do you find yourself protecting me from things that might upset me a lot?"

"No."

"You sure about that?"

"Zsadist, if I do, it's because—"

"I'm not much of a male if I can't be there when you need me."

"You are always there for me. And we did talk about it some."

"Some."

God, he felt like shit for all she had had to do alone, just because of his head fuck.

And yet her voice was strong and sure as she said, "When it comes to the ab-duction, I don't want you to know every little thing that happened. Not because you can't handle it, but because I don't want to give that bastard any more influence over my life than he's already had." She shook her head. "I'm not going to give him the power to upset you if I can avoid it. Not going to happen—and that would be true whether or not you had been through anything traumatic."

Z made a noise to acknowledge that she'd spoken, but he didn't agree with her. He wanted to give her everything she needed. She deserved nothing less. And his past had impacted them. Still did. Christ, the way he'd been about Nalla had been—

"May I tell you something in confidence?" she said.

"Of course."

"Mary wants a baby."

Z's eyes shot up. "She does? That's great—"

"A biological one."

"Oh."

"Yeah. She can't have one of her own, so Rhage would have to lay with a Chosen."

Z shook his head. "He would never do that. He won't be with anyone but Mary."

"That's what she says. But if he doesn't, she can't hold a piece of him in her arms."

Yeah, because IVF didn't work on vampires. "Shit."

"She hasn't talked to Rhage about it yet because she's sorting her own feelings out first. She talks to me so she can ride the peaks and valleys of her emotions without putting him through the wringer. Some days she wants a young so badly, she thinks she can handle it. Other days she simply can't bear the idea on any level and considers adoption. My point is, you can't work out all your stuff with your partner. And you shouldn't. You were there for me afterward. You're there for me now. I never question that. But that doesn't mean I have to drag you into the nitty-gritty. Healing is a multifaceted kind of thing."

He tried to picture himself telling Bella all the ins and outs of the abuse he'd been subjected to. . . . No. . . . no way would he want her to break her heart over the fucked up nightmare he'd been put through.

"Did you talk to someone?" he asked.

"Yes, at Havers's. And I talked to Mary." There was a pause. "And I went back . . . to where I'd been held."

His eyes flipped up and bored into hers. "You did?"

She nodded. "I had to."

"You never told me." Fuck, she'd been *back* there? Without him?

"I needed to go. For me. And I needed to go alone and I didn't want to argue. I made sure Wrath knew when I was leaving and I told him right when I got back."

"Damn . . . I wish I'd known. Makes me feel like a shitty *hellren*."

"You're anything but that. Especially now that you're holding your daughter like you are."

There was a long silence.

"Look," she said, "if it helps any, I've never felt like I couldn't tell you something. I've never doubted that you would man up and support me. But just because we're mated doesn't mean I'm not my own person."

"I know. . . ." He thought for a minute. "I didn't want to go back to where I . . . To that castle. If it hadn't been for the fact that she'd imprisoned another male down in that cell . . . I never would have gone back."

And he couldn't now. The place where he'd been held in the Old Country had long ago been sold to humans, eventually ending up in England's National Trust.

"Did you feel better?" he asked abruptly. "After you went to see where you'd been?"

"Yes, because Vishous had ashed the place. The closure was more complete that way."

Z rubbed Nalla's little round belly absently while staring across at his *shellan*. "I wonder why we haven't talked about it before now."

Bella smiled and nodded at the young. "We've had something else get our attention."

"Can I be honest? The steakhead in me needs to believe that if you'd wanted me to go with you to that place, you know I would have done it in a heartbeat and stayed tight for you."

"I *absolutely* know that. But I still wanted to go alone. I can't explain it . . . it was just something I needed to do. A courage thing."

Nalla glanced in the direction of her mother and made a squirming reach that was accompanied by a little burble of demand.

"I think she wants something only you can give her," Z said with a smile as he got up from the rocker.

He and Bella met in the middle of the room. As they made the handoff, he kissed his *shellan* and lingered a bit, with both of them holding on to their daughter.

"I'm going out, okay?" he said. "I won't be long."

"Be safe."

"I promise. I've got to take care of my girls."

Zsadist armed himself and dematerialized out west of the city, to a stretch of forest dead in the thick of farm country.

The bald clearing was fifty feet ahead, right by a stream, but instead of seeing an empty stretch among the pines, he pictured a single-room building with a plywood exterior and a tin roof.

What was in his mind was clear as the trees around him and the stars in the night sky up above: The facility had been constructed by the Lessening Society quickly and with an eye toward the temporary. What had been done inside, though, had been the stuff of permanence.

He walked over to the clearing, the twigs of the forest floor cracking under his boots, reminding him of a quiet fire in the fireplace.

His thoughts were anything but calming and homey.

When you went through the place's door, there had been a stall shower and a drywall bucket with a toilet seat on it. For six weeks Bella had washed in the four-by-four-foot cubicle, and he knew she hadn't been alone. That bastard *lesser* had watched her. Had probably helped.

Shit, the idea of anything like that happening made him want to hunt the fucker down all over again. But Bella had taken care of the slayer's death, hadn't she. She'd been the one who had shot him in the head while the bastard had stood before her, captivated by his sick love for her. . . .

Fuck.

Shaking himself, Z imagined he was standing once again in the main room of the place. To the left there had been a wall of shelving with tools of the torture trade laid out on flimsy wooden boards held aloft by crude brackets. Chisels, knives, handsaws . . . he could remember how shiny they had been.

There had been a fireproof closet as well, one that he'd ripped the doors off of.

And a stainless-steel autopsy table with fresh blood on it.

Which he'd tossed into the corner like litter.

He could totally remember busting into the facility. He'd been looking for Bella for weeks after that *lesser* had broken into her house and taken her. Everyone thought she was dead, but he'd refused to believe it. He'd been tortured by the need to get her free . . . a need he hadn't then understood but couldn't deny.

The break had come when a civilian vampire had escaped from this "persuasion center," as the Lessening Society called them, and tracked his location by dematerializing out from the clearing at hundred-yard clips through the forest. From the map he'd drawn for the Brotherhood, Z had come here looking for his female.

The first thing he'd found had been a scorched circle of earth right outside the door, and he'd thought it had been Bella, left for the sun. He'd bent at the knees and put his hand to the ashed circle, and when his sight had gone blurry he hadn't known why.

Tears. There had been tears in his eyes. And it had been so long since he'd cried, he hadn't recognized what they were.

Coming back to the present, Z braced himself and stepped forward, his boots crossing over low-napped, weedy grass. Usually, after Vishous used his hand on a place, there was nothing left but ash and small bits of metal, and that was true here. With the forest undergrowth already grabbing hold, soon the clearing would be filled in again.

The three pipes that were set in the ground had survived, though. And would continue to exist no matter how many sapling pines sprang up.

Kneeling down, Z took out his Maglite and angled the beam into the hole Bella had been in. Pine needles and water had filled it in part of the way.

It had been December when he'd found her in the earth, and he could only imagine the cold that had surrounded her down there . . . the cold and the darkness and the tight squeeze of the ribbed metal.

He'd almost missed these earthbound prisons. After he'd thrown the autopsy table across the room, he'd heard a whimper, and that was what had brought him over here, to these three pipes. As he'd popped the mesh cover off the one the noise came from, he'd known he'd found her.

Except he hadn't. When he'd pulled on the ropes that had led into the hole, a civilian male had emerged, a male who was shivering like a child.

Bella had been unconscious in the one she'd been in.

Z had gotten shot in the leg as he'd worked to get her free, thanks to a security system that Rhage had only partially disarmed. Even with the bullet tearing into his leg, though, he hadn't felt a thing as he'd bent down and grabbed onto the ropes and slowly pulled. He'd seen his love's mahogany-colored hair first, and the dizzying relief had been like getting blanketed by a warm cloud. But then her face had become visible.

Her eyes had been sewn shut.

Z got to his feet, his body revolting against that memory, his stomach churning, his throat getting tight. He'd nursed her afterward. Bathed her. Let her feed from him even though giving her the corroded shit in his veins had brought him to the edge of hysteria.

And he'd serviced her in her needing as well. Which was how Nalla had come to be.

In return? Bella had given him back the world.

Zsadist took a last look around, seeing not the landscape but the truth. Bella might be smaller than him and might weigh a hundred pounds less and might be untrained in the martial arts and might not know how to shoot guns . . . but she was stronger than he was.

She had gotten through what had been done to her.

Could the past be like this, he wondered, looking around at the empty clearing. A structure in your mind that you could burn down and get free of?

He moved his foot back and forth over the forest floor. The weeds that had poked up through the skin of the earth were like green whiskers, and they were concentrated in the area that got the most sunlight.

From the ashes came new life.

Z took out his phone and composed a text that he never thought he'd write.

It took him four tries to get it right. And when he hit send, he knew on some level he changed the course of his life.

And you could do that, couldn't you, he thought as he put the RAZR back in his pocket. You could choose some paths and not others. Not always, of course. At times destiny just drove you to a destination and dropped your ass off and that was that.

But on occaision you were able to pick the address. And if you had half a brain, no matter how hard it was or how weird it felt, you went into the house.

And found yourself.

ELEVEN

n hour later Zsadist was in the cellar at the Brotherhood's mansion, sitting in front of the old coal-burning furnace in the basement. The damn thing was a relic from the 1900s, but it worked so well there was no reason to upgrade.

Plus, it took effort to keep the coal burning, and *doggen* loved regular duties. The more chores, the better.

The great iron furnace's belly had a little window in the front, one made from inch-thick tempered glass, and on the other side flames rolled, lazy and hot.

"Zsadist?"

He rubbed his face and didn't turn around at the sound of the familiar female voice. On some level he couldn't believe he was going to do what he was about to, and the urge to bolt was ripping him up.

He cleared his throat. "Hi."

"Hi." There was a pause, and then Mary said, "Is that empty chair next to you for me?"

Now he twisted around. Mary was standing at the bottom of the cellar stairs, dressed as she usually was, in khakis and a Polo sweater. On her left wrist was an enormous gold Rolex, and she had small pearls in each of her earlobes.

"Yeah," he said. "Yeah, it is . . . thanks for coming."

Mary walked over, her loafers making a little clipping noise on the concrete floor. When she sat down on the lawn chair, she repositioned it so it faced him and not the furnace.

He rubbed his skull trim.

As silence meandered around, a blower came on across the way . . . and upstairs someone turned on the dishwasher . . . and the phone rang in the back of the kitchen.

Eventually, because he felt like a fool for not saying anything, he held up one of his wrists. "I need to practice what I'm going to say to Nalla when she asks about these. I just . . . I need to have something ready to say to her. Something that . . . is the right thing, you know?"

Mary nodded slowly. "Yes, I do."

He turned back to the furnace and remembered burning the Mistress's skull in it. Abruptly he realized that was the equivalent of V's ashing the place Bella had been hurt in, wasn't it. You couldn't burn a castle down . . . but there had been a kind of cleansing by fire nonetheless.

What he hadn't done was the other half of the healing stuff.

After a while Mary said, "Zsadist?"

"Yeah?"

"What are those markings?"

His frowned and flicked his eyes over to her, thinking, as if she didn't know? But then . . . well, she had been a human. Maybe she didn't. "They're slave bands. I was . . . a slave."

"Did it hurt when they were put on you?"

"Yes."

"Did the same person who cut your face give them to you?"

"No, my owner's *hellren* did that. My owner . . . she put the bands on me. He was the one who cut my face."

"How long were you a slave?"

"A hundred years."

"How did you get free?"

"Phury. Phury got me out. That's how he lost his leg."

"Were you hurt while you were a slave?"

Z swallowed hard. "Yes."

"Do you still think about it?"

"Yes." He looked down at his hands, which suddenly were in pain for some reason. Oh, right. He'd made two fists and was squeezing them so tightly his fingers were about to snap off at the knuckles.

"Does slavery still happen?"

"No. Wrath outlawed it. As a mating gift to me and Bella."

"What kind of slave were you?"

Zsadist shut his eyes. Ah, yes, the question he didn't want to answer.

For a while it was all he could do to force himself to stay in the chair. But then, in a falsely level voice, he said, "I was a blood slave. I was used by a female for blood."

The quiet after he spoke bore down on him, a tangible weight.

"Zsadist? Can I put my hand on your back?"

His head did something that was evidently a nod, because Mary's gentle palm came down lightly on his shoulder blade. She moved it in a slow, easy circle.

"Those are the right answers," she said. "All of them."

He had to blink fast as the fire in the furnace's window became blurry. "You think?" he said hoarsely.

"No. I know."

Epilogue

Six months later . . .

"And what is going on in here with all this noise, precious one?"

Bella walked into the nursery and found Nalla standing up in her crib, hands locked on the rail, little face red and bunched tight from crying. Everything had been pitched out onto the floor: the pillow, the stuffed toys, the blanket.

"Sounds like your world is ending again," Bella said as she scooped up her wailing daughter and looked at the debris. "Was it something they said?"

Attention just made the tears come faster and harder.

"Now, now, try to breathe—it'll give you more volume. . . . Okay, you just ate, so I know you're not hungry. And you're dry." More howling. "I have a feeling I know what this is about. . . ."

Bella checked her watch. "Look, we can give it a try, but I don't know if it's time yet."

Bending down, she picked Nalla's favorite pink blankie off the floor, wrapped the young in it, and headed for the door. Nalla calmed a little as they left the nursery and went down the hall of statues to the grand staircase, and the trip through the tunnel to the training center was likewise relatively quiet—but when they stepped out into the office and the place was empty, the crying started up again.

"Hold on, we'll just see if—"

Outside, in the corridor, a group of pretrans left the locker room and walked off in the direction of the center's parking area. It was good to see them, and not just because it meant Nalla was probably going to get what she was after: following the raids on the *glymera*, the classes for future soldiers had been halted. Now, though, the Brotherhood was back in business with the next generation—only this time not all of them were aristocrats.

Bella entered the gym through a back door, and she flushed at what she saw. Zsadist was up ahead, working out on a punching bag, his powerful fists driving the thing back until it hung at a stiff angle. His shirtless torso was stunning under the caged lights, his muscles viciously cut, his nipple rings gleaming, his fighting form perfect even to her untrained eyes.

Off to one side, a trainee stood utterly transfixed, a sweatshirt hanging limp in his little hand. His face showed a combination of fear and awe as he watched Zsadist work out, the kid's eyes wide, his mouth open in a little O from his jaw going loose.

The second Nalla's cries echoed up into the vast space, Z spun around.

"Sorry to bother you," Bella said over the wailing. "But she wants her daddy."

Z's face melted into an absolute glow of love, the fierce concentration draining from his eyes and being replaced with what Bella liked to call his Nalla-vision. He met them halfway across the blue mats, dropping a kiss on Bella's mouth as he took the young into his arms.

Nalla settled instantly in her father's hold, the young wrapping her arms around his thick neck and cuddling into his massive chest.

Z looked back across the gym to the trainee. In a deep voice, he said, "Bus is coming soon, son. You better hurry."

When he turned around again, Bella felt her *hellren's* arm come around her waist, and she was pulled tight to his side. As he kissed her on the mouth once more, he murmured, "I need a shower. You want to help?"

"Oh, yes."

The three of them left the gym and went back to the mansion. Halfway through the trip, Nalla conked out, so when they got up to their bedroom, they went into the nursery, put her down in her crib, and enjoyed a shower that was very hot—and not just because of the temperature of the water.

When they were through, Nalla was awake again, just in time for story hour.

While Bella dried her hair with a towel, Z went in, got the young, and father and daughter settled into the big bed. Bella came out a moment later and just leaned back against the doorway and stared at the two of them. The pair were cozied up together so close they were like one person. Z had on a pair of pajama bottoms that were Black Watch plaid, and a muscle shirt. Nalla was in a pale pink onesie that read *Daddy's Girl* on it in white.

"*Oh, the Places You'll Go,*" Zsadist read from the book in his lap. "By Dr. Seuss."

As Z read along, Nalla patted the pages with her palm every once in a while.

This was the new routine. At the end of every night, when Z came home from patrol or teaching, he would usually take a shower as Bella fed Nalla, and then he and his daughter got in bed together and he read to her until she fell asleep.

Whereupon he carefully took her to the nursery . . . and returned for *mahmen*-and-papa time, as he referred to it.

Both the reading and the way he'd grown comfortable holding Nalla were miracles, and Mary had had a hand in both. Z and the female met once a week in the basement by the furnace. The two of them had told Bella about the sessions and sometimes Z would talk a little about what was covered, but for the most part what got discussed stayed in the basement—although Bella was aware that some of what was shared was gruesome: She knew because, afterward, Mary would frequently go into her bedroom with Rhage and not come out for a long, long while. But it was working. Z was easing in a different way, a new way.

It showed with Nalla. When the young grabbed at his wrists he didn't pull away, but let her pat him or kiss him on the bands. He let her crawl over his ruined back and rub her face against his, too. And he'd had his daughter's name added to his skin, carved lovingly below Bella's by his Brothers.

It also showed because the bad dreams had dried up. In fact, months had gone by since the last time he'd shot upright in bed in a fear-sweat.

And it also showed in his smile. Which was broader and more frequent than ever.

Abruptly, the sight of him holding his daughter got a little wavy, and as if he sensed the tears, Z's eyes flipped up to her. He kept reading but frowned with worry.

Bella blew him a kiss, and in response he patted the mattress next to him.

"'So. . . *get on your way!*'" he finished as Bella cuddled up close.

Nalla let out a happy coo and patted the book cover he'd closed.

"Are you okay?" he whispered in Bella's ear.

She put her hand on his cheek and brought his mouth to hers. "Yes. Very much so."

As they kissed, Nalla patted the book again.

"You sure you're all right?" Z asked.

"Oh, yes."

Nalla grabbed at the book and Z grinned, tugging it back gently. "Hey, what are you doing, little one? You want more? You are just too much . . . you . . . oh, no . . . not the quivering lip . . . oh, no." Nalla let out a giggle. "Outrageous! You want more, and you know you're going to get what you want because of The Lip. Jeez, you've got your father wrapped around your little finger, don't you."

Nalla cooed as her dad opened the book again and the story started to roll out of Z's mouth once more, his voice resonant. "'Congratulations! Today is your day. . . .'"

Bella closed her eyes, put her head on her *hellren*'s shoulder, and listened to the story.

Of all the places she'd ever been, this was the best one. Right here. With the two of them.

And she knew Zsadist felt the same way. It was in all the hours he spent with Nalla and all the days he reached through the sheets for Bella when they were alone. It was in the fact that he'd started singing again, and that he'd begun to roughhouse with his Brothers, not for training, but for fun. It was in his new smile, the one she'd never seen before and couldn't wait to see again.

It was the light in his eyes and in his heart.

He was . . . happy with his life. And getting happier.

As if he'd read her mind, Z took her hand in his larger one and gave her a squeeze.

Yes, he felt exactly the same. This was his favorite place, too.

Bella listened to the story and let herself drift off, just as her daughter did, safe in the knowledge that all was where it should be.

Their male had come back to them . . . and was here to stay.

The
Brotherhood
Dossiers

His Royal Highness Wrath, Son of Wrath

"Welcome to the wonderful world of jealousy. For the price of admission, you get a splitting headache, a nearly irresistible urge to commit murder, and an inferiority complex. Yippee."

—DARK LOVER, p. 107

Age:	343
Joined Brotherhood:	Long story on that one . . .
Height:	6'9"
Weight:	273 lbs.
Hair color:	Black, straight, down to small of back
Eye color:	Pale green
Identifying physical marks:	Tattoos on both forearms detailing royal lineage; Brotherhood scar on left pectoral; name ELIZABETH carved in skin across upper back and shoulders in Old English letters.
Note:	Eyesight is weak—eyes hypersensitive to light, likely due to his purebred lineage. Wears sunglasses at all times.
Weapon of choice:	Hira shuriken (martial arts throwing stars)
Description:	*Wrath was six feet, nine inches of pure terror dressed in leather. His hair was long and black, falling straight from a widow's peak. Wraparound sunglasses hid eyes that no one had ever seen revealed. Shoulders were twice the size of most males'. With a face that was both aristocratic and brutal, he looked like the king he was by birthright and the soldier he'd become by destiny.*

—DARK LOVER, p. 3

Mated to:	Elizabeth Anne Randall

Personal Qs (answered by Wrath):

Last movie watched:	*Meatballs* (Rhage's fault)
Last book read:	*Goodnight Moon* by Margaret Wise Brown (for Nalla)
Favorite TV show:	NBC *Nightly News* with Brian Williams
Last TV show watched:	*The Office* (also a fave)
Last game played:	Monopoly
Greatest fear:	Death
Greatest love:	Beth
Favorite quote:	*Rule by the heart and the fist.*
Boxers or briefs:	Boxers, black
Watch:	Braille
Car:	Beth drives me in her Audi, or Fritz takes me out
What time is it while you're filling this out?	2 p.m.
Where are you?	In my study
What are you wearing?	Black leathers, black Hanes T-shirt, shitkickers
What's in your closet?	More of the same, in addition to one black Brooks Brothers suit, and whites for audiences with the Scribe Virgin
What was the last thing you ate?	Lamb sandwich made by Beth
Describe your last dream?	None of your business
Coke or Pepsi?	Coke
Audrey Hepburn or Marilyn Monroe?	Beth Randall
Kirk or Picard?	Kirk
Football or baseball?	Rugby
Sexiest part of a female?	My *shellan's* throat

What do you like most about Beth?	Everything. Yeah, that covers it
First words spoken to her were:	"I thought we'd try this again."
Her response was:	"Who are you?"
Last gift given to her:	Canary diamond earrings from Graff to match the ring I gave her
Most romantic thing you've ever done for her:	You'd have to ask her
Most romantic thing she's ever done for you:	The way she woke me up about an hour ago
Anything you'd change about her?	Just that I would have met her a couple of centuries before I did
Best friend (excluding *shellan*):	Lost him 'bout three years ago. 'Nuff said.
Last time you cried:	None of your biz
Last time you laughed:	'Bout twenty minutes ago, because I got to watch Nalla discover her toes

J.R.'s Interview with Wrath

Here's the thing about the king. He'll allow himself to be interviewed, but it's on his terms. Which is Wrath in a nutshell. He's all about his terms, but then I guess when you're the last purebred vampire on the earth and king of your race and . . . well, when you're as big as he is and have a stare that can cut through glass like a diamond, the world is a place you dictate, not dodge around in.

Did I mention that I'm wearing waders at the moment, and I'm thigh-high in an icy Adirondack stream?

Yeah, the king's taken up fly-fishing.

On this frosty November night, Wrath and I are standing in the midst of rolling, sluggish water that is cold. I have long underwear on, and I'm pretty sure he doesn't, as he's not the type to be bothered by a chill. He did, however, make a concession to a set of gigantic waders, which Fritz custom-tailored for a pair of legs that are each about the size of my upper body. I'm to the side of the king; I figured if I were in front or behind I'd be in hook range, and considering I had to pester him for weeks for this audience, I don't want to risk a trip to an ER for some kind of tackle-ectomy.

On a side note, Wrath looks worn-down. Mind you, he still out-ranks 99.9 percent of any of the males I've ever seen on the Holy Shit Hot Scale, but then, honestly, can you get sexier than a guy with hip-length black hair, a widow's peak, and wraparound sunglasses? Not to mention the tats on his forearms and those green eyes and his . . .

Listen, I have never measured his backside. Ever. Not once. Or the tremendous width of his shoulders. Or his six-pack.

Oh, don't look at me like that.

Anyway, where were we? Right, the stream. Fly-fishing.

The king and I are about a half mile from Rehvenge's safe house in the Adirondack Mountains near Black Snake State Park. Wrath is standing about fifteen feet from me, whisking his right arm back and forth in a gentle rhythm, pulling a gossamer-thin fishing line through the stream, then letting it be taken, through the stream, then letting it be taken. The water sounds like wind chimes as it chatters past smooth brown and gray rocks, and the pine trees on either side of the banks whistle as the wind tickles through their branches. The air is cool and crisp, making me think that I'm glad I have a Macintosh apple in the backpack we brought with us—fall just goes with those tart, juicy little buggers.

Oh, and one last salient point. Wrath has a forty strapped under each arm and throwing stars in his pockets. I can see the forties. He told me about the stars.

J.R.:	Can I be honest with you?
Wrath:	You'd better be. 'Cause I'd smell it if you weren't.
J.R.:	True enough. Ah . . . I'm surprised you have the patience for this. The fishing, that is.
Wrath:	(shrugging) It's not a matter of patience. It's calming. And no, I'm not taking up yoga. That's Rhage's deal.
J.R.:	He's still doing that?
Wrath:	Yeah, he's still namaste-ing his ass into a million different contortions. Swear that fucker's retractable.

J.R.:   Speaking of Rhage and Mary, is it true what I heard?

Wrath: The adoption thing? Yeah. When Nalla came, they both kind of sat up and were like, We want one of those.

J.R.:   How long will it take? And where are they going for the young?

Wrath: You'll hear about it when it's done. But it's going to be a while.

J.R.:   Well, I'm happy for them. (There's a stretch of no talking, during which Wrath reels in his line, then casts it out into another part of the stream.) Do you want—

Wrath: No. I'm still not pushing the children thing. After what Bella went through . . . (Shakes head.) Nope. And before you ask, Beth's okay with that. I think she'll want one in the future, though. Just hope it's later rather than sooner. Although, honestly, she hasn't even gone through her first needing, so it's not a huge issue.

J.R.:   Suppose you'd like me to change the subject?

Wrath: Up to you. You can ask anything, doesn't mean I'll answer. (Shoots a look over his shoulder and smiles at me.) But you know how I do.

J.R.:   (laughing) Yeah, I'm familiar with the way things go. So let me ask you about the whole Chosen thing and Phury. What do you think about the changes he made?

Wrath: Man . . . he impressed the shit out of me. He really did. And not just about what he did with the Scribe Virgin. For a while there, I was sure we were going to lose him.

J.R.:   (thinking about Phury and the heroin) You nearly did.

Wrath: Yeah. (There's another stretch of silence, which I spend watching his arm go back and forth, back and forth. The line makes a lovely sound through the cool forest air, as if it is breathing.) Yeah. Anyhow, that's why we're here, at Rehv's house. I come up with Beth every two weeks or so and meet with Phury and the Directrix and check in on how things are going with the Chosen. Christ, can you imagine what the transition's like for those females? Going from total lockdown to being able to explore a world you've only read about?

J.R.:   I can't, no.

Wrath: Phury's fantastic with them. It's like overnight they've all become his daughters. And they love him. He is the perfect Primale, and Cormia's now their den mother. As she's had more time to assimilate, she's doing a lot of transitioning them herself. I'm really glad it's gone down like it has.

J.R.:   Talking about parent stuff, what's life like at the mansion now that Nalla's around?

Wrath: (laughing) Okay, for real? That kid's a star. She's got us all wrapped around her little finger. The other day I was working at my desk, and Bella was on walkabout with the young—she does this because lately Nalla only sleeps when she's moving? Anyway, Bella brought her into my study and the two of them were pacing. Nalla's head was on Bella's shoulder and she was out like a light—by the way, the kid's got eyelashes longer than your arm. So, Bella? She finally sinks down on the couch to take a breather, and two seconds later, I kid you not, Nalla's eyes flip open and she starts fussing.

J.R.:   Poor thing!

Wrath: Bella, right?

J.R.:   Yup!

Wrath: (laughing) So I got to hold Nalla. Bella let me hold her. (This is said with no small amount of pride.) I walked the young around. I didn't drop her.

J.R.:   (hiding smile) Of course you didn't.

Wrath: She went back to sleep. (Shoots grave stare over his shoulder.) You know, young only sleep if they trust you to keep them safe.

J.R.:   (softly) Anyone would be safe with you.

Wrath: (looks away quickly) So, yeah, kid's a gem. Z's a little uneasy around her still, I think because he's afraid he's going to break her—not because he doesn't love her. Rhage handles her like a sack of potatoes, hauling her any way he pleases, which Nalla loves. Phury's a natural. So's Butch.

J.R.:   What about Vishous?

Wrath: Meh. I think Nalla makes him nervous. He made her a dagger, though. (laughs) Fucking hard-ass. What kind of crack bastard makes a dagger for an infant?

J.R.:   Bet it's lovely, though.

Wrath: Shit, yeah. He put all these . . . (The king pauses and flicks at the line as if he thinks he's got something hooked.) He put all these diamonds on the hilt. Spent three days working on it. Says it's for when she starts dating.

J.R.:   (laughing) I'll bet.

Wrath: Might go to waste. Zsadist says she's never dating. Ever.

J.R.:   Uh-oh.

Wrath: Yeah. Z's little girl? You want to be the male coming to call on her? Shiiiiiiit.

J.R.: I'd pass.

Wrath: I know I would. Like my balls right where they are, thank you very much.

J.R.: (after another stretch of quiet) Can I ask about Tohr?

Wrath: Figured you would.

J.R.: (waits for him to say something) So I'm asking about him.

Wrath: (annoyed) Look, what do you want me to say? He went into the woods to die. Lassiter brought him back to people who remind him every day of his dead *shellan*. He needs to feed, and of course he's refusing, and I don't blame him for that at all. He's weak and angry and he just wants to be dead. That's how he's doing.

J.R.: (knowing not to push any more) Is it weird having Lassiter around?

Wrath: (laughs tightly) That angel is a thing all right. I don't mind him all that much, and I think he knows it. He took a bullet for me once.

J.R.: I'd heard. Do you feel like you owe him?

Wrath: Yeah.

J.R.: He and V don't get along.

Wrath: No, they don't. (laughs) That's going to be fun to watch. It's like two pit bulls in a cage whenever they're in the same room. And before you ask, no, I don't know all the ins and outs, and I'm not asking.

J.R.: Talking about ins and outs . . . about the *glymera*—

Wrath: Shit, why do you want to ruin a perfectly nice evening.

J.R.: Well, I was going to ask you how you felt about Rehvenge being appointed *leahdyre* of the Princeps Council.

Wrath: (roars with laughter) Okay, you're so forgiven. Man, what a trip that is. Who the fuck would have thought that'd happen? A *symphath*. Leading that group of insular, prejudicial bastards. And they have no idea he is one. Plus, come on, Rehv's on my side in this growing civil unrest they're trying to stir up after all the raids by the Lessening Society. They've just appointed someone who thinks the aristocrats are as nuts and as destructive as I do.

J.R.: But do you trust Rehv?

Wrath: As much as I trust anyone who's not my brother or Beth.

J.R.: So the fact that he's half *symphath*—

Wrath: Hold up. He's a *symphath*. Whether his blood's half-and-half is irrelevant. You got any of that shit in you, you're a *symphath*. That's why that colony up north of here was created. They are dangerous.

J.R.: So that's why I'm asking if you trust him. I thought they were all sociopaths.

Wrath: They are, and so is he. Here's the thing, though . . . with *symphaths*, the one thing you can take to the fucking bank is their self-interest. Rehv loves his sister. Bella's married to a Brother. Therefore, Rehv will do nothing to hurt them or me. That math holds in all situations.

J.R.: Do you think the *glymera* poses a threat to you as king?

Wrath: Look, straight up? I don't like them and never have, but shit knows I don't want them dead. Right now they're fragmented, out of Caldwell, and they're scrambling. The longer that goes on, the better for me, because it gives me time to gather the reins as best I can and try to give people a vision to get through this. As long as I have a base of support among the larger group of civilians, I'm fine. And let's face it, the *glymera* isn't about inclusion, so it's not as if your average vampire feels an allegiance to them.

J.R.: What is your vision for the future?

Wrath: Change. Phury's absolutely right, we need to adapt if we're going to survive, and the old rules are killing us. I've already outlawed slavery. I'm changing the rules about soldiers and the Brotherhood. The Chosen have been set free. And there are a hundred other things I need to recast, rethink, redo.

J.R.: About the Brotherhood. So that means Blay and Qhuinn could be Brothers?

Wrath: Assuming they get enough experience under their belts and can rise to the level. The threshold for being a Brother is going to be set very high in terms of skills. Blood's not going to get you in anymore, how you fight will. And I'm freeing up other restrictions. You know, Qhuinn is John's private guard, and in the past that would have disqualified him, but not anymore.

J.R.: I'm surprised that you let him and Blay into the house. Glad, actually.

Wrath: (after a moment) Well . . . Darius built that place, and he loved having people around. Those two boys are tight, and shit knows, Qhuinn did right by John. S'all good. Thing is, the training program is on hiatus for God only knows how long. The *glymera* took what sons were left with them when they went, and besides, we've had our hands full dealing with the war. I need soldiers, and Blay and Qhuinn are good fighters. Excellent, really. So we're going to want them.

(Long silence.)

J.R.: Are you happy? I mean, I know things are hard right now, but are you happier than you were a couple of years ago?

The line suddenly goes taut, and Wrath focuses on bringing in what turns out to be a freshwater trout. The fish is gleaming and slippery in the king's big hands, and he almost loses it while trying to get the hook out of its gaping mouth.

J.R.: He's beautiful.

Wrath: Yeah, full of fight, too. (He leans down and puts the fish to the water, holding it carefully.) You ask me if I'm happy? Well . . . after this, we're going back to a warm house and my *shellan*'s waiting for me there. We're going to eat, assuming Layla hasn't burned down the kitchen, and then I'm going to get into bed with Beth. I'm going to mate with her for an hour, maybe longer, then I'm going to fall asleep with her on my chest. (He releases the trout and watches it tear off through the sluggish current.) You ready to go?

J.R.: Yeah. And I appreciate your doing this.

Wrath: Not a problem. Except you think you're going to drive down to Caldwell now to do the others?

J.R.: That's the plan.

Wrath: (shaking head) No, you're staying here tonight. Tomorrow you'll leave late afternoon. It's a long drive, and the Northway's got deer.

J.R.: (because you do not argue with the king) All right. That's what I'll do.

Wrath: Good.

At this point the two of us wade over to the bank. Wrath gets out of the stream first and offers me his hand. I take it and he pulls me up. He picks up the backpack, opens it, and holds it out to me.

Wrath: You want your apple?

J.R.: Oh, I'd love it.

I reach in and take the thing. Its red-and-green skin is shiny in the moonlight, and when I bite into it, it cracks like hardwood. The juice drips down onto my palm as the two of us go through the woods together, our waders flapping against our legs.

J.R.:   (as we come out of the forest and see the glowing lights of
        Rehv's rustic safe house) Wrath?
Wrath: Hm?
J.R.:   Thank you.
Wrath: It's your apple.
J.R.:   I'm not talking about the apple.
Wrath: (after a moment) I know. I know, *challa*.

He gives me a short, tight hug that lasts for two footfalls, and then the
pair of us separate, but keep walking side by side toward the warm, welcoming home.

Dark Lover

The People:

Wrath, heir to the throne of the vampires
Beth Randall, newspaper reporter
Darius, son of Marklon, son of Horusman
Tohrment, son of Hharm
Wellasandra, blooded daughter of Relix, mated of the Black Dagger warrior
    Tohrment
Rhage, son of Tohrture
Zsadist, son of Ahgony
Phury, son of Ahgony
The Scribe Virgin
Marissa, blooded daughter of Wallen
Havers, blooded son of Wallen
Fritz (Perlmutter), butler extraordinaire
Mr. X(avier), *Fore-lesser*
Billy Riddle, son of Senator William Riddle
Cherry Pie, a.k.a. Mary Mulcahy
Butch O'Neal, detective in the Caldwell Police Department, Homicide
    Division
José de la Cruz, detective in CPD's Homicide Division
Dick, Beth's editor at the *Caldwell Courier Journal*
Doug, the attending at the hospital
Unnamed blond male, Billy Riddle's partner in the attempted rape of Beth
Loser (unnamed youth whom Mr. X takes out with Billy)
Abby, bartender at McGrider's Bar
Boo, the black cat

Places of Interest (all in Caldwell, NY, unless otherwise specified):

Screamer's on Trade Street
Offices of the *Caldwell Courier Journal (CCJ)* on Trade Street
Beth's apartment—1B, 1188 Redd Avenue
Caldwell Police Department on Trade (six blocks from *Caldwell Courier Journal*)
Darius's House—816 Wallace Avenue
Caldwell Martial Arts Academy (across from Dunkin' Donuts)
Mr. X's farm, off Route 22
Havers's clinic—undisclosed location
McGrider's Bar on Trade Street
ZeroSum (corner of Trade and Tenth streets)

Summary:

In this, the first book of the series, Wrath, unascended king of the vampires and the last purebred vampire on earth, reluctantly assumes responsibility for seeing a half-breed female through her transition. Beth Randall is unaware of her vampire heritage and fights both her own truth and her attraction to the dark stranger who comes after her.

Opening line:	*Darius looked around the club, taking in the teeming, half-naked bodies on the dance floor.*
Last line:	*"Please, if you would," the butler said, "no throwing the linens. Peaches, anyone?"*
Published:	September 2005
Page length:	393
Word count:	118,833
First draft written:	September–November 2004

Craft comments:

Dark Lover remains the book of which I'm most proud. In my opinion, the pacing is as good as I'll ever get it, and it was the place where I found my voice. Of course, writing the damn thing scared the ever-loving pants off me because it was a huge stretch for me as an author. Huge. I'd never tried multiple POVs and plots before or done a series or given world building a shot. I had no clue what I was doing when it came to . . . well, just about everything in the story: Even though *DL* was the fifth book I'd written for publication, it was such a departure from the ones that came before it, I might as well have been starting from scratch again.

And I hadn't been an expert before then by any stretch of the imagination.

My first four books were single-title contemporary romances. Published under the Jessica Bird name, they were very much a product of years of reading and loving Harlequin Presents and Silhouette Special Editions. Well, that and the fact that I was born a writer. It's just part of my makeup, something I have to do if I'm going to be happy—and sane. But that's another saga.

I loved writing the Jessica Bird books, but my contract wasn't renewed . . . which meant I didn't have a publisher anymore. I knew I had to change directions if I were going to still have a job, and I tried my hand in a couple of different subgenres. I pulled together a romantic-suspense proposal, but the material just wasn't strong enough. I thought about doing women's fiction and chick lit—except they weren't what I read, probably because the subject matter wasn't my bag. I also considered staying with contemporary romance and trying to find another publisher, although I knew the chance of someone else picking me up was unlikely.

It was in my darkest moment, when I had nothing particularly fresh and interesting in my brain save for an abiding realization that if I didn't reinvent myself I was toast . . . that Wrath showed up. Although I had always been a horror fan, it had never dawned on me to try my hand at paranormal romance. All of a sudden, though, I had over two thousand pounds of male vampire stuck in my head, and the Brothers wanted out like they were locked in a house that was on fire.

Okay. Right. Horror meets romance meets erotica meets fantasy meets hip hop. Throw in some leather and some *Miami Ink* shit, stir with a baseball bat and a tire iron, sprinkle on some baby powder, and serve over a hot bed of Holy-Mary-mother-of-God this-has-to-work-or-I'm-going-to-be-a-lawyer-for-the-rest-of-my-natural-life.

No problem.

Damn it, I remember thinking, *why don't I drink? Or at least eat chocolate?*

Which brings me to my first rule for writers: PR is mission critical for survival, and I'm not talking about public relations.

Persist and *Reinvent*. If you're not selling, or if you're not getting a good response to your material from agents or publishers, try something else, whether it's a new voice or subgenre or even genre. Keep at it. Keep trying. Look for new avenues that interest you. Find a different path.

It was the only thing that saved me.

That didn't mean P&R was fun. As I sat down to tackle Wrath's proposal and sample chapters, I was at once singularly inspired and totally stalled. All I had was a tangle of visions in my head, a burning panic that no one would get the series, much less buy it, and the near conviction that I couldn't possibly pull off something as complicated and interconnected as the Brotherhood's world.

Nothing like trying to fly a plane when you can barely handle a bicycle.

Facing a whole lot of blank screen on my computer, I knew I had to tamp down my anxiety, and considering the fact that putting my skull in a vise wasn't a viable solution, I made an agreement with myself: I would write the story that was in my head exactly as I saw it, and I would do it for me and me alone. I wouldn't allow any you-can't-do-thats or that's-against-the-rules or better-play-it-safes to get in the way. Whatever I saw in my mind's eye was going on the page.

My rule number two? *Write. Out. Loud.*

Take your vision and execute it to the fullest extent of your capabilities. It is always easier to pull back than to push forward in revisions, and I think that the bolder you are in your first draft, the more likely you are to be honest with what's in your head.

So, yeah, that was the plan, and I felt pretty good about my resolution. Except right out of the box, I had a problem.

How was I going to work the plan?

With all that I was being shown, and the number of POVs and subplots, I was at a loss when it came to drafting the story. After doing the panic-and-pace thing for a little while, I ended up falling back on my legal training. In law school, you study by creating these voluminous outlines of the material presented in class. By the time you're done putting everything in order, you've actually learned the material—so it's the process, not necessarily the outcome, that is the big benefit.

Outlining extensively was, and continues to be, the single most important tool I use in my process.

Before the Brothers, I started with nothing more than a high-level summary of my story, the sole goal of which was to give my editor a clue as to where I was headed. Most of my thinking was done while I was drafting—which was totally inefficient and a little dangerous. For example, I'd take the hero and heroine into emotional places that didn't work, or get their motivations and conflicts muddled, or lose track of the book's momentum . . . or sometimes all of these at once. Sure, I'd figure my way out eventually, but I'd end up scrapping tons of pages and be too much of a burden on my editor during the revision process. Further, because of all the struggling, the choices I made were not the best ones because I was brain-dead from all the confusion and lack of clarity.

My all-important third rule is a corollary to number two and the overriding theme to everything I do as an author:

Own your own shit (or *work*, if we're going to be a little more classy).

And it ain't called *shit* 'cause it don't stink.

Do not rely on your editor or your agent or your critique partner to identify and solve your plot, character, pace, context, pagination, or any one of the thousands of problems you have to work through when you write a book. Educate yourself on craft by critiquing the books you read, both the good ones and the bad ones. Ask yourself, What works? What doesn't? Study the standard texts on writing, like *Story* by Robert McKee and *Writing the Breakout Novel* by Donald Maass and *The Writer's Journey* by Christopher Vogler. Talk to other writers about their books and how they wrote them.

Then, when you look at your own work, approach it like you're a drill sergeant facing off at a bunch of unruly, lazy slobs. For me, being nice to my tender little inner artist and soaking in the mother's milk of praise is a surefire way to get soggy and fatheaded. Discipline and a clear assessment of my strengths and weaknesses as a writer are the only things that work for me. Ego is not my friend and never has been.

Back to *Dark Lover* and the outlining. The images in my head were so clear and demanding that it took me only two weeks to draft the outline and the rules of the world (as well as the first sixty-nine pages of the book). Of course, I barely slept or took any breaks at all. I was totally caught up in this undeniable momentum and didn't have any interest in slowing it down.

I still don't.

And when I was finished getting everything I saw out of my head . . . the outline was forty-four pages long. I was stunned. Previously? I topped out at ten pages.

My big concern was that when my agent took the proposal to market, the editors wouldn't read the entire thing. When you've been published previously, generally you sell projects on spec with three sample chapters and an outline—but I felt like I was turning in . . . well, the whole book. Of course, that was also the good thing. I really knew where I was going and what each and every character arc was going to be. I'd done all my thinking and reordering along the way—and learned that changing around a paragraph or two in an outline is a hell of a lot easier than wiping out whole chapters and putting new ones in during drafting.

Fortunately, the proposal for the series was bought (by the most spectacular editor I've ever worked with), and I knew I was going to get a shot to write at least three books. Man, I was excited, but I was also terrified, because I wasn't sure whether I could carry it off. Of course, I told myself my gorgeous, heavyweight outline was my savior. Figured that as long as I had that, I was all set. Ready to pound away on the keyboard.

Riiiiiiiight.

The execution turned out to be far trickier than I could have imagined, for a variety of reasons.

For me, one of the big challenges of *Dark Lover* was learning how to handle multiple plotlines and multiple POVs (points of view). The way I see it, there are three major plotlines in the book: Wrath and Beth's; Mr. X and Billy Riddle's; and Butch's. In each of them, different aspects of the world are introduced, giving the reader an insight into the vampire race, its secret war with the Lessening Society,

and its under-the-radar existence with humans. Which is a lot. And to compli-
cate things even further, these plots were presented to the reader in the voices of
no fewer than eight people.

Lot to handle. Lot to keep up with.

Lot to advance from chapter to chapter.

Rule number four for me as a writer? *Plotlines are like sharks:* They either keep
moving or they die.

With so much going on, pacing was going to be critical: To be successful, I
had to make sure that everything kept progressing, and here was my new reality
as a writer—while I was trying to make sure I showed Wrath and Beth inching
closer both emotionally and physically, I had to keep tabs on Butch and José de
la Cruz's homicide investigation, which simultaneously brought Butch into the
Brotherhood picture and kept the reader up on Mr. X's nasty deeds. Meanwhile,
the other Brothers had to be introduced, I had to give an overview of the war, and
then there was rolling out the welcome mat to the Scribe Virgin and the nontem-
poral world.

And I had to do all this without losing cohesion between the scenes, and
keeping the emotions realistic and vivid without sinking into melodrama.

As a further example, Butch was going to be in the Brotherhood, and his
road in was through Beth's connection with Wrath. Butch was also going to end
up with Marissa. Fine. Dandy. Rock on. The thing was, though, how did I interweave his scenes with the ones of Beth and Wrath's romance along with all the
stuff with Mr. X and the Lessening Society . . . without having the book come out
choppy and incomprehensible?

Also, the plots had to "peak," in an emotional sense, in the right sequence.
Beth and Wrath had to have the most dynamic ending—and going by the pictures in my head they certainly did. But Butch's situation and that of Mr. X and
Billy Riddle had to be resolved . . . but only in a way that didn't drain the drama
from Beth and Wrath.

Brain. Cramp.

The cure? Rule number five, which is a corollary to rule three (Own Your
Own Work): *Sweat. Equity.*

After I finished the first draft, I went through that book over and over and
over and over again. And then I'd take a week off and come at it one more time.
I spent hours and hours repositioning the breaks and the chapters and trimming
things and sharpening the dialogue and making sure that I showed, not told.

And even when I read through the galleys, which is the last stage of production, I still wanted to change things. The book has its strengths and weaknesses,
just like they all do, but I learned a ton writing *Dark Lover.* And I needed those
lessons for what was coming in the series like you read about.

Enough on craft, let's talk about the King and Beth. . . .

Wrath was the first of the Brothers to turn up in my head, and he was the one who showed me the world of the Black Dagger Brotherhood. The thing I like best about him is summed up in the beginning of *Dark Lover:*

> With a face that was both aristocratic and brutal, he looked like the king he was by birthright and the soldier he'd become by destiny.
>
> —DARK LOVER, p. 3

I love that combination—a blueblood who's also a fighter—and I believe Wrath is the perfect leader for the vampires: strong, brutal when necessary, possessing both logic and passion. He just needed to wake up to the fact that he could lead.

And Beth was the one who helped him get there.

Beth was and is Wrath's perfect match. She's strong-minded, warm, and willing to stand up to him. Their dynamic is shown to perfection in what is one of my favorite scenes between them. The two of them are talking about his take on what happened when his parents were slaughtered in front of him. He condemns himself for not saving them, but he was a physically weak pretrans, so realistically there was nothing he could do. Beth loses it and hammers him for being too hard on himself—which is something he needed to hear, even if he clearly wasn't receptive to what she was saying. The thing I love is that she wasn't dissuaded from speaking her mind even with him looming over her. And Wrath, even though he doesn't agree with her, becomes still more attracted to her. When she's finished being frustrated with him, there's an awkward stretch:

> *Ah, hell.* Now she'd done it. The guy opens up to her and she throws his shame back at him. Way to encourage intimacy.
> "Wrath, I'm sorry, I shouldn't have—"
> He cut her off. Both his voice and his face were like stone.
> "No one has ever spoken to me as you just did."
> *Shit.*
> "I'm really sorry. I just can't understand why—"
> Wrath dragged her into his arms and hugged her hard, talking in that other language again. When he pulled back, he ended the monologue with something like *leelan.*
> "Is that vampire talk for *bitch?*"
>
> —DARK LOVER, p. 248

The thing is, Wrath is all about strength, and the fact that Beth can stick up for herself and what she believes puts them on equal footing. The gift of his respect is as significant as the gift of his love, and she's worthy of both.

Another of my favorite scenes in the book is when Beth comes up from

Wrath's underground bedroom at Darius's, fresh from her transition. She's wondering how he'll be with her in front of his Brothers and is prepared to play it cool as she comes into the dining room where the warriors are. Turns out Wrath's just fine with PDA (public displays of affection), and he embraces her in front of a stunned Brotherhood, who had never seen him with a female before. After he explains her significance in the Old Language, he leaves to get her the two things she's craving, chocolate and bacon, and the Brothers greet her in a special way:

> There was a loud scraping noise as five chairs slid backward. The men rose as a unit. And started coming for her.
>
> She looked to the faces of the two she knew, but their grave expressions weren't encouraging.
>
> And then the knives came out.
>
> With a metallic *whoosh*, five black daggers were unsheathed.
>
> She backed up frantically, hands in front of herself. She slammed into a wall and was about to scream for Wrath when the men dropped down on bended knees in a circle around her. In a single movement, as if they'd been choreographed, they buried the daggers into the floor at her feet and bowed their heads. The great *whoomp* of sound as steel met wood seemed both a pledge and a battle cry.
>
> The handles of the knives vibrated.
>
> The rap music continued to pound.
>
> They seemed to be waiting for some kind of response from her.
>
> "Umm. Thank you," she said.
>
> The men's heads lifted. Etched into the harsh planes of their faces was total reverence. Even the scarred one had a respectful expression.
>
> And then Wrath came in with a squeeze bottle of Hershey's syrup.
>
> "Bacon's on the way." He smiled. "Hey, they like you."
>
> "And thank God for that," she murmured, looking down at the daggers.
>
> —DARK LOVER, p. 284–285

The Brothers are greeting their new queen here, although Beth is unaware of the role she'll play in the future, so she actually had two transitions that night: the first her becoming a vampire, and the second this welcome into Wrath and the Brotherhood's private world as his *leelan*, his "dearest one."

One of the most erotic scenes in the book? Aside from the first time they hook up, I think it's when they're having their date at Darius's. The evening starts off rough (thanks to, among other things, Wrath getting into an argument with Tohr, whereupon Tohr feeds him the classic line, "Nice. Fucking. Suit"). However, the couple's private time ends with . . . well, Wrath talking about how much he loves peaches. The mood goes from dark and tense to sensual with this:

> Beth tilted forward in her chair, opened her mouth, and put her lips around the strawberry, taking it whole. Wrath's nostrils flared as he watched her bite down. When some of the sweet juice escaped and dropped onto her chin, he hissed.
> "I want to lick that off," he muttered under his breath. He reached forward and took hold of her jaw. Lifted his napkin.
> She put her hand on his. "Use your mouth."
> A low sound, from deep inside his chest, cut through the room.
> Wrath leaned toward her, tilting his head. She caught a flash of his fangs as his lips opened and his tongue came out. He stroked the juice from her skin and then pulled away.
> He stared at her. She looked back at him. The candles flickered.
> "Come with me," he said, holding out his hand.
> —DARK LOVER, p. 201

Most touching scene? For me, it has to be the one at Havers's clinic at the end. Wrath is still pretty wiped after having been shot in the stomach, and he's just come out of a coma. Beth is trying to communicate with him because he's agitated and upset, but he's having trouble talking. She's asked him if he needs her to get the doctor or food or drink or blood, and none of that is what he's looking for:

> His eyes fixated on their linked hands and came back to her face. Then his gaze locked on their hands and returned again.
> "Me?" she whispered. "You need me?"
> He squeezed and wouldn't stop.
> "Oh, Wrath . . . You have me. We're together, love."
> Tears poured out of him in a mad rush, his chest quaking from the sobs, his breathing jagged and raw.
> She took his face in her hands, trying to soothe him. "It's all right. I'm not going anywhere. I'm not going to leave you. I promise you. Oh, love . . ."
> Eventually he relaxed a little. The tears slowed.
> A croak came out of his mouth.
> "What?" She leaned down.
> "Wanted to . . . save you."
> "You did. Wrath, you did save me."
> His lips trembled. "Love. You."
> She kissed him gently on the mouth. "I love you, too."
> "You. Go. Sleep. Now."

And then he closed his eyes from exhaustion.

Her vision went blurry as she put her hand over her mouth and started to smile. Her beautiful warrior was back. And trying to order her around from his hospital bed.

—DARK LOVER, p. 373

I think that pretty much says it all about them. So I'll leave it at that.

Dark Lover was the launching pad for all the Brothers, not just for Wrath and Beth. I was very clear, even way back then, where the original seven in the Brotherhood were headed and who else was going to join the ranks. And as with all the books, the plotlines of things that wouldn't see the light for years were started. This wasn't because I was brilliant—but a case of scenes landing in my head that would come into play much later.

As I said, Wrath's story is the book I'm proudest of—it was a totally fresh start that was, for the first time, truly authentic to what's in my head. It would shock me if I ever do something like it again and pull it off to the extent I did. Wrath was a complete about-face of subject matter, tone, and voice coupled with an incredible stretch for me in terms of craft—written at a time when I was basically out of a job.

I'm really grateful Wrath came in for a landing and brought the Brothers along with him. His book is dedicated to him—with good reason.

Rhage, Son of Tohrture

a.k.a. Hal E. Wood

He wanted to give her another word to say,
something like luscious *or* whisper *or* strawberry.
Hell, antidisestablishmentarianism *would do it.*

—LOVER ETERNAL, p. 63

Age:	165
Joined Brotherhood:	1898
Height:	6'8"
Weight:	280 lbs.
Hair color:	Blond
Eye color:	Neon blue-green
Identifying physical marks:	Multicolored tattoo of clawed dragon covering entire back; Brotherhood scar on left pectoral; name MARY MADONNA carved in skin across upper back and shoulders in Old English letters.
Note:	Possesses inner dragon that comes out when he is stressed due to punishment issued by Scribe Virgin (which he has retained in order to save Mary). He is now able to exert some control over his alter ego, which has been tamed by his *shellan*.
Weapon of choice:	His beast

Description: *. . . As the guy walked along, there was something about him that wasn't WASPy handsome in spite of his amazing looks. Something . . . animalistic. He just didn't carry himself as other people did.*

            Actually, he moved like a predator, thick shoulders rolling with his gait, head turning, scanning. She had the discomforting sense that if he wanted to, he could wipe out everyone in the place with his bare hands.

                              —LOVER ETERNAL, pp. 81–82

Mated to: Mary Madonna Luce

Personal Qs (answered by Rhage):

Last movie
watched: *La Vie en Rose* (Mary's fault—she maintained it was necessary to balance out my Bill Murray festival.)

Last book read: *The Very Hungry Caterpillar* by Eric Carle (to Nalla)

Favorite
TV show: *Flavor of Love, Rock of Love,* or pretty much anything on the Food Channel—P.S. I want New York to come back and do another season

Last TV show
watched: *Talk Soup*

Last game
played: You don't want to know

Greatest fear: Loss of Mary

Greatest love: Mary

Favorite quote: *Mangia bene!*

Boxers or briefs: Anything that Mary likes taking off me!

Watch: Gold Rolex Presidential

Car: Deep Purple GTO

What time is it
while you're
filling this out?   6 p.m.

Where are you?   In my bed, naked.

What are you
wearing?   See above.

What's in your
closet?   Black stuff, fighting leathers, whites to see the Scribe Virgin. And one lone Hawaiian shirt Mary is trying to get me to

wear. Okay, it's not a Hawaiian shirt, but it's, like, blue, and honestly, color makes me scratch when it comes to clothes. She is, however, willing to bribe me to get me to wear it—which is always fun!

What was the last thing you ate?

Buttermilk pancakes (5) with butter and maple syrup; pot of coffee; six sausages; two servings of hash browns; a box of strawberries; a cinnamon bagel with cream cheese; pink grapefruit halved (ate both halves); and three cherry Danishes. And I'm feeling a bit peckish.

Describe your last dream?

Let's just say I rolled over and acted it out about a half hour ago <VBG>.

Coke or Pepsi?

Coke

Audrey Hepburn or Marilyn Monroe?

Marilyn Monroe, I guess. But it's totally moot, and not because they've both passed. Mary's it for me.

Kirk or Picard?

Kirk. He was the lothario of space, man, and props for that!

Football or baseball?

Football, because it's a contact sport!

Sexiest part of a female?

Depends on my mood . . . I guess I'm an omnivore. Which means I like to nibble—on anything and everything.

What do you like most about Mary?

The sound of her voice. The way she can roll over beside me in bed and talk to me in the darkness of the day and I know that I'm safe.

First words spoken to her were:

"Who are you?"

Her response was:

"My name . . . my name is Mary. I'm here with a friend."

Last gift given to her:

I brought a single white rose to her last night. She was thrilled. See, she's not a big, showy kind of female, my Mary Madonna. Like . . . okay, I bought her an engagement ring before our mating ceremony, because she's a human and that's how they do. It's a diamond, 'cause, you know, only the best for my Mary. The thing's seven carats. D. Flawless. Fritz got it for me in Manhattan from the Diamond District. When I gave it to her, Mary was very polite and grateful, but it's in the drawer. What's on her finger? A single gold band. V made one for both of us, because, like I said, Mary's human and she wanted us to have wedding bands to wear after our mating ceremony. Funny, I didn't understand the whole wedding ring thing until I got one. I mean, for us, for male vampires, we carve skin to show that we're mated. But the great thing about a ring is that folks can see it even when you're fully clothed. I keep mine on always—unless I'm out fighting.

Most romantic
thing you've
ever done
for her:

She seemed to really like the rose. I tell you, the way she smiled at me made me feel like I was ten feet tall.

Most romantic
thing she's ever
done for you:
Anything you'd
change about
her?

The way she thanked me for the rose.

Nothing except for her taste in movies! GOD. I mean, honestly, that female will watch anything with foreign subtitles. And I try to get into the kind of ones she likes, I do . . . but it's a struggle. I understand what she means, though. After watching something she likes, I have to clear my palate with a little dose of Bruce Willis or maybe an encore screening of *Superbad*.

Best friend
(excluding
shellan):
Last time you
cried:
Last time you
laughed:

Butch/V

This afternoon. I thought *La Vie en Rose* would never end.

While I was eating. Butch was the one who made the pancakes, and you should have seen Fritz's expression when he saw what kind of shape the kitchen was in afterward. Butch is tight behind the stove, although not as good as V, but, man, my boy don't know the meaning of clean-as-you-go. The place wasn't just messy, it was like . . . defiled or some shit. We helped take care of the mess, me, V and Butch— along with a bunch of *doggen*, who, after Fritz got over his

shock, had a great time tidying up. *Doggen* love to clean like I love to eat.

J.R.'s Interview with Rhage

The afternoon following my interview with Wrath in that stream, I left Rehvenge's safe house around five. I was glad I'd spent the night. Wrath and Beth and Phury and Cormia, along with the Chosen, were a great group to hang out with, and after hours of chatting I'd slept like a rock—proving that as usual the king was right: My other interviews with the Brothers were going to be better because I wasn't half-dead from travel.

The car ride down through the Adirondacks to Caldwell was lovely. The Northway is one of my favorite highways, cutting as it does through the mountains I spent my summers in while growing up. With the leaves just past their autumnal peak, the jagged ridges on either side of the two lanes I drove were still awash in red and gold and green, the colors glowing like jewels as the sun set.

While I went along in my rental car, I thought how different the Brothers were compared to three autumns ago when their stories all started. I mean . . . so many losses and gains. So many ups and downs. I remembered that first meeting in *Dark Lover*, when they were in Darius's living room right after his death . . . and then pictured them coming out of the woods to reclaim Phury as their own at the end of *Lover Enshrined*. Lot of changes, both good and bad.

I meet Fritz in the parking lot of a Marriott in Albany. He's there with the Mercedes, and after locking up my rented Ford Escape, I get into the S550's backseat and the butler drives south for at least an hour. He's very chatty, and I love the sound of his voice: slightly accented, like Marissa's, and with the chirpy cadence of a Mozart concerto.

I know we're getting close when he puts up the divider and we talk through the car's voice-activated speaker system.

When we eventually pull up in front of the mansion, night is starting to fall, and I'm glad for the courtyard's lighting so I can see everything as he puts down the divider. He parks between Beth's Audi and Z's iron gray 911 Carrera 4S. On the other side of the Porsche there's a black Hummer I don't recognize with no chrome on it whatsoever—even the hubs are black. Without Fritz telling me, I know it has to be Qhuinn's. It is a total spank ride, and no doubt useful for the fighting, but man, what a damn shame the thing leaves a carbon footprint like a T. rex.

Fritz confirms my unspoken conclusion about who owns it, and as I pass by, I see that the SUV has a dent in its brand-new hood . . . a dent the size of a body. A quick sniff and I smell something sweet as baby powder. This reminds me that the "boys" are now soldiers, and I get a little nostalgic for no good reason.

Fritz lets me into the mansion, takes my coat, and reports on everyone's whereabouts—or at least where they were when he left to pick me up: Mary is over at the Pit with V and Marissa, working on a database for Safe Place. Butch, Qhuinn, and Blay are at the pistol range in the training center. John is in Tohr's room sitting with the Brother. Rhage is upstairs, lying flat on his back next to a twelve-pack of Alka-Seltzer.

Ah, the beast.

The butler asks who I want to see first, and I ask whether he thinks Rhage would be up for talking. Fritz nods and informs me that Hollywood's been looking forward to the distraction—so we head upstairs.

When I get to Rhage's door, Fritz leaves and I do my own knocking.

Rhage: (muffled) Yeah?
J.R.:   It's me.
Rhage: Oh, thank God. Come in.

I open the door and the bedroom is so dark, the stretch of light that slices in from the hall is consumed by a hungry blackness. Before I step forward, though, candles flare on the bureau and a table next to the bed.

Rhage: Can't have you tripping over things.
J.R.:   Thank you . . .

Man, Rhage doesn't look good. He is indeed flat on his back, and there's a lot of Alka-Seltzer next to him. He's naked, but there's a sheet pulled up to his waist, and as I look at him I'm reminded that he's the biggest of the Brothers in terms of heft. He's positively huge, even on a bed that seems big as an Olympic pool. But he is not well. His lids are down over his Bahama blue eyes, his mouth is slightly open, his belly distended as if he's swallowed a weather balloon.

J.R.:   So the beast came out, huh.
Rhage: Yeah . . . last night right before dawn. (He groans as he tries to
         turn over.)
J.R.:   Are you sure you want to do this right now?
Rhage: Yup. I'm dying for distraction, and I can't watch TV. Hey,

could you get me some more Alka-Seltzer? Mary hit me with six before she left about half an hour ago, but they don't seem to last long.

J.R.:   Absolutely.

I'm relieved to do something to help him, and I head over to where four boxes of the stuff are lined up next to a pitcher of water and a glass. I fill the glass, crack open three foil packets, and drop the chalky disks in.

J.R.:   (watching the plop-plop, fizz-fizz go to work) Maybe you should take something stronger?

Rhage: Doc Jane tried me out on some Prilosec. Didn't help as much.

When I turn to him, he lifts his head and I put the glass to his lips. As he drinks slowly, I feel guilty about noticing how gorgeous he is. He truly is the most beautiful male anything I've ever seen . . . you almost want to touch his face to make sure it's real and not some artist's rendering of the absolute standard of masculine splendor. He has Mount Everest cheekbones and a jaw that's straight as an I beam and lips that are full and soft. His hair is blond with curls that go this way and that way on the pillow, and he smells amazing.

    As I take the empty glass away from his mouth, Rhage opens his eyes. And I am reminded that his brilliant teal stare is even more of a knockout than his bone structure.

Rhage: (laughs quietly) You are blushing.

J.R.:   No, I'm not.

Rhage: (singing along to the tune of na-na-na-na-na-naaaaa) You are blushing. You are blushing.

J.R.:   How is it possible I want to strike you while you're down?

Rhage: (grins) Aw, you say the sweetest things.

J.R.:   (laughing because you just have to, he's that endearing) Wait, I thought your vision was off afterward?

Rhage: It is, but your cheeks are THAT red. But really, enough about you, let's talk about me. (bats his mile-long lashes) Come on, what do you want to know? What burning questions do I get to answer?

J.R.:   (laughing again) You're the only Brother who likes to get interviewed.

Rhage: Glad to know I've managed to distinguish myself from that ratty bunch of fools.

J.R.:   What happened? (sits down on edge of bed)

Rhage: I followed the lead on another *lesser* "persuasion" house, and
         let's just say I found what I was looking for and then some.

J.R.:   (swallowing) Were there a lot of them?

Rhage: Meh. Enough. There was some lead exchanged, and one of
         the bullets landed somewhere I didn't appreciate.

J.R.:   Where were you hit?

Rhage: (sweeps sheet off his legs, revealing a bandage around his
         thigh) Me and the beast get along much better now, and he
         doesn't like me getting plugged. (laughs) But Qhuinn, John
         Matthew, and Blay came as backup—like they did for me and
         Z last week. Man . . . (laughs) that threesome was a little sur-
         prised at my alter ego.

J.R.:   What did the boys think of the beast?

Rhage: When I came back as me, I woke up with them standing
         around my head, looking like they'd been victims of a hit-and-
         run. They were white as boxer shorts and about as solid.
         (laughs) Guess the beast took care of the squadron of slayers
         who'd been called in as reinforcements. (rubs tummy) Must
         have been quite a number of them.

J.R.:   So you still have to recover afterward. (Rhage shoots me
         a well-DUH expression and rubs his stomach again.) Okay,
         silly question. Is it easier now for you? Dealing with the beast,
         that is?

Rhage: Well . . . yes and no. I don't fight it anymore when it comes
         out, and that seems to decrease the owie time afterward. But I
         still have to go through this to some extent—especially if
         there's been, how do we say, a snack. The good thing is, I don't
         worry so much about the damn thing turning my brothers or
         the boys into a Happy Meal. It's weird . . . ever since Mary's
         come along, the beast is tuning in to people. I don't know if
         that makes any sense. It's like, when he bonded with her, it
         made him capable of seeing folks as friend or foe instead of
         everyone being food, you know?

J.R.:   That's a relief.

Rhage: Man, I used to spend all my time worrying about that shit. So
         yeah, it's better on a lot of fronts. I mean, for real? I'd still be
         way out of it at this point, you know, doing the recovery thing
         hard-core. Now? I'll be up and around in another three hours
         or so. Still will have the indigestion, but those god-awful body
         aches don't last nearly as long. (shakes his head) Have to say,
         though, even if it were still really tough to deal with . . .
         wouldn't matter to me.

J.R.:   No?

Rhage: Got me my Mary. So even if the beast split me apart to get out, as long as I could put myself back together enough to be with her, it's fine for me.

J.R.:   That's beautiful.

Rhage: So is she.

J.R.:   Speaking of couple stuff . . . I've heard that you and she . . .

Rhage: Have baby on the brain? (laughs) Yeah, we do. Go fig. Thing is, it's not clear to me how to work it. There may be an opportunity, but we'll see. We're still just talking about it.

J.R.   (not wanting to press) Well, I think you two would be great parents.

Rhage: You know, I do too. There are some issues that we need to work out. Between you and me . . . Mary is . . .

J.R.:   What?

Rhage: (shaking head) No, it's private. Anyway, if it happens, it would be great, and if not, I'm not missing anything because I have her. I mean, shit, look at Tohr.

J.R.:   He's really not doing well, is he.

Rhage: No, he's not. And to be honest, it's fucking with all of our heads. Thing is, you can't help but put yourself in his position, because he's your brother and you're feeling where he's at and you don't want him hurting so bad. And you can't help but think about yourself. Me without Mary . . . (Eyes close, mouth narrows.) Yeah, what else were you going to ask me.

In the silence that follows, I think about what the *shellans* go through every night that these males of theirs go out to fight. It's sad to realize that there is a fair turnabout. Without their mates, the Brothers are the living dead—and that has got to be equally terrifying to these strong warriors. To some degree, Rhage doesn't have to worry about losing Mary, but it must be hard to live among guys who aren't as fortunate as yourself.

Before I can ask some kind of fluffy nonsense thing, like whether he and V's practical-joke war is continuing, there's a knock on the door. Before it opens, Rhage lets out a purring sound, so I'm not surprised as Mary walks in. As always, Mary's dressed simply in a pair of khakis and a polo shirt, but her arrival brings Rhage to life as if she were Miss America in a sparkling gown. She also flips some kind of switch inside of him. He really looks at her, focusing on her sharply. And he's a flirt with everyone, but with her he's serious, underscoring for me that she is the special exception and the rest of us are the rule.

Oh, and his bonding scent positively roars. Did I mention that he smells great?

Mary and I say hello, and I'm reminded that three's a crowd when Rhage pulls himself up off the mattress and holds his arms out to her. As he envelops her with his great big arms and stays put, I make some pleasantries with Mary and turn to leave.

Rhage says my name softly, and I look over my shoulder. As he stares out over her head, he shoots me a small, sad smile. Like the reason he's holding on to her so hard is because he's won the lottery with his mate and doesn't understand why he got to be the lucky one. I nod once . . . and leave them to themselves.

Lover Eternal

The People:

Rhage
Mary Madonna Luce
John Matthew, aka Tehrror (Darius reincarnated)
Zsadist
Phury
Bella
Wrath and Beth
The Scribe Virgin
Mr. X, *Fore-lesser*
Mr. O(rmond)
Mr. E, who gets hung up in the tree
Caith, vampire female who has oral interlude with Vishous at One Eye
Dr. Susan Della Croce, Mary's oncologist
Rhonda Knute, the Suicide Prevention Hotline's executive director
Nan, Stuart, Lola, and Bill, workers at the hotline
Amber, the waitress at T.G.I. Friday's

Places of Interest (all in Caldwell, NY, unless otherwise specified):

Suicide Prevention Offices on Tenth Street
One Eye, bar on the far side of Caldwell off Route 22
T.G.I. Friday's in Lucas Square
Mary's house, which is a converted barn on the edge of Bella's property
Bella's farmhouse, located on a private road off Route 22

Tohr and Wellsie's home
John's apartment
Brotherhood's training center, under Darius's (now Beth's) mansion,
    undisclosed location
Mr. X's cabin, on the edge of Caldwell
Lessening Society persuasion center—east from Big Notch Mountain, thirty-
    minute drive from downtown

Summary:

Rhage, the Brotherhood's most dangerous member, falls in love with a dying human—who is the only one who can tame his beast and his heart.

Opening line: *Ah, hell, V, you're killing me.*
Last line: *And reveled in all the love.*
Published: March 2006
Page length: 441
Word count: 125,574
First draft written: December 2004–August 2005

Craft comments:

Perfect men (males) are just not all that interesting to me. You know the ones I'm talking about, the BMOC types? The gorgeous guys with the pearly-pearlies and the big laughs and the overload of sexual confidence (like they're packing a rocket launcher in the cup of their boxer-brief Calvins)? Well, those numbers have always left me cold.

While I was writing *Dark Lover*, Rhage struck me as one of these beautiful males I wouldn't give you a plug nickel for. He was full of bravado and so self-assured and all over the place with the ladies that I wasn't really feeling him as a hero. After all, what kind of journey could someone like that have for his story? *Fabulous guy meets girl. Fabulous guy gets girl. Um . . . fabulous guy keeps girl, and keeps keeping girl and then she hangs on even longer because, hello, he's the Perfect Man, and she likes having sex with the lights on.*

I'd be done at, like, the second chapter. Largely due to disgust. I mean, what's the happily-ever-after for them? She installs mirrors over their marital bed and he . . . well, hell, he's already happy because he's perfect.

The truth was, I was disappointed that Rhage was book two in the series.

I found out he was up after Wrath about three-quarters of the way through the writing of *Dark Lover*. It became clear to me during that scene down in Dari-us's underground rooms, the one where Beth gets Rhage those Alka-Seltzers and soothes him as he tries to recover from the beast having come out again. It was while I was writing those pages that I started getting visions for Hollywood's book: I saw Rhage and the beast and how hard it was for him to live with his curse. Saw that to him all the sex he had was hollow, simply a way to keep himself level. Saw him fall for Mary and sacrifice for her.

He was not perfect. He suffered. He struggled.

By the time I was through outlining his story, Rhage not only interested me, I loved him. He was so much more appealing for the fact that he and his life weren't a playboy's paradise.

Which brings me to rule number six: *Conflict is king.*

One of the things I think works in *Lover Eternal* is its conflicts. Mary and Rhage must overcome a hell of a lot to be together: They've got to confront her disease; deal with the fact that she's human and he's not; come to terms with his beast and what he must do to control it; and get through her transition into the world of the Brotherhood. Each time they made it through one of these road-blocks, they became stronger.

Take, for example, the reccurrence of Mary's leukemia. At the end of the book, when it's clear she doesn't have a lot of time left, Rhage goes to the Scribe Virgin and begs her to save the woman he loves. The Scribe Virgin considers the request and presents him with a heartbreaking solution. She tells him that she will take Mary out of the continuum of her fate, thus rescuing her from death. But in return, to preserve the universal balance, Rhage must keep the curse of his beast for the rest of his life and never see Mary again. Further, Mary will not remember him or the love they'd shared:

> His voice trembled. "You are taking my life from me."
>
> "That is the point," she said in an impossibly gentle tone. "It is yin and yang, warrior. Your life, metaphorically, for hers, in fact. Balance must be kept, sacrifices must be made if gifts are given. If I am to save the human for you, there must be a profound pledge on your part. Yin and yang."
>
> —LOVER ETERNAL, p. 428

That's some serious internal conflict. He has the power to save Mary's life, but only at great cost to himself.

Conflict is the microscope of a book. When it's trained on a character, you see what's underneath the narratives of physical description. You see whether someone is strong or weak, principled or apathetic, heroic or villainous.

In the Scribe Virgin/Rhage exchange over Mary's disease, Rhage's conflict is both external, because it's being forced upon him by a third party—namely the Scribe Virgin, in the form of her proposal—and internal, because he must con-front how badly he wants to get rid of the beast and how much he loves Mary. He proves he's a hero because he sacrifices his own happiness for his love's benefit—

and on a broader level, it's the culmination of his journey from the self-centered male he once was to the connected, compassionate guy he is now.

See why I ended up loving him?

Conflict is absolutely critical in every story. And I think of the ins and outs of getting through it as the chessboard across which the people in the book must move: What they do and where they go to reach resolution are just as significant as what first put them between their rock-and-a-hard-place.

Rule number seven: *Credible surprise is queen to conflict's king.*

Credible surprise is the ultimate play on the chessboard for an author. Plenty of things are surprising, but without prior context to give them weight, they're not credible. To really make a resolution sing, you need both halves—a really strong conflict and an unpredictable, but believable outcome.

Take, for example, *Lover Eternal*'s end result. When Rhage accepts the Scribe Virgin's bargain to save Mary's life, he and his *shellan* are done. Permanently. And yet his love comes back to him (thanks to some rock-star driving from Fritz—who knew the *doggen* had had a Jeff Gordon injection?) both cured of her disease and with all her memories of him and what they've shared intact. Great! Fabulous! Except that's not possible according to the agreement Rhage made with the Scribe Virgin.

Hello, credible surprise. It turns out that the sacrifice for Mary's salvation has already been made. When the Scribe Virgin goes to Mary to rescue her from her fate, she discovers that the woman has been rendered infertile as a result of her treatments for leukemia. In the Scribe Virgin's mind, this is enough of a loss to balance the gift of ever-life. As she states:

> . . . The joy of my creation sustains me always, and I take great sorrow that you will never hold flesh of your flesh in your arms, that you will not see your own eyes staring at you from the face of another, that you will never mix the essential nature of yourself with the male you love. What you have lost is enough of a sacrifice. . . .
>
> —LOVER ETERNAL, p. 438

Who could have guessed that Mary's infertility was the key to the ending that kept the heroine and the hero together? I didn't . . . but then, surprise! And here's why it's credible. Mary's infertility had been mentioned before (see pps. 218 and 328), and the Scribe Virgin has always been about balance. Her gifts cannot be made without cost (think of Darius's token of faculty at the end of *Dark Lover*, for instance), so the reader understands that there must always be a payment, because there was precedent for that.

As I said, the resolution surprised me—and was a source of great relief. When I was outlining the book, I got to the scene with Rhage and the Scribe Virgin, when all appeared to be lost, and I wanted to bang my head into my monitor. I mean, I was writing paranormal ROMANCE. And the only way separation works at the end of a ROMANCE is if it involves ditching a nasty mother-in-law. I was in an absolute panic, as I couldn't see how the two of them were going to get an HEA together.

Except they did, thanks to the credible surprise.

Strong conflict and resolutions that are satisfying and not obvious are the name of the game. The problem is, at least for me, I'm never sure until I'm finished getting the scenes in my head outlined whether both halves are going to present themselves. To be honest, I have no clue where my ideas come from, and I feel as if I complete each story by the skin of my teeth. The endings are always a Hail Mary for me, because I never know for certain whether the magic is going to happen. I feel lucky and grateful when it does, but do not take for granted that such boons will come again.

A couple of other things about Rhage's book. After I got through with his outline and started writing him, I felt like something was wrong. The tone struck me as different from Wrath's story. The vibe was just . . . well, more Rhage, less Wrath.

To me, this was a little alarming. I guess I thought all the books would feel the same as I wrote them, but they haven't, and along the way I've learned that a series shouldn't be about identical. Similar context, sure. Same cast of folks, absolutely. But each story is going to have its own rhythm and pace and zeitgeist. Wrath's had a real sharp edge on it, with quick, nimble pacing and pared-down dialogue. Rhage's struck me as softer and more romantic, funnier, too, with more sex in it. Z's book was dark all around. Butch's tone was closer to Wrath's, with its edge, and there was a lot of the world in it. V's vibe was sleek and uncluttered and a little dangerous. Phury's was romantic and evocative and warm.

Which brings me to rule eight: *Listen to your Rice Krispies*.

I don't know where my ideas come from. The pictures in my head have always been there, and they are in charge. I didn't want Rhage as book number two, but he was. I wanted Rhage's tone to be just like Wrath's. It wasn't. I didn't know how Rhage and Mary were going to end up with each other for centuries considering he was a vampire and she was not. They did. (And P.S., I wanted *Lover Eternal's* writing process to be easier, because I'd just spent nine months getting the world straight. It was just as tough, only in a different way. More on that later.)

All went well and goes well, though, because I let what's in my head be the driver. Even when I get lost, I trust the stories . . . largely because I don't have a choice. What I'm shown is always infinitely better than what I try to deliberately construct.

Here's a minor example of how I listened to my Rice Krispies when it came to Rhage's book. As I started to write *Lover Eternal*, Vishous, keeper of visions of the future, popped up and told Rhage that he ended up with a virgin. When I saw this, I was like, *Er . . . that's going to be kind of tough, given that Mary's been with someone before she met Hollywood.* Still, I was like, *Okay, V said it, so it's going on the page.* And then, throughout the book, V kept hinting about Mary's name having a special significance. I had no idea what the hell he was going on about, but I kept seeing him in my head, always with the name. I figured, *Well . . . just throw it in, and when it goes nowhere, I'll trim it out.*

It wasn't until I got to the end of the book when it all became clear. Mary and Rhage were holding each other after being reunited in his bedroom:

> She lifted her head. "You know, my mother always told me I'd be saved whether I believed in God or not. She was convinced I couldn't get away from the Grace because of what she named me. She used to say that every time someone called out for me or wrote my name or thought about me, I was protected."
>
> "Your name?"
>
> "Mary. She named me after the Virgin Mary."
>
> —LOVER ETERNAL, p. 440

I remember typing that and laughing out loud. Vishous is never wrong!

Now, though, let me give you an example of when being true to what was in my head wasn't so easy.

In the course of doing Rhage's outline, which was fifty-eight pages long, I saw a scene that ran counter to one of the big unspoken rules of romantic convention. In the vast majority of romance novels, the hero is never with another woman after he meets and gets physically involved with the heroine. It makes sense. After all, who in their right mind could fall in love with someone who goes around bed-hopping?

Except Rhage went out and was with another woman after he and Mary had been together. The two of them had yet to make love, but the attraction was there and the bonding was in place—at least on Rhage's part. The issue was his beast. In order to keep his curse under some measure of control, he was forced to burn off his excess energy with fighting and sex, using both as release valves. The night the "adultery" happened, he was in a tough crack. Being around Mary juiced him up because of his attraction for her, and he'd tried and failed to find a fight, so he was reaching a critical, dangerous level. He hated what he did and hated himself for his curse—and it was obvious that what happened was mandated by circumstance, never something he would have chosen. What went down was definitively not a case of a loose-moraled player just out for tail.

The scene where Rhage comes back to their room was heart-wrenching to write. I can still picture him after he'd had his shower, sitting on the edge of the bed. He had a towel around his waist and his head was hanging down and he was utterly defeated, trapped by the realities of his curse and his love for Mary. The situation was tough all around, and it did create a stunningly difficult conflict between the two of them. Together they were able to get past it, but I knew this particular part of the story was not something all readers were going to be comfortable with. And I could understand why. Accordingly, when I wrote the book, I was very careful with how I handled the whole thing.

When I started working on the Brotherhood series, I didn't set out to be a firebrand or a convention breaker, and that is still not my goal. However I did, as I said, vow to keep true to what I see, and that remains my operating principle. The difficulty for me always is, How do I show what's in my head without offending the genre I respect so much? It's always a balance, and it's the thing my editor and I spend the most time on in the revision process. Sometimes, with Rhage, I think I do a good job of walking the line. Other times . . . I wish I could have done better. But more on this later.

Speaking about revision . . . a word on Butch. Originally the story of the cop and Marissa was supposed to be in *Lover Eternal*. The two were going to fall in love, and he was going to be made a Brother after his transition was jump-started—and that was that. As I started drafting Rhage, I was excited to write about Butch and Marissa because I thought they had great chemistry, and there were a lot of good scenes with the two of them in my head.

Two hundred pages into the manuscript, though, I realized I had a problem. Butch and Marissa were competing for airspace against Rhage and Mary to such a degree that I was basically writing two separate books.

The cop was no subplot.

The idea of taking those scenes out terrified me, though, because I was afraid that a lot of the depth of the world would be compromised. I was also worried that I would lose the scenes forever and they were great—at that point, I wasn't sure how many of the Brotherhood books I was going to get to do, and I totally wanted to put Marissa and Butch on the page. Finally, I just really, really, really liked what I had written. I mean, I really *liked* it. Removing those pages seemed like I was giving the material a demotion.

But the book wasn't working. No matter how much I hemmed and hawed and tried to make excuses, it just wasn't coming together right.

Let's hear it for rule number three: *Own your own work*.

If you know something isn't working, no matter how much you like it, get rid of the stuff. Don't wait for your editor to tell you what you know in your heart is true—and make those hard choices because it's the right thing to do for the book you're currently working on.

I'm not saying it's easy.

Even though I knew Rhage's story was in danger of losing focus, I just couldn't bring myself to make the cuts, and the *I-don't-want-to*s went on for weeks. What finally tipped the scales was that the nagging conviction I was fucking the book up refused to go away—and in fact just got louder and more persistent. When I finally grew a set and decided to man up, I put my work gloves on and did some heavy lifting. I cut the hell out of that manuscript, just sliced it to pieces, and in the process scared the crap out of myself because, as always, I was under a serious deadline: I knew if I robbed the book of its texture, I wouldn't be able to fix things and still get Rhage in on time (which would lead to all sorts of scheduling complications for my publisher).

The thing was, though, after I put Rhage's material back together again, I read it through and knew I'd taken the correct action. The focus was where it needed to be, and the book worked better.

The point is, listen to your internal editor like you listen to your Rice Krispies. Just because you think something is brilliant, don't let it compromise the story you're writing. I try to keep that in mind always, because there are so many moving parts to the Brotherhood books—I'm always in jeopardy of spiraling away from the main story or stories. And balance of plotlines remains tough.

Let's see, my favorite scene in *Lover Eternal*? Hard to say, but if I had to pick . . . I'd go with the one with the moon—that second one, after Mary has broken up with Rhage, left the Brotherhood's mansion, and moved in with Bella. It happens right after Rhage goes to see Mary at the farmhouse and they have the official we're-done conversation. Rhage leaves her in the bedroom upstairs and goes out the front door. He's utterly ruined, completely at a loss. Up in the night sky there's a big moon, and as he looks at it, he's clearly thinking about what Mary did when they were in the park on their second date:

Instead he stopped dead in his tracks. Ahead, the moon was rising just above the tree line, and it was full, a fat, luminescent disk in the cold, cloudless night. He extended his arm toward it and squeezed one eye shut. Angling his line of sight, he positioned the lunar glow in the cradle of his palm and held the apparition with care.

Dimly, he heard a pounding noise coming from inside of Bella's. Some kind of rhythmic beat.

Rhage glanced behind him as it got louder.

The front door flew open, and Mary shot out of the house, jumping off the porch, not even bothering with the steps to the ground. She ran over the frost-laden grass in her bare feet and threw herself at him, grabbing on to his neck with both arms. She held him so tightly his spine cracked.

She was sobbing. Bawling. Crying so hard her whole body was shaking.

He didn't ask any questions, just wrapped himself around her.

"I'm not okay," she said hoarsely between breaths. "Rhage . . . I'm not okay."

He closed his eyes and held on tight.

—LOVER ETERNAL, p. 309

I think it's a great scene because it's so poignant to see him echoing what she did during a happier time. And then when she comes out of the house and grabs on to him, it marks a turning point for her. She's reaching out to Rhage, finally including someone in her life and her illness.

The most erotic scene? Er . . . the bed scene. You know the one . . . with the chains? I'll just put this passage in to remind you. This is right before it all goes down, and Rhage is over in the Pit looking for something to keep himself on the bed:

> Rhage nodded. "I only want Mary. I couldn't even get hard for any-one else at this point."
>
> "Ah, shit, man," Vishous said under his breath.
>
> "Why's monogamy a bad thing?" Butch asked as he sat down and popped open the can of beer. "I mean, that's a damn fine woman you got. Mary's good people."
>
> V shook his head. "Remember what you saw in that clearing, cop? How'd you like that anywhere near a female you loved?"
>
> Butch put down the Bud without drinking from it. His eyes traveled over Rhage's body.
>
> "We're going to need a shitload of steel," the human muttered.
>
> —LOVER ETERNAL, pp. 386–387

And this reminds me of one of my favorite lines from the book. It happens fairly early on, when V and Butch have taken cover in the Escalade while Rhage's beast goes postal on some *lessers* in a field:

> In short order, the clearing was empty of *lessers*. With another deaf-ening roar, the beast wheeled around as if looking for more to consume. Finding no other slayers, its eyes focused on the Escalade.
>
> "Can it get into the car?" Butch asked.
>
> "If it really wants to. Fortunately, it can't be very hungry."
>
> "Yeah, well . . . what if it's got room for Jell-O," Butch muttered.
>
> —LOVER ETERNAL, p. 41

One of the other scenes I love is when it becomes clear that the beast is a danger to everyone but Mary. The final showdown with the slayers has played out at her place, and the beast has done its thing with the *lessers*. After the carnage, it approaches her:

> Without warning, the beast whirled around and knocked her to the ground with its tail. It leaped into the air at her house, crashing its upper body through a window.

A *lesser* was pulled out into the night, and the beast's roar of outrage was cut off as it took the slayer between its jaws.

Mary tucked into a ball, shielding herself from the tail's barbs. She covered her ears and closed her eyes, cutting off the juicy sounds and the horrible sight of the killing.

Moments later she felt her body being nudged. The beast was pushing at her with its nose.

She rolled over and looked up into its white eyes. "I'm fine. But we're going to have to work on your table manners."

The beast purred and stretched out on the ground next to her, resting its head between its forelegs. . . .

—LOVER ETERNAL, p. 409

Mary has captured both Rhage's and the beast's hearts, and the two of them are utterly devoted to her. And as she says, she loves the beast—'cuz he's cute in a Godzilla sort of way.

In the scenes that I've seen of Rhage and Mary and the beast since the end of *Lover Eternal*, it's been great to find that Rhage and his alter ego have become more integrated. The beast is never going to be an escort for a debutante ball (his table manners haven't improved much at all), but he's not as uncontrollable as he was. Rhage is happier and calmer. Mary is fulfilled and living her life. S'all good.

Which brings me to a final thought. After each of the Brothers' books, they and their *shellans* continue to live their lives and keep changing and evolving as people do over the course of time. I wish I could show more of where they are and what new challenges they are facing and how their relationships have deepened. The Slices of Life (SOLs) that I post from time to time on the message board give me the opportunity to put out these new scenes, and to me, it's comforting to see everyone continue on and keep living. Just as we all do.

So that's Rhage . . . and now thoughts on my favorite Brother, Z.

Zsadist, Son of Ahgony

"I was dead until you found me, though I breathed. I was sightless,
though I could see. And then you came . . .
and I was awakened."

—LOVER AWAKENED, p. 424

Age:	230
Joined Brotherhood:	1932
Height:	6'6"
Weight:	270 to 280 lbs.
Hair color:	Multicolored, skull-trimmed
Eye color:	Yellow when at rest/black when angry
Identifying physical marks:	Slave bands tattooed in black around neck and wrists; scar running down face from forehead to mouth that distorts the upper lip; extensive scarring on back; nipples pierced (by self); gauge in left earlobe; Brotherhood scar on left pectoral; names BELLA and NALLA carved in skin across upper back and shoulders in Old Language.
Note:	Is now literate following years of not knowing how to read. Has an identical twin, Phury.
Weapon of choice:	Twin SIG forties. Used to be hands.
Description:	*Zsadist knelt down over one of the* lessers, *his scarred face distorted with hatred, his ruined upper lip curled back, his fangs long as a tiger's. With his skull-trimmed hair and the*

hollows under his cheekbones, he looked like the Grim Reaper; and like death, he was comfortable working in the cold. Wearing only a black turtleneck and loose black pants, he was more armed than dressed: The Black Dagger Brotherhood's signature blade holster crisscrossed over his chest, and two more knives were strapped on his thighs. He also sported a gun belt with two SIG Sauers.

Not that he ever used the nine-millimeters, though. He liked to get personal when he killed. Actually, it was the only time he ever got close to anyone.

—LOVER AWAKENED, p. 2

Mated to: Bella

Personal Qs (answered by Z):

Last movie watched:	*Meatballs* (thanks, Rhage)
Last book read:	*Oh, the Places You'll Go!* by Dr. Seuss, to my baby girl
Favorite TV show:	Don't really have one
Last TV show watched:	*The Simpsons*—which I do like
Last game played:	Monopoly with Wrath
Greatest fear:	Waking up and finding all this has been a dream
Greatest love:	Bella
Boxers or briefs:	[left blank]
Watch:	Timex—I'm into function
Car:	Porsche 911 Carrera 4S, dark gray—like I said, I'm into function
What time is it while you're filling this out?	Midnight (I'm off tonight)
Where are you?	Office in training center
What are you wearing?	[left blank]
What's in your closet?	[left blank]
What was the last thing you ate?	Granny Smith apple

Describe your last dream?	[left blank]
Coke or Pepsi?	Coke
Audrey Hepburn or Marilyn Monroe?	Oh, please. That's ridiculous.
Kirk or Picard?	Who?
Football or baseball?	Sports bore me.
Sexiest part of a female?	No one's business but Bella's.
First words spoken to your *shellan*:	"Don't know what you're doing here, other than fucking up my workout."
Her response was:	"I'm sorry. I didn't know."
Last gift given to her:	Part of me wants to front and be like it was an object or something. But I think the last and best gift I ever gave to her was manning up and starting to be a true father to Nalla.
Most attractive thing about her is:	Everything. Every inch of her skin, every strand of her hair, every hope and dream in her eyes, and all the love in her beautiful heart.
Last time you laughed?	When Bella tickled me about ten minutes ago.
Last time you cried:	No one's business but Bella's.

My Interview with Zsadist

After I leave Rhage's room, I stand for a moment in the hall and listen to the sounds of the mansion. Down below, I hear T-Pain rolling out of the billiards room, and pool balls knocking into each other. On the other side of the foyer, in the dining room, *doggen* are clearing the dishes after First Meal, their voices soft and supercheerful—which I take to mean there is a lot of china and silverware to clean up. Behind me, through the closed doors of Wrath's study, the king and Beth are discussing—

Zsadist: Hey.
   J.R.:   (wheels around) Hi—
      Z: Didn't mean to spook you.

Zsadist makes a hell of an impression in person. He's really big now, so very different than he was before he met Bella. If I were to put my hand on his chest? It might cover one of his pecs, but it would be a stretch. Along with his body, his face has filled out, and that scar, though very noticeable, as always, doesn't seem as stark because his cheeks aren't cut so sharply. Tonight he's wearing low-slung jeans (Sevens, I believe) and a black TEAM PUNISHMENT shirt. He has shitkickers on his feet and holstered SIGs under each arm.

   J.R.:   Didn't mean to jump like I did.
      Z: You want to interview me?
   J.R.:   If it's okay with you.
      Z: (shrugs) Meh. I don't have any real problem with it. As long as I can choose what to answer.
   J.R.:   Of course you can. (Looks over balcony.) We could do it in the lib—
      Z: Let's go.

When a male like Z says, Let's go, you follow for two reasons: One, he's not going to hurt you, and two, he's not going to let anything hurt you. So there's no reason not to go. Also no reason to ask about the whole where thing. Sure, he's not going to hurt you, but do you really want to bug him? Nope.

We go down the grand staircase at a brisk pace, and when we hit the foyer, we cross over the depiction of the apple tree, heading in the direction of the vestibule. The doggen in the dining room look up, and though they are dressed in formal black-and-white butlers' uniforms, their smiles are as easy and relaxed as a summer day. Z and I wave back at them as we pass.

Z holds both of the vestibule's doors open for me.

Outside in the courtyard, I take a deep breath. Fall air in upstate New York is like ice-cold sparkling water. It gets into your sinuses and down to your lungs with a sizzle. I love it.

      Z: (Taking out car key from his pocket.) Thought we'd take a drive.
   J.R.:   What a fabulous idea. (Follows him over to iron gray Porsche 911 Carrera 4S.) This car is . . .

Z: My only possession, really. (Opens my door and waits as I slide into the passenger seat.)

As he comes around to the driver's side and gets in, I have a serious case of the joneses. Porsches are luxury sports cars, but their roots are in racing, and you can tell. There's no over-the-top gadgetry cluttering things up on the dash. No flabby seating. No fussy styling. It's all about high-level function and power.

This truly is the perfect car for him.

Z starts the engine, and the calibrated vibration that comes from the back is a loud-and-clear about the number of horses in the trunk. As he K-turns on the pebbles, working neatly around the fountain which has been drained for the winter, he works the clutch and the gearshift seamlessly.

We head out past the compound's gates, and the trip down whatever mountain we're on is a blur to me because of the *mhis*. After we get level there are turns and straightaways, and when the landscape comes into focus again for me, we're at one of the countless intersections on Route 22. Z hangs a left and floors it. The Porsche is psyched by the demand and digs into the pavement like its tires have metal spikes and its engine is powered by jet fuel. As we blast forward, my stomach pools in the cradle of my hips and I grip the door handle, but not from fear that we'll crash—even though Z doesn't have the headlights on and the dashboard isn't lit. No, in the moonless night, there is nothing but the Porsche and the smooth road, and I feel like I'm flying. My grip is an attempt to ground myself against the weightlessness.

Except then I realize, I don't want to be tied down. I release my hand.

J.R.: This reminds me of Rhage and Mary.
Z: (without taking his eyes off the road) How so?
J.R.: He took her for a ride in his GTO one night when they were falling in love.
Z: He did?
J.R.: Yeah.
Z: Romantic bastard, isn't he.

We drive along the road, or it could have been the galaxy, and though I can't see the turns and hills, I know he can. The metaphor for life is unavoidable: Each of us in the seat of our destiny, driven along a road we cannot see, by someone who can.

J.R.:   You're taking us somewhere.

Z: (laughs softly) Oh, really.

J.R.:   You aren't the type to just drive.

Z: Maybe I've turned over a new leaf.

J.R.:   No. It's your nature, and not something that needs fixing.

Z: (looking over at me) And where do you think I'm going?

J.R.:   Doesn't matter to me. I know you'll get us there and back safely and that it'll be worth the trip.

Z: Let's hope it is.

We drive in silence, and I'm not surprised. You don't interview Z. You sit and open up a space and maybe he fills it, maybe he doesn't.

The next biggish city from Caldwell is a good thirty minutes from the bridges downtown but only about twelve minutes from the Brotherhood's compound. As we roll into its fringes, Z turns on the headlights to be legal. We pass by an Exxon gas station and a Stewart's ice-cream shop and a McDonald's and a host of nonchains like The Choppe Shoppe hair salon and Browning's Printing and Graphics and Luigi's Pizzeria. The parking lots are lit like something out of an Edward Hopper painting, pools of light congealing around parked cars and ice machines and Dumpsters. I'm struck by how many wires are suspended from telephone pole to telephone pole and the way the traffic lights dangle above the intersections. It's the neuropathways of the city's brain, I think to myself.

The silence is not awkward. We end up at Target.

Z pulls into the parking lot and heads to a secluded space away from the six parked cars clustered around the bank of doors in the front. As we approach the spot he picks, the massive light over us goes dark—probably because he willed it off.

We get out, and while we walk to the toffee-colored building with its red bull's-eye, Z gets closer to me than he ever has. He's about two feet behind me on my right, and it feels, because of his size, like he's on top of me. He's doing his guard thing, and I take it as a gesture of kindness, not aggression. Going along, our footsteps over the cold pavement are like two different voices. Mine are Shirley Temple. His are James Earl Jones.

Inside the store, the security guard doesn't like us. The rent-a-cop straightens up from the partition demarcating the food section and puts his hand on his pepper spray. Z ignores him. Or at least, I assume Z does. The Brother is still walking behind me, so I can't see his face.

J.R.:   Which section?

Z: Over to the left. Wait, I want a cart.

After he gets one, we head for . . . the baby department. When we get to the displays of onesies and tiny socks, Z steps ahead of me. He handles the clothes on the racks in the most gentle way, as if they are already on Nalla's sturdy little body. He fills the cart. He doesn't ask me what I think of what he's buying, but that's no disrespect to me. He knows what he wants. He buys little shirts and ruffled diaper pants in all kinds of colors. Tiny shoes. A pair of mittens that look like they belong on a doll. Then we go to the toy section. Blocks. Books. Soft stuffed animals.

Z: Automotive next, then music and DVDs. Also books.

He's in charge of the cart. I follow. He buys Armor All and a bunch of chamois cloths. Then the new Flo-Rida CD. An Ina Garten cookbook. When we pass by the food section, he gets a bag of Tootsie Pops. We pause at the menswear section, and he chooses two *Miami Ink* baseball caps. In the stationery department he picks up some lovely thick white paper and a set of colored pencils. He takes a deep red knitted scarf from ladies' accessories, and then pauses by a display of silver chains that have charms dangling off of them. He picks one out that has a small quartz heart hanging from the chain and is careful as he lays it out on top of his neat pile of onesies.

I thought he was being careful with the way he touched the baby clothes because of what they were, but in fact, he treats all the merchandise with the same respect. He looks like a straight-up killer, and his expression is as dark as the black in his eyes, but his hands are never rough. If he picks something up off a shelf or a rack or a display and doesn't want it, he returns it where it was. And if he finds a sweater that's just been crammed back into a stack or a book that's been misshelved by another customer or a shirt that's cockeyed on a hanger, he rights it.

Z has a kind soul. At heart, he's just like Phury.

We go to check out, and the twenty-year-old guy who's manning the cash register looks up at Z like the Brother is a god. As I watch all of the items being scanned, I realize the purpose of the trip is not just to get the things, but to send a message. These items are his interview. He's telling me how much he loves Nalla and Bella and his Brothers. How grateful he is.

J.R.:   (softly) The red scarf's for Beth, right?
Z: (shrugs and takes out a black wallet) Yeah.

Ah . . . because a present for Beth is a present for Wrath. And I bet the Armor All is for the three boys to massage Qhuinn's Hummer with. But there's nothing for . . .

> Z: There's nothing to get him. There's nothing he wants, and a gift would make him feel worse.

Tohr. God, Tohr . . .

After Z pays with a black AmEx, we walk past the security guard, who looks at the red-and-white bags like he has X-ray vision and there could be guns in them—even though the store doesn't sell click-click-bang-bangs.

Outside, I help Z put his purchases in the minuscule backseat of the Porsche. They overflow, and I end up sitting with some at my feet and on my lap.

We're silent the whole ride home, until we get to the *mhis* that surrounds the compound. As the landscape blurs again, I look over at Z.

> J.R.:   Thank you for taking me.

There's a pause, one that lasts so long, I figure there's going to be no response. But then he downshifts as we come up to the mansion's gates.

> Z: (glancing over and nodding once) Thank you for coming along.

Lover Awakened

The People:

Zsadist
Bella
Phury
John Matthew
Rehvenge
Mr. O
Mr. X
Mr. U(stead)
Wellsie
Tohr
Sarelle, Wellsie's cousin

Lash, son of Ibex
Qhuinn, son of Lohstrong
Blaylock, son of Rocke
Catronia (Z's Mistress when he was a blood slave)

Places of Interest (all in Caldwell, NY, unless otherwise noted):

The Brotherhood mansion—undisclosed location
Bella's farmhouse—private road off Route 22
Lessening Society persuasion center—east from Big Notch Mountain, thirty-
    minute drive from downtown
Tohr and Wellsie's home
Rehvenge's family home
ZeroSum (corner of Trade and Tenth streets)

Summary:

Zsadist, a former blood slave and the most feared member of the Black Dagger Brotherhood, finds love as he rescues a beautiful aristocratic female from the
obsessive hold of a violent *lesser.*

Opening line:	*"Goddamn it, Zsadist! Don't jump—"*
Last line:	"Bella . . . And Nalla."
Published:	September 2006
Page length:	434
Word count:	136,807
First draft written:	November 2005–March 2006

Craft comments:

I think with Z, I'll start with something from *Dark Lover.* This is from the beginning of the book, when Wrath has called the Brotherhood together following
Darius's assassination by the *Fore-lesser,* Mr. X. Zsadist makes his arrival, so to
speak, thusly:

> The front door swung open, and Zsadist strode into the house.
> Wrath glared. "Nice of you to show up, Z. Busy tonight with the
> females?"
> "How about you get off my dick?" Zsadist went over to the corner,
> staying away from the rest.
>
> —DARK LOVER, p. 30

When I first saw Zsadist walk into that house like that, I assumed he was an antagonist. Had to be. His vibe was too legitimately fuck-off for him to be a hero. And then the impression he made got even worse with this scene of Beth waking up to find him with her:

> The man towering over her had black, lifeless eyes. A harsh face with a jagged scar running down it. Hair that was practically shaved it was so short. And long, white fangs that were bared . . .
>
> "Pretty, aren't I?" His cold stare was the stuff of nightmares, of dark places where no hope could be found, of hell itself.
>
> Forget the scar, she thought. Those eyes were the scariest thing about him.
>
> And they were fixated on her as if he were sizing her up for a shroud. Or for some sex.
>
> She moved her body away from him. Started looking around for something she could use as a weapon.
>
> "What, you don't like me?"
>
> Beth eyed the door, and he laughed.
>
> "Think you can run fast enough?" he said, pulling the bottom of his shirt free from the leather pants he had on. His hands moved to his fly. "I'm damn sure you can't."   —DARK LOVER, p. 226–227

Yeah, okay, so not a hero. The thing was, though, the voices in my head were shouting that he was getting his own book and he was going to end up with an HEA.

Oh, great. Fantastic. And not the last time in the course of writing this series when I've been like, *You have GOT to be kidding me—I can't pull that off.*

By the end of *Dark Lover*, however, I was seduced . . . and totally driven to write Z's story. The turning points for me were two scenes in that book. One is of Beth meeting up with Zsadist in the pantry as they get the food ready for her mating ceremony (p. 318). In this exchange, Z reveals that he has no intention of hurting Beth and that he doesn't like to be touched. The other scene is just after the ceremony. The vows have been spoken and the carving done and the Brotherhood is serenading the couple:

> But then, in a high, keening call, one voice broke out, lifting above the others, shooting higher and higher. The sound of the tenor was so clear, so pure, it brought shivers to the skin, a yearning warmth to the chest. The sweet notes blew the ceiling off with their glory, turning the chamber into a cathedral, the Brothers into a tabernacle. . . .
>
> The scarred one, the soulless one, had the voice of an angel.
>
> —DARK LOVER, p. 334

By the end of *DL*, I needed to write Z so badly that for the only time yet, I dictated book order against what I saw in my head. Z was supposed to be the last in the series, the end cap of the ten books (which included Wrath, Rhage, Butch, V, Phury, Rehvenge, Payne, John Matthew, and Tohrment). But the thing was, when I sold the Brotherhood series, the first contract was for three books. At the time the deal was made, paranormals were hot, but people were already beginning to speculate when the market would hit its crest and begin to fall off in terms of popularity. I wasn't sure I'd get to write all of them.

Call me an optimist, huh.

It was with that mindset that I approached the future, and as I finished *Dark Lover* and started to outline *Lover Eternal*, I knew if I didn't put Zsadist on the page I would never get past it. So I bumped him forward.

Writing him was gut-wrenching, and there were times when I had to stand up and walk away from my computer. But he came out as I saw him in my head, and I love him more than any hero I've ever written. He was tricky, though. Z was an honest-to-God sociopath. The difficulty was presenting him in a way that was at once true to his pathology and yet sympathetic enough for readers to see what I saw in him and understand why Bella fell for him.

There were two keys. One was his reaction to Bella's abduction, and the other was his past as a blood slave and its sexual repercussions. Gaining sympathy for Z with readers was a classic show-not-tell situation. The book opens with Z on a single-minded mission to get Bella back. Very heroic, and the altruism is justified in spite of its being contrary to his nature because it's obvious that he sees her situation through the lens of his own captivity and abuse: He couldn't help himself, but he sure as hell can help her. And after he gets her out, he treats her with great gentleness. Bella becomes the catalyst to his expressing something warm and protective, and his interactions with her balance out his more sadistic and masochistic scenes.

And then there is the sexual side of things. By showing Z under the Mistress's ownership through a series of flashbacks, the reader can see for themselves that he was made into the monster he became, not born like that. Z's sexual issues with Bella, which were introduced in *Lover Eternal*, are evidence that the traumas he suffered are not only with him to the present day, but they own and define him as a male. At least until Bella comes into his life.

There was real potential for Z not coming across as heroic, and I was really nervous when my editor read him for the first time, because I wasn't sure whether I'd pulled it off. She loved him, though, and so did the readers. So do I, although I have to say that I haven't reread him since I reviewed his galleys—and he's the only book of mine that I haven't cracked open when he came back to me bound.

I think it's going to be a lot longer before I read him. And I might never.

A word on the editorial/publishing process. Lots of people, prepublished authors and readers alike, ask me how exactly the different stages of production work and how long each takes. For me, the whole thing is about nine months.

Once I finish my outline, which takes at least a month, I send it to my editor, who reads it. After we touch base, I get down to work, taking what is in the outline and fleshing it out with description, dialogue, and narration. I tend to write half of the book, then go back and read and edit my way through that block of material. This reread is critical for me. In the Brotherhood books there's so much going on that I don't want to risk losing track of all the plot arcs and character development. When I get to the halfway point again, I finish the book all the way through. This whole first drafting process usually takes about four months of seven-day-a-week writing.

Typically I take a week off and let the manuscript sit while I work on other things. This break is really important so that when I go back I have fresh eyes—and if I don't get the downtime, I really don't think the draft finishes as well as it should. When I return to the book, it usually takes me another six weeks to do the heavy lifting associated with getting scene order correct and chapter breaks at the right point and the proper intensity of emotion. Then it's another couple weeks to smooth, smooth, smooth.

At this point I'm blurry eyed and dizzy, because the closer to the end I get, the longer my days are—usually the two weeks before I turn anything in, I'm working fourteen to sixteen hours a day. When it comes to whatever Thursday night is the deadline for mailing (it's always Thursday so the manuscripts drop on Friday), I print the whole book out, get into my car in a zombie state and a pair of wilted sweats, and drive across town to Kinko's, where I FedEx the thing overnight to my editor.

Usually the manuscript boxes weigh about eight pounds and cost a hundred dollars to send off.

After my editor reads the material, she and I go over what we think comes through well and what could be even stronger. We also touch base on whatever might go a little far for the market either sexually or in terms of violence. What I love most about my editor is that she lets me be true to what I see and doesn't dictate. It's a collaboration focused on making sure that what's in my head gets onto the page with the best impact possible—and any changes or additions are my choice and my choice alone.

After that editorial meeting, I go back and rework the manuscript, tightening it, getting the words more precise, amplifying where necessary. By this time the chapters are set, the scene order is solid, the peaks and valleys in emotion and action are really humming along, so it's pretty much just tweaking. That and line editing. I am incredibly anal about words and dialogue and flow, and I go over every single word in the manuscripts over and over again. Nothing ever feels good enough.

For this phase of the process I typically take six weeks, and the manuscript will grow in page length with each succeeding pass I make. A first draft for me is about five hundred pages, double-spaced Times New Roman twelve point. (I can't write in Courier for some reason, although a lot of authors do—that font screws with my voice.) By the time I finish the revised draft, the manuscript is usually around the six-hundred-page mark.

When I'm finished with the revisions, it's another trip to Kinko's on a Thursday evening, pulling a *Night of the Living Dead* in sweats again. Usually my editor and I do only one revision cycle, not because I'm a miracle worker or a genius, but because I'm really critical about my own work and beat the hell out of the material before she gets to see it.

Next up are copyedits. After my editor reads the book through again and approves it for publication, the manuscript goes to a copy editor, who checks it for dropped words, grammatical issues, trademark spellings, continuity glitches between scenes, and time line stuff. She also puts in the typesetting notations—which are like a Morse code of dots and dashes made in red pencil.

I should probably confess that I don't think I'm a joy to copyedit. In my books I use a lot of vernacular. Personally, I think so-called "common language" is more interesting and apropos than "proper English"; it's passionate and powerful in ways that "wherefore art thou ass and thy elbow" just isn't. I'm very grateful to the copy editor we tend to use because she doesn't try to beat me over the head with *The Chicago Manual of Style* (the reference bible for grammatical propriety).

When the copy edits come back, I go through the manuscript, answer any queries on the margins, stet or accept any word additions or subtractions (*stet* is the word you use to reject what the copy editor has done), and address any issues that my editor and I have come up with on the revisions. Usually my manuscripts are pretty clean, but I still manage to find things that bug me. When I read my writing, it's like running my hand down a cloth that should be seamless. Things that aren't smooth irritate the ever living hell out of me, and I have to work and rework the words until I don't feel rough spots anymore.

After I send the copyedited manuscript back, the next step is galleys. Galleys are an eight-and-a-half-by-eleven printout of exactly what will be in the bound book—think of opening a book up to any page split, and the galleys are the left and right sides reproduced. I go through the whole thing in this form, and I always want to fuss over and change too much. I'm truly never satisfied.

So that's my process, and I've got to say it was complicated by Zsadist, because some of the scenes in him I didn't want to write, much less edit. Even for this compendium, when I've pored through all the other books picking out passages for the dossiers . . . I can't do that with Z.

Which is kind of weird, because out of all the males and men I've ever written about, he's my favorite. Bar none. But there's a lot in his story that's really upsetting.

What scenes got to me? They're still in my head so vividly I don't need to open *Lover Awakened* to remember them. One of the hardest for me to write was the sequence where Z is led down into what was going to be his cell for the next hundred years by the private guard he used to serve ale to when he was a kitchen boy. He's just been raped by the Mistress for the first time and is so innocent and hurt and terrified. None of the males will look at him or touch him or take pity on him. They think of him as unclean even though he is a victim. As he walks along, crying, with the remnants of what the Mistress had used on him still on his body, my heart absolutely broke.

It's just awful.

Another scene that absolutely killed me was when Bella finds Z on the floor of his shower, scrubbing at himself, trying to get clean enough for her to feed from him. He's rubbing his skin raw, but no matter how much soap and friction he uses, he still feels absolutely filthy.

Then there was the scene where Z forced her to hurt him so that he could finish sexually.

But there are also sections I don't want to read over again that aren't about Z.

I knew going into the book that Wellsie's death was going to be hard on readers. It was hard on me. I cried when I wrote the scene where Tohr is down in the training center's office with John Matthew and is calling home, hoping that Well-sie will pick up, praying that she's okay. Just as he dials their number once again, the Brotherhood shows up at the office's door. Wellsie's voice comes out of the speakerphone as the call flips into voice mail and Tohr is told she's been killed.

I've had some readers and other authors say that I was courageous for killing a main character off. I've had others be really disappointed at my creative choice. Although I totally respect both perspectives, the thing is, to me it wasn't courage or a choice at all. It was just what happened. I knew all along that Wellsie would be killed; the only thing that surprised me was that it happened as early as it did in terms of the series. I thought it would be farther along in the books, but the thing is, the scenes I see don't always come chronologically, so I don't always know the *when*.

As a side note, I will say that those who had problems with her death had less trouble when I explained that it wasn't a melodramatic calculation on my part and that it basically crippled me. I think if you work with characters whom readers feel a close connection with, and bad things happen, as long as you show that you are far from indifferent, that in fact you are heartbroken and worried and sad, then readers are less likely to feel capriciously manipulated.

Some other thoughts on Z . . .

Bella should have gotten more airtime.

In the Brotherhood books, my heroines don't always get enough attention or page space, and I know why. One of my weaknesses as a writer, and it comes out in the series, is that I get so far into the heads and the lives of my heroes that the female leads are in danger of being eclipsed.

See, the good thing about the Brothers is that I see them with such clarity. The bad thing about the Brothers is that I see them with such clarity.

Choosing what to put in and where to filter is hard for me, and not only in terms of the Brothers' lives. The series as a whole is always progressing in my head: changes in the war are happening; Wrath is at greater and greater odds with the *glymera*; challenges are coming into the previous Brothers' relationships and being surmounted. Nothing is static in the world, and I don't always know what to put to the side.

Back to Bella as a case in point. I wish I'd spent more time showing how her experience being held at the hands of Mr. O affected her emotionally and psychologically. There was some mention of the aftermath, but there could have been more. Sure, she gets the (dubious) satisfaction of killing her captor at the end, but I think I might have shown more of her processing her abduction in front of the readers so they knew where she was and how she was coming along.

As for the romance? Bella was perfect for Zsadist—pretty much the only female I could picture getting through to him (and he's really the only male strong enough for her to respect—I mean, hello, Rehvenge is her brother!).

They're just a great pair. . . . I'm reminded of the very first time they meet in *Lover Eternal*. Z's punching that bag down in the gym, and Bella stumbles upon his workout. She's instantly attracted to him as she watches him from behind, and even after he turns around and she sees his scarred face and gets a load of his nasty attitude, she's still drawn to him (p. 70).

The beginnings of their mutual connection came through toward the end of that book. At the party Rhage throws for his Mary at the Brotherhood's mansion, Bella reaches up and touches Phury's hair out of curiosity. Z is watching from the shadows and comes over to her:

> In a burning rush, she imagined him looking down at her while their bodies were merged, his face inches from her own. The fantasy had her lifting her arm. She wanted to run her fingertip down that scar until it got to his mouth. Just to know the feel of him.
>
> With a quick jerk to the side, Zsadist dodged the contact, eyes flaring as if she'd shocked him. The expression was buried fast.
>
> In a flat, cold voice he said, "Careful there, female. I bite."
>
> "Will you ever say my name?"   —LOVER ETERNAL, p. 346

Phury comes over and separates them. Taking Bella aside, he makes a statement that was so very true before she comes into Z's life:

> "My twin's not broken. He's ruined. Do you understand the difference? With broken maybe you can fix him. Ruined? All you can do is wait to bury him."   —LOVER ETERNAL, p. 346

Later in the evening, Bella ends up following Z to his bedroom. The visit doesn't end as she hopes, with them together in bed. Instead she learns something about this hard-core warrior she's so attracted to. This is from after he nearly takes her, when he stops and rolls off her onto the tiled floor:

> Jesus, his body was in rough shape. His stomach was hollow. His hip bones jutted out of his skin. He must indeed only drink from humans, she thought. And not eat much at all.
>
> She focused on the tattooed bands covering his wrist and neck. And the scars.
>
> *Ruined. Not broken.*
>
> Although she was ashamed to admit it now, the darkness in him had been the largest part of his allure. It was such an anomaly, a contrast to what she'd known from life. It had made him dangerous. Exciting. Sexy. But that was a fantasy. This was real.
>
> He suffered. And there was nothing sexy or thrilling about that.
>
> —LOVER ETERNAL, p. 365

As I said before, Bella's abduction was part of the reason they ended up together, because it opened Z emotionally to her in a way that wouldn't have happened otherwise. But I think Bella still would have gotten to him, because she's a great combination of strength and compassion. She's a realist, though, and does pull out of the relationship toward the end of their book, when Z pushes her away. Their parting, along with other forces in his life, are what prompt Z to make some important changes.

I have to say that, to me, the way *Lover Awakened* ended with its epilogue was so great. Z's back working out in the gym where Bella first saw him, but as she comes in and brings little Nalla to her daddy, you get a sense of how far they've come. I swear, when Z turns back and winks at the trainee while he has Nalla in his arms?

sigh

But here's the thing: As I've said, the reality for me in this series is that these people's lives don't stop just because their book is finished. And that is what the novella in this compendium was all about. It's logical that Z would have trouble bonding with his daughter, and I really value the opportunity of getting to show that part of his development as a male and a *hellren* and a father.

And speaking of family . . . Phury. You can't talk about Z without mentioning Phury. Phury has fascinated me ever since that scene in *Lover Eternal* when he comes back from having beaten Z at Z's request. Phury's hollow eyes as he emerges from the training center's tunnel were what stuck with me, and I was dying to see where he ended up and how he fell in love. And then, in *Lover Awakened*, he goes even farther for his twin. I think the scene when Phury scars his own face really gets to the core of the trouble he's in, both psychologically and emotionally. All his life he has been consumed by his twin's abduction and slavery, and his rescue of Z doesn't save either one of them from their suffering. When Phury shaves his head and puts a dagger to his own face in order to take his twin's place at the hands of the *lesser* who abducted Bella, he becomes the physical embodiment of Zsadist.

More on Phury later, but he was almost too heroic, overbalancing Z's anti-hero with a personality that was self-sacrificing to a detrimental degree.

One last thing . . . Rehvenge . . . oh, Rehv. Getting a chance to show him off was one of the great joys of this book. He was and is just so flat-out hot and such total and complete bad news that I was jonesing to write his book even back then.

And Rehv was significant for another reason.

He was, in *Lover Awakened*, the first time I'd ever tried to deliberately obscure a character's identity. The Reverend, club owner and drug dealer, and Rehvenge, aristocratic, overbearing brother of Bella, were the same person, but I didn't want the reader to know it until the end, when Z and Bella go to her mother's house. The way I managed the sleight of hand was that I showed Rehv mostly through other people's points of view, and if there was anything in his POV, I was careful there were no revelations on his part that left the reader making the connection. It was, as Butch would say, wicked tricky. I literally went through every single word in the Rehv sections to make sure that there were no tip-offs and that the presentations made him believable in both roles.

Okay, I guess I've gone on long enough about Zsadist and his book. Butch is, as always, wanting some attention, and then there're still Vishous and Phury to go through.

I think I'll close with the fact that I'm still in love with Z and always will be.

And that just about says it all.

Dhestroyer, Descended of Wrath, Son of Wrath

a.k.a. Butch O'Neal

*"You've got some of me in you, cop." Wrath's smile stuck around as he slid
his glasses back on. "Course, I always knew you were a royal.
Just didn't think it went past the pain-in-the-ass part, is all."*

—LOVER REVEALED, p. 321

Age:	38
Joined Brotherhood:	2007
Height:	6'7"
Weight:	260 lbs.
Hair color:	Brown
Eye color:	Hazel
Identifying physical marks:	Black tattoo at base of spine in the form of grouped lines; Brotherhood scar on left pectoral; name MARISSA carved in skin across upper back and shoulders in Old English letters; pinkie on right hand is slightly deformed following transition; scar on abdomen.
Note:	Is the fulfillment of the Lessening Society's Destroyer Prophecy. Following his abduction by the Society, and the Omega's tampering with him, he is able to consume *lessers* by inhalation—which, contrary to stabbing, circumvents the slayers' return to their master and thereby threatens the Omega's very existence.
Weapon of choice:	Dry, scintillating wit. (When pressed, he indicated it was a forty-millimeter Glock.)

Description: *Butch took a turn in front of a full-length mirror, feeling like a pansy, but unable to help himself. The black pinstripe fit him well. The bright white, open-collared shirt made his tan come out. And the sweet pair of Ferragamo loafers he'd found in a box were just the right amount of flash.*

He was almost handsome, he thought. As long as she didn't look too closely at his bloodshot eyes.

The four hours of sleep and all that Scotch showed.

—DARK LOVER, p. 316

Looking deeply into his hazel eyes, she stroked back his thick, dark hair. Then traced his eyebrows with her thumbs. Ran a fingertip down his bumpy, broken-too-many-times nose. Tapped lightly on his chipped tooth.

"Kind of battle-worn, aren't I?" he said. "But you know, with some plastic surgery and a couple caps I could be a high-flier just like Rhage."

Marissa glanced back at the figurine and thought about her life. And Butch's.

She shook her head slowly and leaned in to kiss him. "I wouldn't change a thing about you. Not one single thing."

—LOVER REVEALED, p. 451

Mated to: Marissa, blooded daughter of Wallen

Personal Qs (answered by Butch):

Last movie
watched: *Scrooged* with Bill Murray, excellent Christmas flick.
Last book read: *Green Eggs and Ham* by Dr. Seuss, to Nalla.
Favorite
TV show: Old episodes of *Columbo* or anything on ESPN
Last TV
show watched: "Murder by the Book" from *Columbo*'s first season—the episode was directed by Steven Spielberg. Fantastic shit right there. I know the lines, I've watched it so many times.
Last game
played: Foosball with V
Greatest fear: Not being who Marissa believes me to be.
Greatest love: Marissa.
Favorite quote: "Bad deeds, like beauty, are in the eye of the beholder."
Boxers or briefs: Emporio Armani boxer briefs.

Watch:	I have a lot of them—forty-nine at last count. I'm all about *haute horlogerie*. Right now I'm wearing Corum's Golden Tourbillon Panoramique.
Car:	Escalade, black. Started as V's, now it's both of ours.
What time is it while you're filling this out?	2 a.m.
Where are you?	In the Pit on one of the leather sofas. *SportsCenter* is on. So is Ludacris. V is looking over my shoulder. He doesn't seem to believe me when I tell the cribbing bastard that my answers won't help him pass his test— Ow.
What are you wearing?	Diesel jeans, white button-down by Vuitton, black Brunello Cucinelli cashmere sweater, and Acqua di Parma cologne. Oh, and Gucci loafers. The belt is Martin Dingman.
What's in your closet?	That would be closets. I have a clothes addiction—more fun than the Scotch thing I had going on, and I look better—but, shit, it's expensive. I have formal stuff from Tom Ford, Gucci, Vuitton, Hermès, Zegna, Marc Jacobs, Prada, Isaia, Canali— all the regulars. Casual and sport shit's from a variety of designers like Pal Zileri, Etro, Diesel, Nike, Ralph Lauren, Affliction—I'm not a snob. For knits it's Lochcarron of Scotland. Phury and I compare notes a lot—and compete. Fritz helps us get things. The *doggen*'ll head down to Manhattan and pick up a moving van's worth of threads in our sizes— stuff we order or things he thinks we'll like. He does our tailoring. For hand-sewn shirts and suits and slacks we have relationships with a couple of shops and have given them models to work off of. Look, if having nice clothes makes me a metrosexual? Fine, I'll take the hit—but I still have my chipped front tooth, and every night I go out and kick ass. So there you go.
What was the last thing you ate?	Buttermilk pancakes with butter and maple syrup and a cup of coffee. With Rhage. He always makes me feel like a lightweight around food, but then, the brother could eat a pack of wolves under the table—and go back for seconds.
Describe your last dream?	It involved a long, dark tunnel and a train going into it. Over and over again. Do the math.

Coke or Pepsi?	Lagavulin. What? That's liquid in a bottle, what do you want from me? Fine—Coke.
Audrey Hepburn or Marilyn Monroe?	I vastly prefer class to flash. Audrey all the way. P.S. Marissa is even more elegant than AH, and that is saying something.
Kirk or Picard?	Kirk. Abso.
Football or baseball?	Member of the Red Sox Nation. 'Nuff said.
Sexiest part of a female?	Would be indiscreet to spell it out. But use your damn brain.
What do you like most about Marissa?	I love her skin and her hair and the way she crosses her legs at the knee and folds her hands together. I love her accent and her pale blue eyes and the way she's the most proper lady you've ever seen but still makes me— Er, anyway. She has perfect style and exquisite taste and she wakes up smelling good. More than that . . . she's always loved me for who I am, never wanted me to be different. Which makes her an angel.
First words spoken to her were:	"No . . . don't go back there. . . . I'm not going to hurt you."
Her response was:	"How do I know that?"
Last gift given to her:	A desk chair. Two days ago. The one she had before squeaked when you turned in it and didn't have any lumbar support. So I took her to Office Depot and had her try out a bunch and bought her the one she liked best.
Most romantic thing you've ever done for her:	Dunno. I don't think I'm good at the romantic shit. Jesus . . . I have no idea.
Most romantic thing she's ever done for you:	Waking me up every day with a smile. I've got expensive tastes, but one small smile from her is priceless.

Anything you'd change about her?	Sometimes I wish she didn't work so hard. Not in terms of hours, more like the pressure she puts on herself to save every single person who comes to Safe Place. It reminds me of when I was in Homicide. Not all outcomes are what you hope. I do my best to be there for her and talk things through with her. She asks me a lot of questions about the murder cases I worked on and how I dealt with the families. What she does now and what I did then—there's a lot of parallels. It brings us closer.
Best friend (excluding *shellan*):	Vishous, then Rhage. And Phury, too.
Last time you cried:	I don't cry. Ever.
Last time you laughed:	Little while ago, when V changed Nalla's diaper. I'm going to get hit for that, but shit it was— Ow.

My Interview with Butch

After Zsadist and I get home from Target, I help carry the bags into the mansion. We are just finishing the fetch-and-carry routine when Butch comes out of the door under the stairs. He's dressed in a black Izod sweater with a white shirt underneath and a pair of superbly cut black trousers. His shoes are Tod's. Black with no socks. He's got a duffel bag on his shoulder and a monster grin on his face.

Butch: My turn!

    Z: (bending over a bag and taking out one of the *Miami Ink* hats) For you.

Butch: Okay, that's hot. (Takes it and puts it on.) Thanks, man.

    Z: Got one for your boy, too.

Butch: Which is actually another gift to me, because we won't have to fight over this one. (Turning to me.) You ready?

  J.R.: Absolutely. Where are—

Butch: Out the back. (Sweeps arm toward library.) This way.

I smile a good-bye to Z and he returns my expression, his ruined lip twitching up briefly and his eyes flashing yellow. I think for a moment

how lucky Bella and Nalla are; then I follow Butch out of the foyer
and into one of my favorite rooms in the house. The library is walled
with books, the only breaks coming for the windows and the bank
of doors and the fireplace. Oil paintings of landscapes are hung over
the tomes here and there, giving an English-manor-house feel to the
space.

Butch:	(over his shoulder) Betcha can't guess where we're going.
J.R.:	It's not just the library.
Butch:	(goes to one of the French doors and opens it) Right you are. And out you go!
J.R.:	What's in the duffel?
Butch:	(shooting me his trademark smile, the one that totally eclipses his busted nose and the chip in his front tooth, the one that turns him into the most attractive man on the planet) It's not a potato launcher.
J.R.:	Why does that not reassure me? (stepping out and stopping short)
Butch:	(with pride) I'd like you to meet Edna.
J.R.:	I . . . didn't know you could do that to a golf cart.

Edna is your standard-issue links transport—except she's had a makeover right out of the *Robb Report*. She's got a Cadillac hood ornament
and a grille modeled after the Escalade's. Painted black, her rims are
twenty-fours, her bumpers are chromed, her seating leather, and it
wouldn't surprise me in the slightest to discover that she's turbo-charged.
Hell, if you could nitro an electric engine, I'd be looking for the injector
button on the console.

Butch:	Isn't she spank? (puts duffel in the back and gets behind the chrome wheel) I was going for an updated Elvis vibe.
J.R.:	Mission accomplished. (Gets in beside him. Am surprised when my butt tingles.) Seat warmers, too?
Butch:	Shit, yeah. Wait'll you hear the sound system.

Kanye West blares out over the gardens and we take off across the rolling lawn, passing by flower beds that are battened down for the coming
winter. As we go, I grab onto the lip of the top and start to laugh. Rolling
bat-out-of-hell in a golf cart guarantees a trigger of your inner six-year-
old, and I can't help but get a case of the tickle-giggles as we bounce
along. The fact that we are being accompanied by Kanye singing about
the good life is just about perfect.

Butch: (yelling over the righteous bass) You know what's great about
          using this thing at night?!
J.R.:   (yelling back) What?!
Butch: (points to teeth) No bugs!

Deer scamper out of the way at a dead run, their tails flipping up with
white undersides flashing. Like Z, Butch doesn't have the headlights on,
but given how loud Kanye is, I don't think there's any chance of catching one of those lovely animals frozen in our path.

Eventually, Butch slows Edna down right in front of the forest edge.
Kanye quiets and the night's silence rushes forward as if it's a good host
and we've just arrived at its party. Butch grabs the duffel and together we
walk about twenty feet, heading in the direction of the mansion, which
is in the far distance.

Butch puts the duffel on the ground, unzips it, and wades around inside. What comes out is a series of thin metal sections, which he begins
to fit together.

J.R.:   Can I help you? (Even though I don't have any idea what he's
          doing.)
Butch: Two secs.

When he's finished, he's built an odd kind of platform. The base is a foot
off the ground, and it supports a metal rod that's about two feet high.

Butch: (going back to duffel) The critical thing is trajectory. (Returns
          to platform and measures with leveler. Makes adjustment.)
          We'll start small. (Again goes over to duffel and this time
          takes out . . .)
J.R.:   Oh, my God, that is fantastic!
Butch: (beaming) I made it myself. (brings rocket over to me)

The model rocket is about two feet in length from pointed tip to flared
bottom, and it has three sections. White, with a Red Sox logo painted
on the side, its top is fluorescent, no doubt to track its path and increase
the chances of recovering it in the dark.

J.R.:   I didn't know you were into this.
Butch: I used to make models when I was a kid. Airplanes and cars,
          too. The thing is, some people like to read, but I'm slightly
          dyslexic, so that was never relaxing—too much work to get
          the letters to come out right. But models? It's a way to get my

brain to shut off when I'm awake. (Shoots me a sly grin.) Plus I get to do something with my hands, and you know how much I feel that. (Takes rocket over to launching pad and slides it down vertical shaft. Makes more adjustments.) Can you bring me the ignition wires? They're the two bundles tied with twists?

J.R.   (goes to bag) Holy . . . crap. You have, like, three more in here.

Butch: I've been keeping busy. And here, take the flashlight, you'll probably need it. I told V to shut off the motion-sensitive security lights in this section of the acreage.

J.R.:   (catches penlight he throws over and finds wire bundles) You want this box with the switch, too?

Butch: Yes, but leave it there. We're going to want to be a distance away when we fire them off.

J.R.:   (brings over wires and, as he reaches up to take them, I notice his bent pinkie on his right hand) May I ask you something?

Butch: Hell, yeah. That's the point of interviews, ain't it?

J.R.:   Do you miss any part of your old life?

Butch: (hesitates briefly in unrolling the wires) My knee-jerk answer is no. I mean, that's the first thing that comes to mind. (resumes unrolling, then takes rocket off of launcher and attaches wires at bottom) And the core truth is that I'm happier where I am now. But that doesn't mean I don't wish I could do some of the things I used to. Red Sox game on a Saturday afternoon? With the sun on your face and a cold beer against your palm? That was pretty cool.

J.R.:   What about your family?

Butch: (voice gets tight) I don't know. I suppose I miss the next generation . . . like, I wouldn't mind finding out what Joyce's kids look like and where they end up. The others' as well. I wish I could go back to see my mom every once in a while—but I don't want to add to her dementia, and I think my visit didn't help. (slides rocket back onto base) I do go to Janie's grave still.

J.R.:   Really?

Butch: Yup.

J.R.:   (I give him some space to speak. He doesn't.) Were you surprised you ended up here? With the Brothers, I mean.

Butch: Let's get some distance between us and flyboy, shall we? (As we walk back toward the duffel, he strings the wires across the short grass.) Was I surprised? Yes and no. I was surprised at a lot of shit in my life before I ever met the Brothers. The fact that I ended up a vampire? Fighting the undead? In a way, how's that any more shocking than the fact that I managed to live through all the self-destructive crap I did to myself before I met any of them.

J.R.:   I can understand that. (Pauses.) What about—

Butch: By the *oh-god-how-do-I-ask-this-question* in your voice, I'm as-suming you mean the Omega and his little implant surgery?

J.R.:   Well, yes.

Butch: (repositioning *Miami Ink* hat) This is going to come out wrong . . . but in some ways, to me, it's like I have cancer they can't operate on. I can still feel what he put in me. I know ex-actly where it is in my body, and it's wrong, it's bad. (Puts hand on stomach.) I want it out, but I know if it's removed, assum-ing that's even possible, I can't do what I do. So . . . I deal.

J.R.:   Has the aftermath gotten any easier? After you inhale a—

Butch: (shaking head) No.

J.R.:   So . . . aside from that . . . (shifting the subject, because clearly he's uncomfortable) what's been the thing that's surprised you most since coming into their lives?

Butch: (kneeling down next to ignition box) You ask such serious damn questions, woman. (Looks up at me and smiles.) Thought this was going to be more fun.

J.R.:   I'm sorry, I don't mean to make you—

Butch: It's okay. How about we shoot off a rocket or two and then get back to the inquisition stuff. I'll let you push the butttttttttton. . . .

I'm pretty sure at this point he's waggling his eyebrows at me, but I can't see under the brim of the *Miami Ink* hat. I smile anyway because . . . well, some things you çan't help but do.

Butch: Come on, you know you wanna.

J.R.:   (kneeling down) What do I do?

Butch: The way this works is this. . . . (Holds up blue box.) Inside here are four double-A batteries. I turn the ignition key and this light (points to glowing yellow spot) tells us we're ready. We pull out the key (pulls it out), and when you hit this (points to red button), the wires take the charge to the rock-et's igniter, and we're talking a whole lot of zoom-zoom-zoom. Which is why we have over sixteen feet of cord between us and it. You ready? Okay. Let's count this shit down. Three . . .

J.R.: (when he doesn't go further) What? Is there something wrong?

Butch: You're supposed to say two.

J.R.: Oh, sorry! Two.

Butch: No, we have to start over. Three . . .

J.R.: Two . . .

Butch: One . . . Fire in the hole!

I press the buttttttttton, and a moment later there's a spark and a flash and a whizzing fizzle that's like a hundred Alka-Seltzers in a glass. The rocket shoots up to the autumn sky, an arcing trail of light and smoke streaming behind the glowing point at its tip. The angle is perfect, taking it precisely toward the center of the mansion. Its descent is just as smooth, and about three hundred feet from the ground the parachute unfurls. We watch the rocket as it slowly eases down, wagging from side to side like a lazy dog's tail. In the lights from the library I see that it lands in a rose bed.

Butch: (quietly) V.

J.R.: I'm sorry?

Butch: You ask what's surprised me most, and it's him. (Takes another rocket out of the duffel. This one is much larger and has the Lagavulin label repro'd on the side.) Now, this bad boy's got some extra payload in him. He'll go almost twice as high as the first, which is why I brought these. (takes out binocs) My eyesight and night vision are so much better than when I was a human, but I'm nowhere near where the Brothers are, so I need these. I like to watch the parachutes come out.

J.R.: (desperate to ask him to explain about V, but respecting his distance) How long does it take you to build them?

Butch: 'Bout a week. Phury paints the exteriors. (Goes over to launching platform and sets up rocket. When he returns, he nods at the ignition box.) Ladies should do the honors, don't you think?

We count it down, and this time we're coordinated. As we rise to our feet and watch the rocket shoot to the heavens, I can feel that he's about to say something.

Butch: I am in love with Marissa. But without V I'd be dead, and not just because of the whole healing thing.

J.R.: (glancing over) And that's what surprises you most?

Butch: (trains binocs on rocket) Here's the thing, that relationship with V? It doesn't fit into any neat buckets, and it doesn't have to . . . although sometimes I wish it did. I feel like it would be smaller and less important if it was just best friends or brothers or some shit. It's hard enough to be wicked vulnerable to one person, like your wife. But to have this other guy out there in the world, banging and crashing into *lessers* . . . See, I worry about losing them both, and I hate that. V'll go out on his own sometimes and I can't be with him, and I check my phone constantly until he gets home safe. There have been nights when Jane and I have sat side by side on my sofa in the Pit and just stared straight ahead. (Pauses.) It's a pain in the ass, to tell the truth. But I need them both to be happy.

Butch goes back, gets another rocket, and explains to me the ins and outs of its construction. This one is about the same size as the Lag and is painted black with silver bands. We go about shooting it off, and he's funny and charming and irreverent, and you'd be hard-pressed to imagine that just minutes before he'd shared something so deeply personal. I assume the serious conversating is done for the night, yet when we launch number three, he returns to the subject of Vishous—as if the rocket's flaring rise and parachuted fall creates a special zone for talk.

Butch: It's not a creepy incest thing, by the way.

J.R.:   (eyes bulge) Excuse me?

Butch: V and I being tight. I mean, we were tight like that way before the Omega . . . you know, did that shit to me. Sure, Vishous is the Scribe Virgin's son and I'm . . . what I am thanks to Her brother, but there's nothing sleazy about it.

J.R.:   I never thought that.

Butch: Good. And P.S., I like Doc Jane a lot. She's a real ass-kicker, that one. Man . . . (laughs in a bark), she'll hand him his head on a plate if she has to. Damn fun to watch—although he behaves himself most of the time around her, which is disappointing.

J.R.:   And Marissa? How's she dealing with another roommate?

Butch: She and Jane get along like a house afire, and Jane's been a real help. She does the checkups at Safe Place now. It's much better to have a woman physician doing the exams. The nurses Havers sent over were nice enough . . . but it's easier with Jane, and she has more medical training.

J.R.:   Have Marissa and Havers had much contact?

Butch: No reason to. He's just another physician. (looks over at me)

Family is what you make it, not who you were raised with.
(turns back to duffel)

Butch sets up our last rocket, and this is my favorite of all of them. It's
the biggest and has David Ortiz's Sox uniform and the words *Big Papi*
painted on the side. We do our countdown and I press the button . . .
and there's the whiz and fizzle as what Butch built goes barreling up to
the sky. As I watch the glow at the tip rise, I see that this one is going really high. At its apex, it becomes the only star in the cloudy night sky.

Butch: (softly) Pretty, isn't it.
 J.R.: Lovely.
Butch: You know why I build them?
 J.R.: Why?
Butch: I like to watch them fly.

We stand side by side as the parachute comes out and the rocket drifts
back to earth and into the rose garden. As it floats down, swinging gently from side to side, the glow at its tip tells us its location relative to the
house . . . and abruptly I know without asking the reason why he likes to
aim them toward the mansion. With all the security lights, he could easily find them anywhere on the grounds. But Butch likes home . . . and he
wants to send these models he spends hours working on back to where
he loves and needs to be. After having been without a family or a place
in the world for so long, now he has his parachute, his slow, easy ride after a blistering meteoric rise . . . and it's the people in that mansion.

Butch: (grinning at me) Damn, wish we had another, don't you?
 J.R.: (wanting to hug him) Absolutely, Butch. I absolutely do.

Lover Revealed

The People:

Butch O'Neal
Marissa
Vishous
The Scribe Virgin
The Omega
Mr. X
Van Dean

Wrath and Beth
Zsadist
Rehvenge
John Matthew
Blaylock
Qhuinn
Xhex
Lash
Ibex, Lash's father and the *glymera*'s *Leahdyre*
Havers
José de la Cruz
Mother and child
Joyce (O'Neal) and Mike Rafferty
Odell O'Neal

Places of Interest (all in Caldwell, NY, unless otherwise specified):

The Brotherhood mansion, undisclosed location
The Tomb, on the mansion property
Havers's clinic, undisclosed location
Brotherhood training center, on the mansion property
ZeroSum (corner of Trade and Tenth streets)
The Commodore, luxury high rise
Blaylock's bedroom
Ibex/Lash's home
Safe Place, undisclosed location

Summary:

Butch O'Neal finds his true destiny as a vampire and a Brother while falling in love with Marissa, a beautiful aristocrat.

Opening line:	*"What if I told you I had a fantasy?"*
Last line:	*The very staff of life.*
Published:	March 2007
Page length:	455
Word count:	144,321
First draft written:	March 2006–September 2006

Craft comments:

Butch O'Neal had me from the moment I first saw him in *Dark Lover*, when he's investigating Darius's bomb scene. This description of him is from Beth's point of view, and what I liked so much about him was how he tackled his gum:

> "So, Randall, what's doing?" He popped a piece of gum in his mouth, wadding up the foil into a tight little ball. His jaw went to work like he was frustrated, not so much chewing as grinding.
>
> —DARK LOVER, p. 26

Butch's aggression was palpable, and in my opinion that's hot. And my attraction to him only deepened when he arrested Billy Riddle, the young guy who attacked Beth on her way home from work. Here, Billy, who maintained Beth "wanted it," is facedown on the floor in his hospital room, and Butch is reading the kid his Miranda rights while cuffing him:

> "Do you have any idea who my father is?" Billy yelled, as if he'd gotten a second wind. "He's going to have your badge!"
> "If you can't afford [an attorney], one will be provided for you. Do you understand these rights as I've stated them?"
> "Fuck you!"
> Butch palmed the back of the guy's head and pressed that busted nose into the linoleum. "Do you understand these rights as I've stated them?"
> Billy moaned and nodded, leaving a smear of fresh blood on the floor.
> "Good. Now let's get your paperwork done. I'd hate not to follow proper police procedure."
>
> —DARK LOVER, p. 37

Butch O'Neal was absolutely my kind of guy—a hard-ass renegade who, although he didn't always follow the rules, had his own code of honor.

Plus he's a Red Sox fan, too, so there you go.

The heroes in the Brotherhood books are not perfect, not by a long shot: For example, Wrath almost kills Butch in *Dark Lover*, and Rhage had a sex addiction, and Zsadist was a misogynistic sociopath before he met Bella, and Phury's got a drug problem. The thing is, however, they have heroic qualities in addition to these faults, and that's what makes them attractive.

I write alpha males. Always have. The Brothers, though, are ALPHA males, if that makes sense. Maybe part of it is me getting in touch with rule two (*Write Out Loud*) such that everything in the BDB books is pushed as far as it can go, including the heroes and their actions. But most of it is golden rule eight (*Listen to Your Rice Krispies*). The Brothers in my head are just over-the-top, hyperaggressive, and, in my opinion, utterly compelling.

Butch fits right in with the other heroes in the series: He's got a god-awful past that has shaped who he is, as well as a complex interweave of faults and virtues. With respect to his early years, some of the details of it come out in the scene when he finally tells Marissa a little about his background (*LR*, pp. 322–326.) It's been clear all along that he's driven to self-destruction by his sister's abduction and murder and that he's a cop with a razor edge because of what he sees as his culpability in that crime. As he tells Marissa about his drug use and the violence in his life and the fact that he's always felt alienated from everyone around him, it brings into focus how critical the Brothers and their world are to him as a person—the mansion is the only place he's ever felt comfortable in, and he doesn't want to be on the fringes of the Brotherhood's world as an outsider. (When you think of John and Beth, Butch is very similar to them in this regard. All three have always sensed that there is something that separates them from the humans around them, but they are unaware of the why of it all.)

From a character standpoint, I was aware that for Butch the need to belong and be true to an inner self he could only guess at were key aspects of his makeup. And from a story perspective, I knew two things about him: He was going to end up with Marissa and his and V's destinies were inextricably intertwined. In my mind, Marissa was the perfect heroine for him, refined, ladylike, incredibly beautiful—someone he can put on a pedestal and revere and worship. As for him and V . . . well, more on that later.

As I mentioned before, Butch and Marissa's love story was originally going to be a major subplot in *Lover Eternal*, but they demanded so much attention that I cut out their scenes and put them aside. When I got to the end of drafting *Lover Awakened*, my editor and I touched base about what book was next. I wanted to do Butch, but she felt it was better to stick with the Brothers that were vampires, and I agreed—which meant the next in line was Vishous (because at that point Tohr was gone, John Matthew hadn't been through his transition, and Phury couldn't have his book come after Bella had given birth).

Trouble was, when I started to outline V, I realized something that I had known since *Dark Lover*: There was no way you could do Vishous's book before Butch's. V's relationship with the cop, and the emotions he felt for the human, were what opened him up emotionally so that he could fall in love. Additionally, in order for him to be vulnerable to someone else, he needed to come to terms with his feelings for Butch and I couldn't see all that happening in one book for a couple of reasons. First, I try to show as much as I can (as opposed to telling)—so V's book would have been full of scenes between him and Butch, especially in the beginning—which would be dangerous, because that kind of plotting runs the risk of being seriously misbalanced (i.e., a ton of scenes of Butch/V, V/Butch,

Vishous and Butch . . . then suddenly switching to scenes of female/V, Vishous/
female, Vishous and female). Further, with Butch unattached romantically, Vishous wouldn't be able to let him go sufficiently to find love with someone else—to
really get V bonded with his heroine, Butch needed to be happy and committed
with Marissa.

I tried to do V, though. Gave it my best shot.

The outline didn't work.

After a couple of weeks of banging my head, I followed rule eight (*Rice
Krispies*) and called up my editor in classic Houston-we-have-a-problem style.
When I explained to her what the issues were, she understood and agreed. Which
is only one of the billion reasons I worship her: She gets how it is with me and the
Brothers.

So Butch was up next. And, boy, talk about your corkscrews.

When I started to outline him, I had no clue about the Destroyer Prophecy
or the transformative role the cop was going to play in the war with the Lessening
Society. I thought that the thrust of the book was going to be about the ancestor
regression and Butch having the change jump-started on him.

Ah . . . no.

After I took the scenes I had already written concerning him and Marissa
falling in love, and sketched out the other things I saw in my head, it was clear
something was missing. The book just wasn't as big as I sensed it was.

I stewed about it. Worried. Stewed some more . . . and then I got the image
of the Omega cutting off his finger and putting it into Butch's abdomen.

Actually, I got both the image and the sound of the carrot crack when the
Omega did the knife action on himself.

Ew.

Once I tuned in to that, all these scenes came hammering down on my head.
As I followed the story, it was fascinating to see how the original scenes of the
book morphed. For instance, I'd known that Butch was going to get abducted by
the *lessers*, and had seen him and Marissa reuniting in the clinic, but suddenly he
was under quarantine and the consequences were much, much more dire. So
there weren't huge shifts in content, per se, but more in implication and scope
within the world.

The big theme for the book is transformation, and with respect to Butch, I
love the parallel tracks of his story. Both good and evil transform him—first when
the Omega has at him, and then when the change is brought on him and his
vampire nature comes out. It's as if the Lessening Society and the Brotherhood
are both fighting for control of his destiny and his soul, and it's not immediately
clear who wins. For a while after Butch leaves quarantine, neither he nor the
Brothers are sure whether or not he's been turned into a *lesser* or what exactly he's
doing when he inhales a slayer.

The thing I like most about where Butch ends up in terms of the world is that he's a significant player in the war, arguably turning the tables on the Omega because he puts the evil directly at risk. The Brothers have been picking off *lessers* for centuries, but Butch is actually degrading the Omega's finite being each time he takes care of business. I think this is a great ending for the cop. It gives him a place where, although he's not purely of the Brotherhood bloodlines, he's an equal participant in the fight to protect the species.

And Butch isn't the only one who changes. Marissa, too, is transformed from a cloistered female of the *glymera* into someone who has her own life.

I think, of all the females, Marissa's probably the one who resonates with me most personally, because I, too, am from a conservative, establishment background and have had to break a few molds and expectations to be who I really am. Her scene in the beginning of *Lover Revealed* (the one that starts on page seven), with her having a panic attack in the bathroom during that party at her brother's, shows clearly the toll of her having lived her life in the *glymera*. She's sublimated so much of herself and borne burdens for which she didn't volunteer for so long, that she's nearing her breaking point.

I get asked a lot whether there are parts of me in the books and whether I take people I know and put them in. Both are a no. I'm very private, and I strictly separate my personal life from my writing life, and additionally, I would hate to think any of my friends or family would feel used. That being said, there are definitely things that happen in the books that I've had personal experience with. For example, as someone who's had panic attacks, Marissa's interlude in that bathroom really resonated with me. I didn't put the scene in because I was revealing something of myself, but I did empathize with my heroine in the way you would when you talk to someone else who's been through what you have.

For Marissa, the real turning point for her as an individual comes when she burns all of her dresses in the backyard. I thought this was a great way to symbolically mark her break with tradition:

> It took her a good twenty minutes to drag each one of her gowns out into the backyard. And she was careful to include the corsets and the shawls in the pile as well. When she was finished, her clothes were ghostly in the moonlight, muted shadows of a life she would never go back to, a life of privilege . . . restriction . . . and gilded degradations.
>
> She pulled out a sash from the tangle and went back into the garage with the pale pink strip of satin. Picking up the gas can, she grabbed the box of matches and didn't hesitate. She walked out to the priceless swirl of satins and silks, doused them with that clear, sweet accelerant, and positioned herself upwind as she took out a match.
>
> She lit the sash. Then threw it.
>
> The explosion was more than she'd expected, knocking her back, scorching her face, flaring into a great fireball.

> As orange flames and black smoke rose, she screamed at the inferno.
>
> —LOVER REVEALED, p. 266

I had such a clear image of that fire, with her running around those burning dresses, screaming—it was such a temporal representation of the internal shift she was going through, a wiping clean of the past in preparation for her moving forward.

And man, does she get her act together. One of my favorite scenes in the whole series is when Marissa slaps down her brother and the whole Princeps Council during its vote on mandatory *sehclusion* for unmated females of the aristocracy (which starts on p. 419). Rising to her feet, she asserts her status as head of her bloodline, because she is older than Havers, and votes no, putting an end to the discussion and the restriction. It was a total reversal for her from where she was in that bathroom, no longer under the *glymera*'s control, but asserting control *over* them.

I also like where she ended up. She's perfectly suited for running Safe Place and is making a real contribution to the race that way. Plus it's nice that after years of strife, she and Wrath get to work together—because it gives him a chance to prove to her over and over again that he truly does respect her.

On a side note, when it comes to the females in the series, it's significant that at the end of *Lover Revealed*, the *shellans* all come together in Marissa's office, and Beth gives out the little statues of the owls. It shows a side of the *shellans* that I hadn't been able to work into a book yet—namely that they are, like the Brothers, bonded to one another in a special way.

Back to Butch. At the end of the book, when he's being inducted into the Brotherhood, it's clear that he isn't complete, even with the new role he has in the world:

> Wrath cleared his throat, but still, the king's voice was slightly hoarse. "You are the first inductee in seventy-five years. And you . . . you are worthy of the blood you and I share, Butch of mine blooded line."
>
> Butch let his head fall loose on his shoulders and he wept openly . . . though not out of happiness, as they must have assumed.
>
> He wept at the hollowness he felt.
>
> Because however wonderful this all was, it seemed empty to him.
>
> Without his mate to share his life with, he was but a screen for events and circumstance to pass through. He was not even empty, for he was no vessel to hold even the thinnest of air.
>
> He lived, though was not truly alive.
>
> —LOVER REVEALED, p. 446

Without Marissa he is less than zero, and that is true for all the Brothers. Once they bond they are completed, and severing that relationship leads to a breakdown that is irreparable (I'm thinking of Tohr now). Fortunately for Butch, Marissa and he work everything out and are reunited at the end.

Speaking of unions . . . let's talk about sex. Butch made me blush. A lot.

Maybe it was because, of all the Brothers, he tended to talk the most when he was making love. Or maybe it was the way he handled Marissa and her virginity. Or maybe it was just that, quite frankly, I think he's monster hot. Whatever the reason, of all the series so far, I think his book is the hottest of the bunch.

So it makes sense I'd cover the whole sex thing when discussing him.

I get asked in interviews every now and again how I feel about writing "hot" books, and whether I do it to meet the market demands for more and more erotic content. Certainly, over the past five years or so, romance novels have been getting more and more sexual, and the erotic market has grown substantially. Back when I started writing the Brothers, a lot of the now-popular e-pubs were starting to gain momentum, and soon thereafter a number of New York houses developed hotter lines as well. The marketplace was in transition—which was lucky for me.

From the get-go, I knew the Brothers were going to be more sexually explicit than my previous contemporary romances. And I was aware that the series was going to take readers in directions that my other books hadn't (i.e., Rhage's sex addiction, Z's sexual dysfunctions, V's predilections). That being said, I didn't specifically target the erotic market. The Brothers are just very sexual, and the scenes I see of them with their females are hot. In keeping with rule eight (yes, it's the Rice Krispies again), I write what I see in my head. Do I sometimes think, OMG, *I can't believe I just typed that*? Yes! But the thing is, the sex scenes always advance an emotional imperative, and that's why, however graphic they become, I don't feel they are gratuitous.

Take, for example, Rhage being chained down to his bed . . . or when Z services Bella in her needing . . . or Butch and Marissa in the back of the Escalade when she finally feeds from him. All of these scenes are highly erotic, but the dynamic within the relationships changes afterward, either for the worse or the better. I think maybe that's one difference between romance and strict erotica. With romance, sex affects the emotional bonds of the characters and propels those connections forward. With strict erotica, the sexual act or sexual exploration itself is the focus.

Do I think the market will stay as hot as it is? It wouldn't surprise me if it did. Predicting is a dangerous sport, but there seems to be a sustained appetite for books with heat in them. I'm quite certain that subgenres will continue to rise and fall in relative popularity, and that some new ones will come along that we can't begin to guess at. But I think the overall trend of sexuality will probably remain where it is.

And speaking of sexuality . . . now a word on Butch and V.

Where to start.

The first inclination I had that there was going to be a sexual component to their relationship was in *Dark Lover,* when the two of them spent the day together in Darius's guest room. There was something so intimate about the pair of them lying in those beds, drunk, talking. And then they moved into the Pit with each other and became inseparable. To be honest, I was clear from the beginning what V felt toward Butch, and I was also aware that Butch was clueless about it— but I sat on the dynamic, keeping it to myself. I wasn't sure how to handle it. Or how readers would feel about it.

I do that sometimes. I have whole plotlines that happen in the world that I don't put in the books, and I leave them out for a variety of reasons. Most of the time it has to do with story-focus and book-length issues. For instance, the short story in this compendium about Z and Bella and Nalla has been in my mind for about eighteen months now, but there was nowhere I could put it in any of the books.

Sometimes, though, I leave plotlines out because I'm not sure how to deal with them. As I wrote the first three books, there were all these scenes between Butch and V, both on the page and in my head, and they fascinated me. The whole time, I was like . . . *Okay, when's Butch going to tweak to what's doing with his roommate, and what's his reaction going to be to the way V feels about him?*

As I kept banging away at the keyboard, the question in my mind was, *Do I bring the dynamic out on the page? And if so, when?* Eventually I decided to make the leap. The way I saw it, I had already tiptoed into some tricky waters over the course of the first three books, and it went okay—but more important, the story deserved that kind of honesty.

Lover Revealed was the logical choice for it in terms of timing.

When Butch was abducted at the beginning of his book, the single-minded focus with which V approached the rescue is reminiscent of the way Z went after Bella in *Lover Awakened.* The thing was, though, the obsession could have been explained by him and the cop being best friends. I knew I had to make it clear that things were beyond friends on V's side, and the scene where he comes to see Butch to heal him in quarantine, and catches Butch and Marissa together, was when I exposed the feelings to the reader in V's POV:

> Butch shifted and rolled Marissa over, making a move to mount her. As he did, the hospital johnny broke open, the ties ripping free and revealing his strong back and powerful lower body. The tattoo at the base of his spine flexed as he pushed his hips through her skirts, trying to find home. And as he worked what was no doubt a rock-hard erection against her, her long, elegant hands snaked around and bit into his bare ass. As she scored him with her nails, Butch's head lifted, no doubt to let out a moan.

> Jesus, V could just hear the sound. . . . Yeah . . . he could hear it. And from out of nowhere an odd yearning feeling flickered through him. *Shit*. What exactly in this scenario did he want?
>
> —LOVER REVEALED, p. 103

It was pretty clear what (or who) he wanted by the description—and it wasn't Marissa. I have to admit I was a little trepidatious. I'd previously hinted at V's "unconventional interests," but I had always led with the BDSM stuff, not the fact that he'd also been with males. And here he was, a primary hero in the series . . . who's attracted to another primary hero.

Butch is not bisexual. He's never been into men. He is, if I were pushed to define him, a V-sexual, as it were. There's something about his relationship with Vishous that crosses the line on both sides, and to the cop's credit, he doesn't bolt or get freaked out. He's with Marissa, and he's committed to her, and the V thing hasn't made anyone uncomfortable because boundaries are respected.

I have to say, I think the scene of Butch's induction into the Brotherhood, when V bites him, is off-the-chain erotic:

> Without thinking, Butch tilted his chin up, aware that he was offering himself, aware that he . . . oh, fuck. He stopped his thoughts, completely weirded out by the vibe that had sprung up from God only knew where.
>
> In slow motion Vishous's dark head dropped down, and there was a silken brush as his goatee moved against Butch's throat. With delicious precision, V's fangs pressed against the vein that ran up from Butch's heart, then slowly, inexorably, punched through skin. Their chests merged.
>
> Butch closed his eyes and absorbed the feel of it all, the warmth of their bodies so close, the way V's hair felt soft on his jaw, the slide of a powerful male arm as it slipped around his waist. On their own accord, Butch's hands left the pegs and came to rest on V's hips, squeezing that hard flesh, bringing them together from head to foot. A tremor went through one of them. Or maybe . . . shit, it was like they both shuddered.
>
> And then it was done. Over with. Never to happen again.
>
> —LOVER REVEALED, p. 443

As I've said, I wasn't sure how readers were going to take the whole V/Butch thing, and after the book came out I was surprised. Overwhelmingly, folks wanted more of the two of them! The fact that the readership was so incredibly supportive is a testament to their open-mindedness and I'm very grateful for it. I'm also thankful for trailblazers such as Suzanne Brockmann, who, with her Jules Cassidy character, paved the way so that males like Blay can get their happily-ever-afters, too, and Brothers like V are accepted for just who they are.

And now a couple of random thoughts about *Lover Revealed* . . .

Butch didn't just make me blush; I had my first case of writer's block with him.

It wasn't because he was getting naked all the time, though.

With each succeeding title the books were getting longer, and I was becoming concerned. If the trend kept going? I'd be turning in tomes. The issue appeared to be that the world had started developing its own plot—something that was particularly true with Butch's story—so the events weren't just about the heroes and heroines anymore.

For me as the author, the fact that I have the freedom to explore the ins and outs of the Omega and the Scribe Virgin and the war with the Lessening Society is part of what I like about the series. Bigger, however, is not necessarily better. During the revision process, my editor and I always check the pacing just to make sure there's no fat on the page. It's rewarding when we don't find any—but also daunting when you see those little numbers in the upper corners getting higher and higher.

Anyway, when I started drafting *Lover Revealed*, I decided I was going to be "smart," given the complexity of all the plotting. I decided that I was going to consolidate a bunch of the up-front scenes to save page space.

Right.

Sure, this made sense practically, but the Brothers didn't like it at all. As I tried to retrofit the beginning scenes, cramming them in together, the voices in my head dried up. It was the eeriest thing. Everything went dead quiet, and I confronted what I've always feared the most: Because I have no clue where my ideas come from or how I do what I do or why certain things happen in the world, I'm always afraid the Brothers will pack up their leathers and their daggers and leave me with nothing.

Four days. The dead zone lasted for four days. And because I can be dense, it wasn't immediately clear to me what the problem was. Finally, after I was going half-psychotic from the silence, it dawned on me . . . *Huh, you don't suppose I'm trying to jockey these scenes around too much just to save on page count?*

As soon as I stopped worrying about length, everything flowed again and the Brothers came back. Takeaway? Good old rule number eight trumps just about every other concern I might have. Every story demands different things, whether it's pacing or description or dialogue . . . or page count. The best thing you can do is remain true to what you see. I'm not saying you should be inflexible during revisions. Not at all. But be brutally honest in that first draft—then you can worry about editing things out later.

On another subject . . . a lot of people ask me what the deal with Butch's father is. Specifically, they want to know if he'll play a role later in the series. The answer is, I don't know. I can see a pathway where there could be some very interesting family ties, but it's a wait and see situation. I am quite sure of one thing, though: Butch's father had to be a half-breed. The male had to either have gone through the transition, but been able to endure sunlight as Beth can, or the change didn't hit him and he functioned in the world as an aggressive human.

The other question that I often get about Butch's background has to do with the rest of his family and whether he ever reunites with them. That answer I do know, and it's no. He's said his good-bye to his mother, and his brothers and sisters have been shutting him out for years. The one person from his old life he does miss is José de la Cruz—although something tells me the two of them aren't done yet.

Finally, of all the books, male readers tend to like Butch's best, and that doesn't really surprise me. It's got a lot of good fight scenes, and the world building is more extensive than in some of the other stories, where the romance might take up more space. And some of the guys have commented that they love the idea that there is a great force inside of them, one that rocks the world and puts them in a position of power, and with the Omega's tinkering, Butch certainly has that.

Plus, they think Marissa is hot.

So that's my take on Butch. Now . . . for V.

sigh

Vishous, Son of the Bloodletter

"Vishous, could you stop grinning like that?
You're beginning to freak me out."

—LOVER UNBOUND, p. 443

Age:	304
Joined Brotherhood:	1739
Height:	6'6"
Weight:	260 lbs.
Hair color:	Black
Eye color:	White with navy blue rims
Identifying physical marks:	Scar of the Brotherhood on left pec; tattoo on right temple; tattoos on groin area and thighs; JANE carved across shoulders in Old English. Partially castrated. Wears black glove on right hand always. Goateed.
Note:	Is born son of the Scribe Virgin and carries her glow in his right hand—which is a powerful energy force capable of vast destruction. Sees visions of the future. Possesses healing capabilities.
Weapon of choice:	His right hand.
Description:	*After having talked with V at the party, [Bella] liked him tremendously. He had the kind of smarts that usually sucked the social skills right out of a vampire, but with that warrior, you had the whole package. He was sexy, all-knowing, powerful,*

the kind of male that made you think of having babies just to keep his DNA in the gene pool.

She wondered why he wore that black leather glove. And what the tattoos on the side of his face were about. Maybe she'd ask him about those, if it seemed okay.

—LOVER ETERNAL, p. 375–376

Mated to: Dr. Jane Whitcomb

Personal Qs (answered by V):

Last movie
watched: *Flicka* with Dakota Fanning
Last book read: *The Secret of the Old Clock* by Carolyn Keene
Favorite
TV show: *The Golden Girls*
Last TV show
watched: *The Young and the Restless*
Last game
played: "This little piggy goes to market . . ."
Greatest fear: Being by myself in the dark
Greatest love: Knitting
Favorite quote: "The plane! The plane!"
Boxers or briefs: Panties
Watch: Ladies' Seiko
Car: Don't have a car—I ride a Vespa
What time is it
while you're
filling this out?   1:16 a.m.
Where are you?   In the bath
What are you
wearing?   Suds that smell like coconut and vanilla
What's in your
closet?   Floral prints, no stripes (because I'm a bit "hippy"), pumps in size 16, and a dresser full of Spanx
What was the
last thing you
ate?   An entire bag of Lindt dark chocolate truffles. I think I'm about to go into my needing soon. I always get cravings right before it hits.

Describe your last dream?	I was in a field of wildflowers, running about—nay, frolicking—with a unicorn who had a pink mane and tail. I had gossamer wings and a wand, and everywhere I went I left clouds of fairy dust.
Coke or Pepsi?	Orangeade
Audrey Hepburn or Marilyn Monroe?	Audrey, because I want to BE her
Kirk or Picard?	Riker. Goatees are SO attractive
Football or baseball?	I'm not really interested in sports. All I can think about is how much laundry will need to be done at the end—all those yucky grass stains and ground-in dirt. I mean, honestly.
Sexiest part of a female?	Her underwear drawer
What do you like most about Jane?	The way she polishes my nails
Best friend (excluding *shellan*):	Rhage. Definitely Rhage. He is the strongest, smartest vampire I've ever met. I worship him. In fact, I'm starting a religion based on him, because everyone needs to know how perfect he is.
Last time you cried:	Yesterday. That meanie Butch took my knitting needles and hid them. I curled up into a little ball on my bed and wept for HOURS.
Last time you laughed:	Yesterday, when—

*At this point, the answer is scribbled out and below is written:

Actually, it was ten minutes ago, when I beat the ever-living shit out of Rhage for macking my interview, thank you very much. What a freak. Here's my real answers—oh, and BTW, Dakota Fanning isn't in *Flicka*—and I know it because I looked the DVD up NOT because I saw the damn movie.

Last movie watched:	*Stripes* (great flick, Rhage is a fidiot, but he knows his films)
Last book read:	Richard Scarry's *Lowly Worm Storybook* to Nalla
Favorite TV show:	*CSI* (LV, of course) or *House* if you're talking, like, fiction shit. Otherwise, *SportsCenter*.
Last TV show watched:	Some fakakta episode of *Columbo* with Butch (actually it was good, just don't tell him that)
Last game played:	Pin the tail on the ass—guess who was the donkey?
Greatest fear:	Don't have one anymore. Lived through the worst thing that could happen to me, and now I don't need to worry about it.
Greatest love:	Duh
Favorite quote:	"Rhage is a fucktwit."
Boxers or briefs:	Commando
Watch:	Nike Sport in black
Car:	Escalade, black, I share with the cop
What time is it while you're filling this out?	9:42 a.m.
Where are you?	The Pit in front of my Four Toys.
What are you wearing?	Leather mask, ball gag, restraining harness, latex uni, hand-cuffs, and some metal clips, the strategic placement of which I'll detail only if you ask nicely. Kidding. Black muscle shirt and nylon sweats.
What's in your closet?	Leathers, shirts, shitkickers, and weapons.
What was the last thing you ate?	I bit Rhage's head off just now. Does that count?
Describe your last dream?	It was about Rehvenge. So it's none of your biz, true?
Coke or Pepsi?	Coke.
Audrey Hepburn or Marilyn Monroe?	Neither.
Kirk or Picard?	Both.

Football or baseball?	Baseball.
Sexiest part of a female?	I'll tell you what the sexiest part of Jane is: her grip.
What do you like most about Jane?	Her mind.
First words she spoke to you were:	"Are you going to kill me?"
Your response was:	"No."
Last gift given to her:	Was nothing special.
Most romantic thing you've ever done for her:	I don't do romance. It's schmaltzy.
Most romantic thing she's ever done for you:	I don't know. Like, I said, I'm not into romance. Shit . . . well, I guess it's what she did with that thing I made her, even though it was nothing special. It's just a necklace made of these gold links . . . see, she likes my name for some reason. The way it's spelled. So I took the characters from the Old Language and turned them into links for a necklace down in my forge. I wanted the chain to be delicate enough so she wouldn't feel like she had a noose around her throat, but still readable. . . . man, it took for-fucking-ever to get the weight right and the design correct. I ended up having to spell out my name twice, and there still wasn't enough length on the thing. So I added her name in the Old Language in the middle—so she's surrounded by me. Anyway. She never takes it off. Whatever.
Anything you'd change about her?	Yes, but it's private.
Best friend (excluding *shellan*):	Butch, then that asshole Rhage. Plus I get along okay with Wrath when we don't want to kill each other.

Last time you cried:	Yeah right I'm answering that.
Last time you laughed:	I dunno, cracking Rhage was kind of fun—put a smile on my piehole just fine, true?

My Interview with Vishous:

Out on the compound's lawn, Butch and I pack up the duffel and take Edna back to the mansion, where we spend about fifteen minutes weeding through the rose garden picking up the rockets. After we find all four and detach their parachutes, we go into the library and Butch gives me a hug. He smells good.

Butch: Himself is waiting for you in the basement.

J.R.: I'm not looking forward to this.

Butch: (smiles a little) Neither is he. But look at it this way, it could be worse. You could have to write another book on him.

J.R.: (laughs) Roger that.

I head off, crossing the foyer and going into the dining room, which has been cleaned up. On the other side of the flap door into the kitchen, Fritz, butler extraordinaire, is polishing silver with two other *doggen*. I chat with them and end up trying to fend off offers of food and drink. I fail. As I go down into the basement, I have a mug of coffee and a homemade raisin scone wrapped in a damask napkin. The scone is delicious and the coffee is just the way I like it: superhot with a little sugar.

At the bottom of the basement stairs I look left and right. The cellar is huge, with great stretches of open space broken up by storage rooms and HVAC piping. I have no idea where V could be, and I listen, hoping for direction. At first all I hear is the sound of the ancient coal furnace that is up ahead, but then I catch a beat.

It's not rap. It's a rhythmic, metal-on-metal clanging.

I follow the sound all the way down to the far end of the basement. It takes me a good five minutes of walking to get to where V is, and along the way I finish the scone and the coffee. As I go, I try to think what the hell I'm going to ask him. He and I don't really mix all that well, so I figure this is going to be short and not-so-sweet.

As I come around the last corner I stop. V is seated on a stout wooden stool wearing heavy leather chaps and a muscle shirt. In front of him is an anvil on which is a deep red dagger blade that he's holding with a pair of calipers. He has a blunt hammer with a special grip in his glowing hand and is pounding the tip of the weapon. Between his lips is a hand-rolled, and my nose registers the woody smell of Turkish tobacco, the sharp acid of hot metal and dark spices.

Vishous: (without looking up) Welcome to my workshop.
    J.R.: So this is where you make the daggers. . . .

The ovenlike room is about twenty by twenty and has whitewashed concrete walls like the rest of the basement. Black candles are lit all around, and next to the anvil is an ancient brass pot full of sparkling sand. Behind V is a sturdy oak table on which are a variety of daggers in various stages of creation, some just the blades, others with handles.

V turns and thrusts the still-red metal slice into the sand, and I'm struck by how strong he is. His shoulders are roped with muscle, and so are his forearms.

As he waits, he releases a stream of smoke from his lips and taps the hand-rolled on the edge of a black ashtray.

I am uneasy around him. I always have been. It makes me sad.

    V: (without looking at me) So you survived the rocket-man routine with the cop, huh.
    J.R.: Yes.

I stare at him as he takes the blade from the sand and wipes it with a thick cloth. The metal stretch is irregular in shape and consistency, clearly in the process of being birthed. He examines it, tilting it around, and as he frowns the tattoos on his temple move closer to his eye. Putting the hammer down, he brings his glowing hand back to the blade and clasps it. Light flares, pulling sharp shadows out of the softer candlelight, and a hissing sound sizzles into the air.

When he removes his hand the blade is brilliant orange, and he lays it down on the anvil. Picking up the hammer, he strikes the hot metal over and over again, the clanging sound ringing in my ears.

    J.R.: (as he pauses to look at the blade) Who are you making that for?
    V: Tohr. I want to have his daggers ready.
    J.R.: He's going to fight again?
    V: Yup. Doesn't know it yet, but he is.
    J.R.: You must be glad he's back.
    V: Yup.

Vishous hits the nascent blade with his glowing hand again and then repeats the banging. After a while he thrusts the metal slice back into the sand and finishes his cigarette.

While he stabs out the hand-rolled, I feel as though I'm intruding and also not getting the job I came to do done. As the silence continues, I think of all the questions I could ask him, like . . . how does he feel about Jane being a ghost? Is he worried that he can't have children? How are things with his mother? What's it like for him to be committed to one person in particular? Does he miss his BDSM lifestyle? Or is he still practicing it with Jane? And what about Butch? Has their relationship changed?

Only thing is, I know that the answers would not be forthcoming, and the silences that follow each inquiry would be deeper and deeper.

I watch him work the blade, alternating the heat and the pounding, until he's evidently satisfied and puts the dagger on the oak table. I wonder for a moment if now isn't when the interview will really start . . . except he just stands up and goes to some smaller lengths of metal rodding that are in the corner. He's going to start another blade, I realize.

J.R.:   Guess I better go.
V: Yup.
J.R.:   (blinking quickly) Take care of yourself.
V: Yup. You too.

I leave his workshop to the sound of the hiss as his hand comes into contact with metal. I go more slowly than I came, maybe because I'm hoping he'll have a change of heart and come after me and at least . . . well, what would he do? Nothing really. A union between the two of us is my aspiration, not his inclination.

As I meander along, the empty mug and wrinkled napkin in my hand, I find myself truly and honestly depressed. Relationships require effort, sure. But you need to have one in the first place in order to work on them. V and I have never clicked, and I'm beginning to realize we never will. And it's not that I don't like him. Far from it.

To me, V is like diamond. You can be impressed and captivated by him and want to stare at him for hours, but he will never reach out and welcome you. As with him, a diamond exists not to be shiny and sparkly or because of who bought it to put on someone's hand—those functions are simply by-products of the results of the incredible pressure inflicted upon its molecules. All that brilliance comes from its—and his—hardness.

And both will also be around long after all of us are gone.

Lover Unbound

The People:

Vishous
Dr. Jane Whitcomb
Phury
John Matthew
Wrath and Beth
Butch and Marissa
Zsadist and Bella
Cormia
The Directrix
Amalya (who becomes the new Directrix of the Chosen)
Layla
Qhuinn
Blaylock
Rehvenge
Xhex
Dr. Manny Manello
The Scribe Virgin
Payne
The Bloodletter
Grodht, solider in the war camp

Places of Interest (all in Caldwell, NY, unless otherwise specified):

St. Francis Hospital
Brotherhood mansion, undisclosed location
The Tomb,
ZeroSum (corner of Trade and Tenth streets)
Jane's condo
The Commodore
The Other Side (the Chosen's Sanctuary)

Summary:

Vishous, son of the Scribe Virgin, falls in love with Dr. Jane Whitcomb, the human surgeon who saves his life after he is shot by a *lesser*.

Opening line: "*I am so not feeling all this cowhide.*"
Last line: *Without another word he dematerialized back to the life he'd been*

given, the life he was leading . . . the life he now, and for the first
time, was grateful he'd been born into.

Published: September 2007
Page length: 502
Word count: 159,404
First draft written: July 2006–April 2007

Craft comments:

God, where to start.

Vishous was, hands down, the single worst writing experience of my life. Getting his story on paper was a miserable exercise in torture and was the first and thus far only time I have ever thought to myself, *I don't want to go to work.*

The *whys* are complicated, and I'll share three of them.

First of all, each of the Brothers is a separate entity in my head, and they've all had their own way of expressing themselves and their story: Wrath is very dictatorial, very blunt, and I have to race to keep up with him. Rhage is always a cutup—even when the serious parts come rolling through, there's a goofy sidebar going on. Zsadist is reserved and suspicious and chilly, but we've always gotten along. Butch is a total party—with a lot of sex talk thrown in.

V? Vishous is and has always been—and excuse me for being blunt—a prick. A self-contained, defensive prick who doesn't like me.

Putting his story on the page was a nightmare. Every single word was a struggle, particularly when it came to his first draft—most of the time I felt as if I were having to pry the sentences from bedrock using a kiddie hammer and a salad fork.

See, for me, drafting is really a two-part enterprise. The pictures that I have in my head guide the story, but I also need to hear and smell and sense what's going on while I'm doing the writing. What this usually means is that I step into the shitkickers of the Brothers or the stillies of their *shellans* and go through the scenes as if I were living the events through whoever's POV I'm in. To do this, I play the scenes backward and forward, like you would a DVD, and just record, record, record on the page until I feel as though I've captured as much as I can.

Vishous gave me next to nothing to work with, because I couldn't get behind his eyes at all. The scenes that were in POVs other than his were fine, but his? Nothing doing. I could watch, but only from afar—and as a lot of the book is from his perspective, I felt like banging my head against the keyboard.

Look . . . yes, this is fiction. Yes, it's all in my mind. Except, believe it or not, if I can't get into a POV deeply, I feel like I'm making stuff up—and that isn't a happy place. Honestly, I'm not that bright—I'm not going to get it right if I just guess. I have to be inside a person to do things right, and having the V-door slammed in my face was the root of most of my misery.

Things did break eventually, though. More on that in a little bit.

The second reason *Lover Unbound* was a hard book to write was that there was content in it that made me nervous, because I wasn't sure whether the market would bear it. Two things in particular worried me: Bisexuality and BDSM (bondage, dominance, sadomasochism) are topics that not everyone is comfortable with even in terms of subplots, much less when they involve the hero of a book. But that wasn't the full extent of it. In addition, V had been partially castrated and had forcibly taken a male after he'd won his first fight in the war camp.

The thing was, V's complex sexual nature colored a lot of his life—including his relationships with Butch and Jane. In order to show him properly, I felt like I had to present all sides of him. ·

In the first draft of *Lover Unbound*, I played things so conservatively that the book was flat. I went very light on the bondage scene with him and Jane right before he lets her go, and I didn't put anything about him and Butch in at all.

In the process, I totally violated my own rule number two (*Write Out Loud*). And, big surprise, the result was something that was about as appealing as a dead sunfish on a summer dock—nothing moved and it stank. I stewed and hemmed and hawed for a week or so, just tinkering with scenes involving John Matthew and Phury. In my heart I knew I had to jump off the cliff and stretch some boundaries, but I was exhausted and uninspired from the effort of trying unsuccessfully to drag V's POV out of him.

Talking to my editor was what got me off my ass and back in the game. She and I discussed the things that were weighing on me, and she was like, "Go for it—just get it all in there and let's see how it plays out on the page."

She was, as usual, right. In fact, the message she gave me that day was the message she's always given me since way back in the *Dark Lover* era: "Push it all the way, go as far as you can, and we can evaluate later."

When I went back into the manuscript, I was one hundred percent committed to balls-to-the-walling it—and was surprised that there were really only three scenes that I markedly changed. Two were with Butch and V, with the newer content beginning on pages 209 and 369 respectively, and then I added the scene with V in the war camp that starts on page 287.

The rest of the alterations or additions were relatively minor, but changed the tone of the Butch/V interactions entirely—proving that a little goes a long way. Take, for example, the opening pages of chapter thirteen (p. 135). Butch and V are in bed together, and V is healing Butch after the cop did his business with a *lesser*. If you read through the second, third, fourth, and fifth paragraphs of my first draft, you'll note that V is admitting to himself he needs soothing in the form of another warm body next to his. It's not Butch's body specifically, however, and there is no mention of anything sexual. It's purely a comfort thing:

. . . With the visit from his mother and the shooting, he craved the closeness of another, needed to feel arms that returned his embrace. He had to have the beat of a heart against his own.

He spent so much time keeping his hand away from others, keeping himself apart from others. To let down his guard with the one person he truly trusted made his eyes sting.

—LOVER UNBOUND, p. 135

What I added in the second draft were these two paragraphs:

As Butch stretched out on Vishous's bed, V was ashamed to admit it, but he'd spent a lot of days wondering what this would be like. Feel like. Smell like. Now that it was reality, he was glad he had to concentrate on healing Butch. Otherwise he had a feeling it would be too intense and he'd have to pull away. [p. 135]

Butch shifted, his legs brushing against V's through the blankets. With a stab of guilt, V recalled the times he'd imagined himself with Butch, imagined the two of them lying as they were now, imagined them . . . well, healing wasn't the half of it. [p. 136]

Much more honest about what was really going on. Much better. Could have gone even farther, but it was enough—so much so that it required me to add the few sentences that followed, to clarify for the reader that Jane was the object of V's desire now.

That's the thing with writing. Books to me are like ships on oceanic courses. Small, incremental changes can have huge effects in their ultimate trajectory and destination. And the only way to get it right is to constantly reread and double-check and make sure that what's on the page takes the reader where they have to go. Once I made those changes (there were a number of other places where I did a little tinkering—including, for example, the dagger scene in the beginning of the book where Butch lifts V's chin up with the weapon Vishous just made for him), the writing in V's POV got much easier.

Bottom line? I look at the whole mess as yet another example of rule number eight at work: Once I was more true to what was in my head, the writing block was lifted.

As for the scene from the war camp where V loses his virginity by taking another male? Man, I just wasn't sure how people would view him after that one. The thing was, he wasn't given a choice, and it was the standard of the camp: In hand-to-hand combat practice, losers were sexually dominated by winners. The key, I decided, was to show as much context as possible—and to depict V's internal commitment after it was over that he would never do it again.

After my editor read the new material, I was relieved when she said that it worked for her, but I remained concerned what the overall reader reaction was going to be. For me as an author, reader response is something that weighs on me, but in a curious way. It's in my mind because unless people buy the books I write, I'm out of a job. But the thing is, I can't write to please readers, because I truly don't have much control over my stories. The best I can do, as I've said, is always be mindful and respectful and thoughtful with the challenging content. I suppose I kind of live by the motto, *It's not what you do, but how you do it.*

Funny, though. Little did I know that the negative reaction about V's book would concern something else entirely.

Which brings us to Jane.

The third reason the book was so agonizing to write was because I got Jane wrong on the first pass. I'll admit, I was so concerned with V that although I had plenty of scenes with Jane in the initial draft, the dynamic between the two of them was relatively lifeless. The problem was, I interpreted Jane as a cold scientist. What happened, then, was that there were two chilly, reserved people interacting, and that is about as much fun to write/read about as an ingredient list on a soup can.

My editor figured it out, though. Jane was a healer, not a white lab coat. She was a warm, caring, compassionate woman who was more than just a repository for medical knowledge and know-how. On the second trip through the park with the manuscript, I tapped into Jane's core, and the relationship between her and V started to sing, reflecting more what was in my head.

On a side note, one of the first scenes that I saw for V and Jane hit me way back when I was writing *Lover Awakened* in 2005. I was running at the time, and this vision of V standing in front of a stove, stirring hot chocolate, suddenly came to me. I watched as he poured what was in the pan into a mug and handed it to a woman who knew he was going to leave her. Then I saw her standing at the window of her kitchen, looking out at V, who was outside in the shadows cast by a street lamp.

That, of course, became the good-bye that starts on page 322 of their book.

When the scenes from the Brothers come to me, they do not arrive in chronological order. For instance, visuals of Tohr and where he ultimately ends up hit me before Wellsie even died on the page. So, in the case of the hot-chocolate exchange for *Lover Unbound,* I was stuck wondering how in the hell Jane and V were going to end up together. The thing was, I knew she was a human, and I wanted for them what the others had, namely a good seven or eight centuries of mating. But with Jane not being a vampire, I had no clue how that was going to happen—plus I knew she got shot, because I'd seen V's visions and knew what they meant, even if he didn't. . . .

When I outlined *Lover Unbound,* I just kept wondering how the two of them were going to have an HEA, and I was really worried. What if there wasn't one at all? But then I got to the end . . . and saw Jane standing in V's doorway as a ghost.

I was actually relieved and thrilled. I was like, *Oh, this is great! They get the long time frame!*

Unfortunately, some readers didn't see it that way, and part of that I blame on myself.

Usually when I get to the end of a book, I feel that although I wish I could refine the line-by-line writing even more (I'm never satisfied), I'm confident that the scenes themselves and the way the plotlines flow is rock-solid. I'm also fairly certain that I've given sufficient context and grounding for the reader so that they can see where things started, what happened, and how everything ended up.

For me, I was so relieved about Jane and V's future (with her life-span issue being resolved), that I took for granted readers would feel the same way. My mistake was that I underestimated the challenge to romantic convention with her being a ghost, and I was unaware that it would be a problem to the extent it was for some. I've been over and over the disconnect in my mind (the one between the market and my internal radar screen) and have decided that part of it is my background in reading horror and fantasy—because the resolution worked within the world and provided the hero and heroine with a solution, I just assumed it was okay.

Except here's the thing: Even if I had realized it was going to be a problem for certain folks, I wouldn't have changed the ending, because anything else would have been a copout and a lie. I don't write to the market and never have—the stories in my head are in charge, and even I don't get to see what I want to happen in the world occur. That being said, if I were writing the book again, I'd put in another ten pages or so at the end with V and Jane interacting to show the happiness they both felt—so readers were superclear that in the couple's minds things ended up just fine.

The way I view it? This series has pushed a lot of boundaries, pushed them hard, but I've always been careful about the *hows* and the *whys*. I truly try to be respectful of the genre that gave me my start and has long been my book of choice—and romance is and will continue to be the basis of each of the Brotherhood books.

On that note . . . V and Jane as a couple. Man, they were hot. I didn't blush as much at the computer as I did with Butch, although whether that was because the cop brought me to a new level or I just expected that kind of stuff from V, I'm not sure.

The scene where V's in his bed and Jane is giving him a sponge bath was really erotic, and I saw everything about it so clearly. Especially this part where she's, ah, attending to a certain place:

. . . but then he moaned low in his throat and his head kicked back, his blue-black hair feathering over the black pillow. As his hips flexed upward, his stomach muscles tightened in a sequential rush, the tattoos at his groin stretching and returning to position.

"Faster, Jane. You're going to do it faster for me now."

—LOVER UNBOUND, p. 178

For V, before Jane came along, sex and emotions were not linked at all. In fact, except for Butch, and to some extent the Brotherhood, emotions were just not a part of his life, and that makes sense. Growing up in the war camp left him with an attachment disorder that persisted into adulthood and colored his relationships. The question is, then, what made Jane—and for that matter Butch—different?

I think Jane and Butch are a lot alike—for one thing, they've both got the smart-ass thing down. Take for instance this little volley between V and Jane, which is one of my favorite exchanges in all the books:

"Don't want you near that hand of mine. Even if it's gloved."

"Why is—"

"I'm not talking about it. So don't even ask."

Okaaaay. "It nearly killed one of my nurses, you know."

"I'm not surprised." He glared at the glove. "I'd cut it off if I had the chance."

"I wouldn't advise that."

"Of course you wouldn't. You don't know what it's like to live with this nightmare on the end of your arm—"

"No, I meant I'd have someone else do the cutting if I were you. You're more likely to get the job done that way."

There was a beat of silence; then the patient barked out a laugh. "Smart-ass."

—LOVER UNBOUND, pp. 171–172

I also think V's into Jane because she's no weak and floundering woman. The scene of her abduction from the hospital shows that, especially here when Rhage has her over his shoulder, and Phury is trying to calm her using his mind control tricks:

"You gotta knock her cold, my brother," Rhage said, then grunted.

"I don't want to hurt her, and V said she had to come with us."

"This was not supposed to be a kidnap operation."

"Too fucking late. Now knock her out, would ya?" Rhage grunted again and switched his grip, his hand leaving her mouth to catch one of her flailing arms.

Her voice came through loud and clear. "So help me, God, I'm going to—"

Phury took her chin in his hand and forced her head up. "Relax," he said softly. "Just ease up."

He locked his stare on hers and began to will her into calmness . . . will her into calmness . . . will her into—

"Fuck you!" she spat. "I'm not letting you kill my patient!"

—LOVER UNBOUND, p. 103

At that moment, Jane reminds of me of Butch back in *Dark Lover,* after he brings Beth to Darius's mansion and faces off at the Brothers. Even outnumbered, he's still a fighter. And so is Jane.

I also believe that both Jane and Butch are driven to do good in the world. Between her being a surgeon and Butch being a cop, the two of them are cut in the hero mold—so V has a lot of respect for them.

Finally I suspect, as appears to be true for all the Brothers, there is a pheromone thing happening. The Brothers, and indeed all the males I've seen thus far, seem to bond instantaneously and irrevocably when they get into the vicinity of their mate. So I can only assume there's some kind of instinctual component at work.

But back to V and Jane. From my perspective, one of the strongest emotional exchanges in the book comes when V allows Jane to Dom him at his penthouse, right before he lets her go. For him to put himself at the mercy of someone sexually, considering what had been done to him the night of his transition when he was held down and partially castrated, is the biggest commitment he can make to another person. The scene, which starts on page 315, really shows him for the first time in his life choosing to be defenseless. Back in the war camp, as a pre-trans, he was vulnerable by circumstance and physical design, and he's spent the rest of his life making sure he's never at the mercy of anyone. With Jane, however, he is willingly giving himself over to someone else. It's a declaration of love that goes farther than words.

And again, that's my point about sex scenes. Yes, that stuff between them was hot, but it's manifestly significant to their character development.

Now for a word about the Scribe Virgin and V.

Talk about mother issues, huh? When V first sauntered onstage in *Dark Lover,* I knew that hand of his was significant, but I had no idea just how important it was or what its larger implications were. In fact, during the writing of the first two books, even I didn't have a clue that Vishous was the son of the Scribe Virgin. It's kind of like Boo or the coffins: When I see something really vividly, I put it in, in spite of the fact that I might not know what it has to do with anything.

It wasn't until *Lover Awakened*–ish that it clicked: white light equals Scribe

Virgin. V has white light. Therefore V equals Scribe Virgin. I thought it was a great twist, and I was so good about not blabbing about it on the message boards or at signings when my leaf (the one that keeps secrets inside) dropped. Frankly, once I tweaked to V's lineage, I was surprised that no one else really caught the connection. (I think there might have been one or two speculations on the boards that got close, but I deflected them with lawyerly nonanswers.)

In *Lover Unbound*, V and his mom had a hard time relating, which, given what she'd kept from him and what she'd been complicit in subjecting him to, is understandable. But things worked out, and for a lot of people, their favorite scene in the book is the one at the end, where Vishous goes to see his mother:

> "What have you brought?" [the Directrix] whispered.
>
> "Little present. Nothing much." He walked over to the white tree with the white blossoms and opened his hands. The parakeet leaped free and took to a branch as if it knew that was its home now.
>
> The brilliant yellow bird shuffled up and down the pale arm of the tree, its little feet gripping and releasing, gripping and releasing. It pecked at a blossom, let out a trill . . . brought a foot up and pedaled its neck.
>
> V put his hands on his hips and measured how much space there was between all the blossoms on all the branches. He was going to have to bring over a shitload of birds.
>
> The Chosen's voice was rife with emotion. "She gave them up for you."
>
> "Yeah. And I'm bringing her new ones."
>
> "But the sacrifice—"
>
> "Has been made. What's going on this tree is a gift." He looked over his shoulder. "I'm going to fill it up whether she likes it or not. It's her choice what she does with them."
>
> The Chosen's eyes gleamed with gratitude. "She will keep them. And they will keep her from her solitude."
>
> V took a deep breath. "Yeah. Good. Because . . ."
>
> He let the word drift, and the Chosen said gently, "You don't have to say it."
>
> He cleared his throat. "So you'll tell her they're from me?"
>
> "I won't have to. Who else but her son would do such a kindness?"
>
> Vishous glanced back at the lone yellow bird in the midst of the white tree. He pictured the branches filled once again.
>
> "True," he said.
>
> —LOVER UNBOUND, pp. 501–502

The Scribe Virgin is not one of the most popular forces in the series. Personally, I respect her, and to see her giving up her one personal attachment (her birds) to balance the gift she gives her son (in the form of Jane coming back) really got to me. I've had people ask why she can't just fix everything, i.e., with respect to Wellsie and Tohr (even John Matthew broaches this issue, too), but the thing is, she's not a total free agent in the world she created. Absolute destiny is always at work—and is the purview of her father, I suspect.

V and his mother are reconciled to some degree at the end of *Lover Unbound*. But what remains to be seen is what happens when V's twin, Payne, comes forward. Somehow I don't think V is going to take that well to the way his sister's been treated—or the fact that his mother has never mentioned Payne to him previously.

So that's *Lover Unbound*.

They say that every author in the course of a career has a couple of books that are just grueling, and Vishous's was definitely that way for me. Each one of the Brotherhood books has been a unique challenge, and getting them out is WORK. I struggle at the computer every day, but there's always some small reward, whether it's a dialogue exchange that really sings, or a great description, or a really good chapter ending. With V, the rewards were delayed, to be sure. It wasn't until the final product was done that I sat back and was like, *Okay, this works. This is all right.*

I'm proud of *LU*, and I think it is a good book. . . . I'm just really grateful that the Brother who came next was true to his nature—a total gentleman.

Because if it had been another like V?

I don't know that I could have gone through that kind of struggle again right away.

Phury, Son of Ahgony

"I am the strength of the race. I am the Primale. And so shall I rule!"

—LOVER ENSHRINED, p. 484

Age: 230
Joined
Brotherhood: 1932
Height: 6'6"
Weight: 275–285 lbs.
Hair color: Multicolored
Eye color: Yellow
Identifying
physical marks: Star-shaped scar of the Brotherhood on left pec; missing lower half of right leg; name CORMIA carved across shoulders in the Old Language.

Weapon of
choice: Dagger.

Description: *Phury dragged a hand through his outrageous hair. The stuff fell down past his shoulders, all blond and red and brown waves. He was a handsome Joe without it; with that mane, he was . . . okay, fine, the Brother was beautiful. Not that Butch went that way, but the guy was better-looking than a lot of women. Dressed better than most of the ladies, too, when he wasn't in his ass-kicking clothes.*

Man, it was a good thing he fought like a nasty bastard or he might have been taken for a nancy.

—LOVER AWAKENED, p. 44

. . . Phury knew damn well he was stuck in an endless loop, going around and around like the head of a drill, digging further and further underground. With each new level that he sank to, he tapped into deeper and richer veins of poisonous ore, ones that spidered up through the bedrock of his life and enticed him down even farther. He was heading for the source, for the consummation with hell that was his ultimate destination, and each lower plateau was his malignant encouragement.

—LOVER ENSHRINED, p. 68

Mated to: The Chosen Cormia

Personal Qs (answered by Phury):

Last movie
watched: *What About Bob?* with Bill Murray

Last book read: *Horton Hears a Who!* by Dr. Seuss (to Nalla)

Favorite
TV show: Can't really think of a favorite—I'm not big into TV, to be
                       honest.

Last TV
show watched: *Unwrapped* on the Food Channel—with the Chosen—
                       they love to see how things are made. I think it was on
                       potatoes?

Last game
played: Gin rummy with Layla and Selena.

Greatest fear: Letting down the people whom I love.

Greatest love: Cormia

Favorite quote: "Heroes are made, not born."

Boxers or briefs: Depends on the cut of the trousers.

Watch: Cartier men's Tank in gold.

Car: BMW M5 dark gray/silver.

What time is
it while you're
filling this out?   10 p.m.

Where are you?   Rehvenge's Great Camp in the Adirondacks.

What are you
wearing?   Canali dress slacks, in cream, bright white button-down from
                       Pink with citrine studs as cuff links (present from my *shellan*),
                       black Hermès belt, black Hermès loafers (no logo because of
                       the one on the belt), no socks.

What's in your closet?	How much time do you have? I like Italian designers, for the most part. I wear a lot of Gucci. Have some Prada, of course, and the old standbys Armani and Valentino for men. Zegna and Canali. But I also have Isaia, who's a real up-and-comer, although the ordering process is complicated, and Tom Ford, who, thank God, got back in the game. I go through English moods as well and get out my Dunhill and Aquascutum. Not a lot of French, I'm afraid. No, wait . . . I'm getting some Dior later this week. The artist in me loves beautiful clothing. I like how it hangs off your body and the silhouettes it creates. And there's no need to be uncivilized if you have the choice. By the way, it's hard to believe Butch and I have the same taste. We actually bond over it.
What was the last thing you ate?	Cranberry scone with clotted cream.
Describe your last dream?	I was shopping. And not for clothes. I was in this supermarket with a cart full of laundry detergent and fabric softener, going up and down the aisles looking for the way to check out. It was truly bizarre. Weirder still when I woke up, because Layla said she wanted to learn how to use the washing machine. (The lesson didn't go well, unfortunately. I love that female, but the domestic arts? Not her thing. She does, however, have a spectacular skill of which we're all in awe.)
Coke or Pepsi?	Neither. I don't like sodas.
Audrey Hepburn or Marilyn Monroe?	Audrey. Hands down.
Kirk or Picard?	Picard.
Football or baseball?	Neither. I'm not a huge sports guy. Better to ask me Leonardo or Michelangelo. And it would be Michelangelo.
Sexiest part of a female?	I'm going to pass on this one. I'm just not comfortable answering that kind of thing.
What do you like most about Cormia?	The way she looks at me.

Most romantic thing you've ever done for her:	You'd have to ask Cormia. But I make certain that every day I do a little something that is just for her. Whether it's making sure that she has enough of the toothpaste she likes, or taking her for a driving lesson, or finding a perfect hawk feather out in the woods and bringing it back to her, or surprising her with a flat stone I found in a riverbed. The small things matter—especially as she's just getting used to the idea of having property that is hers and hers alone. And, you know . . . my *shellan* doesn't favor fancy jewelry or clothes. She likes to dress in my shirts and doesn't fuss over herself, so I guess I'm the girl in this mating. You know . . . to her credit, she has a true affinity for the simple things . . . like that feather. She was enthralled. It was from a red-tailed hawk, and I found it when I came back from NA one night and was out for a walk by myself. I brought it home and disinfected the tip and gave it to her. She loves things with color.
Most romantic thing she's ever done for you:	Funny that you should ask that. The hawk feather? She took it to Fritz and with his help made a quill pen out of it for me. The nib is sterling silver and gold. The pen sits in a stand on my desk. I use it to sign things for my brokerage accounts and whatnot, and also to draw her. It's probably the best thing anyone's ever given me.
Anything you'd change about her?	No. Nothing.
Best friend (excluding *shellan*):	My twin, Z.
Last time you cried:	I'll keep that private, if I may.
Last time you laughed:	Not long ago. With Cormia. But the context is private.

J.R.'s Interview with Phury:

After my noninterview with V, I head up to the kitchen and hand over my mug and napkin, along with my compliments, to Fritz and his staff. I'm informed that Phury has arrived and is waiting for me in the library, and I head there.

Breaching the room's majestic entrance, I find Z's twin facing the stacks. He's got on a spectacular pin-striped black suit, and the contrast of his wavy, multicolored hair with the precisely tailored dark wool is arresting. He turns as I arrive. His shirt is blush pink with white collar and cuffs, and his tie is one of those Ferragamo small prints in red and pink . . . birds, I believe the pattern is birds.

Phury: (frowning) What's wrong?
  J.R.:   Oh, nothing. (Looking around deliberately to avoid his yellow eyes.) God, I love this room. All the books . . .
Phury: What's happened?

At this point I head for one of the silk couches and sit down facing the fire. The cushions curl up around me, and the crackling of the cedar logs makes me think of winter things, like snow falling and canopy beds that are heavy with comforters and pillows.

Phury joins me on the sofa, jogging his trousers up at the thigh before sitting down. When he crosses his legs it's in the European fashion, knee over knee, not ankle to knee. His hands link in his lap, his massive diamond pinkie ring flashing . . . and making me think of V.

Phury: Let me guess . . . the interview with tall, dark, and icy didn't go very well.
  J.R.:   I'm not surprised, though. (trying to shake self out of it) So tell me, how are the Chosen liking this side?
Phury: (eyes narrowing) If you don't want to talk about him, we won't.
  J.R.:   I appreciate the kindness, but honestly, that's just the way it is. I'll be fine.
Phury: (after a long pause) Okay . . . the Chosen are doing surprisingly well. All but five have come for a visit on this side, and what they do here varies based on their personality and predilections. The way it works, we usually have anywhere between six and ten in the house up north and . . . You're not tracking.
  J.R.:   Between six and ten. Personality. Predilections.

Phury: (standing up) Come on.
  J.R.:   Where?
Phury: (holds out hand) Trust me.

Like Z—and all the Brothers for that matter—Phury is someone you can
put your faith in, so I lay my palm in his and he pulls me to my feet. I
hope we're not going to see V, and am relieved when, instead of heading
back to the kitchen, we go up the grand stairs. I'm surprised when he
takes me into his old bedroom, and the first thing I think of is that it
smells of red smoke, all coffee and chocolate together.

Phury: (stops in the doorway, frowning) Actually . . . let's go to the
          guest room next door.

Clearly he's noticed the scent too, and I'm happy to help him avoid
what is no doubt a trigger for him. We step out into the balconied hall
and go into the room Cormia stayed in when she was at the mansion. It's
grand and lovely, just like his, just like all of theirs. Darius had spectacular taste, I think to myself as I look at the lush silk drapery and the
museum-quality Chippendale dressers and the glowing landscapes. The
bed isn't so much a place to sleep, but a sanctuary to be absorbed in—
with its canopied top and acres of red satin bedding, it is exactly what
was in my mind when we were downstairs by the fire.

Phury: (taking off his suit jacket) Sit here. (points to floor)
  J.R.:   (planting it, cross-legged) What are we—
Phury: (mirroring me on the floor and putting palms out) Give me
          your hands and close your eyes.
  J.R.:   (doing what he asks) Where are—

The sensation that comes next is something like submerging your body
in a warm bath—except then I realize that in fact I've become liquid; I
am the water and I'm flowing somewhere. I panic and start to—

Phury: (voice coming from far distance) Don't open your eyes. Not yet.

A century later I feel like I'm condensing again, becoming whole . . . and
there's a new smell, something like flowers and sunshine. My closed lids
diffuse a sudden light source, and my weight is absorbed by a soft pad as
opposed to the short-napped Oriental I'd first seated myself on.

Phury: (taking his hands away) Okay, you can open now.

I do . . . and am overwhelmed. I blink not from disorientation, but from too much orientation.

When I was little I spent my summers on a lake in the Adirondacks. My mother and I would move up there at the end of June and stay straight through until Labor Day—and my father would come on the weekends and for a block of two weeks at the end of July and the beginning of August. Those summers were the happiest times in my life, although part of that, I'm realizing as I get older, is the glow of nostalgia and the simplicity of youth. Still, for whatever cause, colors were brighter back then and watermelon on a hot day was wetter and sweeter and sleep was deeper and easier to come and no one ever died and nothing ever changed.

I have been far away from that special place for many years now—distanced in a way that a trip up the Northway can no longer cure. Except . . . I am there now. I am sitting in a meadow of long grass and clover and there are monarch butterflies drunkenly skipping from milkweed to milkweed. A red-winged blackbird is letting out its call as it heads for a row of shagbark hickory trees. And up ahead . . . there is a red barn with a flagpole and a massive stand of purple lilacs in front of it. A dark green Volvo from the eighties is parked to one side, and woven wicker lawn furniture marks the pale stone terrace. The window boxes are the ones my mother planted every year with white petunias (to match the white trim on the barn), and the porch pots have red geraniums and blue lobelia in them.

I can see the lake on the other side of the house. It's deep blue and sparkling in the sunshine. Farther out in its midst is Odell Island, the place where I'd take my boat and my friends and my dog for picnics and swimming. If I turn my head, I see the mountain that rises up from the meadow, the one on which my family going back for generations is buried. And if I look behind me, I see across the meadow my great-uncle's white house and then my best friends' house and then my cousin's Victorian manse.

J.R.:   How did you know about this?
Phury: I didn't. It's just what's in your mind.
J.R.:   (looking back to the barn) God, it feels like my mother's in there getting dinner ready, and my dad'll be here soon. I mean, it really . . . is my dog still alive?
Phury: Yes. That's the beauty of memories. They don't change and they're never lost. And even if you can't recall all of them

anymore, the pathways they created in your brain are always with you. They're the infinity for mortals.

J.R.:   (after a while) I'm supposed to ask you a lot of questions.

Phury: (shrugging) Yeah, but I thought you'd appreciate this answer.

J.R.:   (smiling sadly) Which is?

Phury: (puts hand on my shoulder) Yes, it's still all here. And you can come back anytime you like. Always.

I stare out over the landscape of my childhood and think . . . *well, shit. Isn't this just like Phury.* I've been totally sniped by his kindness and thoughtfulness.

Bastard. Lovely, lovely bastard.

But this is the essence of him. He knows what you need more than you do, and he delivers. And he's also flipped the interview on its head, making it about me, not him. Which is also his way.

J.R.:   I'll bet you give fantastic birthday presents, don't you. The really freaky-thoughtful kind.

Phury: (laughing) I think I do all right.

J.R.:   You wrap well, too, don't you.

Phury: Actually, Z's the best bow man you ever want to see.

J.R.:   Who in your life would do something like this (sweeps arm around) for you?

Phury: Lots of people. Cormia. My Brothers. The Chosen. And also . . . myself. Like the whole recovery thing? (Pauses.) This is going to come out way wrong, just totally nancy, but the whole stop-using thing? That's my gift to me. For instance, right now, you're glad you're here, but it's hard too, right? (I nod.) Well, recovery hurts like hell sometimes, and it gets lonely and sad too, but even at its most difficult moments, I'm grateful for it and I'm glad I'm in it. (Smiles a little.) For Cormia, it's the same. Making the transition out of the strict traditions of the Chosen has been a real challenge for her. It's not easy to completely restructure everything about your life. She and I . . . we kind of bond over that. I'm redoing the way I've lived, you know, as an addict for the last two hundred years, and I'm discovering who I really am. She's doing a lot of the same work. We flounder and triumph together.

J.R.:   Is it true Cormia's going to design Rehvenge's new club?

Phury: Yup, and she's finished. They're starting construction on it as we speak. And Wrath's commissioned a new Safe Place facility from her as well. She's thrilled. I bought her a CAD program and taught her how to use it . . . but she likes to do everything on paper. She has an office in Rehv's Great House with an architect's desk—no chair, she stands up when she's drafting. I've bought her every book on architecture I can think of, and she's devoured them.

J.R.:   Do you think the other Chosen will find mates?

Phury: (frowning) Yes . . . although any males who come sniffing around are going to have to get through me first.

J.R.:   (laughing) You're going to be as bad as Z with Nalla, huh?

Phury: They're my females. Every one of them. Cormia is my mate, and I love her in a deeper, very different way, but I am still responsible for the futures of the others.

J.R.:   Something tells me you're going to do an outstanding job taking care of them.

Phury: We'll see. I hope so. I can tell you one thing, when it comes to their *hellrens*, I'm going to choose character over bloodline every time.

There's a long silence that's companionable, and after a while I let myself fall back in the grass and stare at the sky. The blue positively glows, and the white of the cotton-puff clouds is brilliant and a little blinding. The pair together remind me of fresh laundry for some reason, maybe because it's all so sparkling clean and the sun is warm on me and everything smells so good. . . .

Yes, I think to myself, *these are the colors I remember* . . . the ones from childhood, their vividness enhanced by the wonder and the excitement of just taking them in.

J.R.:   Thank you for bringing me here.

Phury: I didn't do anything. This is just where you wanted to go. And it's a lovely trip, by the way.

J.R.:   I couldn't agree more.

The other questions I might have asked him drift out of my mind and into the fair skies above. When I hear a rustle of grass beside me, I realize he, too, has lain down. Together we stretch out on the grass, hands behind our heads, legs crossed at the ankles.

Eventually we return to the mansion and the bedroom we'd been in, and we talk about nothing special. I know that Phury's giving me a chance to reorientate and I appreciate his thoughtfulness.

When it's finally time for me to leave, he and I go down the hall to the study. I say good-bye to Wrath and Beth, and Phury stays there to have a meeting with the king and queen. As I put the grand staircase to use, I hear the voices of the *doggen* once again coming from the dining room. They're setting up for Last Meal, laying out the place settings for the Brothers and the *shellans*.

Fritz comes forward, opens the vestibule's door, and leads me back out to the Mercedes. Before I get into the sedan, I glance up at the mansion's dour gray facade. Lights glow in almost every single window, evidence that in spite of the grim, bulwark-like exterior, there is great life and joy inside.

I slide into the backseat of the car, and as Fritz shuts the door I see that there's a small black leather pouch on the place where I should be sitting. After the butler gets behind the wheel, I ask him what it is, and he says that it's a present for me. When I start to thank him, he shakes his head and tells me it is not from him.

As the partition rises between me and Fritz, I take the satchel, pick apart the tie at the top, and spill its contents out into my palm.

It's a small black-bladed dagger, still warm from the forge. The workmanship is breathtaking. . . . Every detail, from the hilt to the razor-sharp tip, is perfectly wrought, and the miniature weapon gleams. It took its maker a long time to create it . . . and he cared about the outcome, cared greatly.

I curl my palm around the gift just as the Mercedes eases forward and we descend from the mountain, heading back for the "real world."

Lover Enshrined

The People:

Phury
Cormia
The Wizard
Rehvenge
Xhex
Lassiter
Tohrment
Zsadist and Bella
John Matthew
Qhuinn
Blaylock
Wrath and Beth
Fritz

Butch O'Neal
Rhage
Doc Jane
iAm
Trez
The Scribe Virgin
The Omega
Lohstrong (Qhuinn's father)
Lash
Mr. D
Havers
Amalya, Directrix of the Chosen
Selena
Pheonia
The Princess
Payne
Low (the biker)
Diego RIP (gang member in the jail)
Skinhead (unnamed man in the jail)
Eagle Jacket (the human drug dealer)
Stephanie (the manager at Abercrombie & Fitch)

Places of Interest (all in Caldwell, NY, unless otherwise specified):

The Brotherhood mansion, undisclosed location
The Other Side (the Chosen Sanctuary)
Havers's clinic, undisclosed location
ZeroSum (corner of Trade and Tenth streets)
Screamer's
The Caldwell Galleria
Cabin in the woods, Black Snake State Park, Adirondacks
Rehvenge's Great Camp, Adirondacks
The farmhouse (Lash's birthplace), Bass Pond Lane
Lash's parents' house
Blaylock's parents' home
The Caldwell Police Department

Summary:

Phury finds love and conquers both his addictions and his race's restrictive social and spiritual constructs.

Opening line:	*Time was not, in fact, a draining loss into the infinite.*
Last line:	I love you forever *didn't always need to be spoken to be understood.*
Published:	June 2008
Page length:	534
Word count:	162,403
First draft written:	December 2007–March 2008

Craft comments:

I love Phury. He was a dream to write, he truly was. And as I said, boy, did I need the break.

On that note, some thoughts about my daily working patterns.

My writing schedule is pretty much set in stone. I write seven days a week, no excuses, no compromises: sick days, holidays, travel days—my butt is in the chair. I've kept this up for about ten years now, and I think I've missed three days in that decade—due to extremely extenuating circumstances. I've gotten up at four-thirty in the morning in Manhattan in hotel rooms to write. Sat down after root canals. Stayed inside when it's sunny. My point is—writing is a priority, and I make it clear to everyone around me that writing time is nonnegotiable. It's not that I'm a superhero. I'm just very disciplined, for one thing, and for another, I need to write. If I don't, it's like not exercising. I just get antsy to do it.

Were all these days stellar examples of drafting at its finest? Absolutely not. I can write crap just like everyone else does sometimes. But I keep after it and re-work it and just hammer away until the words feel right. Often, it's slow going, and tedious. When I'm laying down a first draft, I can do only about six to ten pages a day. When I revise those pages, the first trip through is usually no more than ten pages a day. Then it's fifteen. Then it's twenty. After my editor reads the manuscript, I'll go through it again and again, doing no more than twenty-five pages a day. If I'm hitting copy edits, maybe I'll do forty. For galleys? It's hard for me to do more than fifty or seventy-five.

The thing is, I don't write fast, I write long—which means I just put the hours in.

My normal day starts when I get to the computer upstairs around eight. I write for two hours. Take a break to make more coffee (during which I sometimes check e-mail downstairs), then go back up for another two hours. After that I run and come back and spend the rest of the day editing and dealing with business-related stuff. This all changes, however, if I'm under deadline—which means nothing except a run takes me away from the computer.

I do not have Internet access on either computer I write on, and I strongly urge folks, if they can afford the luxury, to draw that line and keep Web and e-mail distraction far, far, far away from their writing machines. See, for me, the writing uses a very specific part of my brain. If I stop working to deal with other issues, it can be a struggle to get back to the zone I was in before I put on my business head.

No one goes up into my working space except my dog (who's always welcome) and my husband (who's usually welcome). I don't describe it anywhere, and there are no pictures of it. I will say that it is extremely uncluttered and has a tremendous amount of light. I think part of the reason I'm so territorial about the physical space is that keeping the real world out helps me to focus on what's in my head. I'm also by nature, as I said, rather private, and the writing is very personal to me—so I'm quite protective of it.

In addition to my agent and my editor (and all the spectacular folks at my publisher's who are incredible), I work with a lot of absolutely amazing people. My personal assistant makes sure everything runs smoothly and keeps me in line by being thoroughly unimpressed by any of the J. R. Ward stuff and liking me for me (well, most of the time it's about our friendship—sometimes I drive her insane and she stays only because she loves my dog). My research assistant is a walking, talking Brotherhood encyclopedia who can find obscure pieces of knowledge and know-how with amazing alacrity—he's also endlessly patient with me and one of the kindest people I've ever met. I also have a six-foot-ten-inch consigliere with a metal fetish—because everyone who writes about vampires needs one of those—and a woman who, even when six months pregnant, is willing to hump bags around hotel lobbies and go to conferences and make sure the trains run on time (we call her the APA).

My critique partner, Jessica Andersen (who writes fabulous paranormals), and I met like eight years ago, and we've been through a lot of ups and downs (the downs are what we call roadkill periods). She writes plot-driven stories and I'm into character sketches, so we don't have a thing in common when it comes to material—which is one of the reasons I think we work so well together. I call her my CP, but because I don't really share my content much, she's more like a brain trust. I run a lot of business as well as writing issues by her, and she never fails to give me good advice.

My two assistants run the J. R. Ward message boards and the BDB Yahoo! Group and work with a tremendous team of volunteer moderators, most of whom have been with the Brothers from the very beginning. Our mods are amazing, and I'm so grateful for what they do just because they like the books.

Everything's a team effort. And I couldn't get the time and space to write like I do without the help of these folks.

Usually my days end around nine at night, when my husband and I get to spend a little time together before we pass out and get up and do it all over again. The truth is, I'm actually kind of boring. I'm mostly in my head all of the time—

writing consumes my life, and the solitary existence nourishes me as nothing else could or has: I'm happiest at the computer by myself with my dog at my feet and it's been that way since day one.

I kind of believe writers are born, not made—but that's not specific to writing. I think it's true of athletes and mathematicians and musicians and artists and engineers and the hundred million other endeavors that humans pursue. And in all my life, I believe the single best thing that's ever happened to me, aside from having the mother I do, is that I found my niche and have been able to make a living out of doing what I love (my husband has had a *huge* hand in this whole publishing thing, so I thank him for that).

Now, before I nancy out completely and get all mushy with gratitude, let's talk about Phury.

I have always seen Phury as a hero. From day one. I'd also been aware all along that his book was going to be about addiction—which was going to be tricky. To be honest, I was very concerned about the heroin thing. I remember, when I got the image of Phury passed out next to the toilet in that bathroom, going, *Oh, God, no . . . I can't write that. How are people going to be able to see him as a hero if he shoots up and ODs?* And my problems weren't just about him doing it, either.

The thing is, heroes are not always right, but they are always strong. Even if they tear up or break down, the context that brings them to that state is so overwhelming that we excuse them for their brief unraveling. With Phury abusing red smoke and exhibiting an addict's need to protect his habit (with all the lying that implies), I was really concerned that if I didn't portray him correctly, readers would view him as weak, instead of tortured.

Tortured is okay for heroes. Weak, in terms of constitution, is really not.

I think it's understandable that Phury has some serious problems getting through the day. Considering all the stuff with Zsadist, and the complex interweave of guilt and sadness and panic that Phury's had to live with all these years, the red smoke was a way of self-medicating his feelings. The first step to depicting him sympathetically was bringing the Wizard out before the readers so they had an idea of what Phury was trying to shut up with all the blunt rolling and lighting. Once again, like V's actions at the war camp, it was all about context.

The Wizard is the voice that drives Phury's addiction, and it lives in Phury's head:

> In his mind's eye, the wizard appeared in the form of a Ring-wraith standing in the midst of a vast gray wasteland of skulls and bones. In its proper British accent, the bastard made sure that Phury never forgot his failures, the pounding litany causing him to light up again and again just so he didn't go into his gun closet and eat the muzzle of a forty.

You didn't save him. You didn't save them. The curse was brought upon
them all by you. The fault is yours . . . the fault is yours. . . .
                                        —LOVER ENSHRINED, pp. 5–6

The next thing that needed to be shown was Phury beginning to realize that
he is an addict. For him to be a hero, he had to conquer his drug use, and the first
step of recovery is recognizing you have a problem. The initial inkling for him
comes when he and a *lesser* are looking for some privacy to fight downtown and
they interrupt a drug sale. When it looks as if the transaction won't go through,
the desperate buyer ends up attacking the dealer, killing him and cleaning him
out before taking off:

> The rank joy on the addict's face was a total head nailer. The guy
> was clearly on the express train to one hell of a bender, and the fact that
> it was a free fix was only a small part of the buzz. The real boon was the
> lush ecstasy of super-surplus.
> Phury knew that orgasmic rush. He got it every time he locked him-
> self in his bedroom with a big fat pouch of red smoke and a fresh pack of
> rolling papers.
>   —LOVER ENSHRINED, p. 47

Identifying with another addict was the start for Phury. But things had to get
worse before they got better:

> "Am I still a Brother?"
> The king just stared at the dagger—which gave Phury the three-
> word answer: *in name only.*
>   —LOVER ENSHRINED, p. 87

Phury's getting the boot from the Brotherhood was not just about his addiction,
but also about his other method for dealing with his emotions—torturing *lessers*
before he kills them.

This was, originally, something I thought Zsadist was doing. I even alluded to
it on the message board. Except I was wrong. It was Phury who was cutting up
slayers before stabbing them—which is pretty hard-core. Funny, when I saw the
scenes, I just thought that Phury, the nice one, the kind one, wouldn't do something as base and cruel as torture. But here's the thing—and I think to some degree it's one of the points of Phury's book: Even people who dress well, come from
titularly good backgrounds, and look put-together can be totally unhinged on the
inside.

Speaking of backgrounds, a word on Cormia. The parallels between her and

Marissa are obvious. Both are high-stationed females suffering under the load of social expectations they were born into—and both transform themselves, becoming agents not only of their own liberation, but of others' as well (the vote at the Council meeting and her work at Safe Place for Marissa; helping Phury to transform the Chosen for Cormia).

As a couple, I think Phury and Cormia work on a lot of levels, and in this passage I think she sums up her side of the connection well:

> . . . But that wasn't what really compelled her. He was the epitome of all that she knew to be of worth: He was focused always on others, never on himself. At the dinner table, he was the one who inquired after each and every person, following up about injuries and stomach upsets and anxieties large and small. He never demanded any attention for himself. Never drew the conversation to something of his. Was endlessly supportive.
>
> If there was a hard job, he volunteered for it. If there was an errand, he wanted to run it. If Fritz staggered under the weight of a platter, the Primale was the first out of his chair to help. From all that she'd overheard at the table, he was a fighter for the race and a teacher of the trainees and a good, good friend to everyone.
>
> He truly was the proper example of the selfless virtues of the Chosen, the perfect Primale. And somewhere in the seconds and hours and days and months of her stay here, she had veered from the path of duty into the messy forest of choice. She now wanted to be with him. There was no *had to, must do, need to*.
>
> —LOVER ENSHRINED, p. 18

Of course, this puts her in direct conflict with her role as First Mate—who under the traditions of the Chosen must share the Primale with her sisters. This clash between Cormia's upbringing and who she is and what she truly wants is the core of what she struggles with, not only romantically but individually.

On Phury's side, I think that in addition to the instinctual bonding thing he has going on, Cormia really sticks by him. She is incredibly steadfast and accepting, and the two of them go through a lot. She is also instrumental in his recovery—more on this later.

Phury's decent into the dark hell of his addiction truly bottoms out after he's with Cormia sexually. The scene where he takes Cormia's virginity was a hard one to write, because I knew I had to be very careful with what I saw, and I didn't want there to be any confusion: Cormia absolutely wanted what happened to go down, but Phury, in his haste, truly believed he had hurt her.

There is nothing sexy about rape. Period.

Phury's misconception about his actions drives him right into the Wizard's playground. He'd had a near miss with heroin already (in *Lover Awakened*), and I suppose his doing H was inevitable, given his addiction and his emotional instability. It did break my heart, however:

> This shit was definitely not red smoke. There was no mellow easing, no polite knock on the door before the drug stepped into his brain. This was an all-guns-blazing assault with a battering ram, and as he threw up, he reminded himself that what he'd gotten was what he'd wanted.
>
> Dimly, in the far background of his consciousness, he heard the wizard start laughing. . . . heard his addiction's cackling satisfaction get rolling even as the heroin took over the rest of his mind and body.
>
> As he passed out while throwing up, he realized he'd been cheated. Instead of killing the wizard, he was left only with the wasteland and its master.
>
> *Good job, mate . . . excellent job.*
>
> —LOVER ENSHRINED, p. 431

It was a wonder Phury lived through it, and I shudder to think what would have happened if Blay hadn't come to stay at the mansion and he and Qhuinn and John hadn't walked into that spare bedroom.

So that was Phury's bottom, and to his credit he didn't stay there. The first significant step he took in his recovery was the choice he made the following day. He goes to complete the Primale ceremony with Layla, but instead of laying with her, he sits on the steps in the vestibule of the Primale Temple and makes a personal resolve to stop drugging:

> As the wizard started to get pissed and Phury's body milk-shaked it something fierce, he stretched out his legs, lay down on the vestibule's cool marble floor, and got ready for a whole lot of going-nowhere.
>
> "Shit," he said as he gave himself over to the withdrawal. "This is going to suck."
>
> —LOVER ENSHRINED, p. 459

This in turn led to what was for me the most significant scene between Cormia and Phury as a couple—the one where she helps him through his detox hallucinations. By taking him around his parents' overgrown garden and directing him to clean it up (the scenes start on page 468), Cormia is a hero in her own right, being strong when her male can't be and providing him with leadership when he needs to be led.

The symbolic nature of the ivy, when Phury's either remembering how it covered the statues in his parents' garden or using it to do away with one of his drawings, is obvious. The past has been choking him all along, and I loved the fact that during those hallucinations, not only does he free the statues, but he frees himself—and gets to see his parents in a happier place.

As a result of the detox, Phury then has the lucidity and the gumption to rehaul the whole construct of the Chosen—which was about fricking time. I love this part when he becomes resolved:

> After a lifetime of watching history unfold in a bowl of water, Cormia realized as she measured the medallion being held aloft that for the first time she was seeing history made right in front of her, in live time.
> Nothing was ever going to be the same after this.
> With that emblem of his exalted station waving back and forth under his fisted grip, Phury proclaimed in a hard, deep voice, "I am the strength of the race. I am the Primale. *And so shall I rule!*"
> —LOVER ENSHRINED, p. 484

That is Phury's inner heroic nature being truly realized—and man, does he go to town with it when he goes to see the Scribe Virgin.

About that confrontation. During his conversation with the Scribe Virgin, I think he hits on what is her essential failing when it comes to the race she created and loves. She's too overprotective and has to, as Phury says, have faith in her creation. The traditions of the vampire race are hindering their survival as much as the war with the Lessening Society is, and things must change: The pool of candidates for the Brotherhood must be opened up so that more warriors can be brought on, and the Chosen need and deserve to be liberated.

A note on all the social and religious restrictions within the vampire race. There were those at the beginning of the series who criticized the books for being too male-dominated and chauvinistic. But that was the point.

Rule four: *Plotlines Are Like Sharks.* They must move or die.

The series needed to start at a place where there were things to be fixed, otherwise there would be no struggles, no conflict, no evolution and resolution. And even with the improvements made in *Lover Enshrined,* the world remains ripe with strictures that need changing or areas where conflict is going to breed— Rehvenge's *Lover Avenged* is going to have a lot of that.

A *symphath* working with the Brotherhood? Pow.der.keg.

The thing is, plotlines must advance across a credible playing field of people. Always. For example, to me, the most powerful scene in Phury's book comes when he leaves the Scribe Virgin's private quarters after having freed the Chosen. Here, he returns to Chosen's sanctuary:

> He froze as he threw open the door.
> *The grass was green.*

The grass was green and the sky was blue . . . and the daffodils were yellow and the roses were a Crayola rainbow of colors . . . and the buildings were red and cream and dark blue. . . .

Down below, the Chosen were spilling out of their living quarters, holding their now colorful robes and looking around in excitement and wonder.

Cormia emerged from the Primale temple, her lovely face stunned as she looked around. When she saw him, her hands clamped to her mouth and her eyes started to blink fast.

With a cry, she gathered her gorgeous pale lavender robe and ran toward him, tears streaming down her cheeks.

He caught her as she leaped up to him and held her warm body to his.

"I love you," she choked out. "I love you, I love you . . . I love you."

In that moment, with the world that was his in transformation, and his *shellan* safely in his arms, he felt something he never would have imagined.

He finally felt like the hero he had always wanted to be.

—LOVER ENSHRINED, pp. 492–493

I'll be honest: I bawled like a baby right there. It was just the most perfect moment for Phury—and it couldn't have happened if there hadn't been something huge to fix in the world.

And speaking of things that needed to be fixed, a word on Phury and Z. The relationship between the twins had to be addressed in the course of the book, and there was some serious stuff to deal with. Phury had a lot of pent-up frustration and anger, and it eventually came out (I'm thinking of that scene in front of the mansion that starts on page 277, where the two of them go at it). I will say that I think Z's lack of gratitude was more about the current suffering he was dealing with—namely the concern about Bella and her pregnancy—than a fundamental resentment over the fact that he had been saved. After all, it's hard sometimes to be grateful that you're walking the planet when the very foundation of your life is unstable.

Phury needed the acknowledgment from his twin, and needed the thank-you, though. Hands down for me, one of the most moving scenes in the series—and the one I absolutely *wept* at when I wrote it—was the reunion of the twins following the birth of Nalla. By this point, Phury's on the road to recovery and has redefined his role as the Primale—and Bella and Nalla have lived through the birth, so Z's in a much better place as well. The twins, however, remain estranged. At least until Zsadist comes up to Rehv's house in the Adirondacks and approaches his brother while singing Puccini:

Phury got to his feet as if his twin's voice, not his own legs, had lifted him from the chair. This was the thanks that had not been spoken. This was the gratitude for the rescue and the appreciation for the life that was lived. This was the wide-open throat of an astounded father, who was lacking the words to express what he felt to his brother and needed the music to show something of all he wished he could say.

"Ah, hell . . . Z," Phury whispered in the midst of the glory.

—LOVER ENSHRINED, p. 531

If you look throughout the book, you'll see that here and there I put in a line about things not needing to be said to be understood. We're talking about scenes between John and Cormia, Phury and Wrath, Phury and Cormia. I wanted it all to lead up to this moment, when Z's emotions are too complex and overwhelming for him to explain, so he must sing to get his point across. And his message is received in exactly the manner it is given: The grand thank-you voiced in song is lovingly embraced by the one being thanked. Perfect.

The theme of silent communication also comes into play in the last line of the book. Here Phury is holding Cormia close to his heart after suggesting they get mated back at the Brotherhood mansion:

The hooting and hollering and backslapping of the Brotherhood cut off the rest of what he was going to say. But Cormia got the gist. He'd never seen any female smile as beautifully and broadly as she did then while looking up at him.

So she must have known what he meant.

I love you forever didn't always need to be spoken to be understood.

—LOVER ENSHRINED, pp. 533–534

And that just about sums up Phury and Cormia.

Some thoughts about John Matthew and Lash.

One of the great things about John Matthew (who is Darius reincarnated) is that in the earlier books I could introduce parts of the world to the reader through his eyes. As he is unfamiliar on all levels with the vampire thing, what was new to the reader was new to him. John has also lent great continuity from book to book: On balance, the POVs change with each story, and thus far, once I've done a hero and heroine, except for in Slices of Life outside the books, I do not return to them (although I think in Rehv's story that might change—I can see where Wrath might come back in a huge way). John, however, has been a constant—as well as constantly evolving as he goes through his life.

As I begin to prepare for John's book (which might well be coming after Rehvenge, I'm not sure), I wanted to show readers how the whole time thing works with respect to the Omega and the Scribe Virgin—as a way of anticipating the Darius reincarnation issue. To this end, Lash as the Evil's son, which I knew about much earlier, was the perfect way to do this. At the end of *Lover Revealed*, when the Omega says to Butch: "Lo, how you inspire me, my son. And may I say you would be wise to search for your blood. Families should congregate." (p. 427), the Omega is making a reference to his defensive reaction to Butch's changing the dynamic of the war. Having "spawned" Butch, in a sense, and being at the cop's mercy, the Omega realizes that he needs to do something to counteract the threat to his survival. What he does is this. After *Lover Revealed*, the Omega went back in time, impregnated a female vampire, and created Lash. Lash was not in existence prior to the time between *Lover Revealed* and *Lover Enshrined* (the lapse of a matter of months reflected the Evil's failed attempts at procreation, which were not detailed), but was created when the Omega went back to the early eighties at the start of Phury's book.

This, of course, created a problem. For me as the author, bringing in a major character like Lash and having to explain why all of a sudden everyone knew him was just not going to work—it would have involved way too much exposition. So I had to work off of absolute time—which is different from the fungible time the Scribe Virgin and the Omega can manipulate at will. Absolute time is the absolute destiny that is the sole province of the Scribe Virgin and the Omega's father. This absolute truth and time in the vampire world reflects the culmination of all the choices ever made by all actors in that universe, and the books have to run on that absolute—otherwise it's a mess (or, more accurately, a boring stretch of explaining and flashbacks).

Lash is therefore shown from the day John Matthew first meets him on the bus. Which is, in absolute time, exactly what happens.

It's on this same absolute time that the John Matthew and Darius thing went down. When Darius is killed in *Dark Lover*, and he goes to the Scribe Virgin in the Fade, John Matthew does not exist. But after the Scribe Virgin and Darius strike a deal, the Scribe Virgin steps back in time and plants John Matthew/ Darius in that bathroom in the bus station as an infant. John Matthew then develops over the course of those years independently of the vampire world—until his destiny brings him in contact with Bella through Mary in *Lover Eternal* (after Darius is dead). Technically, therefore, John Matthew and Darius coexist for a period of years, but there is no contact between them.

A mind-bender for sure. But kind of cool.

Anyway . . . I could keep going on and on, but I might as well end here. Get me started on the Brothers and their world and I'm a windup toy with no end of enthusiasm.

So that's *Lover Enshrined* . . . and the series so far.

On some level, I can't believe I've actually written the first six books already.

It's been a blur, a strange, fascinating, terrifying ride that's taken me to places, both in terms of writing and on a personal level, that I couldn't possibly have predicted.

I'm grateful for all of it. Even the really hard parts (and there have been some).

Next up is Rehvenge.

And if you thought the first six were humdingers . . . wait'll you get a load of him.

For Writers

Advice and FAQs

A s this section is for writers, I think I'll start by listing my eight writing rules up front in a nice little group:

I. P & R—PERSIST AND REINVENT
II. WRITE OUT LOUD
III. OWN YOUR OWN WORK
IV. PLOTLINES ARE LIKE SHARKS
V. SWEAT EQUITY IS THE BEST INVESTMENT
VI. CONFLICT IS KING
VII. CREDIBLE SURPRISE IS QUEEN
VIII. LISTEN TO YOUR RICE KRISPIES

Writing is hard stuff, and publishing is a difficult business to break into and survive, much less thrive, in. But here's the thing. I don't really know much in life that isn't hard. Being a mother is difficult, and so is being a teacher or an accountant or an athlete or a student. My point is, I'm not sure whether writing is any more scary and heartbreaking and exhilarating than anything else. I do know that the eight rules above have taken me this far—and I hope they'll continue to see me through the ups and downs of my endeavors.

I've had a lot of writers, both prepubbed and published, come to me for advice. I'm always flattered, but also a bit at a loss in describing how I do what I do or why it's worked thus far (and I never take for granted that it's going to keep working). Routinely, however, I make a couple of recommendations for each of the various stages of the process, which follow below. I would like to note, however—and this is important—this advice is for people who are trying to get published. You DO NOT have to write solely to get published. I wrote for years just for myself and was perfectly happy doing so. What is laid out hereafter is for folks who are doing something that is quite specific—and it must be said that a published book is a very distinct animal and NOT THE BE-ALL AND END-ALL.

I'll try to get off my soapbox now. But I just think it's important for folks to know that if you write, you are an author. Period. You don't need a publisher or consumers to validate what you are doing. Getting a book on the retail shelves is just one avenue some people choose to explore—but not the only one. Collecting the oral history of your family for the next generation or writing in journals to record your thoughts for yourself or jotting down descriptions of a thunderstorm for no other reason than you like how the lightning travels across the black sky—that all counts and it all matters.

Right, advice for those who want to get published:

1. *Finish a book.* Even if you don't like it, or you don't think it's good enough, see one of your projects through to the end. Discipline is mission critical to publication, and no matter how enticing the other ideas in your head may be, get to the final page on at least one of your WIPs (works in progress). If you find yourself getting distracted by the buzz of new characters or concepts, write them down in a notebook or Word document to save for later. But teach yourself to finish what you start. Writing can be a drag. It can be nothing more than a series of tiny, incremental steps that drive you nuts. In every single Brotherhood book, particularly while revising, I've wanted to scream from frustration because I'm convinced that what I was working on was the longest book in history and it was NEVER going to be finished. That's just part of the process.

2. *Find other writers.* I joined the Romance Writers of America (www.rwanational.org) after I'd finished my first marketable project, and I've met all my writer friends through RWA. There are local chapter meetings across the country, e-mail loops you can participate in, contests you can enter your writing in, regional conferences, and a magazine that comes every month with tons of information in it. Additionally, every year there's a big national convention, which is great for networking with other writers and which offers opportunities for appointments with editors and agents, as well as classes taught by experts. RWA also has on its Web site incredible resources on craft and business—essentially everything that has to do with romance writing. If you want to get published, I strongly recommend joining, but RWA isn't the only group available. And if you want to get pub-

lished in another genre, there are other nonprofits that likewise encourage content-specific networking (like mystery or horror or sci-fi).

3. *Don't write to the market, but be strategic.* In terms of subgenres (like paranormals or romantic suspense or historicals), if there's something that's hot that publishers are buying, it never hurts to put your hat in the ring if what's being bought is something you've legitimately got in you to write. The Brothers and I are an example of this. By the same token, if there's something that you want to write but isn't selling very well, if your goal is to get picked up by a publisher, you might consider exploring some of your other ideas and seeing if they're in a subgenre that's moving a little bit more. HOWEVER, that all being said, if you write what you're passionate about, your enthusiasm is going to come through on the page and make for a better reading experience—and things change. What's hot now may be replaced with something else in another year. Hold on to your rejected manuscripts—you never know when you might resubmit to someone else or in another form in the future.

4. *Write your book for you, then see who it fits with.* It's a good idea to know what individual publishers/editors are buying, and it does make sense, once you're finished with a project, to send it to the right place: For example, you wouldn't want to get a medieval romance to an editor who's looking for paranormals (more on how to find out who's buying what in a little bit). The great thing about having a good agent is that they'll know on whose desk to place your work. Some editors like to work with dark stuff, others like comedy, and personality matches are always a plus in the editor/author relationship. If you haven't found an agent yet and are submitting without one, ask other authors whose material is similar to yours who they're working with (but, again, more on agent/editor searches in a little bit).

5. *Category or single title is a personal choice.* There are a couple of different avenues to explore when it comes to getting published in romance, and I'm not talking in terms of subgenre. The two big ones for print books are categories versus single titles. Categories, such as Silhouette Special Editions or Harlequin Intrigues, are shorter stories that fit into clear guidelines laid out by the publisher in terms of content and page count. Single titles are the longer, stand-alone books. There are pluses and minuses to doing both: You don't need an agent to approach category editors, whereas for the most part, if you want to sell a single title, you're going to need representation. Categories, therefore, can be a really good place to break into (and a TON of supersuccessful authors like Elizabeth Lowell, Suzanne Brockmann, Lisa Gardner, and Jayne Ann Krentz got their start with them). Also, categories can help you find

your niche in the marketplace a little quicker, because the guidelines for submission are so clear—there are lines that feature suspense, paranormal, humor, you name it. I tell folks to check out www.eharlequin.com for the list of category lines and their submission guidelines. EHarl, as we call it, also has terrific resources on craft.

In my career, I kind of started out bass-ackwards, doing single titles first, then going to category when I wanted to keep doing contemporary romances while the Brothers were getting started. I love writing my categories (Silhouette Special Editions under the Jessica Bird name), and they're a great break from the Brotherhood books—lighter and quicker, they clean my palate. I will say, though, that I do not find them appreciably easier to write just because they're shorter—good work is hard no matter what the page count is.

As for the single-title market, compared to getting picked up in category, it can be more competitive, and as I said, there is most often the rate-limiting step of needing an agent. However, you do have more freedom in single title in terms of page length, content, and subplots, as well as the potential for earning more money—although there is more risk, too. If you don't sell, there is a perception out there that you will get dropped more quickly than in category.

The choice depends on where you are in your writing and the kind of stories you want to write. And it's not a one-or-the-other kind of thing. You can try a single title or start out in category, it's really just what appeals and what you think your material is best suited for.

6. *A note on e-pubs.* I don't have a ton of knowledge on e-pubs, so I usually refer folks to friends of mine who have been brought out by them and have firsthand knowledge of which ones are the best in terms of author support and business ethics. I think e-pubs can provide a really good opportunity for professional editing and are a great avenue to bringing your name forward to the market much more quickly than would otherwise be possible. I also think they can be groundbreaking in terms of what kind of content they'll publish and can be an outstanding place to see through a project that might otherwise be deemed too racy or too controversial. I do think authors should be careful—going with those companies that are more established and getting an independent read on contracts before you sign is only smart (as well as apropos in ANY business endeavor).

7. *Agents are desirable.* From what I understand from the editors whom I know, their slush piles have grown geometrically over the past few years. I'm not exactly sure why—maybe it's the advent of computers, who knows. But this phenomenon, in addition to the squeeze publish-

ing is currently under, means that editors are understandably even more overloaded and cautious than ever before.

This is where agents come in. The editors I know use agents as a kind of gateway for screening projects, and they rely on recommendations from them when it comes to choosing which material to review and perhaps bid on. A good agent has relationships with editors in every house at every level and knows where to place proposals. In addition, they can vouch for your project with their reputation, giving you even more credibility.

A good agent doesn't have to be your friend and they shouldn't be. They should tell you the things you don't want to hear and be honest about where you are in your career and where you're going. Each one is different, just like each author is different. Some want to have a say in content, others stress promotion; some are hand-holders, others are bulldogs. The key thing is to find a connection that works for you. And remember it's a relationship like any other. Be professional and honest and expect the same, and never, ever shoot the messenger. If your agent is doing their job right, you're going to hear things you don't like or wish were different. The key thing is working together to solve problems and getting your work out to as many people as possible.

8. *How do I find an agent or a publisher?* The best advice I can offer here is go out and get the most recent version of *Writer's Market*. This yearly reference volume is a great guide to what agents and publishers are looking to buy. The listings are grouped by agent (or agency) and by publisher as well, and give names, addresses, and statements as to who is looking to represent or acquire what. RWA also does a yearly report on agents and publishers that is specifically geared toward romance (another great boon that comes with membership). Further, if you know published authors, it also helps to ask around and find out who they are represented and published by, how they like their agent and editor(s), and what kind of experiences they've had. Sometimes you can even get someone to pass your work on to their representative, which can be very helpful—although this is something you should wait to have offered to you, not something you should pressure another author for.

It may take several tries to get represented or picked up by a publisher, but it's a case of persist and reinvent until it works. And when it comes to agents, if you can't find one to take you on, that doesn't necessarily mean you are out of luck, because again, some publishers don't require them.

9. *Multiple submissions require full disclosure.* Certainly sending out the same project to a couple of different agents (or publishers, if you are unrepresented) at a time can potentially reduce the duration of the process, but it can also land you in hot water if more than one of the folks

wants to represent or publish you. If you do choose to multiple-submit, disclose the fact right up front—and be sure you do not send it to agents or editors who refuse multiple submissions.

10. *Be professional.* And this is about everything. Make sure your submissions are spell-checked and properly paginated with appropriate typeface and margins (Times New Roman 12 or Courier 10, double-spaced, one-inch margins all around)—as well as bound with a rubber band. When talking to folks, be polite and concise. If you're going to an editor or agent appointment at a conference, dress appropriately. Be on time—if you tell someone you'll get something to them by a certain date, leave yourself wiggle room for emergencies and have the material drop on the day you committed to. Write thank-you notes. Speak well of others or shut your piehole. Sure, a lot of this is no-shit-Sherlock, but it matters. God willing you're going to have a career in this business, so you might as well start building your reputation and good name from day one.

11. *Do not submit too early.* This one was HUGE for me. What I'm talking about is your material. There is a tremendous temptation to finish whatever you're working on and get it out to an agent/editor as quickly as possible—or at least there was for me. The thing is, though, you can make a first impression only once, and you'd be surprised at the kind of faults you can find in your work if you go back one more time with fresh eyes. My rule of thumb was (and is) to FORCE myself to sit on whatever project I was working on until I could give it one final read-through. It was brutal, because of course I was curious about what the editor or agent was going to say and whether I would get bought. But the thing was, I was never sorry I waited.

    Here's a perfect example. My first published book, *Leaping Hearts*, was not the one I got my first agent with. I wrote it during the process of trying to find representation. By the time I was picked up, I knew *LH* was much stronger than what I'd sent out, so I told my agent at the time to wait until I could get the new material to her. I actually delayed what went to market by a couple months in order to get *LH* right. But it was the correct thing to do, and my agent agreed with me. *Leaping Hearts* was a much stronger book and it was sold quickly.

    The thing is, it's in my nature to want to beat deadlines, but rushing compromises the work. I'm not saying that you should get caught up in analysis paralysis, where you go over the material so many times you crush it by overediting. But there is a ripening period for the writing that has to occur, and over time you'll figure out what that is for you and how many revisions you need.

12. *Promotion.* Once you're sold to a publishing house and have gone

through all of the editorial and production steps that culminate in your book being bound within a cover, you're going to want to consider the various options for promotion.

I've talked to a ton of authors and agents and editors about promotion because, like everyone else, I'm still trying to figure out what works and what doesn't. And you know what the consensus appears to be? (And this is after convos with hugely successful authors and very powerful publishing houses, mind you.)

No. One. Has. A. Clue.

There seems to be no quantifiable link between any one author-driven promotional activity and book sales. That being said, however, there are things that authors can do to help support what their publisher does for them.

A. *Brand yourself, and build your promotions around that brand.* Ask yourself what kind of books you write and create a definition. For example, dark erotic paranormals are J. R. Ward, and everything I've done for promo has the dark erotic paranormal vibe.

B. *Definitely establish a Web presence.* Get a Web site that reflects your brand, and get an e-mail address where readers can reach you and you can respond to them.

C. *Consider an interactive forum.* Whether it's a message board for your readers or a Yahoo! Group or a blog (either by yourself or with others), be active and engaging and enthusiastic about your work on the Net.

D. *Offer a newsletter.* I'm a little behind the boat on this, only just now having developed one, but at least I had my message boards and Yahoo! Group to get word out about my releases and appearances beforehand. For better or worse, the initial two weeks of a single-title release are a make-it-or-break-it time, and the more folks who know you have something new on the shelves, the more likely they are to buy during those critical first fourteen days.

E. *Do guest days at other blogs/message boards/Yahoo! Groups.* Network with your friends and see who will host you for a day around your release time. Conduct a contest to generate traffic, or talk about an interesting subject concerning either your books or yourself.

F. *Signings and conferences.* Attend them and be outgoing.

G. *Merchandising and promo items.* Bookmarks and pens and other giveaways can help keep you in readers' or booksellers' minds.

All of the above can certainly help—but all of it is also a time suck. For me, the writing must come first, and I've had to take the guilt out of all the other things I could be doing on the promotion front. The bottom line is, you need to write the best book you can . . . then worry about how to promote it. There are a lot of times when I've had to make choices about what not to do because I've needed to write. It's hard, though, and I know a lot of authors who struggle with this issue. You have to do well in the marketplace if you're going to stay published—but there's a lot that we as authors don't have control over, and promo sometimes feels as if it is the only thing we can do to increase sales.

And now . . . for the single most important piece of advice I've ever been given.

The Golden Rule: *Do the best you can for where you are.* This deceptively simple concept transformed me, and it was a gift that came at just the right time: If you check out the acknowledgments in my books, you'll see that I always thank "the incomparable Suzanne Brockmann." There's a good goddamn reason for it.

Let me paint a picture. Way back in July of 2006, I went to the RWA National Convention in Atlanta, Georgia. At that point, *Dark Lover* had come out in September of 2005 and, against all odds and expectations, had hit the *New York Times* extended list three weeks after its release. Which made NO sense on a lot of levels. Then *Lover Eternal* was released in March 2006 and it did even better, staying on the extended list even longer and selling spectacularly well. Readers were starting to get a head of steam up about the Brothers, and my publisher was really excited and my agent was totally thrilled and *Dark Lover* was up for the RITA for best paranormal. . . .

And I was . . . about to have a nervous breakdown.

See, one year prior to all this, I'd assumed I was never going to be published again.

When I went to Atlanta, I was losing it. I had no clue why the Brothers appeared to be working in the marketplace, I had no control over whether they would continue to do well, and it was incredibly difficult to go from being myself (grotty little writer in her boxers and her slippers) to being J. R. Ward (this, like, wunderkind thing).

Now, I'd had the good fortune of meeting Suz Brockmann through the New England chapter of RWA a couple of years before, and was, like most people I knew, in awe of her and her success. I was also a total fangirl over her work, having read it for years.

Plus, she was (and is), as they say, wicked nice.

By some stroke of luck, Suz agreed to see me for a quick one-on-one at that RWA in Atlanta, and my mom and I met her in a quiet hidey-hole in the hotel's massive lobby. As we all sat down, I wanted to make a good impression and try to not show how clueless and terrified I was. And I was terrified. Good news is in some ways harder for me to deal with than bad news because I trust it less . . . and at the moment I truly was at the end of my rope from self-doubt and fear and disorientation.

So Suz and I are talking and she's giving me all this great business advice and everything . . . and in the back of my mind I'm thinking, *Don't lose it, don't embarrass yourself.* . . .

I almost made it. Until she sniped me with kindness.

Toward the end of the meeting, Suz puts her hand in this little cloth bag she'd brought with her and takes out this book. Leaning forward, she says, all casual no-big-dealy, "Hey, I brought you an ARC of my new book."

I looked down at what she was holding out to me. To this day, I remember precisely what the cover of it looked like: shiny white with a little red pattern, the title in bold with her name underneath.

I reached forward and carefully took the book.

The thing is, I've read Suz for years. She's like Elizabeth Lowell to me. She's the author I curled up with at night and read until my eyes went double from exhaustion . . . and I still kept going. She's the one who I can remember seeing at a conference with a hundred people standing in line just to meet her—for two hours straight. She's the gold standard for being kind and nice to readers. And she's the one who wrote the book that I read and then walked around my condo for hours in tears over because I was convinced I would never be as good as her on her worst day.

I fucking lost it. Took that damn ARC to my chest, curled around it, and cried all over myself.

In. Front. Of. Suz. Brockmann.

And my mother.

On the third floor of the lobby of that hotel in Atlanta . . . so it was in public.

I still cringe.

Suz, of course, handled it graciously, and listened as I blubbed on about the fact that I was fricking losing it and I didn't know if I could keep the quality of my writing up and I wasn't sure whether I would be able to meet the deadlines and I was worried about not doing the very best job that any author now or in the past or in the future could do with the opportunities I'd been given.

Suz let me go on and on, and when I'd worn myself out like a hamster on a spinning wheel, she looked at me and said she knew exactly what all that was like. She knew precisely how it was to want to be perfect and do a perfect job and somehow earn the success you'd been gifted with. The thing was, she said, as time passed she learned that if you shoot for absolute perfection, you're going to fail by definition—and that "perfect" simply cannot be the standard, because you will burn yourself out.

Doing the very best you can with where you're at is what matters.

When I was younger, particularly when I was doing the lawyer/corporate America thing, I nearly killed myself trying to be perfect, and I was on the same path back then with the writing. But Suz opened my eyes—and I figured what worked for her was good enough for me.

(Note: I asked her to read this part before this book went to print to make sure she was comfortable with being mentioned—and she said that the advice she

gave me was a "pay it forward kind of thing"—it was first given to her by a wonderful Harlequin writer, Pat White, who got it from a book called *The Four Agree-
ments* by Don Miguel Ruiz. Now I'm passing it along. Kind of cool, huh.)

So, look, on the publishing journey . . . don't beat yourself up. Do the best
you can. Inevitably, real life is going to get in the way of the quality or the quantity of your writing . . . or your enthusiasm or your faith in your dream . . . or your
success. Know this going in, and find yourself some good support, whether it's
friends or other writers or your family or your dog—and remember that there are
only guidelines, no hard-and-fast rules for anything, whether it's craft or business
or success. I always temper whatever advice I give with the caveat that what's
worked for me may not be right for someone else, and that everything is just an
educated guess. And that's okay.

Because miracles happen.

Every day.

The thing is, if you don't put yourself out there, it makes it a lot harder for
them to find you. So, please, take a chance and see where it leads. And be kind
to yourself along the way. At the end of the day, all we can do is believe in our-
selves and work hard . . . the rest is left to fate.

Oh, and be grateful.

I know I am.

The Black Dagger Brotherhood Proposal

The Black Dagger Brotherhood Proposal

A lot of writers who are starting out on their journey to get published ask me questions about query letters (which are the correspondence you send out introducing you and your project to agents and/or editors) and proposals. *Writer's Market* has some good examples of query letters. Bottom line is keep it on one page, detail your project succinctly, but with enthusiasm, and list your writing credentials (such as any publishing credits you have, contests you've won, and professional memberships [like RWA]). Include also any relevant personal information that pertains to the particular material (i.e., you're a pediatric nurse who's writing about a heroine who's a pediatric nurse).

Proposals are generally the outline of your book, which is all about telling, not showing, and the first three chapters of the manuscript. What follows is the exact proposal I sent out for the Brotherhood through my agent (you can read the first three chapters in the book if you like). Right off the bat, I'm going to tell you it's way too long—so if you follow this example, I encourage you to do one full version for yourself, then pare it down for agents/editors. I made up the format myself—I'd never seen anyone else's proposals at that point and just focused on what I would want to know about the series if I were an editor. I will say that I think the layout works especially well with paranormals—you'll note I include the rules of the world as well as an overview of every major character and their role not only in the book, but in vampire society.

For me, it's cool to go back and read it through and see the changes in content. The vast, vast majority of the discrepancies that show up are because I misinterpreted what I saw, or because I saw more later which changed the implications of these original scenes. In a few cases, however, the differences came about because there were holes in what I was shown and I filled them in with stuff I made up. For example, when I first saw Phury and Z, I didn't know they were twins, didn't know much about them at all. Rather than leave the slate blank, I developed some background for them both that I thought was suitably dramatic. The truth came out though as I actually drafted the full manuscript.

And the same was true for the way *Dark Lover* ended. While I was outlining, the scenes stopped coming to me at the point that Wrath was in the clinic after he got shot. That just didn't seem like the right way to end the book, however, although it was all I had. I tried to come up with more—and I put in some things—except I sensed that wasn't what really happened. Fortunately the rest of the scenes downloaded during the writing, and the Brotherhood ended up together, still in Caldwell, at Darius's compound.

You will see that I made no mention of the Omega—that was because he wasn't clear to me. At least not until the drafting! Then I knew more than enough.

You'll also note, particularly in the introductory section, that I talk about my having "given" Wrath a critical weakness or "constructed" a situation to bring a woman into his life. This was, of course, not how things went down at all—but I was understandably wary of telling editors that these vampires were in my head, telling me what to do! I figured it was a good idea to present the story as though I was at least nominally in control of the material. Even if the truth was anything but that.

And I never did use *uta-shellan* in the series. I just went with *shellan*.

Oh, and the anticipated word count? *Waaaaaaaaaaaaaay* off on that one!

Last word: I've reproduced the file below right off my computer and it's not going to be copyedited as part of the editorial process of this insider's guide—what you see is exactly what went out to market, mistakes and all. The purpose is to show that I did my very best to make sure there were no errors, but there are and though that's not desirable, it still sold. This is not to encourage laziness—but part and parcel of the whole no-one's-perfect thing.

Dark Lover

By J.R. Ward
Single Title, approx. 100,000 words

OVERVIEW/THEMES

A well-constructed world of vampires can amplify the very best elements of romance: hot sex, high stakes, and soaring emotion can come together in a unique, contemporary setting. For this kind of book to work properly, the Rules of the World have to be firm and unyielding and these laws must be constructed to encourage acts of heroism and sacrifice for love. Contrasts are critical and have to play strongly through out the plot: strength vs. weakness; righteousness vs. evil; loyalty vs. betrayal; love vs. hatred; loss vs. communion; these essential forces must all be represented. The heroes need to be supermen facing foes of worthy stature. And the heroines need to have strong backbones and sharp intelligence.

And did I mention there has to be lots of fantastic sex over the course of steamy nights? Yeah, I guess that comes under the hot sex part.

In planning this book, I started with a warrior hero who needs to be healed by love. Wrath is a four hundred year old vampire, the last of his line, the only pure bred of his race left on earth. He has incredible physical strength, he's menacing and sexy, and he's blind. With respect to his disability, I thought it would be important to give him a critical weakness. His lack of sight forces him to rely on others and provides a good contrast to his otherwise physical invincibility. His poor vision does not hinder his ability to fight, however.

Wrath has been at war with members of a dark arts society of vampire hunters since he went through his transition. Vampires in this series are born without their race's characteristic features: fangs, super strength, longevity, photophobia, and the need for blood don't come to them until some time around their twenty-fifth birthday when they undergo an agonizing physical transformation. To survive, they don't drink from humans, they need a vampire of the opposite sex.

Prior to his transition, Wrath was scrawny, prone to sickness, weak. As a result of his poor health and eyesight, he was unable to save his parents when they were attacked by the vampire hunters. This contrast between Wrath's earlier feebleness and his current status of super-strength is at the crux of his internal conflict. His inability to protect those he loved is a failure he has never forgiven himself for. His vengeance and self-hatred have consumed his soul and shut out all avenues of love and caring.

Wrath is a menace to be sure, but he's worthy of being liberated from his emotionally barren world. The trouble is, in order for his salvation to occur, he's got to learn that he can take care of someone and that he is worthy of love.

Because he avoids personal relationships, I had to construct a situation whereby he was forced to have a woman come into his life.

Beth Randall, the heroine, is resilient, super-smart, physically beautiful and the half-human daughter of one of Wrath's band of warrior brothers. When her father is killed by their enemies, Wrath is forced to accept Beth as a responsibility and help her through her transition. Through being with Beth, and supporting her, Wrath is compelled to relive his own transition and the deaths of his parents. Beth helps him process the events more accurately and he is able see how his perceived failure to protect those he loved from death was not in fact the result of a lack of honor or internal weakness of his. This helps to free him of his burden of self-hatred and heals his emotional scars, leaving him able to love her with passion and commitment.

As for Beth, when we meet her at the beginning of the book, her life is as lonely and emotionally barren as Wrath's. Having grown up in the foster care system, she has no idea who her parents were and she has no familial support system whatsoever. She's stuck in a nowhere job. She longs for a relationship but can't seem to make the right connections with men. She also has no clue that she's half-vampire. When Wrath enters her life, she's swept up into a new world that gives her the opportunity to love and be loved as well as to find a family. And through Wrath, she finally gets that critical link to a parent she's always wanted. She also gets a good dose of excitement and passion.

The secondary romance features Wrath's *shellan,* or titular wife, Marissa and a hardened homicide detective. Marissa has loved Wrath for centuries but he's always been out of her reach emotionally and physically. She's a gentle soul who's lonely and she longs for the day when Wrath finally sees all she has to offer. Marissa's a tricky character to portray. She can't come across as a doormat because that's boring. But she needs to be a foil to Wrath's dark menace and their incompatibility has to be believable.

In the course of the book, Marissa realizes Wrath will never love her and this frees her to find her heart's other half in Detective Butch O'Neal. Butch is a good man who, not unlike Wrath, can tread the edge of madness when he lets his anger out. His daily life is a bleak stretch of death and red tape and he's been slowly losing his soul, figuratively speaking, for years. He meets Marissa and her inner purity refreshes him and gives him an optimism about life and love that he's lost. He also finds the vampire culture to be more compatible with his temperament. The complications inherent in him being a human and Marissa a vampire will only be partially solved by the end of the book. Their future will not be clear.

A note on Wrath's foes. In large measure, the average vampire in this series (apart from the heroes) simply wants to live in peace and co-exist with humans without being discovered. Vampires have been hunted systematically since the Middle Ages out of intolerance and a lack of understanding over their race's need to drink blood. Terrible acts of violence have been perpetrated by members of the so-called Lessening Society and vampires have been driven nearly to extinction. A select corps of vampire warriors are the defenders of the race and Wrath is the strongest arm among this band of brothers.

The band of brothers offers avenues for development of a series. Each one of the six of them have a crucial weakness. They have lost family, been betrayed by friends and lovers, suffered and endured great pain. They fight for their race, facing their enemies with courage and skill, but at the end of the night, all but one go home alone. The manner in which love tames a savage beast of man, revealing his caring, nurturing core, is a universal tenet of romance. Each of these men are in need of salvation and deserving of the love they require in order to be healed.

This story is set in a large town in upstate New York that is located on the Hudson River. It's the beginning of July and the weather is hot with thunderstorms sweeping through the area regularly and marking the nights with lightening flashes and the deep rumbling of thunder. In the book, the interior settings are urban and in large measure gritty: dance clubs; apartments; the police station; a diner; a martial arts academy. The contrast is where Wrath stays. The chamber he uses is housed in a lavish mansion. The exteriors are likewise mostly stark: dark streets; back allies; parking lots; a stretch under a suspension bridge. I believe the sober tone of the book's scenery sets off the contrast of love's warmth, comfort and light to its best advantage.

Again, I'm convinced that vampire love stories have the perfect blend of fantasy and romance. The format is elastic enough so that magic and ritual can be present in contemporary settings but the themes are universal and enduring. I am thrilled to be working on this project and excited by the characters and their lives.

And did I mention that the vampires are just plain sexy hot?

Thank you for your consideration.

MAIN CHARACTERS

Beth Randall

Beth Randall is turning twenty-five and unhappy in her life. She was raised in the foster care system and she's been unable to find any information on either of her parents. The only thing she knows is that her mother died in childbirth. This lack of knowledge has been difficult bear and she feels groundless, wondering if she'll ever really know who she is. Or where she belongs.

Her job as a reporter is an outlet for her frustrated searching and she takes satisfaction in finding the answers to other people's lives. She covers the police blotter for the *Caldwell Courier Journal* and she spends a lot of time down at the station with the cops. A couple of them have asked her out but she's never been too interested. On the whole, men find her extraordinarily attractive but ultimately they leave her cold. She wonders sometimes if she isn't a lesbian because she just doesn't seem too interested in having sex with men. Then again, she isn't attracted to women, either.

When she looks ahead ten years, she can't picture anything changing. She sees herself going to work day after day, getting nowhere fast at the paper, and going home to her cat. She longs for family, for love, for connections to people, but she just can't seem to relate to the men and women around her.

Lately, Beth hasn't been sleeping well. She's also been hungry all the time and eating constantly but at least she's not putting on any weight. She can't shake the feeling that something bad is about to happen to her and the fact that she has no one who she can really talk to makes her ever present feelings of loneliness all the more acute.

Wrath

Wrath was born in the 17th century to a pair of adoring parents. His father was the chief of their race and a respected leader. His mother was a kind, compassionate female. Wrath's birth was celebrated throughout their world as vampires rarely conceive and many of their infants are still born. The race took relief in knowing that their traditions would survive after his father's death and they intertwined their hopes and dreams with Wrath's future as chief.

But Wrath was sickly as a child, scrawny as a teenager, and there was concern he wouldn't survive until his middle twenties when his transition would finally strengthen his body. His eyes were of particular concern as his sight was poor even before he matured. His parents and their servants watched over him constantly and he grew up believing that the world was a safe, orderly place in spite of his health problems.

On the night of the slaughter, no one was prepared for the attack. Vampires had coexisted with humans with few problems up until the late Middle Ages in Europe. With human society fragmented and warring, and communication being limited by geography and language barriers, vampires were able to successfully evade notice. This peaceful era changed with the religious and intellectual developments of the 17th century in human culture. At that time, a secret society was established to hunt vampires down.

Wrath's parents were tortured and killed in front of him. He survived only because his father forced him into a crawl space and locked him inside just before the attackers came in. Wrath watched the slaughter with horror, and when he was released by the servants the next day, he buried his parents according to custom and vowed revenge. It was a pathetic covenant. With his under-developed body he knew he was no warrior. During the mourning period, as his people came by to pay homage to him as the last surviving member of a pure bloodline and the new chief of their race, he despised himself and his weakness even more.

Wrath set off alone and traveled Europe for three years, trying to find out more about the men who killed his family. He had no money, having left all his worldly goods behind, and with his pitiful body, he had no way to earn from his labor. He was attacked and beaten, mugged, threatened, and left for dead by humans a number of times. Somehow he managed to scrounge by, eating scraps and fetid animal carcasses until he finally found work as a servant.

When his transition hit, it caught him unaware because his parents had sheltered him and not told him what to expect. After drinking from a female vampire who materializes before him, he grows six inches, his muscles develop into rugged flesh, and he finally has the physical force necessary to exercise his vengeance.

Wrath spends the next four hundred years hunting members of the society and being hunted by them. He despises humans both for their cruelty to him before his change and for the fact that their race has spawned the society of vampire hunters. He lives a warrior's life with few possessions other than his weapons and no ties except to his band of brothers.

Marissa, the female vampire who came to him on the night of his change, was chosen by his parents to be his mate but he has no love in him to give her. He never sees her unless one of them must feed and he knows their relationship is slowly killing her. He's asked her to find someone else but she's refused and her loyalty makes him uncomfortable because he knows he hasn't earned it.

His band of brothers are six other vampires he's met through the centuries. They fight mostly alone but they share information and coordinate strategy when they need to. He's aware that the others look to him as their leader because of his bloodline and his strength as a fighter but it's a position and an adoration he doesn't want. He prefers the sting of hatred to any warmth and he sees himself not as a hero for defending his race but as someone who's just marking time until death puts him out of his misery.

Marissa

Marissa is Wrath's *shellan,* or wife, but her gentle nature makes her wholly unsuited for him. As Wrath and her do not share the kind of relationship that most vampires have with their mates, she lives with her brother. She is utterly devoted to Wrath and hopes that someday he will stop fighting and find that he loves her. She's a virgin, has never even been kissed, and she's socially isolated. Other males will not approach her out of deference to Wrath and the females pity her. She feels as though she exists in the shadows, watching other people's lives unfold while her days and nights are stagnated by her paralyzing hope.

Brian "Butch" O'Neal

Butch is a homicide detective who's strong sense of justice and passion for victim's rights can at times take his temper over the edge. He's tough on perps, protective of the innocent, and no one's fool. He's a good man but he's living a hard existence and he's lost his faith in humanity. His life revolves around his work, he's never been married, nor has he ever had a meaningful relationship with a woman. He's very lonely and sometimes he thinks that if he gets killed in the line of duty that's alright.

Havers

Marissa's brother, Havers, is a vampire physician, a dedicated healer. As Havers and Marissa's siblings have died of a disease specific to vampires years ago, and their parents are likewise dead, Havers has always looked after her. A year ago, he lost his *shellan* when she died trying to give birth to their stillborn son. Now, he feels as if his sister is all he has left. He's compassionate by nature and the pain that Marissa suffers in her relationship with Wrath really upsets him. He wishes that she could find a mate who truly cared for her.

The Band of Brothers

Darius, Tohrment, Rhage, Vishous, Zsadist and Phury are a band of warriors who revere Wrath. They are a deadly group who have sworn their lives to protect their race and they are revered and somewhat feared by other vampires. Darius had an affair with a human woman twenty-five years ago and the woman died in childbirth. He's lost two sons to his enemies and he's worried that his half-human daughter, Beth, won't survive her transition. Tohrment is the only one with a living *uta-shellan,* or first and only wife, and he worries about the safety of his family. Zsadist has a scar running down his face from having been tortured after his own brother betrayed him. Rhage is fiery in his personality, capable of flying off the handle at any moment, and he loves women. Vishous is the strategist of the group, possessing a frighteningly powerful mind but being haunted by dark visions which often come true. Phury had his children and *uta-shellan* killed by his enemies fifty years ago and has an artificial leg as a result of a battle injury.

A note on the names. The English words such as rage, fury, vicious, sadist, torment and wrath are derived from the traditional vampire warrior names which came first.

The Lessening Society

The Lessening Society is a totally self-contained, self-supported group of vampire hunters that operates outside of the law. Members of the society, called *lessers,* are humans who have traded their souls in return for a hundred years of sanctioned killing. They are vicious sociopaths, soulless killers with violent backgrounds or psychiatric pathologies who hunt for pleasure and like to torture. They have a high death rate so there is a constant demand for new society members. These recruits are drawn from a number of arenas, typically self-defense- or sports-related because the society favors the physically strong. In this book, a martial arts academy provides a fertile training and proving ground for new recruits.

Lessers can move around freely during the day. On occasion, they fight with each other over territory. They are physically stronger after their indoctrination and live to be a hundred while showing no signs of aging. They are also impotent and smell a little like baby powder.

Joe Xavier, a.k.a. Mr. X

Mr. X is an up and coming leader in the Lessening Society. He started training in the martial arts when he was in his teens, and when he was indoctrinated as a *lesser*, he went through a spec ops military program and then returned to the Society. He's brought a new level of technology and violence to the society's endeavors.

RULES OF THE WORLD

-Vampires are a completely different species from humans
-They live much longer lives than humans but are not immortal
-At around age 25, they 'turn', meaning they must feed from a vampire of the opposite sex to survive
-They will feed from humans but the strength they take from a man or woman doesn't last long
-After their transition, they are sensitive to light and blinded and burned by the sun
-Vampires can dematerialize at will but only if they are at the height of their strength
-When they dematerialize, they may not take others with them
-Vampires can read emotions in others
-Vampires are able to sense the geographic location of their mate
-Vampires heal quickly but maybe killed by a catastrophic injury
-They reproduce very infrequently and sometimes with humans
-Half-breeds, if they survive the transition, are subject to all of the above

STORYLINE

Darius, one of the band of brothers, asks Wrath to meet him out at a Goth bar in downtown called Screamer's. He knows that Wrath's unlikely to help his half-human daughter through her transition to a vampire. But Darius is desperate. He loves his daughter and she has a better chance of surviving the transition if she can be with Wrath because his blood is pure. Darius waits for Wrath to arrive, thinking of how much he hopes she's spared agony of the change and the life of a vampire.

At the same moment, his daughter, Beth Randall, walks home from her job at the local paper down Trade Street. She walks by the bar her father is in. While she's thinking about the lonely evening ahead, she's followed by two college boys. At first, she's not afraid when they approach and start to harass her. But then one of them grabs her and drags her into an alley. She fights but ultimately they pin her against a building behind a dumpster. While one holds her arms, the other rips her shirt off and starts to fondle her. Even though she's terrified, she forces herself to pretend that she's willing to have sex with the primary attacker. When he lets his guard down, she strikes him where it hurts most and then knees him in the nose as he doubles over. His friend is so surprised that he doesn't stop her escape. She runs home.

Back at Screamer's, Wrath finally appears. As he makes his way to Darius, humans trip over themselves to get out of his way. He takes a seat with Darius and waits for the other vampire to speak. When he hears what Darius wants, he flat out says no. He hates himself for turning his warrior brother down, but he wants no part in the transition of a half breed. That would require a compassion that he just doesn't have.

Wrath leaves the bar because he has to meet Marissa, his *shellan,* or female mate. Unlike most vampires, he does not have a sexual relationship with her, they merely feed off each other as they need to. Because he's consumed with hunting his enemies, there's no room in his life for. Her brother, Havers, with whom she lives, disapproves of the relationship which was established by Wrath's parents four centuries ago. So Marissa won't have to deal with her brother, Wrath frequently meets her in a room in Darius's mansion.

Wrath is headed for a dark alley to dematerialize to Darius's when he senses he's been tracked. It's a member of the Lessening Society, a group of humans who have sold their souls to become vampire killers. He draws the *lesser* into the shadows, slits its throat with a martial arts throwing star, and takes its wallet and cell phone. Wrath stabs the *lesser* through the heart, causing it to disintegrate. Wrath then dematerializes to Darius's guest chamber. Marissa comes to him and feeds. In their scene, the dynamics of their relationship are very clear. Marissa is very attached to him, hoping that someday he will turn to her and realize that her love is what is missing from his cold, warrior existence. He's strained by her devotion and loyalty and loathes himself for all he cannot give her. Before he can take her back to her brother's house, there's a knock on the chamber door. It's Darius's butler. Darius has been killed by a car bomb outside of Screamer's. Wrath tames his rage so that he can get details and asks Fritz to call the band of brothers together. Before the butler leaves, he gives Wrath an envelope from Darius. When Wrath is alone, he lets out his vengeance, causing a black whirlwind of anger to swirl around him.

When Beth gets home, she takes a forty-five minute shower and finds that though her nerves are shot, her body is recovering. She's starving. After she eats, she's sitting with her cat, thinking that she should file a report with the cops, when the phone rings. It's Jose De La Cruz, one of the policemen who's taken her under his wing. He tells her about a car bomb that's just exploded outside a bar downtown. He urges her to be careful when she shows up on the scene because Hard Ass, a.k.a., Homicide Detective Butch O'Neal, is on the case. Though she tries, Beth finds herself unable to talk about what happened for fear of breaking down. She tells Jose she can't go to the crime scene tonight and has to reassure him that she's fine when he gets worried about her. After she hangs up, she decides she must make a report after all and heads out, taking pepper spray with her.

The band of brothers show up at Darius's. Wrath must give the wallet and the cell phone to someone else because he can't see well enough to go through them. The wallet yields a driver's license and the cell phone has a call log that one of the brothers says he'll investigate. The brothers are looking to Wrath for leadership and for once this doesn't annoy him. He tells them that they are going to go raiding in retaliation. Typically, large scale battles with *lessers* are to be avoided because the carnage attracts the notice of human police. But Darius's death can not go un-avenged. The immediate quest for the brothers therefore is to find the nearest Lessening Society training and recruiting facility and take it out. These facilities move often and typically take the form of some kind of legitimate business in the human world as a shield.

When the brothers leave, Wrath takes out Darius's envelope and opens it. Inside is a sheet of paper and a picture of what appears to be a dark-haired female. Wrath calls Fritz in to read the note to him. Darius has left his mansion, Fritz and his half-breed daughter in Wrath's care. Wrath curses.

Downtown, Beth arrives at the bomb scene, looking for Jose. She's not there as a reporter, she's come to file a report on her attacker so that he can't hurt some other woman. Jose's not around but Butch O'Neal comes over, annoyed that she's arrived on the scene. When he sees her split lip, he pulls her into a quiet corner and demands to know what the hell happened to her face. She prevaricates and asks to talk with Jose. She doesn't want to relive the trauma of the attack with someone like Hard Ass O'Neal. Butch pressures her and doesn't back off until she threatens to do an expose on his heavy handed interrogation techniques. He leaves her and she goes back to her apartment in a cab.

An hour or so later, Beth is getting ready for bed when her cat starts acting oddly. He's pacing in front of the sliding glass door which opens out to the cruddy little courtyard behind her place. A knock on her front door gets her attention. She looks through the peephole and groans. It's Butch O'Neal. She opens the door and he barges in, looking around and taking a seat. Earlier in the night, Butch responded to a report of a guy down and bleeding in an alley off Trade Street. Putting it all together, he's deduced that Beth was attacked on her way home and he's come to try and help.

Outside, in the courtyard, Wrath is in the shadows watching. When Beth opens the sliding door to let some air in, he catches her scent and is enthralled. He also recognizes that the change, her transition, is coming on fast. He overhears her and the cop talking.

When Beth finishes recounting her attack, Butch leaves her place and goes to the local emergency department. He finds her assailant, who's dressed exactly as she described, and does a hard number on young Billy Riddle. At the end of the meeting, Butch has Billy pinned on the floor of the hospital room and is rubbing the kid's nose into the linoleum. He arrests Billy.

After the cop leaves Beth's apartment, Wrath comes into her home. He terrifies her so badly, he's forced to erase the memory of him from her mind so he can try again. Early in the morning, she wakes up from what she assumes is an awful nightmare, grateful that the horrible night is finally over.

Wrath goes back to Darius's house and down into the guest chamber. He showers and shaves and then takes out a black marble slab. After pouring pebble-sized, rough cut diamonds onto the platform, he knees on the rocks naked, prepared to observe the death ritual in honor of Darius. He will sit in the position unmoving for the whole day and reflect on the proud warrior who's now gone. Before Wrath goes into his trance, he thinks of Beth and vows that not only will he protect her, he will help her through her transition.

After Butch books Billy Riddle into holding, he leaves his office, headed for his squalid apartment. On the way out, he meets up with a prostitute named Cherry Pie who's a regular overnight guest in the women's holding cell. They talk and go their separate ways. On impulse, Butch heads back to the Screamer's neighborhood and pulls up in front of another bar. A woman comes out and they drive over to the river, parking underneath the bridge over the Hudson River. While the woman is having sex with him, Butch looks out at the river, thinking how beautiful the sunlight on the water is. When she asks him if he loves her, he says, yeah, sure. He knows she doesn't care that he's lying and he feels the desperation of his life intensely.

The next scene features the *lesser* who set up the bomb under Darius's car. Mr. X is a martial arts instructor working out of an academy in town. He's decided that to win the war against the vampires, spec ops techniques should be used and he posts the details of his bombing on a secured Lessening Society website. His good mood lasts all day long. When his four o'clock Kung Fu class arrives, he's still smiling. He's about to start his students sparing when one comes in late. It's Billy Riddle. His nose is bandaged and he has to sit out the session. Mr. X lets Billy lead the class's warm-up.

Towards the end of the day, Beth goes to the police station. Butch tells her that her attacker's been sprung on bail. Butch has discovered that Billy has a juvenile record and is the son of a powerful businessman. Beth tells him that she will take the stand and testify if the plea bargaining negotiations fall through. When Butch asks her how she's doing, she deflects his concern by asking about the bombing. He counters by asking her whether she's had dinner. She tells him she's not eating with him but he dangles a detail about the bombing in front of her and walks out of the office. She ends up following him.

Across town in Darius's mansion, Wrath is getting ready to go out when Marissa materializes in his chamber. She's sensed his pain over his loss and has come to try and ease his suffering. Caught up in his drive to avenge Darius, and his need to get to Beth to talk to her about her transition, Wrath tells Marissa to go home. He goes to Beth's apartment, and while he waits in the shadows for her, he reflects on his own transition. This flashback is important to establish one of his essential internal conflicts. Prior to his transition, he was a weakling, incapable of protecting his parents when they were slaughtered by *lessers* in front of him. After the deaths of his mother and father, he struck out on his own, unable to bare the reverence with which he was held by other vampires solely by the accident of his birth and his pure blood. When he emerged from the change, his body having mutated into a tower of strength, he was on his way to becoming a warrior. But it would be a cold, hard path.

Beth comes home having found dinner with Butch to be surprisingly relaxing. She changes for bed and gets annoyed with her cat who's back to pacing and purring at the sliding door. She's about to get in bed when Wrath comes into her home. This time, he's smoking a drug which has relaxing properties, and as he exhales into the air, Beth finds that she can't run from him. Her body won't move. And then she discovers she's not all that interested in bolting. As he comes up to her, she's overwhelmed with lust for him. They end up making love and it's explosive. An important note: the drug Wrath uses has no aphrodisiac properties, it's just a relaxant and the reader knows this. I thought it would be very unattractive of him to seduce her with some kind of sex drug and take advantage of her.

Across town, Mr. X heads out into the night. He approaches Cherry Pie and they strike up a deal for sex. In a dark alley, she starts to come on to him and he cuts her throat. His plan is to capture a vampire, using her blood as bait. Sure enough one of them, not a solider but a civilian, approaches. Mr. X shoots him with a tranquilizer gun but it has no affect and the vampire turns on him. Mr. X uses a throwing star in the course of their combat. He prevails against the vampire but is disappointed that his plan failed.

Meanwhile, in the basement laboratory under another mansion in town, Marissa's brother Havers looks up from his work on vampire blood typing. The grandfather clock in the corner has started to chime. It's time for a meal and Havers goes to his sister's room. He finds her staring off into the night and her sorrow cuts at his heart. Marissa is incredibly precious to him, especially since his *shellan* died. He feels as if, because of his sister's gentle nature, she needs to be with a civilian male who will care for her, not just use her for her blood. He asks her to come down to eat but she declines. He senses that she's been to see Wrath, even though she just fed the night before. He asks her why she puts herself through this. She tells him it's fine. Havers counters that Wrath shows her no respect, no doubt forces her to feed in some back alley. That's not true, she protests. She tells him that they meet at Darius's a lot of the time because Wrath stays there. You don't have to do this to yourself, he says. She doesn't answer him and he leaves her, feeling his own brand of loneliness as he goes down to a sumptuous table and finds himself having another meal by himself.

In her apartment, Beth stirs when she feels something soft on her face. It's Wrath. He's running his fingertips over her features, desperately wishing he could see her. He tells her she's beautiful and for once the comment doesn't turn her off. Wrath's cell phone goes off and he leaves the bed. It's one of the brothers. There's a number of businesses in the call log of the phone Wrath lifted off the *lesser* he'd killed the night before. They're going to go check them out and want Wrath to come in the event they find a facility and all hell breaks loose.

Wrath starts to dress. Beth watches him and is surprised when her cat, Boo, leaps up into his arm and purrs. A low sound comes out of this menacing man as he purrs back. Beth asks what his name is. He tells her and recites his cell phone number, making her repeat it until she remembers it. He tells her he has to go and may not be able to get back to her tonight but she should call him if she gets followed or if she feels afraid at any time. Wrath drops Boo and straps on a shoulder holster. That's when it hits her. Obviously, Wrath's been sent by the boys at the police station to protect her. She asks him if Butch sent him. Wrath comes over and sits next to her. He debates telling her it was her father but he has to meet his brothers and doesn't want to open that issue without having the time to really talk to her. Wrath kisses her and asks her to come to him in the day. He gives her Darius's address and she agrees to drop by in the morning. He figures that they'll be able to talk in the chamber and there'll be time to answer all of her questions then.

After he leaves, she falls asleep, totally sated. She wakes up in the morning, and when she steps out into the sunlight, her eyes ache. She figures it's a hangover from whatever he was smoking around her. She goes to her office because it's too early to go see Wrath. She gets a call from Jose. A prostitute was killed in an alley over night. When Beth arrives at the police station, Butch is there and he tells her that there was a throwing star found in the alley, similar to one found around the car bomb. There's probably some kind of turf war going on between the pimps, he says. They talk a little more and he asks her out to dinner again. She tells him no but thanks him for sending his friend to her. Butch asks what the hell she's talking about.

Beth leaves, disturbed by the ramifications of what she did the night before. She's had sex with a total stranger. Who looks like a trained killer. It felt somehow different if Butch or one of the cops was involved and suddenly the idea of going to some address to meet that man strikes her as foolhardy. Just as night is falling, she calls up Butch and asks him if he still wants to have dinner with her. She doesn't want to be alone and eating with him is better than being jumpy at home.

At Darius's house, Wrath's been prowling around his chamber all day long, waiting for Beth to arrive. And his temper was on a short leash before she blew him off. The night before he and his brothers had cased several places including a monastery, a prep school, a martial arts academy, and a meat packing plant. It wasn't clear that anything suspicious was going on in any of them. They also went through the dead *lesser's* apartment, learning nothing.

The moment the sun goes down, Wrath leaves the mansion and goes on the hunt for Beth through the city. He's aware as he moves around that he feels fatigued but he shrugs off the sensation, consumed with the need to find her. He ends up waiting for her behind her apartment. When Butch pulls up to the front of the building with her, Wrath senses her presence and approaches the car. Butch leans over to kiss Beth just as Wrath looks inside. Even with his poor eyesight, he recognizes what's happening. His first instinct is to rip the door off, drag the human male out, and bite him. But he controls himself with discipline and sticks to the shadows. Jealousy and possessiveness are two emotions he's not real familiar with and he's surprised at the depth of his feelings.

Beth is not attracted to Butch and tells him so. She gets out of the car and walks across the street to the front door of her building. Butch waits to make sure she gets inside safely, but just before he takes off, he sees a giant of a man heading around to the back courtyard. Butch gets out of the car and follows.

When Beth walks in her apartment, Wrath is at her back door. He's about to enter when Butch cocks his gun and tells him to freeze. Wrath turns and confronts Butch just as Beth opens the door and runs outside. Butch demands that Wrath put his hands on the building and spread his legs. Wrath toys with the idea of killing the cop but he doesn't want to terrify Beth. Besides, not even Wrath can survive a bullet to the head fired at point blank range. With Beth looking on, Butch pats Wrath down and starts peeling weapons off him. Daggers, blades, and throwing stars get spread out on the picnic table. Butch tries to get Beth to go inside but she won't leave. He asks what the hell Wrath was doing casing the building. Wrath says he was just out for a walk. Butch presses Wrath into the wall, drags his arms behind him, and puts cuffs on him. Wrath asks what he's being arrested for and Butch says concealed weapons, trespassing, stalking, and maybe murder. He tells Wrath that throwing stars like his have been found at two murder sites.

As Butch starts to lead Wrath off, Beth wonders if Wrath killed that prostitute after he left her apartment the night before. She just can't understand how a man can have such different sides. He was so gentle with her when he held her after they'd made love. She jumps in front of the men and demands a chance to talk with Wrath. Butch tells her to go inside and lock her doors. He drags Wrath off with Beth jogging along side. She asks Wrath why he's come to her. Wrath looks over at her and tells her that her father sent him. She stops, stunned.

Butch puts Wrath in the back of the car and drives him down to the station. Butch keeps an eye on him in the rear view mirror because something tells him that even handcuffed the man is deadly dangerous. They pull up to the back of the station. As Butch gets him out, Wrath steps back into the shadows. Butch is trying to pull him forward when Wrath breaks free of the cuffs like they're made of twine. Wrath grabs Butch, lifts him off the ground, and holds him against the building. For the first time in his adult life, Butch is sure he's about to be killed. And how ironic that he can see the window of his office while it's happening.

Wrath is tempted to end the man's life but there's something intriguing about the guy. He's not terrified as most human males would be. He's resigned, like he's looking forward to death, and Wrath sees a little of himself in Butch. Wrath tells Butch that he's not going to harm Beth. On the contrary, he's come to save her. At that moment, Beth leaps out of a cab and runs over to them. She tells Wrath to put Butch down. Butch is dropped to the ground, dazed.

Beth is determined to find out about her father and urges Wrath away from the station before Butch regains his wits. She hails a cab and Wrath tells the driver to take them to Darius's mansion's neighborhood. He has them dropped off a block or two away and they walk to Darius's. Fritz, the butler, greets them at the door.

Wrath leads Beth into the drawing room and down to the guest chamber. She's frightened but determined to learn about her father. Wrath's bedroom is a foreign place with its spooky black walls and candles but she doesn't feel as if he presents a danger to her.

Before she can demand that he talk, he starts asking her a bunch of weird questions. Has she been more hungry than usual? Has she been eating a lot but not putting on weight? Are her eyes more sensitive to light? Does she feel achy? Are her front teeth sore? She thinks he's crazy and asks what any of that has to do with her father.

Wrath takes off his jacket and tosses it on the bed. He paces around before taking her hand and sitting her down on the sofa. He tells her that her father's name was Darius and that he has recently died. She says that she was told her father died before she was born. Wrath shakes his head and explains that Darius and he have fought together for many years and that her father's love for her was very strong. She asks why, if her father care for her so much, he never bothered to introduce himself. Wrath doesn't answer but smoothes back her hair. You're going to get sick soon, he says softly. You're going to get sick and you're going to need me.

Beth loses track of what he's saying. He's going on about how he's going to help her through some kind of illness but she's only interested in her father. Who was he, she demands. He was as I am, Wrath says. He takes her face in his hands. And slowly opens his mouth.

Beth takes one look at his fangs and pushes him away, horrified. She leaps from the sofa and runs for the stairs. He lets her go, dematerializing to the front of the house just as she bolts out of the door. She takes his appearance in with utter disbelief and veers away wildly. Wrath lets her run her fear out, keeping close behind. When she finally exhausts herself, he picks her up from the ground and holds her as she starts to cry. She just keeps saying, over and over again, that she doesn't believe him. She just can't believe him.

Back at the police station, Butch drags himself inside and immediately puts out an APB for Wrath and for Beth. He goes to Beth's apartment but she's not around. He goes trolling downtown, but when he can't find her, he goes back to her apartment.

Wrath carries Beth back to the mansion. Down in the chamber, he draws her against him and holds her. She's numb but eventually her mind clears enough so that she turns and looks at him. He drops a kiss on her mouth, thinking only that he will soothe her but the flame between them leaps to life. Driven by the insanity of what he's told her, Beth unleashes her frustration on his body and they make love with an all consuming passion. As Wrath is entering her, he bares his fangs and nearly sinks them into her neck. He comes dangerously close to feeding from her, something that he shouldn't do because she hasn't gone through her transition. Feeling his desperation for Beth's blood and his increasing fatigue, he knows that he'll have to call on Marissa soon.

The next morning, Butch goes back to the station and is called into the captain's office. He's told that he's being placed on administrative leave for what he did to Billy Riddle. Butch tells his captain that the kid deserved worse. He leaves his badge and his gun and heads out, determined to keep looking for Beth. He calls Jose at home and tells him what happened. He asks if Jose has found anything out about the stars that were picked up at the two crime scenes. Jose tells him he thinks at least one of the weapons was purchased at the local martial arts academy. Butch decides to go over and check the place out.

Back at the mansion, Beth wakes up in Wrath's arms. He's been awake and holding her for hours. She asks softly what her father was like. Wrath tells her that Darius was brave and strong, everything a warrior should be. She asks him what it is that he and Darius are fighting against. He tells her about the Lessening Society and its history of hunting vampires. He tells her that her half-brothers were slaughtered by *lessers*. She asks him who he's lost and he shares with her the horrible deaths of his parents. She strokes his face and says she's sorry. His anguish is utterly apparent and so is his self-hatred. When he tells her he blames himself, she helps him see how powerless he was, given his physical stature and the fact that he was locked in by his father. She tells him that no one in that situation could have stopped the deaths. No one.

There's a knock on the door. Wrath pulls on a robe, puts his sunglasses back on, and answers it. Boo, her cat, bounds through the room and throws himself into her arms. She laughs and hugs him. While she'd been asleep, Wrath had asked the butler to go and get Boo from her apartment.

Wrath thanks the butler and catches sight of her father's door. When they're alone, he tells her he wants to show her something and draws her from the bed. He takes her across the hall to Darius's bedroom. She walks in and is awed by the sight of dozens of photographs of her at various ages. They're everywhere in beautiful frames. (She finds out later that Fritz the butler had taken them.) She also finds a picture of her mother. Wrath waits by the door as she explores her father's room. As he watches her, he realizes that he wants to take her as his *uta-shellan*, his one and only mate. His wife. The thought then occurs to him that she may not survive her transition. He's filled with a cold dread.

Beth is incredibly touched at both her father's obvious adoration of her as well as Wrath's quiet support as she goes through the room. He answers her questions thoughtfully and each bit of information he shares is a precious gift to her. When she finds a diary, she asks him to come over. She can't read the writing because it's in a language she doesn't know. As she holds the journal out to him, she realizes that he's not even looking at it. She puts the book down and reaches to his face. She slowly takes off his sunglasses. Whenever he's been without his glasses previously, it's been dark. Here, in the light from a lamp, she sees that his irises are a pale, milky green, the pupils tiny, unfocused pinpoints. You're blind, she says softly. Wrath feels an instinctive shame at his disability and tries to push her hands away. He worries that she'll think he can't protect her and tells her that he can still take care of her. Somehow, I don't doubt that at all, she whispers while kissing him.

Out in town, Butch arrives at the martial arts academy and sees Billy Riddle leave. Butch goes inside and talks to one of the instructors, a guy named Joe Xavier. Butch can't put his finger on it but there's something not right about the man. Xavier answers his questions about throwing stars and then casually asks Butch who he's looking for. No one in particular, Butch replies. He asks if Mr. Xavier would mind if he bought one of the stars. They're not for sale, the man says, but I'll give you one. Butch takes the star and puts it in his pocket. He leaves and drives over to the newspaper to see if Beth's come in. No one's seen her.

Beth leaves the mansion later that day, thinking she should go to work. She stops by her apartment, changes, and heads downtown. When she gets to the paper, her editor demands to know where she's been. She's missed two deadlines and he threatens to fire her. She sits down and writes two columns but her mind is really on Wrath. As fantastically unbelievable the story he's told may be, it somehow makes sense. It explains why she's always felt so different from the people around her. And how for some reason she's always felt as if someone was looking over her.

As the sun sets, Wrath calls for Marissa. She arrives in the chamber, pleased that he's reached out for her because he's obviously disturbed. On Wrath's side, his mind is consumed by Beth. He's worried that she's out in the city without him, he can't get the memories of making love to her out of his mind, and he's petrified of her coming transition. Marissa offers him her wrist but, as Wrath closes his eyes, he sees Beth. In a surge of remembered passion, he goes for Marissa's neck.

Marissa feels him take her in her artery and she's shocked. His body is fully aroused as he drags her against him. This is what she's always waited for and she grabs onto his shoulders, reaching into his mind with hers. She gets a vivid image of the female he's thinking of and her heart breaks. She finally lets her hope go. She knows that he will never, ever feel this way about her. A tear slips from her eye as he drinks.

Across town, Mr. X sets out in search of another prostitute to use as bait to catch a vampire. This time, he's brought a net with him that's strung with silver cording. He kills another woman in an alley, leaving her to bleed out. When a vampire comes by, he traps the male in the net. Mr. X walks over and shoot several darts into the male. When the vampire loses consciousness, Mr. X drags him over to his car and drives him out into the country where Mr. X lives.

Beth walks back to her apartment to pick up some clothes and checks her messages. Butch has called her several times and she'd also heard at work that he'd been trying to find her. She gets him on his cell phone. He tells her to say put because he's coming over. She's waiting for him when her stomach starts feeling nauseous. She pops a couple of TUMS but the feeling just gets worse.

Wrath finishes with Marissa, and when he pulls back, she tells him that she's releasing him of their covenant. He takes her hands in his and tells her he's sorry. She murmurs that they were a bad match from the beginning. He vows to always protect her but she tells him that she'll find someone else to do that. She dematerializes.

Wrath goes upstairs and the warrior brothers come to him. While Wrath was with Beth the night before, they were watching the martial arts academy. They noticed a steady stream of *lessers* going in and out at three a.m. and believe that it is the center.

Meanwhile, Butch arrives at Beth's apartment and buzzes the intercom. When she doesn't answer, he goes around to the back. Through the glass door, he sees her laying face down on the floor, curled in a ball. He breaks the glass of a window with the butt of his gun and goes inside. She's writhing in pain. He starts to call 911 when she stops him. She gives him an address and begs him to take her there. He tells her he's not taking her anywhere but an emergency room. She grips his arm and drags his face close to hers. She tells him if he wants her to live, he has to take her to Wrath. It all becomes clear to Butch. Wrath has gotten Beth hooked on heroin and she's in withdrawal. If he takes her to an ER, she could die if she can't get the drug. He picks her up in his arms and carries her to his car. Driving like a bat out of hell, he goes to Darius's house.

Wrath and the brothers are in the drawing room when they hear a pounding on the door. Drawing their weapons, they go over in a group. Wrath opens the door. Butch barges inside with Beth in his arms. Wrath takes her from him as the brothers watch in astonishment. He carries her as if she is utterly precious and disappears into the drawing room.

Across town, Marissa has returned to her room and crawls into her bed. When her brother comes up later, in hopes of bringing her out to a party, he looks in horror at the fresh wounds on her neck and the bruising of her pale skin. Havers is consumed with rage at Wrath. He goes into his laboratory, convinced he has to do something.

Back at Darius's, Wrath lays Beth gently on the bed in the chamber. She's suffering and his hand shakes as he takes out his dagger. He makes a move toward his wrist but stops because he wants to hold her close when she drinks. He makes a small cut in his neck and picks her up, cradling her. As she drinks from him, he rocks her back and forth, ancient prayers he thought he'd forgotten falling out of his lips.

Upstairs, the brothers circle Butch. Butch is distraught about Beth, tired of dealing with drug pushers and their carnage, disillusioned about his job. When one of the brothers pauses in front of him, Butch lets his rage out, taking the larger man down to the floor. In a matter of moments, Butch is flat on his back, totally pinned, with an elbow crushing his wind pipe. The guy sitting on his chest is smiling tightly and commenting to the others that he kind of likes Butch. Just as Butch is about to pass out, one of them comes forward and pulls the man off him.

Butch looks up at his savior while he gasps for breath. The man staring down at him has a scar running over his cheek and the deadliest eyes Butch has ever seen. This is really it, Butch thinks. This time he's finally going to die. But instead of killing Butch, the man pronounces that they will wait for Wrath before deciding what to do. At that moment, a butler dressed in black livery bustles in with some hors d'oeuvres. Butch can't believe his eyes. The guy passes a silver tray around and then tells the men that if they're going to do any killing, would they please be so kind as take their business out into the backyard?

Down in the chamber, Beth finishes drinking and Wrath holds her through the pain. At one point, he's convinced she's dying but she pulls through. Two hours before dawn, the agony finally relents and she falls asleep.

Upstairs, Butch is stripped of his jacket and his captors go through his pockets and find the throwing star. You have a background in martial arts, one of them asks. Butch tells him no. So what are you doing with this is, comes the next question. It's a friend's, Butch replies. They ask him some questions about the marital arts academy in town. For some crazy reason, he almost thinks that they're all after the same thing: the man who set the car bomb and might be killing prostitutes. The butler interrupts with an announcement that dinner is served. While the other men start to head out of the room, the one with the scar hangs back and tells Butch that he's welcome to try and escape. The front door's unlocked. But if Butch leaves, the man's going to hunt him down like a dog and kill him in the street. When Butch is alone in the drawing room, he considers his options. He's worried about Beth and decides, Scar Face's threat not withstanding, he will not leave.

In her bedroom across town, Marissa rolls over fitfully. She feels weird and it takes her a while to realize she's mad. No, she's beyond mad. She's way into fury.

She throws the sheets back and dematerializes. She figures that Wrath will be coming back home soon so she reappears in Darius's drawing room. She's tired of hiding herself away with Wrath and hopes his warriors are with him when he returns. She wants to tell him off in front of an audience.

Butch is walking around the drawing room, pausing to look at the antiques and thinking that drug dealers end up with way too much money, when suddenly, there's a woman in front of him. He feels his breath catch. She's so ethereally beautiful, he almost forgets how to breathe. She has a delicate face, bright green eyes, and cascades of blond waves falling her back. She's dressed in some kind of flowing white gown or robe. With a knee jerk protective instinct, Butch looks out in the hall, thinking he should take her away. He can't imagine what a delicate beauty like her would be doing with a group of rough neck thugs like that. She's so pure, he thinks. She's so utterly pure.

Marissa is surprised at what's in front of her. It's a human. In Wrath's house. And the man is staring at her as if he's seen a ghost. He clears his throat and sticks out his hand. Then he withdraws it and wipes his palm vigorously on the seat of his jeans. He puts the hand out again and introduces himself as Butch O'Neal. She considers the palm he's offered her but takes a step back. He drops his hand and just keeps staring at her. What are you looking at, she asks, bringing the lapels of her gown closer. She wonders if maybe he senses she's a vampire and is disgusted by her. A flush hits his cheeks and he laughs awkwardly. He apologizes and says she's probably sick of men laying eyes on her. She shakes her head. No males ever look at me, she murmurs. To herself, she thinks that this was one of the hardest parts of being Wrath's *shellan*. No males and few females would even meet her in the eye for fear of what Wrath might do. God, if they'd all only known how little she'd been wanted.

The human takes a step closer. I can't imagine the men don't stare, he says. He smiles at her and his eyes, they're so warm, she thinks. She's heard so many stories about humans. How they hate her race, would burn her kind at the stake if they could. This one doesn't seem violent, though, at least not towards her. What's your name, he asks. She tells him and then he wants to know if she lives in the house. She shakes her head.

Butch cannot take his eyes away from her. He knows he's behaving like a perfect ass but he really wants to reach out and touch her, just to make sure she's real. Would you mind—he shuts his mouth. What, she prompts. May I touch your hair, he whispers. She seems shocked and then a look of determination crosses her face. She takes a step towards him and he loves the way she smells. Like clean air. She tilts her head down and one long lock of her hair falls forward. Butch takes the silken strands between his fingers. Soft, he thinks. So soft.

Marissa closes her eyes as his hand grows a little bolder. She feels the touch of his fingertips on her cheek and instinctively she turns her face into his palm. Her body starts to feel warm and time seems to slow. She's confused by the change in herself, a little frightened of the attention of this male. But she likes it. She likes the way he's looking at her.

Back at his home, Havers has spent the night pacing in the garden. He knows how to take Wrath out of his sister's life but the method goes against his principles and his commitment to his race as a healer. Unsure, he goes up to her bedroom. When he finds she's gone again, he makes up his mind. He dematerializes and projects himself to a retched part of the city. Dressed in his expensive clothes, he looks totally out of place among the leather and chain set downtown. He begins to pace the streets and alleys.

With Beth sleeping soundly, Wrath leaves her to go talk with the brothers. When he pushes open the painting and steps into the drawing room, he sees Butch and Marissa standing close together. Wrath is astounded at the attraction he senses between them. It's on both sides. Before he can say anything, Rhage comes in from the dining room, a dagger in his hand. He's heading for Butch, having obviously seen the same thing Wrath has and believing that Marissa is still Wrath's *shellan*. Wrath's commanding voice pulls Rhage, Butch and Marissa up short. Wrath notes with approval the way Butch instinctively protects Marissa with his body. Rhage smiles and tosses the dagger over to Wrath, obviously assuming Wrath wants to kill the human. Relax, Rhage, Wrath mutters. And leave us.

Butch looks up at the bigger man, thinking about Beth and now also worried about the blonde woman behind him. He feels a movement and realizes that Marissa is actually putting herself between him and the drug dealer. As if she could protect him. Butch starts to protest when Marissa speaks sharply in a language he doesn't recognize. She and the dealer talk for a moment and then the dealer actually smiles. He walks over and kisses Marissa on the cheek. And then with a quick movement, the dealer reaches around her body and grabs Butch around the neck. From behind his sunglasses, the man's shooting a glare right into the back of Butch's skull. Marissa starts to push at the dealer's chest but she gets nowhere. The dealer then smiles tightly and whispers in Butch's ear, she's intrigued by you. I don't disapprove. But hurt her and I'll- Butch cuts the man off, tired of having people vow to kill him. Yeah, yeah, I know, he mutters. You'll bite my head off and leave me in the street to die. The dealer's lips open as he grins and Butch frowns. There's something wrong with the guy's teeth, he thinks.

Beth stirs, feeling stiff. She reaches out for Wrath, and when he's not there, she opens her eyes. Her sight is still with her. She gets up, looks down at her body. It feels the same. She does a little jig. Works the same, too. She dresses in a black robe which smells like Wrath and goes upstairs. She notices on the way up that she's not breathless at all from the exertion. Which is a bonus, she thinks. Maybe there are benefits to the whole vampire thing.

When she gets to the top of the stairs, it takes her a minute to figure out how to push the secret door open. And then she steps into the drawing room. Butch is there with a gorgeous blonde woman. The two of them are sitting on the couch and both look up. Butch comes over to Beth and gives her a hug. Beth can feel the blonde watching her closely, as if the woman's measuring every inch of her. There's no hostility in the blonde's eyes, though. Just curiosity and something oddly close to awe. Butch introduces the two of them, and when Beth asks where Wrath is, he tells her he's in the dining room.

Beth walks across the hall and her feet slow when she sees a group of deadly looking men sitting around a table with china on it. The scene is totally incongruous. All these hard ass guys in leather eating with silver. Then she sees Wrath. He's sitting at the head of the table. The moment he sees her in the doorway, he rushes over to her. He takes her into his arms and gently kisses her. Beth is dimly aware that all conversation in the room has ceased and that the other men are staring at her. Wrath asks her softly how she's feeling and it takes her a little time to reassure him. He asks if she's hungry and she says she has the oddest craving for chocolate and bacon. He smiles and tells her he'll bring her some of both from the kitchen. He pulls back and then seems to realize he needs to introduce her. Wrath points at the men around the table, telling her their names and then introducing her. After saying her name, he uses a word she doesn't recognize and then heads for the kitchen.

Beth watches him go and then there's a rush of sound in the room as the men push their chairs back and stand up in a group. Daggers appear in their hands and they start for her, moving with purpose. She panics and backs into a corner. Just as she's about to yell for Wrath, the men drop to one knee in a circle around her, bow their heads to her, and thrust their daggers into the floorboards at her feet. The handles wobble from the force, the blades flashing in the candlelight. Umm, nice to meet you, too, she says lamely. The men look up at the sound of her voice. Their harsh faces are reverent, their eyes shining with adoration.

In the bad part of town, Havers is sensing the coming dawn and worried that he'll lose his resolve when a *lesser* finally starts to track him. Just as the *lesser* is about to attack, Havers stops him by offering information on a great vampire warrior. The *lesser* pauses. Havers points out reasonably that he's small potatoes. If the *lesser* wants to take down a real vampire, he should get reinforcements and go across town. Havers gives the address of Darius's home, where he knows Marissa has been meeting Wrath.

Meanwhile, back in the drawing room, Butch and Marissa are talking when she says that she has to go. Why, he asks. And where? When can I see you again? She says she doesn't know. Can they have lunch? Dinner? What are you doing tomorrow night, he asks. Marissa smiles a little. It feels kind of funny to be pursued. She likes it. She considers the options for places to meet and finds, oddly enough, that seeing the human at Darius's house feels right. She tells Butch that she'll meet him the following night. He then offers to give her a ride home. She says that she'll take herself home. She stands up, and forgetting that he's a human, dematerializes in front of him.

Butch leaps up from the sofa. He looks around. Rushes forward to feel the air where she'd stood. He puts his head in his hands and decides he's losing his mind. At that moment, Wrath and Beth appear in the doorway. Butch wheels around, stuttering. Beth smiles at him and steps forward, taking his hand. Butch, I've got some things to tell you, she says.

As the sun rises, Mr. X opens up the martial arts academy. He's still not where he wants to be with the capturing of vampires. The one he caught last night died too fast. Mr. X signs on to the internet and there's a posting for him. It's from a Mr. C. Mr. X calls the other *lesser,* and when he hangs up the phone, he's grinning. At that moment, Billy Riddle walks into his office. Billy tells him that he's considered his offer and he wants to come on board. Mr. X gets up and puts his arm around the boy. Perfect timing, he says. I could use some help with a new job. Billy asks if they'll go out tonight. Mr. X shakes his head. Tonight, we're going to have to initiate you, son. Then you can go hunting.

That afternoon, Beth wakes up in Wrath's arms to find him staring down at her with a grave face. What's wrong, she asks. He kisses her softly. He tells her he loves her. He wants to be her protector. Her warrior. He wants to be with her for the rest of their lives. She wraps her arms around him and tells him that's exactly what she has in mind. He grins and says that they will have the ceremony as soon as the sun falls. We're getting married, she asks. He nods and tells her he'll have Tohrment's *shellan* Wellsie bring a dress for her. Beth tells him she loves him and they make love.

That night, the brothers assemble at the mansion. Beth meets Wellsie, a gorgeous red head, and likes her immediately. Marissa shows up and Beth is amused at how Hard Ass seems to have a bad case of love at first sight for the delicate blonde. Wrath decides to have the ceremony down in his chamber and the men work to clear the room of furniture. Beth and Wellsie help Fritz get the food ready and Beth marvels at how natural everything feels to her. She feels as though she belongs with these people, even if their ways are a little strange. She's carrying a roast beef out to the dining room table when she sees Fritz pouring a big bag of Morton's salt into a silver dish. She's about to ask him what it's for when Wellsie says it's time to get changed. The men are ready downstairs.

Beth changes into a long white dress and follows Wellsie down the stairs into the earth. When she walks into the chamber, she sees Wrath dressed in a black satin robe and pants. The men are lined up in a row, wearing similar clothes with nasty looking daggers hanging off jeweled belts. Butch and Marissa are also there as is Fritz, the butler. Wrath smiles at her from behind his sunglasses. Tohrment approaches her. We're going to do as much of this in English as we can so you'll understand. She nods. He calls Wrath forward and addresses her. This male asks that you accept him as your *hellren,* Tohrment says. Would you have him as your own if he is worthy? Yes, she says, smiling at Wrath. Tohrment addresses Wrath. This female will consider you're proposal. Will you prove yourself for her? I will, Wrath says. Will you sacrifice yourself for her? I will, Wrath repeats. Will you defend her against those who would hurt her? I will, Wrath repeats. Tohrment steps back, smiling. Wrath takes her into his arms and kisses her. Beth wraps her arms around him and feels as if she's come home.

But then Wrath steps back. He undoes the sash of his robe and takes it off, revealing his bare torso. Wellsie comes up behind Beth and holds her hand. It's going to be okay, Wellsie whispers. Just breathe with me and don't worry. Beth looks around in alarm as Wrath removes his sunglasses and kneels in front of his men. Fritz brings forward a small table with a pitcher and the silver bowl she saw him filling upstairs.

Tohrment stands before Wrath. What is the name of your *shellan*? She is called Elizabeth, Wrath says. Tohrment unsheathes his dagger and bends over Wrath's bare back. Beth gasps and lunges forward but Wellsie holds her in place. You're marrying a warrior, Wellsie whispers. This is how they do things. But it's wrong, Beth exclaims. I don't want him to- Wellsie cuts her off. Let him have his honor in front of his brothers, she says urgently. He's giving his body to you. It's yours now. Beth struggles, repeating that he doesn't need to do this to prove himself to her. But this is who he is, Wellsie says. Do you love him? Yes, Beth says, closing her eyes. Then you have to accept his ways, Wellsie replies.

One by one, Wrath's men step forward and ask him the same question before unsheathing their dagger and bending over his back. When they are finished, Tohrment takes the bowl of salt and pours it into the pitcher. He rinses Wrath's back off and then dries his skin with a pristine white cloth. Tohrment takes the cloth, rolls it up, and puts it into an ornate box. He stands over Wrath. Rise, my lord, he commands. Wrath stands up and Beth sees a pattern on his back, running across his shoulders. Tohrment gives Wrath the box and says, take this to your *shellan* as a symbol of your strength and your bravery, so she will know that you are worthy of her and that your body is now hers to command.

Wrath turns and crosses the room. Beth anxiously scans his face. He seems perfectly fine. In fact, he's positively glowing with love, his pale, blind eyes sparkling. He drops to his knees, bows his head, and holds up the box. Will you take me as your own, he asks. Hands shaking, she accepts the box and is relieved when he stands up and puts his arms around her. She holds onto him tightly as the others break into cheers and applause. Can we not do that again, she whispers. He laughs and says she better brace herself if they have children.

The celebrations last throughout the night and Butch and Marissa spend time talking. As dawn approaches, they are upstairs in the house, looking around. Marissa turns and says she must go. She's grown more relaxed with the human and she thinks he is very attractive. Butch approaches her slowly. He seems terribly serious. All night long she's had the sense that he's working hard to make her feel comfortable. The shift in him intrigues her. What's the matter, she asks. I want to kiss you, he says in a low voice. She senses both his desire and his restraint.

Anxious but not scared, she steps forward and feels his hands land softly on her shoulders. His lips are soft and gentle as they brush against hers. She closes her eyes and leans into him. A sound, something like a growl of satisfaction, rumbles through his chest. He deepens the kiss, his tongue sliding inside her mouth and stroking hers. His hands are warm on her waist, his heart a steady, surging beat against hers, his body stirring wildly but held firmly in check. He pulls back, eyes scanning her face as if he's afraid he's come on too strong. Was that alright, he asks softly. She smiles. It was beautiful, she says. A female couldn't ask for a better first kiss. Butch's eyes flare in surprise. Marissa puts her hands on his face. Let's do it again, she says, drawing him down to her.

Beth and Wrath spending the following day sleeping after their furniture is put back in order. After the sun goes down that evening, Wrath and the brothers talk with Butch who tells them what he knows about the martial arts academy which isn't much. The decision is made that the brothers will go out in a group, in-filtrate the place, and go on the offensive. At Wrath's request, Butch agrees to stay home with Beth and guard her. Wrath tells Beth that he's just going out to take care of some business. He doesn't want to worry her but she's no fool. As the men arm themselves, she tries to keep Wrath home. What can be so important, she de-mands. It's about your father's death, he says. We need to find out who did it. Your father deserves to be avenged. Beth finally lets him go, feeling uneasy.

Out in the suburbs, Mr. X and Billy, who's now known as Mr. R, leave Mr. X's farmhouse. Mr. C doesn't show because he's been killed by another *lesser* in a fight over territory. Their plan is to stake out Darius's house and wait for the legendary warrior vampire who's taken up residence there to return at dawn. Mr. X has brought the net and the darts. He finds it ironic that the house of the warrior he blew up is where he's going. He'd assumed that because the vampire who'd owned it had been killed, no other vampire would stay there because the place is hot. When they arrive, they scope out the mansion. They sense that the warrior vam-pires have left but there appears to be at least one female in there.

Inside, Marissa arrives and she and Butch sit with Beth. Beth feels like a third wheel and begs them to go upstairs. She'll be fine. Butch thinks it over, and after checking the windows and doors and activating the security system, he allows as how he and Marissa will go into the living room across the hall. That's as far as he's willing to compromise. Beth curls up on the couch in the drawing room.

Mr. R trains his binoculars on the house and sees Beth. I'm going to really take that bitch down this time, he says to Mr. X. I want to beat her until she bleeds. Mr. X considers him thoughtfully and suggests a change in plan. How would you like to get her right now, he asks Mr. R.

Beth hears something hit the window. She goes over and looks out. There's no one there. A moment later, an explosion racks the mansion. She's thrown against the wall. As Butch runs into the room, two men come through the hole where the window used to be. One of them calmly shoots Butch. And the other is Billy Riddle.

Wrath and the brothers are battling with *lessers* inside the martial arts academy when he gets a terrible feeling in the center of the chest. He pulls out of the battle as soon as he can and flashes to the mansion. He finds chaos. Butch is down, the security system is going off, Marissa is hysterical, and Beth is gone.

Mr. X and Mr. R arrive at the farmhouse with Beth, having tied her hands and legs together. Mr. X is happy about the unexpected direction things have taken. Given that she's a female, she offers certain new avenues for torture. Besides, the warrior will come after her. She's obviously either his wife or his girlfriend or his sister. So it's a win/win. Two for one. They take her inside.

Because Beth has fed from him, Wrath is able to sense where she is and he materializes in front of the farmhouse. Breaking through the door, he takes both *lessers* on in a ferocious fight. Beth works herself free of her holds, and with a physical strength she's never had before, she attacks Billy Riddle. She slams him down and when Wrath throws a dagger at her, she stabs Billy and he disintegrates. Although Wrath prevails with Mr. X, Wrath is critically wounded. Beth rushes to his side. Using Wrath's phone, she frantically calls Butch's cell phone, hoping someone will answer it.

Marissa picks up. When she hears what's happened to Wrath, Marissa, who's already called upon her brother to help treat Butch's wound, demands that Havers go to Wrath. As her brother refuses to meet her eyes, she has a terrible suspicion that he had something to do with the attack. Filled with rage, she confronts him and demands that he help Wrath. Havers, who's been conflicted all along with his course of action, admits his culpability and flashes out to the farmhouse. It's clear that Wrath is close to death and the only hope is for him to feed. Havers begins to role up his sleeve when Beth pushes him out of the way. Use your wrist, Havers tells her. Wrath eventually takes Beth's blood and stabilizes enough for them to get into a car. They have to drive him because he's unable to project himself. Darius's place is too dangerous to stay in and dawn is coming. They decide to go Havers's house. It takes both of them to carry Wrath down to the laboratory.

After a long day of anxious waiting, Wrath comes around. As Beth holds him and cries, he hates his life as a warrior for the first time. With Beth now being his wife, he doesn't want her exposed to the violence. They hold each other until Havers comes into the lab with Marissa. Havers looks agonized and he admits to Wrath what he did. He volunteers to let Wrath take his revenge in a ritual that will result in Havers's death. Wrath tells him, no. They're even now, for what Wrath did to Marissa all those years.

When the brothers show up at Havers's, Wrath and Beth accept an invitation to go to Tohrment and Wellsie's while Wrath finishes recovering. Wrath is still too weak to dematerialize himself so Beth, Butch and Marissa decide to drive him west. As they get on the highway, Beth smiles at her vampire husband, thinking that she asked for an adventure. And boy did she ever get one.

Epilogue

A month later, at Tohrment and Wellsie's ranch in Colorado, the brothers are in the war room getting ready to go out hunting. Wrath has taken up the role as leader of the brothers and he's accepted his position as the Chief of his race. Vampires have started coming to him, asking him to resolve disputes and bless their children, traditional duties of the Chief that have been missing since the death of Wrath's father. Beth is adjusting to her role as the chief's *uta-shellan*. Butch and Marissa are happy but struggling with the implications of his mortality.

As the brothers ready themselves to go out, Wrath frowns as he sees Beth strap on a dagger. What are you doing, he asks. I'm coming with you, she says. Why, he demands. To fight, she replies. Oh, no, you're not, Wrath counters, because I forbid you from warring. Beth kicks up her chin. Excuse me? You forbid me, she says. As the two of them square off, the brothers quickly file out of the room.

On the other side of the door, the brothers listen to muffled, angry voices. So who do you think's going to win this one, Tohrment asks. The brothers make their wagers. The door opens. Wrath walks out looking fierce, pulling his leather jacket on. A moment later, Beth appears, wearing two guns and a dagger. She's smiling. As the brothers laugh, Wrath puts his arm around Beth and kisses her. None of you look too surprised, he says to his brothers. Yeah, Tohrment replies. We all bet on her.

Together, Wrath and Beth disappear into the night.

Deleted Scenes

Deleted Scenes

The vast majority of things I see in my head get used in the books—which is why the Brotherhood novels are so long! And most of the time, if I do take something out, I use it elsewhere. However, there are some scenes that I have set aside, and I've included some below with commentary.

I trimmed this out of the beginning of Lover Awakened, *due to length issues. I really like the scene and wish I could have taken it further, as it was the beginning of an entire subplot involving the trainees. Reading it again, I'm reminded of how far John has come—at this point in the series, he was just starting to meet all the Brothers and had a lot to learn about his new world.*

Standing in the training center's gym, waiting shoulder-to-shoulder with the other trainees for the next jujitsu position command, John was beat. His brain was blank-slate exhausted, his body aching. He felt like he'd been picked clean and left for dead.

Okay, so that was a little melodramatic. But not by much.

Class had started as usual at four in the afternoon, but they'd had to make up for the time they'd lost the night before. So instead of ending at ten o'clock, it was now two a.m. and they were still being put through their paces.

The other guys looked tired, too, but John was damn aware that no one was as wrung out as him. For some reason, his classmates were handling the training better than he was.

Some reason? Christ, he knew why. Not only did he have to work harder at everything because he was an uncoordinated boob, but after that whole therapist, visit-to-his-past-nightmare, he hadn't been able to sleep, so he'd been groggy and out of it to begin with.

Up front, Tohr was giving the lineup a hard look. Dressed in black nylon sweats and a muscle shirt, the Brother was every inch the drill sergeant, with his military buzz cut and his blade-sharp blue eyes. John tried to stand up straighter, but his spine refused to crank to attention. He was utterly out of gas.

"That's it for today," Tohr barked. As the trainees sagged, he frowned. "Any injuries I don't know about?" When no one spoke up, the Brother glanced at the clock that was mounted in a steel cage on the concrete wall. "Remember we start at noon tomorrow and run until eight p.m. instead of our usual time. Hit the showers. Bus will be ready in fifteen. John, can I have a minute?"

As everyone else dragged their sorry asses across the blue mats toward the locker room, John stayed behind. And said a little prayer.

The bus rides to and from the training center were hell. On a good day, none of the other trainees talked to him. On a bad day . . . he wished for the silent treatment. So even though it made him a coward, he was kind of hoping Tohr would tell him he could stay and work in the office or something.

Tohr waited until the steel door clanged shut before he transformed from drill sergeant into father. Putting a hand on John's shoulder, he said softly, "How we doing, son?"

John nodded briskly even though his dishrag state pretty much said it all.

"Listen, the Brotherhood was late getting out tonight, so I need to leave right now to do patrols. But I was talking to Butch earlier. He said if you wanted to hang with him for a while, that'd be cool. You can shower at the Pit if you want, and he could take you home later."

John's eyes popped. Hanging with Butch? Who was, like, totally the shit? Man . . . talk about prayers answered. The guy had come in just two days before, taught this rip-cool class on forensics, and had every one of the trainees decide they wanted to be a homicide cop like him.

Hanging with him . . . plus not having to deal with the Hades Express to get back home?

Tohr smiled. "So I take it this is a *yeah*, right?"

John nodded. And kept nodding.

"You know how to get there?"

Same code? John signed.

"Yup." Tohr squeezed his shoulder, the big palm transmitting all kinds of warmth and support. "Take care, son."

John took off for the locker room and for once didn't hesitate as he stepped inside the hot, humid maze of metal lockers and social hierarchy. As usual, he made no eye contact with anyone on the way to number nineteen.

Funny, both his locker and he were in the back and on the bottom.

When he grabbed his duffel and slung it over his shoulder, Blaylock, the red-head, who was one of only two who didn't ride him with insults, frowned.

"Aren't you changing for the van?" the guy asked while he rubbed his hair with a towel.

John couldn't help smiling as he shook his head and turned away.

Which, of course, meant Lash had to step into his path.

"Looks like he's going to go chase after the Brotherhood." The blond guy made elaborate work out of strapping on a huge diamond watch that was "from Jacob and Co., you know." "Bet he's gonna polish daggers for them. What are you going to use on their blades, John?"

The urge to flip him off was so strong, John actually lifted his hand, but Christ, he didn't want to dick-toss with the asshole. Not when he was Pit-bound and bus-free. Turning away, he took the long way out of the locker room, going down another whole aisle of benches and lockers to avoid the conflict.

"Have fun, Johnny," Lash shouted. "Oh, and hit the equipment room on your way out. For those knee pads."

As laughter echoed, John pushed open the door and went down to Tohr's office . . . thinking he would give anything for Lash to know what it was like to get picked on.

Or maybe pounded into submission.

Going through the back of Tohr's supply closet and coming out the other side in the underground tunnel was like walking into sunshine: a singing relief. Sure, there were only ten hours of freedom in front of him, but that was a lifetime under the right circumstances.

And being around Butch was definitely the break he needed.

John walked quickly toward the main house, and he paused when he got to the stairs that led up to the foyer. Tohr had said it was another hundred and fifty yards farther down to the Pit . . . so he kept going. When he found another set of stairs, he was relieved. The tunnel was dry and dimly lit, but he didn't like being in it alone.

Sticking his face into the registry field of a video cam, he hit the summons button and resisted the urge to wave like an idiot.

"Hey, man." Butch's voice was clear as a bell as it came through the intercom. "Glad you made it."

The lock was sprung and John took the stairs fast. Butch was standing in the doorway at the top in a black-and-gold smoking jacket.

The guy had the best clothes John had ever seen. He'd taught class in a pin-striped suit that looked like something out of a magazine.

"You can use my bathroom to shower in, because my roommate, who's off rotation tonight, is micromanaging that goatee of his."

"Whatever, cop," a deep male voice called out.

"You know it's true. You so suffer from OBD—" Butch glanced over. "That would be Obsessive Beard Disorder. Hey, listen, J-man, I was going to head into town, you cool with that?"

John so loved it when Butch called him J-man. And he really loved to be asked to go anywhere with a guy like him.

As he nodded, Butch smiled. "Good deal. I'm getting another tat. You have any?"

John shook his head.

"Maybe you'll get one."

A tattoo. With Butch? Man, this night was looking up.

While John nodded, Butch smiled and glanced around. "You ever been in our place, John?"

When John shook his head, the cop gave him a quick tour, and it was clear the Pit was Guy Central. There wasn't a lot of furniture, but there were plenty of gym bags, and a legion of Scotch and vodka bottles. The foosball table was righteous sweet. So was the massive high-def TV and the incredible bank of computers in the living room. The place also smelled great, all smoke and leather and aftershave.

Butch led the way down a hall. "V's in that bedroom."

John glanced through the doorway and saw a huge bed with black sheets and no headboard. Weapons and thick books were all over the place, kind of like a library had been taken over by a squadron of Marines.

"And I'm in here."

John walked into a smaller bedroom . . . that was choked with men's clothes. Suits and shirts were hanging from racks with rollers on them. Ties and shoes were everywhere, and there were easily fifty pairs of cuff links on top of the bureau. It was like the inside of a department store. A very, very expensive department store.

"Bathroom's all yours. Clean towel's on the back of the toilet." Butch took a squat crystal glass of Scotch off the bedside table and put it to his lips. "And you should also think about that tat. Place where I go's top-notch. They'll ink you right."

"You trying to corrupt a youth there, cop?"

John looked to the doorway. A huge man with a goatee and tattoos on his face stood in the threshold. He had on a set of leathers and a black T-shirt and a glove on one hand, and his eyes were the diamond white of a husky's, the rims around the irises superblue.

Staring at him, one word came to John's mind: Einstein. The guy just oozed IQ—it was the eyes, those penetrating, icy eyes.

"This is my roommate, Vishous. V, meet John."

"What's doing? I've heard a lot about you." The guy offered his palm and John shook it.

"And as for the tat," Butch said, "he's of age. Right? Twenty-something."

"He should wait." V turned to John and started signing. Perfectly. *If you get one done before your transition by a human, it's going to distort when you go through the change. Then it's going to fade in a month or two. If you wait, though, I'll ink whatever you want into you, and I'll do it so it stays.*

John could only blink. Then he dropped his duffel and signed, *Wow. Are you deaf?*

Nope. Heard from my man Tohr this is how you communicate, so I taught it to myself the other night. Figured we'd run into each other sooner or later.

As if learning an entire language took no notable effort.

"Hey, I'm feeling left out over here."

"Just giving the man a little advice."

John whistled to get V's attention. *Will you ask Butch what he's going to get for a tattoo?*

"Good question. Cop, what're you getting done tonight, man? Tweety Bird on your ass?"

"I'm adding to an old one." Butch went over and threw open the closet doors, taking off the robe so he was just in his black boxer-briefs. "What to wear . . ."

John tried not to stare and failed. The cop was built. Big shoulders. Thick, fan-shaped muscles flaring out from his spine. Arms that were cut. He wasn't as immense as a vampire like Tohr, but he was easily one of the bigger human men John had ever seen.

And all across the small of his back was a tattoo. Done in black ink, the geometric pattern took up a lot of space. It was a series of lines—no, it was a numerical thing. Groupings of four lines with a diagonal slash. Five of them and one lone line. Twenty-six.

V pointed to John's duffel. "Hey, man, your bag's leaking. You got shampoo or some shit in there?"

John shook his head and then frowned when he saw the stain in one corner. He went over and pulled back the zipper. There was something on his clothes, something white, opaque . . .

"What the hell is that?" V said.

Oh, God . . . had someone . . . ?

Butch nudged John out of the way, put his hand right in there, then lifted his fingers to his nose.

"Conditioner. Hair conditioner."

"Better than what I thought it was," V muttered.

Butch's hazel eyes lifted upward. "This yours, J-man?" When John shook his head, the cop asked, "You got problems at school you ain't talking about?"

The man's face was dark, as if he were prepared to go hunt down whoever was screwing with John and his stuff and pound them into the ground like a tent pole. And for a moment, John entertained a happy little picture of Butch popping Lash a good one and then stuffing the guy into a locker.

But he wasn't about to have his problems solved by someone else.

As he shook his head, Butch's eyes narrowed and he looked at V. Who nodded once.

Then Butch went all smiles, fronting real casual-like. "I'll call Fritz and he'll clean your clothes. And don't worry, we'll find you something to wear tonight. No problem."

John looked at V, not falling for the no-big-deal on the cop's face. *Tell him it's nothing. Tell him I can handle it.*

V just smiled. "Butch already knows that, don't you, cop?"

"That it's no big deal and he'll take care of it? Yeah, I know, J-man."

I thought you didn't understand sign language?

Butch shook his head. "Sorry, don't read hands yet. But I know from assholes, son. Like I said, you don't worry about a thing."

The man kept grinning, his expression entirely pleasant. As if he were going to enjoy getting to the bottom of the problem.

John looked at V for help. Except the vampire just crossed his arms over his chest and nodded again at Butch. Totally onboard with the plan.

Whatever plan it might be.

Oh, crap.

The following scene is not really a deleted one, but something I edited a lot in the revisions of Lover Awakened, *mostly because I didn't like the vibe. (The scene in the book starts on p. 344.) Bottom line, I thought this came across as too rough for Z and Bella's good-bye, but now I wish I'd gone with what I saw in my head. I think the scene in the printed book was good, but this is better:*

Bella packed up her things in less than two minutes. She didn't have much to begin with, and what little she did have she'd moved from Z's room the night before. Fritz would be coming for her things soon and would drive them to Havers and Marissa's. Then in another hour she would dematerialize to their house and Rehvenge would meet her there. With a guard.

Stepping into the dim bathroom, she turned on the lights over the sink and double-checked the counter to make sure she had everything. Before she stepped away, she looked at herself in the mirror.

God, she'd aged.

Under the pool of illumination, she lifted her hair off her neck and turned this way and that, trying to find some way to see her true self. When she gave up after God only knew how long, she let the weight fall and—

Zsadist appeared behind her in the shadows, taking shape from thin air, darkening the darkness with his black clothes and his weapons and his mood.

Or maybe he'd been there all along and only now chose to reveal himself.

She stumbled back, banging into one of the marble walls with her hip. As she cursed and rubbed the sore spot, she refiled through her vocabulary for all the ways to tell him to go to hell.

And then she smelled him. His bonding scent was strong.

Z stayed silent, but it wasn't like he needed to say much. She could feel his eyes. Could see the golden glow out of the corner he was in.

She knew exactly why he was staring at her. And couldn't believe it.

Bella backed even farther away, until she hit the shower door. "What do you want?"

Wrong words, she thought, as he stepped into the light.

As she saw his body, her mouth went lax.

"I want to mate," he said in a low voice. And he was more than ready.

"You think . . . Christ, you think I'd lay with you now? You're deranged."

"No, I'm psychotic. At least, that's the clinical diagnosis." As he took off his dagger holster, the door shut behind him and the lock turned. Because he willed them to do so.

"You're going to have to force me."

"No, I won't." His hands went to the gun belt at his hips.

Bella stared at what was straining against his leathers. And wanted it.

God, she wished he would hold her down and not give her a choice. That way, she could be absolved of what she was about to do and hate him more deeply. She could . . .

Z came forward until he was right in front of her. In the straining silence between them, his chest lifted and compressed. "I'm sorry I'm a bastard. And I wouldn't be pushing you at Phury if I didn't think it was the right thing for both of you."

"Are you apologizing just because you want to be with me right now?"

"Yes. But it's true anyway."

"So if you weren't hard at the moment, you'd just let me go?"

"Think of this as good-bye, Bella. The last time."

She closed her eyes and felt the heat coming off him. And when he put his hands on her, she didn't jump. As his palms locked on her throat and tilted her head back, her mouth opened because it had to.

Or at least, that was what she told herself.

Z's tongue pushed inside of her as his hips came up against her lower belly. As they kissed there was a ripping sound—her shirt as he tore it in half.

"Zsadist," she said hoarsely when he went for the button on her jeans. "Stop."

"No."

His mouth dropped down to her breast and her pants hit the floor and then he lifted her up and carried her over to the counter. He was purring loudly now as he forced her knees apart with his head and knelt before her, his eyes fixated on her sex.

So he knew exactly how turned-on she was.

Bella put her hands between him and where he was going.

"Zsadist, if you do this, I will never forgive you."

"I can live with that." He moved her arms away easily, trapping her wrists. "If it means I can be with you this last time."

"Why the hell do you care so much?"

He pulled her hands forward, flipping them around so they faced upward. When he stared downward, he shook his head. "Phury didn't feed from you, did he. No marks on your neck. Your wrists."

"There's still time."

"He said you couldn't bear it."

Great, that was the last thing she needed Zsadist to know.

"And this is my punishment?" she said bitterly. "You're going to force me—"

Z dove down to her, his mouth going straight to her core. With all his demand, she expected him to eat at her, but instead the soft strokes of his lips were so loving they brought tears to her eyes. As he released her hands, her cheeks went wet, and she held on to his head, bringing him closer still.

His eyes stared up at her while she climaxed against his tongue, watching her as if storing precious memories.

"Let me take you to the bed."

She nodded as he came up her body and buried his glossy lips in her neck. The scrape of his fangs gave her a momentary flash of hope. Maybe he would finally feed—

But then he picked her up and willed the door open . . . and the passion left her. She was leaving. And he wasn't going to stop her.

Wasn't going to take her vein now, either.

He sensed the change in her immediately. "Where have you gone?"

"Nowhere," she whispered as he laid her down on the bed. "I'm going nowhere."

Z paused, looming over her, perched on the precipice. But then he worked his fly, springing loose that huge arousal. As he got up on her, his pants around his thighs, she turned her face to the side.

His hands stroked her hair back. "Bella?"

"Do it and then let me go." She opened her legs wider to accommodate him, and as his erection hit her core, he groaned, his weight shifting in a jerk. When he didn't penetrate her, she closed her eyes.

"Bella . . ."

"I'd reach down and put you inside, but we both know you can't stand to have me touch you. Or do you want me on all fours? More anonymous that way. You'd barely know what you were fucking."

"Don't talk like that."

"Why not? Hell, you're not even naked. Which makes me wonder why this needs to happen at all. Now that you know how to take care of yourself, you don't have to have a female." Her voice cracked. "You most certainly don't need me."

There was a long silence.

She heard a hissing sound. And then he bit her.

Zsadist sank his fangs in deep and shivered at the first rush of Bella's blood. The richness, the thick, heavenly texture pooled in his mouth, and when he swallowed, it coated the back of his throat.

He couldn't stop.

When he'd decided to take her vein, he'd told himself he was allowed only one single, great pull, but once he started he couldn't break the connection. Instead, he gathered her in his arms and rolled her to the side so he could curl himself around her better.

Bella cradled him close, and he was sure she was crying again as she held him, because her breathing was raw.

Stroking her naked back, he tucked her hips into his, wanting to comfort her as he took from her, and she seemed to ease. Even as he didn't. His dick was screaming, the tip about to blow off.

"Take me," she moaned, "Please."

Yes, he thought. Yes!

Except, oh God, he couldn't stop the drinking long enough to get inside her: The strength pouring into him was too addictive and the response of his body was too incredible. As he fed, he felt his muscles knitting together, forming a steel weave over the hardening cage of his bones. His cells were absorbing the essential nutrients he had deprived them of for a century and putting them to immediate use.

Afraid he was going to take too much and kill her, Z eventually forced himself to release Bella's throat, but she just grabbed onto the back of his head and pushed him down. He fought his impulse for a moment, but then growled, the sound loud and low as a mastiff's. With a rough lift and twist, he repositioned her and nailed her on the other side of the neck, biting hard. Now he was crawling over her, trapping her underneath him, the bonding scent pouring out of him in waves. He was the carnivore standing over its prey while it fed, his arms flared and bent while he held himself up, his thighs spread over her lower body.

When he was finished he tilted his head back, took a deep breath, and roared loud enough to rattle the windows, his body twitching with the kind of power he'd known long ago, and only from the vile, forced feedings of the Mistress.

Zsadist looked down. Bella was bleeding from the two wounds he'd given her, but her eyes were shining and the unmistakable scent of the female sex rose from her. He licked up both sides of her throat and kissed her, pushing into her mouth, taking, dominating what was his . . . marking her now not just with his scent but his will.

He was drunk on her, greedy and needy. He was the dark, raw hole that had to be filled. He was the dry pit; she was the water.

Z reared up and whipped off his shirt. Looking down at his nipples, he looped his pinkies into the piercings and pulled at them.

"Suck on me," he said. "Like you did before. Now."

Bella sat up, splaying her hands over his belly as he let himself fall back on the bed. When he was stretched out, she crawled onto his chest, putting her mouth just where he wanted it. As she took one of the hoops in, he roared again, not giving a shit who else in the house might hear him.

He planned on being as loud as he wanted. Fuck it, he planned on yelling the damn door down.

As she sucked, he shrugged out of his leathers and reached down, taking himself in his hand and stroking. He wanted her mouth there, but as wild as he was, he wouldn't force her.

But she knew what he wanted. Her hand took the place of his on his dick, and she fell into a rhythm that nearly killed him. She slid up and down on his shaft, slipping back and forth over his head, all the while licking and tugging at his nipple. She was in total control, playing him hard, and he loved it, loved the suffocation, the sweat, the agony of wanting to come while never wanting her to stop.

"Oh, yeah, *nalla*. . . ." He dug into her hair, panting. "Work me out."

And then she moved down his chest and onto his belly. In anticipation, he bit his lower lip so hard he tasted his own blood.

"Is this okay with you?" she asked.

"If you don't mind—" She covered him with her lips. "*Bella.*"

Her mouth was glorious. Wet and warm. But he wasn't going to last more than thirty seconds like this. He sat up and tried to get her head out of his lap, but she fought him.

"I'm going to come . . ." he moaned. "Oh, God . . . Bella, stop, I'm going to . . ."

She didn't. And he . . .

The first convulsion snapped him in half so hard he fell back on the mattress. The second lifted his hips up, pushing him farther into her mouth. And the third took him to heaven.

As soon as he could pull his shit together, he reached for her, bringing her mouth to his. He tasted his bonding scent on her lips and tongue and liked it there.

Relished it there.

He rolled her over. "Now it's your turn. Again."

"Are you okay?" Zsadist said some time later.

Bella opened her eyes. Z was lying next to her, his head on his curled arm.

God, her neck was sore, and so was the inside of her. But the hedonistic glory he'd let loose was worth the creaks and groans. Zsadist had loved her hard, just as she'd always wanted him to.

"Bella?"

"Yes. Yes, I am."

"You said you didn't want to be avenged. You still mean that?"

She covered her breasts with her hands, wishing real life had stayed away a little longer. "I can't bear the idea of you going out and getting hurt because of me."

When he didn't say anything, she reached out and touched his hand.

"Zsadist? What are you thinking?" The silence went on and on until she couldn't stand it any longer. "Talk to m—"

"I love you."

"What . . . ?" she breathed.

"You heard me. And I'm not going to say it again." He stood up, grabbed his leathers, and pulled them on. Then he went into the bathroom. He came back a moment later fully armed with his daggers on his chest and his gun belt fastened around his hips.

"So here's the damage, Bella. I can't stop hunting that *lesser* who did those things to you. Or the bastards he works with. Can't. So even if I were picture-perfect like Phury, even if I could pull his smooth moves with the polite shit, even if I wouldn't make your family cringe, I can't be with you."

"But if you—"

"I've got war in my blood, *nalla*, so even if I hadn't gotten all fucked-up in the past, I would still need to be in the field fighting. I stay with you, you're going to want me to be different than I am, and I can't turn into the kind of *hellren* you're going to need. Eventually my nature would blow up in both our faces."

She rubbed her eyes. "If I follow that logic, why do you think I can be with Phury, then?"

"Because my twin is wearing out. He's getting tired. I'm part of the reason, but I think it would have happened anyway. He likes teaching those recruits. I could see him training full-time, and we're going to need that. That would be a good life for you."

Bella dropped her hands in anger and glared at him. "I really need you to shut up about what you think would be best for me. I'm totally uninterested in your theories about my future."

"Fair enough."

She stared up at him, focusing on the scar that ruined his face.

No, not ruined, she thought. He would always be beautiful to her. A beautiful horror of a male . . .

Getting over him was going to be as hard as getting past her captivity.

"There's never going to be anyone else like you," she murmured. "For me . . . you will always be the one."

And that was her good-bye to him, she realized.

Z came to her, and knelt by the side of the bed, keeping his yellow, glowing eyes downcast. After a moment he took her hand, and she heard a metallic sound . . . then he pressed one of his daggers into her palm. The thing was so heavy she almost needed two hands to hold it. She looked at the black blade, the metal reflecting light like a pool at night.

"Mark me." He pointed to his pectoral, right above the star-shaped scar of the Black Dagger Brotherhood. "Here."

With a quick lean, he reached to the bedside table for the little dish of salt that had come with her food. "And make it permanent."

Bella hesitated for only a second. Yes, she thought . . . she wanted to leave something that endured on him, some small thing that would serve to remind him of her for as long as he breathed.

She shifted around and braced her free palm on his opposite shoulder. The dagger grew lighter in her hand as she took the vicious point of the weapon to his skin. He twitched as she dug into him and blood welled, trickling down onto his ribbed stomach.

When she was finished, she put the knife aside, licked her palm, and sprinkled salt onto it. Then she pressed her open hand to the cuts she'd made over his heart.

Their eyes held as the B she'd made in the Old Language fused permanently into him.

This scene was taken out of the Butch/Marissa material that was moved from Lover Eternal to Lover Revealed. My reasoning was because of my usual length and pacing concerns—I thought this early visit to his family that I saw in my head was just too much. There was already a lot going on in Butch's book, and leaving this in (and going further with it) was a distraction that was largely unnecessary, given the way the O'Neal dynamic gets tied up at the end of the story.

That being said, it's so cool to read. Remember, this was written back at the beginning of Rhage's story, when Butch is still getting acclimated to the Brotherhood's world—and its restrictions:

Butch caught the remote as it came flying at him without moving from his prone position on the couch. His body was sublimely comfortable: Head on the padded armrest. Legs stretched out. Red Sox throw blanket tucked around his feet. As it was around seven a.m. the shutters were down, so the Pit was dark as midnight.

"You turning in?" he asked as V stood up. "Right in the middle of *Shaun of the Dead*? How can you stand the suspense?"

Vishous arched his back as he stretched his heavy arms. "You know, you sleep less than I do."

"That's because you snore and I can hear it through the wall."

V's eyes narrowed. "Talking about noise, you've been quiet the last couple of days. You want to tell me what's doing?"

Butch picked his glass of Scotch up from the floor, balanced it on his stomach, and reached for the bottle of Lagavulin that was on the coffee table. As he poured himself some more hooch, he watched the brown rush flicker in the blue-gray glow of the TV.

Damn, he was really throwing back the stuff lately.

"Talk, cop."

"My old life came calling."

Vishous scrubbed his hair until it stood up on its ends. "How so?"

"My sister v-mailed me yesterday on my old phone. Her new baby's getting baptized. Whole family's going to be there."

"You want to go?"

Butch tilted up his head and took a long drink. The Scotch should have burned its way to his stomach. Instead it just eased on down the well-trodden path.

"Maybe."

Although he had no idea how to explain what had happened to him.

Yeah, see, I got fired from Homicide. And then I met these vampires. And now I kind of live with them. I'm also in love with one of their kind, but that's sort of dead in the water. Am I happy? Well, it's the first vacation I've ever had in my life, I'll tell you that much. Plus the clothes are better.

"V, man, why me? Why you boys letting me hang in here?"

V leaned forward and took a hand-rolled off the little stack he'd made next to his couch. His gold lighter made a hiss before it spit flame.

The Brother stared straight ahead as he exhaled, his profile getting obscured by the smoke.

Which was the same color as the TV, Butch thought randomly. Blue-gray.

"You want to leave us, cop?"

Well, wasn't that a good goddamned question. The call from his sister had reminded him this couldn't last; this odd interlude with the Brotherhood couldn't be his whole life.

But where did that leave him? And them? He knew all about the Brothers. Where they lived, what the rhythms of their nights and days were. Who their women were, if they had one.

The very fact they existed.

"Didn't answer my question, V. Why'm I here?"

"You're supposed to be with us."

"According to who?"

V shrugged and took another drag. "According to me."

"That's what Rhage said. You going to tell me the why of it?"

"You're in my dreams, cop. That's all I'm going to tell you."

Okay, that was hardly reassuring. He'd heard the moaning sound track to whatever V conjured up when he was asleep. Not exactly the kind of thing that made a guy optimistic about his future.

Butch took another deep one from his glass. "And if I want to leave? What happens then? I mean, my memories are long-term by now, so you can't scrub me. Right?"

The flicker of the TV played over the hard lines of Vishous's face.

"You want to look at me, V?" When that profile didn't turn, Butch cupped his glass and sat up. "Tell me something, if I leave, which one of you is supposed to kill me?"

V put his fingers on the bridge of his nose. Closed his eyes. "Damn it, Butch."

"You, right? You'll do it." Butch drained his glass. Stared into the bottom of it. Refocused on his roommate. "You know, it would help if you'd look at me."

V's ice white eyes flashed across the way. And they glowed with regret.

"It would really kill you, wouldn't it?" Butch murmured. "Putting me in the ground."

"It would absolutely kill me." Vishous cleared his throat. "You're my friend."

"So what's it going to cost me?"

V frowned. "Cost you?"

"To go to my sister's kid's baptism." Butch cracked a smile. "A foot? No, an arm. An arm and a leg?"

Vishous shook his head. "Shit, cop. That isn't funny."

"Ah, come on. It's a little funny."

V laughed in a burst. "You're sick, you know that?"

"Yeah, I do." Butch put his glass back down on the floor. "Look, V, I'm not going anywhere. Not in a disappearing way. Not right now. I've got nothing out there waiting for me, and I never fit in all that well anyhow. I am going to go up to Boston at the crack of dawn Sunday morning, however. I'll be back Sunday night. You got a problem with that, well, tough."

V blew out some more smoke. "I would miss you."

"Don't be a sap. I'll be away twelve hours." When V looked down, Butch grew serious. "Unless . . . we have a problem?"

After a long while V walked over to where all his computer shit was. Picked something off the desk.

Butch caught what was thrown at him.

Keys. To the Escalade.

"Drive safe, cop." V smiled a little. "Don't say hi to the family for me."

Butch laughed. "That's not going to be a problem."

Now it was V's turn to get good and grim. "If you're not back by Sunday night, I'm coming after you. And not to bring you back, true?"

Butch realized in the silence that followed that this was a fish or cut bait moment. He was in the Brotherhood's world for good. Or he was fertilizer.

He nodded once. "I'll be back. Don't you worry about that."

This was taken out of Lover Enshrined. *Originally it was where Phury and Cormia see each other when he comes back from his rescue efforts during the sack of Havers's clinic. What it grew into, however, was their walk down the hall of statues and then his shower and her feeding from him . . . all of which went further than the below in terms of developing their relationship. This is the problem with what I see in my head: I saw the below play out . . . but I also saw all of the scenes that are in the book as well. Fitting everything that happens in together and deciding what's more material to the story to protect pacing is always a judgment call.*

hury left Fritz to keep tidying up Wrath's study. It was just as well the king wasn't there. The head of the Brotherhood should get a report on what went down from a Brother.

As he came up to his room, Cormia was standing in the hallway, hand at her throat, looking as if she were waiting for him. Or maybe he just hoped that was the case.

"Your grace," she said with a bow.

He was too tired to correct her on her formality. "Hey."

As he went into his room he left the door open, because he never wanted her to feel as if she couldn't talk to him, no matter how exhausted he was. He figured if she had something to say she'd follow him, and if she didn't she'd go on to her room.

He went around and sat down on his bed, reaching for his gold lighter and a blunt before his weight had settled on his ass. He lit up, thinking that after a night like tonight there was no way in hell he was going to cut back on the red smoke. This was exactly why he needed the stuff.

As that first draw went down into his lungs, Cormia appeared in his doorway. "Your grace?"

He looked down at the blunt, focusing on the glowing orange tip. It was better, safer, to keep his eyes off her slim body in that long flowing robe. "Yes?"

"Bella is well. Jane says so. I thought you'd want to know."

Now Phury glanced over his shoulder at her. "Thank you."

"I prayed for her."

He exhaled. "You did?"

"It was right and proper to do so. She is . . . lovely."

"You're a very kind person, Cormia." He went back to staring at the hand-rolled, thinking that he was raw tonight. Absolutely wild on the inside, and the inhaling wasn't helping much. "Very kind."

When his stomach growled, she murmured, "May I make you something to eat, your grace?"

Even though his stomach rumbled again, as if it were thrilled with the prospect, he said, "I'm okay, but thank you."

"As you wish. Sleep well."

"You, too." Just as the door was shutting, he called out, "Cormia?"

"Yes?"

"Thank you again. For praying for Bella."

She made some kind of noncommittal noise, and the door clicked into place.

Even though he needed a shower, he slid his legs up onto the mattress and leaned back into the pillows. As he smoked, he was relieved as his shoulders gradually loosened and his thigh muscles relaxed and his hands released from the claws they'd turned into.

Closing his eyes, he let himself drift along, and images played on the backs of his lids, quickly at first, slowing as they continued. He saw the bodies in the clinic and the fight that happened and the rapid evac. Then he was back here looking for Wrath—

A picture of Cormia bending down over the roses barged into his brain.

With a curse he rolled up another chub, lit it, and settled back against the pillows.

Man, she had been so beautiful in that reflected light on the terrace.

And he thought of her standing in the hallway just now, her robing wrapped around her such that it formed a V between her breasts.

In a hot flash of insanity, he fantasized that instead of letting her walk out of his room, he'd taken her hand and drawn her farther inside. He pictured himself tugging her gently over to his bed and laying her down where he was now. Her hair would be all over the pillowcases in gold strands, and her mouth would be parted just as it had been in the movie theater when he'd approached her.

Of course, he'd have to take a shower first. Naturally. There was no way he'd expect her to put up with a male who'd not only been humping boxes of bandages for a couple of hours, but had also been in a fistfight with a *lesser*.

Yada, yada, yada . . . fast-forward through him scrubbing down under the hot water.

He'd come back in his own white robe and he'd sit on the bed next to her. In order to calm her—well, to calm them both—he'd start by stroking her face and her neck and her hair. And when she tilted her head back to give him access, he'd put his lips to hers. At this point his hands would work down the robe's two halves until he got to the sash. He would loosen that slowly, so slowly she wouldn't be shy about the fact that he was about to see her breasts and her stomach and her . . . everything.

He went everywhere with his mouth.

That was what happened in the fantasy. Everywhere. His lips, his tongue . . . every inch of her got attention.

The images were so off the chain that Phury's hand had to find the ache between his own thighs. He meant to just rearrange himself in his pants, but once he made contact it wasn't about relocation . . . it was the only thing that had felt even remotely good in so long.

Before he knew what he was doing, he put the blunt between his lips, unzipped, and let himself wrap a palm around his cock.

The rules of his self-imposed celibacy had held that doing this kind of pump action was a no-no. After all, it seemed pointless to deny himself sex and yet open the door to masturbation. And the only time in his life he'd worked himself out had been during Bella's needing and that was about biological necessity, not enjoyment—he'd had to either relieve himself or go insane, and those orgasms had been as hollow as the empty bathroom he'd had them in.

This didn't feel hollow.

He pictured himself going where he wanted to be most . . . between Cormia's legs with his head . . . and his body went crazy, his skin heating until you could have put a pot on his abs and boiled water. And shit got volcanic as he imagined his tongue finding its way through her core to the sweet, welling center of her.

Oh, God . . . he was stroking himself. There was no denying it. And he wasn't going to stop.

Phury took the blunt from his lips, flicked it into an ashtray, and moaned, his head falling back as he parted his legs. He did not want to think of what he shouldn't do. He just needed one slice of ease and happiness, one small piece of joy . . . just this moment when he was warm. He'd watched his brothers find love and settle down in strong matings, and he'd wished them well from the sidelines—while knowing all along that would not be his future. And that had been okay for a long time. Now, though, it didn't feel okay anymore.

He . . . wanted things. For himself.

Anxiety started to bleed into his pleasure, like an ink stain on pale cloth.

He stopped the spoil by focusing on Cormia in his head. He saw himself treating her with both gentleness and power, handling her body. . . .

"Oh, yeah . . ." he groaned into the still air of his bedroom.

This moment he would steal for himself, and he told his guilty conscience he deserved it for all the hard work he'd done.

He was alone. No one would ever know.

Cormia carefully balanced the glass of milk and the plate of stacked bread and meats while she lifted a hand to knock on the Primale's door. She wished she'd put the "sandwich" together better. Fritz had shown her what to do, and undoubtedly his would have looked less disheveled, but she'd wanted to move quickly, and she'd wanted to make it herself.

Just before her knuckles made contact with the wood, she heard a moan, as if someone were hurt. And then another.

Concerned for the Primale's well-being, she went for the knob and pushed her way into his room—

Cormia dropped the sandwich plate. As the thing bounced on the floor, she stared across at the bed while the door shut by itself.

Phury was leaning back against the pillows, his spectacular, multicolored hair streaming out around his head. His black button-down shirt was pushed up to just below his rib cage, and his pants were undone and shoved down to the tops of his golden thighs. One hand was on his manhood, and his sex was thick and glossy at the broad tip. As he stroked the length hard and strong, his other hand was down below on the potent sac underneath.

Another moan broke through his open, rosy mouth; then he bit down on his lower lip, his fangs punching into the puffy flesh.

His hand started moving fast and his breath came even harder and he seemed to be on the verge of something tremendous. It was beyond wrong to watch, but she couldn't have left to save herself. . . .

His nose flared, the nostrils opening wide as if he were catching a scent. With a growl he convulsed, his stomach muscles tightening up in a rush, thighs striating. As pearly white jets came out of him, his brilliant yellow eyes flipped open and focused on her. The sight of her seemed to hurt him even more as he barked out a curse and his hips thrust upward. More of the satin cream came out of him, and it seemed he would never stop, his neck straining, his cheeks red and flushed.

Except he wasn't in true pain, was he, she thought. His eyes held on to her as if she were the fuel of it all and he didn't want what was happening to him to end.

This was the culmination of the sexual act.

Her body told her so. Because every time the Primale surged, every time he groaned, every time his palm licked over the tip of his sex and shot down to the base, her breasts lit up and what was between her legs wept even more.

And then he was still. Spent. Satiated.

In the silence she felt the wetness on the insides of her thighs and looked at what was all over his stomach and hand and arousal.

What a glorious mess sex was, she thought, imagining what it would be like to have what was on him in her.

As her mind churned, she realized the Primale was staring at her in fuzzy confusion, as if he weren't sure whether he'd dreamed her up or she was really in his room.

She walked forward, because with what had just happened, and the way the room was saturated with his dark scent, his outstretched body was the only destination she was interested in.

His eyes changed as she got closer, as if it were dawning on him that she was actually with him. Shock replaced his dreamy satisfaction.

She put the glass of milk down next to his ashtray, looked at his stomach, and her hand went forward without conscious thought.

He hissed, then sucked in a breath as she made contact. What was on him was warm.

"This is not blood," she murmured.

His head shook back and forth on the pillow, his expression one of amazement, as if he were surprised by her boldness.

She lifted her finger up, recognizing that what had come out of him was the source of the dark spices in the air—and she wanted whatever it was. Glossing her lower lip, she then ran her tongue over what she'd put on herself.

"Cormia . . ." he groaned.

The sound of her name wrapped the room in a private, heated insulation that was tangible, and in the suspended, protected moment, it was just him and her together. There was nothing but their bodies, a stunning simplicity in the complex structure of the way they'd met and come to be mated.

"Let's leave our roles behind," she said. "And our entanglements."

His face tightened. "We can't."

"Yes, we can."

"Cormia . . ."

She dropped her robe, and that pretty much ended the conversation.

But as she got up on the bed, he shook his head and stopped her. "I've been to see the Directrix."

As her name leaving his lips had created a special place, his words now sliced through the warmth and heady promise in the room.

"You set me aside, didn't you."

He nodded slowly. "I wanted to tell you, but then everything went down at the clinic."

Cormia looked at his gleaming sex and had the strangest response. Instead of failure she felt . . . relief. Because he desired her even though he didn't have to. Because it made what she wanted to happen so much more honest. Later she would dwell on the emotional ramifications, but now she just wanted to be with him. Female to male. Sex to sex. No traditions weighing on the act or giving it any larger implications.

She put one knee up on the mattress, and Phury grabbed hold of her wrists, stopping her. "Don't you know what this means?"

"Yes." She put her other knee up. "Let me go."

"You don't have to do this."

She stared boldly at the straining length at his hips as it lay thick as her forearm up his belly. "And neither do you. But you want this, too. So let's take this time." She shifted her eyes up his chest to meet his wary, hot stare, and for a moment she was saddened. "You will have many others. I will only have you. So give this to me now, before . . ."—*her heart was broken over and over again*—"Before you must go on."

His conflict played out in his eyes, and it was a testament to his honor. But she knew what the outcome was going to be. And was not surprised when he gave in, his hands no longer restraining her but pulling her to him.

"Dear God," he whispered, sitting up and taking her face in his palms. "I need a minute, okay? Lie down here. I'll be right back."

He stretched her out with gentle hands, then left the bed and went into the bathroom. The shower came on, and when he returned his hair was in damp ringlets around his shoulders and chest.

He came to her naked, a warrior in his physical prime, his sexual need standing straight out from his spectacular body.

He paused next to the bed. "Are you sure?"

"Yes." Even though she'd been told it was going to hurt, she wasn't turning back. She couldn't explain her resolve, but it was going to carry her through.

She would have him now, and what would come thereafter be damned.

Cormia held her hand out to him, and when he put his palm in hers, she brought him down to her body.

Phury allowed himself to be drawn onto the bed until he lay beside Cormia's stunning naked form. Her bones were tiny compared to his, her body delicate next to his brawn.

He couldn't bear to hurt her. He couldn't wait to get into her.

His hand shook as he brushed a piece of blond hair off her forehead. She was right, he thought: It was better this way for both of them. This was a choice. The Primale obligations were a duty.

This would be his first time, and hers as well.

"I'm going to take care of you," he said. And not just when it came to tonight.

Although . . . damn, he had no clue how to make love to a female. Sex was one thing. Making love was altogether different, and suddenly he wanted to be all about finesse. He wanted to have had scores of lovers so he knew how to make sure Cormia got the most out of him.

He let his hand drift down to her neck. Her skin was soft as the still air, so finely grained he couldn't see the pores.

She arched her back, the pink tips of her breasts surging.

He licked his lips and leaned down to her collarbone. Closing his eyes, he hovered just above her body. He knew the instant he made contact there was no going back.

Her hands went deep into his hair. "Will you not begin, your grace."

He flipped his eyes up to hers. "Call me Phury?"

She smiled, a shy blossoming of happiness. "Phury . . ."

After she said his name, he put his lips to her skin and breathed in her scent. His entire body trembled, he wanted her so badly, and instinctively he pushed his hips until his cock was trapped between his thigh and hers. When she gasped and arched again, he latched onto her nipple.

Cormia's nails went into his scalp, and he growled as he suckled and tugged at her. His hand closed on her other breast, and he twisted his hips so that his arousal got held in an even tighter grip.

Oh, shit, he was going to . . .

Yup. He came. Again.

Groaning wildly, he tried to stop. Except she didn't want him to—instead of pulling back, she shifted herself closer and moved with the surges of his orgasm.

"I love when you do that," she said in a guttural voice.

He found her mouth desperately. That she didn't seem to care that he was a loser who had never done this before and had just prematurely ejaculated all over her thighs meant the world to him. He didn't have to pretend to be strong. In this private moment he could just be . . . him.

"It might happen again," he moaned against her lips.

"Good. I want you to do that all over me."

He growled loudly then, his marking instinct pricking to attention. Yes, he thought. He was going to do that all over her. In her as well.

He swept his hand down her body to her legs, then shifted so he could move up her long, lean muscles to her core. His palm dragged through what he'd left on her, and he took his essence with him as he found her sex.

Which was running with honey, wetter than if she'd just bathed.

Cormia cried out and threw open her legs.

He went for the heart of her with his mouth before he had a clue where he was going. It didn't matter that he had no technique to lead with. He needed to taste her, and that was going to happen only if his lips met hers—

"Oh . . . sweet female," he said into her well. He was aware his fingers were biting into her thighs and that he was holding her splayed open, but he couldn't help himself.

She didn't seem to mind in the slightest. Her hands tangled in his hair and pressed him against herself as he dragged his tongue deep and deeper still. He rubbed his face in a circle, then started sucking and swallowing. He was ragged with thirst, feeding from her sex and off the sexual current between them, carried away—

She'd just started to come when the phone rang—and it was a no-brainer to stay right where he was. He could tell that she was rolling off the cliff of release by the way she stiffened and lifted her head so she could meet his eyes. She was nervous, excited, worried.

"Trust me," he said to her. Then he made a point out of his tongue, tilted her hips up, and penetrated her.

She called out his name as she had her orgasm.

And that was when someone pounded on his door.

The following was taken out of Lover Enshrined *because everyone thought it needed to be scrapped! My editor, my research assistant, and my CP (critique partner) all were like, "You don't need it" . . . and I caved because I understood their point. Phury's book ended powerfully, and tacking on something that happens years later diffused the closure. So here's the epilogue that wasn't:*

Five years later . . .

"I've got her!" Phury called out to Bella as he scooped his niece up into his arms. Nalla giggled and buried her little face in his hair, which she loved to do, holding on to him with her strong grip.

Bella came racing around the corner of the Brotherhood's library and then stopped short, her silver gown settling in a lovely swirl around her legs. The diamonds around her neck sparkled like fire, as did the ones on her wrists and at her ears.

"Oh, thank God," she said. "I swear she's as fast as her father."

"You look so spectacular," Cormia said from behind him.

"Thanks." Bella fiddled with the gown. "This is not my usual style, but—"

"It barely does you justice." Zsadist came into the library, looking like a vicious version of Cary Grant. His tuxedo fit every tight line of his body and mostly hid the SIG under his arm.

He did the stern thing as he shook his finger at his daughter. "Now, are you going to be good for your uncle and your *aumahne?*"

Nalla nodded gravely, as if she had just agreed to assume leadership of the continental United States. "Yes, Daddy."

Z's smile pretty much lit up the galaxy. "That's my girl."

Nalla grinned and held out her arms. "Kisses, Daddy."

Z took her for a hug, and then she was reaching for her mother.

"Okay," Zsadist said, all business as he passed his daughter over to his *shellan*. "We'll be at the Met until eleven. Then we're having dinner back at Wrath's place. I have my beeper, my cell phone, my BlackBerry—"

Phury clapped his twin on the shoulder. "Take a deep one, my brother. In with the good air."

Zsadist did the best he could. "Right. I mean, I know you'll be fine with her. I mean, you'll be fine . . . you're all going to be just fine—"

Phury checked his watch. "And you're going to be late. You'll be lucky to get there by the time the intermezzo starts."

"I'm so excited," Bella said, giving Nalla back to Phury. "Mascagni's *Cavalleria Rusticana*. It's going to be fantastic."

"Assuming you can get your baby daddy out the house." Phury gave his twin a little shake. "Go. Be with your *shellan*. It's your anniversary, for God's sake."

They left the library about twenty minutes later. Maybe twenty-five.

Phury shook his head. "He's got some serious separation issues, that one."

"Oh, and you're much better?"

Phury turned around. Cormia was on the couch, their sleeping son, Ahgony— or Aggie, as he was known—in her arms. The young's fat fist was holding on to his mother's thumb, as was his habit even when he was out like a light.

"I resemble that remark."

"Story, Uncle?" Nalla said. "Please?"

"Of course, which would you like?" Even though he knew.

As he sat down on the couch next to Cormia, Nalla pointed to the book of fables he had made for her. "The one of the warrior."

"Now, that's a surprise." He winked at Cormia. "Do you mean the one with the warrior and the maiden?"

"No, Uncle. T'other one."

"The warrior and the ship."

Nalla giggled. "No, Uncle!"

Phury nodded with grand seriousness. "Right. The warrior and the game of pinochle."

Nalla looked confused. "What knuckle?"

Cormia laughed, her beautiful green stare so lovely Phury couldn't look away. For a moment, he was struck once again by the fact that their son had his mother's eyes, that incredible shade of spring leaves.

As Nalla squirmed, Cormia said, "Phury, don't torture her." ·

Phury settled his niece on his lap, kissed his *shellan*, and brushed the smooth cheek of his son. Then he opened the book and started to read in the Old Language.

"'*There once was a warrior strong of limb and stout of heart, who tarried in the woods upon a windy day. . . .*'"

Aggie's eyes opened and he let out the sound that young did when all was well with them, a kind of contented bubbly sigh. Phury recognized it well, because he'd heard it a lot from Nalla and now from Aggie. The sound was something they did when their bellies were full and their parents were right with them and a voice they found pleasing to the ear was embarking on a story.

As Phury lost the rhythm of his words, Cormia reached out and squeezed his hand.

She always knew, he thought. She always knew. . . . She knew he was thinking of his parents and of his brother, of the past and the future, of hopes and dreams and fears.

She knew everything that was in his head and everything that was in his heart, and none of it put her off. She knew he worried about staying sober, even after all these years. And knew he was glad their son looked like her, because he took it as a sign that whatever biological link to addiction he carried might not have been passed on to the young. And she knew that he still struggled with feeling like he wasn't doing enough for everyone around him.

She knew all of this and she loved him anyway.

He kissed the inside of her wrist and looked at the next generation. He hoped that life had only good things in store for the young, that the moonlit night would always be clear for them, and that the wind would always be gentle, and that their heart's deepest love would be returned by a worthy mate.

But he knew it wasn't going to be easy, and they would face challenges he couldn't even imagine.

Here was the thing, though: He had faith in what he saw in those eyes of theirs. Because they came, on both sides, from survivors. And that, more than any guarantee of an easy life, was going to see them through.

Phury cleared his throat.

And kept on reading to them.

So those are just a few examples of what I've taken out. You'll note there isn't anything from Dark Lover, because Wrath's manuscript was tight from the get-go—with only that scene I've posted on my Web site (www.jrward.com) being deleted. There isn't much from Lover Eternal, because again, I used almost all of the Butch and Marissa material in Lover Revealed. Lover Unbound was likewise tight.

There are a couple more scenes in old files. It was so much fun rereading these, maybe someday I'll go back and see what else I can find!

Kicks and Giggles

Kicks and Giggles

One of the greatest things about writing the Brothers is the way they crack me up. On a regular basis, I'll be at the computer upstairs, laughing my butt off at one thing or another. Butch reliably throws out some good ones, Rhage and Vishous are always quick with the comebacks, and Qhuinn is doing the next generation proud when it comes to being an ass.

I've taken some of my absolute favorite exchanges from the books, the ones that made me bark out loud and caused the dog to look at me funny, and excerpted them below.

Dark Lover

Wrath glared. "Nice of you to show up, Z. Busy tonight with the females?"

"How about you get off my dick?" Zsadist went over to the corner, staying away from the rest.

p. 30

Wrath was dumbfounded.

And he wasn't a vampire who got struck stupid very often.

Holy shit.

This half-human was the hottest thing he'd ever gotten anywhere near. And he'd cozied up to a lightning strike once or twice before.

p. 64

If sex were food, Rhage would have been morbidly obese.

p. 81

Wrath clapped his brother on the shoulder. On the whole, though, the SOB was a total keeper. "Forgiven, forgotten."

"Feel free to hammer me anytime."

"Believe me, I do."

p. 84

God knew the Omega was always receptive to initiative and new directions. And would have benefited from some Ritalin when it came to loyalty.

p. 86

The human reached inside Wrath's jacket and started pulling out weapons. Three throwing stars, a switchblade, a handgun, a length of chain.

"Jesus Christ," the cop muttered as he dropped the steel links on the ground with the rest of the load. "You got some ID? Or wasn't there enough room in here for a wallet, considering you're carrying about thirty pounds of concealed weapons?"

p. 111

Giving in to a shrill instinct, she ran around the side of the building.

Butch was marching toward his car as if he were carrying an unstable load, and she rushed to catch up with them.

"Wait. I need to ask him a question."

"You want to know his shoe size or something?" Butch snapped.

"Fourteen," Wrath drawled.

"I'll remember that at Christmas, asshole."

p. 113

"No, thanks." Rhage laughed. "I'm a good little sewer, as you know firsthand. Now who's your friend?"

"Beth Randall, this is Rhage. An associate of mine. Rhage, this is Beth, and she doesn't do movie stars, got it?"

"Loud and clear." Rhage leaned to one side, trying to see around Wrath. "Nice to meet you, Beth."

"Are you sure you don't want to go to a hospital?" she said weakly.

"Nah. This one's just messy. When you can use your large intestine as a belt loop, that's when you hit the pros."

p. 131

"You have cable?" He nodded toward her TV.

She tossed him the clicker. "Sure do. And if I remember, there's a Godzilla marathon on TBS tonight."

"Sweet," the vampire said, kicking his legs out. "I always root for the monster."

She smiled at him. "Me, too."

p. 166

"And I left the aspirin next to the phone with a tall glass of water. Figured you weren't going to be able to make it to the coffeepot. Take three, turn your ringer off, and sleep. If anything exciting happens, I'll come and get you."

"I love you, honey."

"So buy me a mink and a nice pair of earrings for our anniversary."

"You got it."

p. 168

A hand landed on his shoulder like an anvil. "How'd you like to stay for dinner?"

Butch looked up. The guy was wearing a baseball cap and had some kind of marking—was that a tattoo, on his face?

"How'd you like to be dinner?" said another one, who looked like some kind of model.

p. 258

With a deliberate shrug, he stepped free of the hold on his shoulder.

"Tell me something, boys," he drawled. "Do you wear that leather to turn each other on? I mean, is it a dick thing with you all?"

Butch got slammed so hard against the door that his back teeth rattled.

The model shoved his perfect face into Butch's. "I'd watch your mouth, if I were you."

"Why bother, when you're keeping an eye on it for me? You gonna kiss me now?"

A growl like none Butch had ever heard came out of the guy.

"Okay, okay." The one who seemed the most normal came forward. "Back off, Rhage. Hey, come on. Let's relax."

It took a minute before the model let go.

"That's right. We're cool," Mr. Normal muttered, clapping his buddy on the back before looking at Butch. "Do yourself a favor and shut the hell up."

Butch shrugged. "Blondie's dying to get his hands on me. I can't help it."

The guy launched back at Butch, and Mr. Normal rolled his eyes, letting his friend go this time.

The fist that came sailing at jaw level snapped Butch's head to one side. As the pain hit, Butch let his own rage fly. The fear for Beth, the pent-up hatred of these lowlifes, the frustration about his job, all of it came out of him. He tackled the bigger man, taking him down onto the floor.

The guy was momentarily surprised, as if he hadn't expected Butch's speed or strength, and Butch took advantage of the hesitation. He clocked Blondie in the mouth as payback and then grabbed the guy's throat.

One second later, Butch was flat on his back with the man sitting on his chest like a parked car.

The guy took Butch's face into his hand and squeezed, crunching the features together. It was nearly impossible to breathe, and Butch panted shallowly.

"Maybe I'll find your wife," the guy said, "and do her a couple of times. How's that sound?"

"Don't have one."

"Then I'm coming after your girlfriend."

Butch dragged in some air. "Got no woman."

"So if the chicks won't do you, what makes you think I'd want to?"

"Was hoping to piss you off."

Stunning electric-blue eyes narrowed.

They had to be contacts, Butch thought. No one really had peepers that color.

"Now why'd you want to do that?" Blondie asked.

"If I attacked first"—Butch hauled more breath into his lungs—"your boys wouldn't have let us fight. Would've killed me first. Before I had a chance at you."

Blondie loosened his grip a little and laughed as he stripped Butch of his wallet, keys, and cell phone.

"You know, I kind of like this big dummy," the guy drawled.

Someone cleared a throat. Rather officiously.

Blondie leaped to his feet, and Butch rolled over, gasping. When he looked up, he was convinced he was hallucinating.

Standing in the hall was a little old man dressed in livery. Holding a silver tray. "Pardon me, gentlemen. Dinner will be served in about fifteen minutes."

"Hey, are those the spinach crepes I like so much?" Blondie said, going for the tray.

"Yes, Sire."

"Hot damn."

The other men clustered around the butler, taking what he offered. Along with cocktail napkins. Like they didn't want to drop anything on the floor.

What the hell was this?

"Might I ask a favor?" the butler said.

Mr. Normal nodded with vigor. "Bring out another tray of these and we'll kill anything you want for you."

Yeah, guess the guy wasn't really normal. Just relatively so.

The butler smiled as if touched. "If you're going to bloody the human, would you be good enough to do it in the backyard?"

"No problem." *Mr. Normal popped another crepe in his mouth.* "Damn, Rhage, you're right. These are awesome."

pp. 258–260

"So what'd you do to the lesser?" *a male voice said.*

"I lit his cigarette with a sawed-off," *another one answered.* "He didn't come down for breakfast, you feel me?"

p. 283

"Tohr, relax. I'm a female, I cry at matings. It's in the job description."

p. 329

"Hopefully, you won't have to. Now tell me something. What's your word for husband?"

"Hellren, I suppose. The short version is just hell."

She laughed softly. "Go figure."

p. 347

Rhage nodded. "The place is also big enough. We could all live there without killing each other."

"That depends more on your mouth than any floor plan," Phury said with a grin.

p. 390

"Yeah." Rhage sighed. "All I want is one good female. But I guess I'll settle for quantity until I find her. Life just sucks, doesn't it?"

p. 393

Lover Eternal

"All right, big guy, down you go."

Oh, yeah. Bed. Bed was good.

"And look who's here. It's Nurse Vishous."

p. 47

"So say that."

"What?"

"Nothing. Say nothing. Over and over and over again. Do it."

She bristled, the scent of fear replaced by a sharp spice, like fresh, pungent mint from a garden. She was annoyed now.

"Say it," he commanded, needing to feel more of what she did to him.

"Fine. Nothing. Nothing." Abruptly she laughed, and the sound shot through to his spine, burning him. *"Nothing, nothing. No-thing. No-thing. Nooooooothing. There, is that good enough for you? Will you let me go now?"*

"No."

She fought against him again, creating a delicious friction between their bodies. And he knew the moment when the anxiety and irritation turned to something hot. He smelled her arousal, a lovely sweetening in the air, and his body answered her call.

He got hard as a diamond.

"Talk to me, Mary." He moved his hips in a slow circle against her, rubbing his erection on her belly, increasing his ache and her heat.

After a moment the tension eased out of her, softening her against the thrust of his muscles and his arousal. Her hands flattened on his waist. And then slowly slid around to the small of his back, as if she were unsure why she was responding to him the way she was.

He arched against her, to show his approval and encourage her to touch more of him. When her palms moved up his spine, he growled low in his throat and dropped his head down so his ear was closer to her mouth. He wanted to give her another word to say, something like luscious or whisper or strawberry.

Hell, antidisestablishmentarianism would do it.

pp. 62–63

"Christ. You can be a real pain in the ass, you know that? No impulse control but totally single-minded. Helluva combination."

p. 74

"Okay, whadda we got here," he said, opening his own. "Let's have the Chicken Alfredo. The NY strip, rare. And a cheeseburger, also rare. Double on the fries. And some nachos. Yeah, I want the nachos with everything on them. Double that, too, will you?"

Mary could only stare as he closed the menu and waited.

The waitress looked a little awkward. "Is all that for both you and your sister?"

As if family obligation was the only reason a man like him would be out with a woman like her. Oh, man . . .

"No, that's for me. And she's my date, not my sister. Mary?"

"I . . . ah, I'll just have a Caesar salad, whenever his"—feeding trough?—"dinner comes."

pp. 87–88

"You're getting into some kind of shape, cop."

"Aw, come on, now." Butch grinned. "Don't let that shower we took go to your head."

Rhage fired a towel at the male. "Just pointing out your beer gut's gone."

"It was a Scotch pot. And I don't miss it."

p. 117

"The female threw me out of her house early this morning after doing a job on my ego."

"What kind of hatchet did she use?"

"An unflattering comparison between me and a free-agent canine."

"Ouch." Butch twisted the shirt in the other direction. "So naturally, you're dying to see her again."

"Pretty much."

"You're pathetic."

"I know."

"But I can almost beat that." The cop shook his head. "Last night, I . . . ah . . . I drove out to Marissa's brother's house. I don't even know how the Escalade got there. I mean, the last thing I need is to run into her, you feel me?"

"Let me guess. You waited in hopes of catching a—"

"In the bushes, Rhage. I sat in the bushes. Under her bedroom window."

"Wow. That's . . ."

"Yeah. In my old life I could have arrested me for stalking. Look, maybe we should change the topic."

p. 118

One look at the movie collection and he knew he was in trouble. There were a lot of foreign titles, some deeply sincere American ones. A couple of golden oldies like An Affair to Remember. Casa-*fucking*-blanca.

Absolutely nothing by Sam Raimi or Roger Corman. Hadn't she heard of the Evil Dead series?

pp. 150–151

"Shit, you've bonded with her." Wrath put a hand through his long hair. "For God's sake . . . You just met her, my brother."

"And how long did it take you to mark Beth as your own? Twenty-four hours? Oh, right, you waited two days. Yeah, good thing you gave it some time."

Wrath let out a short laugh. "You gotta keep bringing my shellan into it, don't you?"

p. 200

Oh, the humanity.

The Austin Powers boxed set. Aliens and Alien. Jaws. All the Naked Guns. Godzilla. Godzilla. Godzilla . . . wait, the rest of this whole shelf was Godzilla. She went one lower. Friday the 13th, Halloween, Nightmare on Elm Street. Well, at least he hadn't bothered with the sequels to those. Caddyshack. The Evil Dead boxed set.

It was a wonder Rhage hadn't blinded himself with all that pop culture.

p. 202

She smiled a little. "You are a manipulator."
"I like to think of myself more as an outcome engineer."

p. 246

Phury's laugh came out of the robe on the right. "Only you could try to turn this into a party."

"Well, hell, you've all wanted to nail me a good one for some shit I've popped, right? This is your lucky day." He clapped Phury on the thigh. "I mean, come on, my brother, I've ridden you for years about the no females. And Wrath, a couple of months ago I needled you until you stabbed a wall. V, just the other day you threatened to use that hand of yours on me. Remember? When I told you what I thought about that goatee monstrosity?"

V chuckled. "I had to do something to shut you up. Every damn time I've run into you since I grew it, you ask me if I've French-kissed a tailpipe."

"And I'm still convinced you're doing my GTO, you bastard."

p. 250

"What is your name?" she murmured.
He cocked an eyebrow at her and then went back to staring at his brother. "I'm the evil one, in case you haven't figured it out."
"I wanted your name, not your calling."
"Being a bastard's more of a compulsion, really. And it's Zsadist. I am Zsadist."

p. 271

He took a deep breath: "God, I love you. I really, really love you."
And then he smiled.
She laughed in a loud crack that brought every head in the room around.
The cherry stem was tied neatly around one of his fangs.

p. 354

A male who looked as dangerous as he did, people were bound to talk. Her brother was the same way. She'd heard whispers about Rehvenge for years, and God knew, all of them were false.

p. 356

No one was listening to her.

"God, spare me from heroes," she muttered. "Back the fuck off!"

That got their attention.

p. 408

She shook her head and bent down to pick up a shirt from the floor. "You are the sweetest thug I've ever known."

p. 419

Sweeping her hair back, she laughed. "So your sight's returning?"

"Among other things. Come here, Mary. I want to kiss you."

"Oh, sure. Make up for being a bully by plying me with your body."

"I'll use any asset I've got."

He threw the sheets and duvet off himself and swept his hand down his chest, over his stomach. Lower. Her eyes widened when he took his heavy erection in his palm. As he stroked himself, the scent of her arousal bloomed like a bouquet in the room.

"Come over here, Mary." He twisted his hips. "I'm not sure I'm doing this right. It feels so much better when you touch me."

"You are incorrigible."

"Just looking for some instruction."

"Like you need that," she muttered, taking off her sweater.

pp. 419–420

"I told you, that's fine with me." She smiled. "I mean, come on. He's kind of cute, in a Godzilla sort of way. And I'll look at it as a two-for-one kind of deal."

p. 441

Lover Awakened

Man, it was a good thing he fought like a nasty bastard or he might have been taken for a nancy.

p. 44

. . . The other was behind the desk and hump-ugly: a ragged, avocado green leather monstrosity with dog-eared corners, a sagging seat, and a set of legs that gave new meaning to the word sturdy.

Tohr put his hand on the thing's high back. "Can you believe Wellsie made me get rid of this?"

John nodded and signed, Yes, I can.

p. 73

"Well, I can't read. So we're SOL, you and me."

John worked his Bic quickly. As he showed the pad to Phury, the male with the black stare frowned. "What did the kid write?"

"He says that's okay. He's a good listener. You can do the talking."

p. 94

He grabbed her hand, whipped the pen out of it, and flattened her palm.
I want to talk to you, he wrote.
Then he looked straight into her eyes and did the most amazing, ballsy thing.
He smiled at her.

p. 123

John nodded and looked at the twelve guys who were seated in pairs and staring at him.
Whoa. Really not feeling the love here, fellas, *he thought.*

p. 140

After a moment Blaylock pulled a polite one and introduced the others. They all had odd names. The blond's was Lash. And how fricking appropriate was that?

p. 142

"This place is just too frickin' precious," the cop said, eyeing a guy dressed in a hot pink leisure suit with makeup to match. "Give me rednecks and home-grown beer any day of the week over this X-culture bullshit."

p. 158

"Just want to make sure your needs are served. Customer satisfaction is so damned important." The male moved even closer and nodded at Phury's arm, the one that disappeared into his coat. "Your hand's on a gun butt right now, isn't it? Afraid of me?"
"Just want to make sure I can take care of you."
"Oh, really?"
"Yeah. In case you need a little Glock-to-mouth resuscitation."

p. 159

That female who'd walked in on him and the Reverend clearly had a big mouth and . . . Christ. Butch must have already told Vishous. The two were like an old mated couple, no secrets between them. And V would squeal to Rhage. And once Rhage knew, you might as well have popped the news flash on the Reuters wire.

p. 181

Their eyes met. She was so pretty, she made him dizzy.

"Do you want to kiss me?" she whispered.

John's eyes cracked open. Like a balloon had popped behind his head.

"Because I'd like you to." She licked her lips a little. "I really would."

Whoa . . . Chance of a lifetime, right here, right now, he thought.

Do not pass out. Passing out would be a total buzz kill.

John quickly called on every movie he'd ever seen . . . and got no help at all. As a horror fan, he was swamped by visions of Godzilla stomping across Tokyo and of Jaws chewing on the ass end of the Orca. Big help.

p. 215

. . . The guy was cracking down on the Brotherhood, organizing shifts, trying to turn four loose cannons like V, Phury, Rhage, and Z into soldiers. No wonder he always looked like his head hurt.

p. 219

Phury lit a blunt and eyed the sixteen cans of Aqua Net that were lined up on Butch and V's coffee table. "What's doing with the hair spray? You boys going drag on us?"

Butch held up the length of PVC pipe he was punching a hole in. "Potato launcher, my man. Big fun."

"Excuse me?"

"Didn't you ever go to summer camp?"

"Basket weaving and woodcarving are for humans. No offense, but we have better things to teach to our youngs."

"Ha! You haven't lived until you've gone on a midnight panty raid. Anyway, you put the potato in this end, you fill up the bottom with spray—"

"And then you light it," V cut in from his bedroom. He came out in a robe, rubbing a towel on his wet hair. "Makes a great noise."

"Great noise," Butch echoed.

Phury looked at his brother. "V, you've done this before?"

"Yeah, last night. But the launcher jammed up."

Butch cursed. "Potato was too big. Damn Idaho bakers. We're leading with red skins tonight. It's going to be great. Of course, trajectory can be a bitch—"

"But it's really just like golf," V said, dropping the towel across a chair. He pulled a glove over his right hand, covering the sacred tattoos that marked the thing from palm to fingertip and all across the back. "I mean, you gotta think of your arc in the air—"

Butch nodded up a storm. "Yeah, it's just like golf. Wind plays a big role—"

"Huge."

Phury smoked along as they finished each other's sentences for another couple min-

utes. After a while he felt compelled to mention, "The two of you are spending way too much time together, you feel me?"

V shook his head at the cop. "The brother has no appreciation for this kind of thing. Never has."

"Then we aim for his room."

"True that. And it faces the garden—"

"So we don't have to work around the cars in the courtyard. Excellent."

pp. 259–260

Tohr laughed softly. "Yeah, I'm not much for the emotive crap either—Ouch! Wellsie, what the hell?"

p. 272

He put the bottle on the table next to him and held up his gloved hand. "After all, this godforsaken thing still glows like a lamp. And until I lose this whacked-out nightlight of mine, I figure I'm still normal. Well . . . normal for me."

p. 301

Phury pulled on a pair of nylon warm-ups. "You want food? I'm going to make a kitchen trip."

Butch's eyes blissed out. "You're actually going to bring it up here? As in, I don't have to move?"

"You're going to owe me, but yeah, I'm willing to deliver."

"You are a god."

Phury put on a T-shirt. "What do you want?"

"Whatever's in the kitchen. Hell, make yourself really useful and drag that refrigerator on up here. I'm starved."

pp. 307–308

"Then why are you wearing that bandage like a sash?"

"It makes my ass look smaller."

p. 339

"I don't want to go."

"Well . . . in the words of Vishous, want in one hand, shit in the other—see what you get most of."

p. 358

Phury was lying on the king-size bed, lines plugged into him as if he were a switchboard.

The male's head turned. "Z . . . what are you doing up?"

"Giving the medical staff a workout." He shut the door and weaved into the room, heading for the bed. "They're pretty damn fast, actually."

p. 397

There was no reply. So Z glanced over again—just as a tear slid down Phury's cheek.

"Ah . . . fuck," Z muttered.

"Yeah. Pretty much." Another tear rolled out of Phury's eye. "God . . . damn. I'm leaking."

"Okay, brace yourself."

Phury scrubbed his face with his palms. "Why?"

"Because . . . I think I'm going to try to hug you."

Phury's hands dropped and he looked over with an absurd expression.

Feeling like an utter ass, Z pushed himself over to his twin. "Lift up your head, damn it." Phury craned his neck. Z slid his arm underneath. The two of them froze in the unnatural positions. "You know, this was a hell of a lot easier when you were out cold in the back of that truck."

"That was you?"

"You think it was Santa Claus or some shit?"

p. 399

Butch sighed in relief. "Listen, man, do me a favor. Warn me before you pull another stunt like that. I'd rather choose." Then he smiled a little. "And we still ain't dating."

p. 406

Lover Revealed

. . . When it was finished, the scaled dragon looked around and as the thing spotted V, a growl rippled up to the bleachers, then ended in a snort.

"You finished, big guy?" V called down. "FYI, goalpost over there would work righteous as a toothpick."

p. 22

"For sure. I'm thinking about a future in contracting. Wanted to see how this bathroom was put together. Excellent tile work. You should check it."

"How about I carry you back to bed?"

"I want to look at the sink pipes next."

Respect and affection clearly drove V's cool smirk. "At least let me help you up."

"Nah, I can do it." With a groan, Butch gave the vertical move a shot, but eased back down onto the tile. Turned out lifting his head was a little overwhelming. But if they left him here long enough—a week, maybe ten days?

"Come on, cop. Cry uncle here and let me help."

Butch was suddenly too tired to front. As he went totally limp, he was aware of Marissa staring at him and thought, man, could he look any weaker? Shit, the only saving grace was that there wasn't a cold breeze on his butt.

Which suggested the hospital gown had stayed closed. Thank you, God.

pp. 84–85

"You know you were with the lessers, true?"

Butch lifted one of his busted-up hands. "And here I thought I'd been to Elizabeth Arden."

p. 85

"Sure." Except when V brought up his business hand and started taking off that glove, Butch recoiled. "What are you going to do with that thing?"

"Trust me, true?"

Butch barked a laugh. "Last time you said that I ended up with a vampire cocktail, remember?"

"Saved your ass. That's how I found you."

So that had been the why of it. "Well, then, fly me some of that hand."

Still, as V put the glowing thing close, Butch winced.

"Relax, cop. This isn't going to hurt."

"I've seen you toast a house with that bastard."

"Point taken. But the Firestarter routine isn't going down here."

p. 87

She pulled back the sheet. Good God, his sex was . . . "It's gotten so . . . huge."

Butch barked out a laugh. "You say the nicest things."

p. 117

"Man," Rhage muttered, "someone hit this place with the Hallmark stick."

"Until it broke."

p. 143

"When the females tie you down, do they paint your toenails and shit? Or just do your makeup?" As V laughed in a loud crack, the cop said, "Wait . . . they tickle your pits with a feather, right?"

p. 150

Before Butch knew what was doing, V grabbed his forearm, bent down, and licked the cut, sealing it up quick.

Butch yanked out of his roommate's hold. "Jesus, V! What if that blood's contaminated!"

"It's fine. Just f—" With a boneless lurch, Vishous gasped and collapsed against the wall, eyes rolling back in his head, body twitching.

"Oh, God . . . !" Butch reached out in horror—

Only to have V cut the seizure off and calmly take a drink from his glass. "You're fine, cop. Tastes perfectly okay. Well, fine for a human guy, which really ain't my tail of choice, you feel me?"

Butch hauled back and nailed his roommate in the arm with his fist. And as the brother cursed, Butch popped him another one.

V glared and rubbed himself. "Christ, cop."

"Suck it up, you deserve it."

p. 193

"Shit . . . you're right. I apologize."

"Can we screw the 'sorry' part and let me hit you back instead?"

p. 194

"V, you know I love you like a brother, right?"

"Yeah."

"You feed her and I'll tear your fucking throat out."

p. 218

"That's what I like to hear." The Reverend slid into the booth, his amethyst eyes scanning the VIP section. He looked good, his suit black, his silk shirt black, his mohawk a dark cropped stripe that ran front to back on his skull. "So I want to share a little news."

"You getting married?" Butch tossed back half the new Lag. "Where you registered? Crate and Bury 'Em?"

"Try Heckler and Koch." The Reverend opened his jacket and flashed the butt of a forty.

"Nice little poodle shooter you got there, vampire."

"Put a hell of a—"

V cut in. "You two are like watching tennis, and racquet sports bore me. What's the news?"

Rehv looked at Butch. "He has such phenomenal people skills, doesn't he."

"Try living with him."

pp. 219–220

"You're such a pain in the ass."

"Said the SIG to the Glock."

p. 281

Except when his roommate's palm landed on his bare chest all he felt was a warm weight. Butch frowned. This was it? This was fucking it? Scaring the shit out of Marissa for no good—

He looked down, pissed off.

Oh, wrong hand.

p. 316

"Marissa," he mumbled, taking her hand. "Don't want to see you drink so much." Wait, not really what he'd been going for. "Ah . . . don't you to see me drink so much . . . want."

Whatever. God . . . he was so confused.

p. 320

Wrath smiled broadly, his fangs so very white. "What's doing . . . cousin."

Butch frowned. "What . . . ?"

"You've got some of me in you, cop." Wrath's smile stuck around as he slid his glasses back in. "Course, I always knew you were a royal. Just didn't think it went past the pain-in-the-ass part, is all."

p. 321

Butch looked back at the Scribe Virgin.

"Do you have any idea how relieved—"

As Marissa gasped, V stepped in and slapped his gloved hand over Butch's mouth, yanking him backward by the head and hissing in his ear, "Do you want to get fried like an egg here, buddy? No questions—"

"Ease from him, warrior," the Scribe Virgin snapped. "This I wish to hear."

V's grip slid off his face. "Watch it."

"Sorry about the question thing," Butch said to the black robes. "But I just . . . I'm glad I know what's in my veins. And honestly, if I die today, I'm grateful I finally know what I am." He took Marissa's hand. "And who I love. If this is where my life took me after all those years of being lost, I'd say my time here wasn't wasted."

There was a long silence. Then the Scribe Virgin said, "Do you regret that you leave behind your human family?"

"Nope. This is my family. Here with me now and elsewhere in the compound.

Why would I need anything else?" The cursing in the room told him he'd thrown another question out there. "Yeah . . . ah, sorry—"

A soft feminine laugh came from under the robes. "You are rather fearless, human."

"Or you could call it stupid." As Wrath's mouth fell open, Butch rubbed his face. "You know, I'm trying here. I really am. You know, to be respectful."

"Your hand, human."

He offered her his left, the one that was free.

"Palm up," Wrath barked.

He flipped his hand over.

"Tell me, human," the Scribe Virgin said, "if I asked for the one you hold this female with, would you offer it to me?"

"Yeah. I'd just reach over to her with the other guy." As that little laugh came again, he said, "You know, you sound like birds when you do that chuckle thing. It's nice."

Over to the left, Vishous put his head in his hands.

There was a long silence.

Butch took a deep breath. "Guess I'm not allowed to say that."

The Scribe Virgin reached up and slowly lifted the robes from her face.

Jesus . . . Christ . . . . Butch squeezed Marissa's hand hard at what was revealed.

"You're an angel," he whispered.

Perfect lips lifted in a smile. "No. I am Myself."

"You're beautiful."

"I know." Her voice became authoritative again. "Your right palm, Butch O'Neal, descended of Wrath son of Wrath."

Butch let go of Marissa, regripped her with his left hand, and reached forward. When the Scribe Virgin touched him, he flinched. Though his bones weren't crushed, the awesome strength in her was merely shelved potential. She could grind him to powder on a whim.

The Scribe Virgin turned to Marissa. "Child, give me yours now."

The instant that connection was made, a warm current flooded Butch's body. At first he assumed it was because the heating system in the room was really cooking, but then he realized the rush was under his skin.

"Ah, yes. This is a very good mating," the Scribe Virgin pronounced. "And you have my permission to join for however long you have together." She dropped their hands and looked at Wrath. "The presentation to me is complete. If he lives, you shall finish the ceremony as soon as he is well enough."

The king bowed his head. "So be it."

The Scribe Virgin turned back to Butch. "Now, we shall see how strong you are."

"Wait," Butch said, thinking about the glymera. "Marissa's mated now, right? I mean, even if I die, she will have had a mate, right?"

"Death wish," V said under his breath. "Fucking Death Wish Boy we got over here."

The Scribe Virgin seemed flat-out amazed. "I should kill you now."

"I'm sorry, but this matters. I don't want her falling under that whole sehclusion thing. I want her to be my widow so she doesn't have to worry about anyone else leading her life."

"Human, you are astoundingly arrogant," the Scribe Virgin snapped. But then she smiled. "And totally unrepentant, aren't you."

pp. 347–349

V was halfway down the hall when he heard a yelp. He hightailed it back, barging through the door. "What? What's—"

"I'm going bald!"

V whipped back the shower curtain and frowned. "What are you talking about? You've still got your hair—"

"Not my head! My body, you idiot! I'm going bald!"

Vishous glanced down. Butch's torso and legs were shedding, a rush of dark brown fuzz pooling around the drain.

V started laughing. "Think of it this way. At least you won't have to worry about shaving your back as you get old, true? No manscaping for you."

He was not surprised when a bar of soap came firing at him.

p. 376

As her brother rose from his chair, Marissa rapped her knuckles sharply on the table. All eyes shot to her. "Wrong name."

The leahdyre's eyes went so wide she was quite sure he could see behind himself. And he was so aghast at her interruption, he was speechless as she smiled a little and glanced at Havers. "You may sit down, physician," she said.

"I beg your pardon," the leahdyre stammered.

Marissa got to her feet. "It's been so long since we've done one of these votes . . . not since Wrath's father died." She leaned forward on her hands as she pegged the leahdyre's face with a level stare. "And back then, centuries ago, my father lived and cast our family's vote. So obviously that is why you are confused."

The leahdyre looked at Havers in a panic. "Perhaps you will inform your sister she is out of order—"

Marissa cut in. "I'm not his sister anymore, or so he's told me. Though I believe we can all agree that blood lineage is immutable. As is order of birth." She smiled coolly. "It so happens that I was born eleven years before Havers. Which makes me older than he is. Which means he can sit down, because as the eldest surviving member of my *family, the vote from our bloodline is mine to cast. Or not. And in this case, it is most definitely . . . not."*

Chaos broke out. Absolute pandemonium.

In the midst of which, Rehv laughed and clapped his palms together. "Hot damn, girl. You are so the shit."

pp. 421–422

Then the Omega disappeared in a flare of white. As did the Scribe Virgin.

Gone. Both of them. Nothing remaining except a bitterly cold wind that cleared the clouds from the sky like curtains ripped away by a savage hand.

Rhage cleared his throat. "Okay . . . I'm not sleeping for the next week and a half. How about you two?"

p. 427

"That's you," Wrath said. "You shall be called the Black Dagger warrior Dhestroyer, descended of Wrath son of Wrath."

"But you'll always be Butch to us," Rhage cut in. "As well as hard-ass. Smart-ass. Royal pain in the ass. You know, whatever the situation calls for. I think as long as there's an ass in there, it'll be accurate."

"How about basstard?" Z suggested.

"Nice. I feel that."

p. 445

Lover Unbound

"I am so not feeling all this cowhide."

Vishous looked up from his bank of computers. Butch O'Neal was standing in the Pit's living room with a pair of leathers on his thighs and a whole lot of you've-got-to-be-kidding-me on his puss.

"They don't fit you?" V asked his roommate.

"Not the point. No offense, but these are wicked Village People." Butch held his heavy arms out and turned in a circle, his bare chest catching the light. "I mean, come on."

"They're for fighting, not fashion."

"So are kilts, but you don't see me rocking the tartan."

"And thank God for that. You're too bowlegged to pull that shit off."

Butch assumed a bored expression. "You can bite me."

p. 10

As another martini arrived, Phury tried to remember whether it was his fifth? Or sixth? He wasn't sure.

"Man, good thing we ain't fighting tonight," Butch said. "You're drinking that shit like water."

"I'm thirsty."

"Guess so." The cop stretched in the booth. "How much longer you plan on rehydrating there, Lawrence of Arabia?"

p. 49

Moments later a huge male with a cropped mohawk came out. Rehvenge was dressed in a perfectly tailored black suit and had a black cane in his right hand. As he came slowly over to the Brotherhood's table, his patrons parted before him, partially out of respect for his size, partly out of fear from his reputation. Everyone knew who he was and what he was capable of: Rehv was the kind of drug lord who took a personal interest in his livelihood. You crossed him and you turned up diced like something off the Food Channel.

p. 50

"Okay, so spill," Blay said. "What was your transition like?"

"Screw the change, I got laid." As Blay and John both bug-eyed, Qhuinn chuckled. "Yeah. I did. Got my cherry popped, so to speak."

p. 52

"You so need to lighten up about that potato-launcher incident," Butch said.

Phury rolled his eyes and eased back in the banquette. "You broke my window."

"Of course we did. V and I were aiming for it."

"Twice."

"Thus proving that he and I are outstanding marksmen."

p. 81

"What the guy look like?"

"The vic?" The kid leaned in. "Vic is what the police call the victim. I heard 'em."

"Thanks for the clarification," Phury muttered. "So what did he look like?"

p. 93

. . . Damn it. She had no interest in playing doc. It was a big enough job being kidnap victim, thank you very much.

p. 128

"Didn't we just do this?" Red Sox murmured to the patient. "'Cept I was the guy in the bed? How about we call it even now and not pull this wounded shit anymore."

Those icy bright eyes left her and shifted to his buddy. The frown didn't leave his face. "You look like hell."

"And you're Miss America."

pp. 129–130

Berating herself and them, she took her hand from her pocket, bent down, and grabbed a vial of Demerol out of the bigger duffel. "There aren't any syringes."

"I've got some." Red Sox came over and held a sterile pack out. When she tried to take it from him, he kept a grip on the thing. "I know you'll use this wisely."

"Wisely?" She snapped the syringe out of his hand. "No, I'm going to poke him in the eye with it. Because that's what they trained me to do in medical school."

p. 139

"You're kidding me, right? Like I'm supposed to forget the abduction and the mortal threat and give you a drive-thru order?"

p. 142

V settled back against the pillows and measured the hard line of her chin. "Take off your coat."

"Excuse me?"

"Take it off."

"No."

"I want it off."

"Then I suggest you hold your breath. Won't affect me in the slightest, but at least the suffocation will help pass the time for you."

p. 157

"What job do you have at the end, exactly?" Please let it not be buying Hefty bags to put her body parts in.

"You aren't interested in what I am?"

"Tell you what, you let me go, and I'll ask you plenty of questions about your race. Until then, I'm slightly distracted with how this happy little vacation on the good ship Holy Shit is going to pan out for me."

p. 163

When she drew the cloth downward, he pulled away.

"Don't want you near that hand of mine. Even if it's gloved."

"Why is—"

"I'm not talking about it. So don't even ask."

Okaaaay. "It nearly killed one of my nurses, you know."

"I'm not surprised." He glared at the glove. "I'd cut it off if I had the chance."

"I wouldn't advise that."

"Of course you wouldn't. You don't know what it's like to live with this nightmare on the end of your arm—"

"No, I meant I'd have someone else do the cutting if I were you. You're more likely to get the job done that way."

There was a beat of silence; then the patient barked out a laugh. "Smart-ass."

Jane hid the smile that popped up on her face by doing another dip/rinse routine. "Just rendering a medical opinion."

pp. 171–172

"Sounds like you want a date, Lash," Qhuinn barked. "Good deal, 'cause you keep that shit up, you're going to get fucked, buddy."

p. 196

Red Sox looked around Jane at the patient. "Your mind reading coming back?"

"With her? Sometimes."

"Huh. You getting anything from anyone else?"

"Nope."

Red Sox repositioned his hat. "Well, ah . . . let me know if you pick up shit from me, 'k? There are some things that I'd prefer to keep private, feel me?"

"Roger that. Although I can't help it sometimes."

"Which is why I'm going to take up thinking about baseball when you're around."

"Thank fuck you're not a Yankees fan."

"Don't use the Y-word. We're in mixed company."

p. 199

Gimme an S! A T! *An* O! A C! *Followed by a* K-H-O-L-M! *What's it spell?* HEAD FUCK.

The patient leaned down to her ear. "I can't see you as the cheerleader type. But you're right. We both would slaughter anything that so much as startled you." The patient straightened again, one giant testosterone surge plugged into bedroom slippers.

Jane tapped him on the forearm and crooked her forefinger so he'd lean back down.

When he did, she whispered, "I'm scared of mice and spiders. But you don't need to use that gun on your hip to blow a hole in a wall if I run into one, okay? Havahart traps and rolled newspapers work just as well. Plus, you don't need a Sheetrock patch and plaster job afterward. I'm just saying."

She patted his arm, dismissing him, and refocused on the tunnel ahead.

pp. 199–200

Butch nodded as if he knew exactly what was doing. "Like I said, my man, it's whatever. You and me? Same as always, no matter who you screw. Although . . . if you're into sheep, that would be tough. Don't know if I could handle that."

V had to smile. "I don't do farm animals."

"Can't stand hay in your leathers?"

"Or wool in my teeth."

p. 211

"She is." Butch headed for the door but then paused and looked over his shoulder. "V?"

Vishous raised his stare. "Yeah?"

"I think you should know, after all this deep conversatin' . . . ." Butch shook his head gravely. "We still ain't dating."

p. 213

Standing in front of his locker three hours later, John wished Qhuinn would shut his damn piehole. Even though the locker room was loud from sounds of metal doors banging shut and clothes flapping and shoes dropping, he felt like his buddy had a bullhorn stapled to his upper lip.

"You're flippin' huge, J.M. For real. Like . . . ginormous."

That is not a word. John shoved his backpack in like he usually did and realized none of the clothes he was crushing would fit him anymore.

"The hell it isn't. Back me up, Blay."

Blay nodded as he pulled on his ji. "Yeah, you fill out? You're going to be, like, Brother-sized."

"Gigundous."

Okay, also not a word, asshole.

"Fine, really, really, really big. How's that?"

p. 301

Qhuinn smiled, baring his fangs. "Has anyone ever shown you the difference between good touch and bad touch? 'Cause I'd love to demonstrate. We could start right now."

p. 303

"I came to see if you were dead."
Jane had to smile. "Jesus, Manello, don't be such a romantic."
"You look like shit."
"And now with the compliments. Stop. You're making me blush."

p. 360

V blinked a couple of times, horrified at what he was about to say. "God, you're going for sainthood, you know that? You've always been there for me. Always. Even when I . . ."
"Even when you what?"
"You know."
"What?"
"Fuck. Even when I was in love with you. Or some shit."
Butch clasped his hands to his chest. "Was? Was? I can't believe you've lost interest." He threw one arm over his eyes, all Sarah Bernhardt. "My dreams of our future are shattered—"
"Shut it, cop."
Butch looked out from under his arm. "Are you kidding me? The reality show I had planned was fantastic. Was going to pitch it to VH1. Two Bites Are Better Than One. We were going to make millions."
"Oh, for the love."

pp. 369–370

"You know I'm right."
"Fuck you, Dr. Phil."
"Good, I'm glad we agree." Butch frowned. "Hey, maybe I could have a talk show, since you aren't going to be my June Cleaver anymore. I could call it The O'Neal Hour. Sounds important, doesn't it?"
"First of all, you were going to be June Cleaver—"
"Screw that. No way I'd bottom for you."
"Whatever. And second, I don't think there's much of a market for your particular brand of psychology."
"So not true."
"Butch, you and I just beat the crap out of each other."

"You started it. And actually, it would be perfect for Spike TV. UFC meets Oprah. God, I'm brilliant."

"Keep telling yourself that."

p. 370

"Ten minutes," Butch whispered into Marissa's ear. "Can I have ten minutes with you before you go? Please, baby . . ."

V rolled his eyes and was relieved to be annoyed at the lovey-dovey routine. At least all the testosterone in him hadn't dried up.

"Baby . . . please?"

V took a pull on his mug. "Marissa, throw the sap bastard a bone, would you? The simpering wears on my nerves."

"Well, we can't have that, can we?" Marissa packed up her papers with a laugh and shot Butch a look. "Ten minutes. And you'd better make them count."

Butch was up out of that chair like the thing was on fire. "Don't I always?"

"Mmm . . . yes."

As the two locked lips, V snorted. "Have fun, kiddies. Somewhere else."

p. 445

Lover Enshrined

Shoulda. Woulda. Coulda.

Cute rhyme. The reality was that one of the Ring-wraiths from The Lord of the Rings *drove him to red smoke sure as if the bastard hog-tied him and threw him in the back of a car.*

Actually, mate, you'd be the front bumper.

Exactly.

p. 5

. . . The thing had woken him up as usual, an alarm clock as reliable and stiff off the ground as Big Fucking Ben.

p. 19

The Brother Rhage's voice boomed. "That bunch of self-serving, prejudicial, light-in-the-loafer—"

"Watch the loafer references," *the Brother Butch cut in.* "I have some on."

"—parasitic, shortsighted motherfuckers—"

"Tell us how you really feel," *someone else said.*

"—can take their fakakta ball and blow it out their asses."

The king's laugh was low. "Good thing you're not a diplomat, Hollywood."

"Oh, you gotta let me send a message. Better yet, let's have my beast go as an emissary. I'll have him rip up the place. Serve those bastards right for how they've treated Marissa."

"You know," Butch announced, "I've always thought you had half a brain. In spite of what everyone else has said."

p. 36

Not more than five blocks to the east, in his private office at ZeroSum, Rehvenge, aka the Reverend, cursed. He hated the incontinent ones. Hated them.

The human man dangling in front of his desk had just pissed in his pants, the stain showing up as a dark blue circle at the crotch of his distressed Z Brands.

Looked like someone had nailed him in the hey-nanny-nannies with a wet sponge.

p. 49–50

"You got hair like a girl," Mr. D said.

"And you smell like bubble bath. At least I can get a trim."

p. 60

The king's voice resonated through the wall she leaned against. "Not having fun tonight, Z? You look like someone's shit on your front lawn."

p. 73

You're a freak. But I really can't accept these—

"Were you raised in a barn? Don't be ruuuuuuuuuuuuuuude, my boy. They're a gift."

Blay shook his head. "Take them, John. You're just going to lose this argument, and it will save us from the theatrics."

"Theatrics?" Qhuinn leaped up and assumed a Roman oratory pose. "Whither thou knowest thy ass from thy elbow, young scribe?"

Blay blushed. "Come on—"

Qhuinn threw himself at Blay, grasping onto the guy's shoulders and hanging his full weight off him. "Hold me. Your insult has left me breathless. I'm agasp."

Blay grunted and scrambled to keep Qhuinn up off the floor. "That's agape."

"Agasp sounds better."

Blay was trying not to smile, trying not to be delighted, but his eyes were sparkling like sapphires and his cheeks were getting red.

With a silent laugh, John sat on one of the locker room benches, shook out his pair of white socks, and pulled them on under his new old jeans. You sure, Qhuinn? 'Cuz I have a feeling they're going to fit and you might change your mind.

Qhuinn abruptly lifted himself off Blay and straightened his clothes with a sharp tug. "And now you offend my honor." Facing off at John, he flipped into a fencing stance. "Touché."

Blay laughed. "That's en garde, you damn fool."

Qhuinn shot a look over his shoulder. "Ça va, Brutus?"

"Et tu!"

"That would be tutu, I believe, and you can keep the cross-dressing to yourself, ya perv." Qhuinn flashed a brilliant smile, all twelve kinds of proud for being such an ass. "Now, put the fuckers on, John, and let's be done with this. Before we have to put Blay in an iron lung."

"Try sanitarium!"

"No, thanks, I had a big lunch."

pp. 121–122

Xhex offered him her arm without looking at him because she knew he was too much of a pride-filled dickhead to lean on her otherwise. And he needed to lean on her. He was weak as shit.

"I hate when you're right," he said.

"Which explains why you're usually so short-tempered."

p. 163

In spite of the exhaustion that was dragging at him, he shook his head. "Tell me."

"You don't—"

"You tell me . . . or I'm going to get up and start doing fucking Pilates."

"Whatever. You've always said that was for pansies."

"Fine. Jujitsu. Talk before I pass out, would you?"

p. 228

"Understood. And listen, I'm going to want to help Havers out. It's too much for him to set up the new clinic and care for patients. Thing is, it's going to involve some days off-site for me."

"Vishous okay with that security risk?"

"Not his call, and I'm telling you only out of courtesy." The female laughed dryly. "Don't give me that look. I'm already dead. It's not like the lessers can kill me again."

"That is so not funny."

"Gallows humor is part of having a doctor in the house. Deal with it."

Wrath barked a laugh. "You are such a hard-ass. No wonder V fell for you."

pp. 237–238

The hidden entrance to the escape tunnel was all the way in the far corner to the right and it was shielded by bookshelves that were on a slide. You simply reached out, pulled the copy of Sir Gawain and the Green Knight forward, and a latch released, causing the partition to retract and reveal—

"You are such a moron."

Qhuinn jumped like an Olympian. There, in the tunnel, seated in an outdoor lounger like he was getting a tan, was Blay. He had a book on his lap, a battery-operated lamp on a little table, and a blanket over his legs.

The guy calmly lifted a glass of orange juice up in toast, then took a sip. "Hellllllllo, Lucy."

"What the fuck? You're like lying in wait for me or some shit?"

"Yup."

"What was in your bed?"

"Pillows and my head blankie. I've had a nice little chill sesh hanging here. Good book, too." He flashed the cover of A Season in Purgatory. "I like Dominick Dunne. Good writer. Great glasses."

pp. 270–271

Hell, he expected a fleet of Dobermans to come trucking around the corner with their chompers showing.

Then again, the dogs were probably still gnawing on the bones of the last guest they'd turned into pulled pork.

p. 282

Hey, John signed.

"Hey."

John stepped back, clearing the way. How are you doing?

"I wish I were a smoker." Because then he could put this off for the duration of a cig.

No, you don't. You hate smoking.

"When I face the firing squad, I may rethink that hard line."

Shut up.

p. 283

In quick succession Qhuinn reviewed his answers: No, of course not, the knife was acting of its own volition, I was actually trying to stop it. . . . No, I only meant to give him a shave. . . . No, I didn't realize that slicing open someone's jugular was going to lead to death. . . .

p. 284

"John wants you to stay here."

Qhuinn's eyes shot to the king. "What?"

"You heard me."

"Shit. You can't approve that. No way can I stay here."

Black eyebrows crashed down. "Excuse me?"

"Er . . . sorry." Qhuinn clammed up, reminding himself that the Brother was king, which meant he could do whatever the fuck he wanted, including but not limited to re-naming the sun and the moon, declaring that people had to salute him with their thumbs up their asses . . . and taking roadkill like Qhuinn under his roof if he were so inclined.

King was spelled c-a-r-t-e b-l-a-n-c-h-e in the vampire world.

p. 286

As Qhuinn looked at his friend, he was not about to tell the guy that he was going to jail and then being released into the custody of Lash's parents to be tortured for the rest of his days. "Ah, not too bad."

You lie.

"Do not."

You're the color of fog.

"Well, hello, I had surgery, like, yesterday."

Oh, please. What's happening?

"To tell you the truth, I have no clue—"

p. 288

"You have what I call a 'male brow.' Which is a frown brought on when you're thinking about your male and you either want to boot him in the ass or wrap your arms around him and hold on 'til he can't breathe."

p. 292

But Tudor mansions on manicured grounds didn't look right with their grand front doors wide open to the night. It was like a debutante flashing her bra thanks to a ward-robe malfunction.

p. 302

"Thank you," Qhuinn said as V smoothed on more of that ointment, the fresh ink vivid against his golden skin. "Thank you very much."

"You haven't seen it yet. For all you know, I could have inked 'jackass' back here."

"Nah. I never doubt you," Qhuinn said, grinning up at the Brother.

Vishous smiled a little, his hard face with its tattoos showing approval. "Yeah, well, you aren't a flincher. Flinchers get fucked. The steady ones get the goods."

p. 314

Qhuinn pulled a light jacket from his bag and seemed to gather himself as he put it on. When he turned back around, his characteristic smart-ass smile was back in place. "Your wish is my command, prince of mine."

Don't call me that.

John headed for the exit, and he texted Blay, hoping the guy would show eventually. Maybe if he was bugged enough he'd relent?

"So what should I call you?" Qhuinn said as he leaped ahead to open the door with a flourish. "Would you prefer 'my liege'?"

Give it a rest, would you.

"How about good ol'-fashioned 'master'?" When John just glared over his shoulder, Qhuinn shrugged. "Fine. I'll go with fathead, then. But that's your damage, I gave you options."

pp. 315–316

"You want me to open your door," Qhuinn said dryly as he cut the engine.

John looked over. If I say yes, would you do it?

"No."

Then by all means, open my door.

"Damn you." Qhuinn got out of the driver's seat. "Ruining my fun."

John shut his door and shook his head. I'm just glad you're so manipulate-able.

"That's not a word."

Since when have you been in bed with Daniel Webster? Hello? 'Gigunda'?

Qhuinn glanced to the house. He could just hear Blay's voice filling in, That would be Merriam-Webster. "Whatever."

pp. 351–352

"Long time no see," the angel said.

"Not long enough."

"Always with the hospitality."

"Listen, GE." Rehv blinked hard. "Mind if you dim your disco ball?"

The glow drifted away until Lassiter appeared normal. Well, normal for someone with a serious-ass piercing fetish and aspirations for being some country's gold currency standard.

Trez shut the door and stood behind it, a wall of you-fuck-with-my-boy-and-angel-or-not-ima-show-your-ass-a-beatdown.

"What brings you onto my property?" Rehv said, cradling his mug with both hands and trying to absorb its warmth.

"Got a problem."

"I can't fix your personality, sorry."

Lassiter laughed, the sound ringing through the house like church bells. "No. I like myself just as I am, thank you."

"Can't help your delusional nature, either."

"I need to find an address."

"Do I look like a phone book?"

"You look like shit, as a matter of fact."

"And you with the compliments." Rehv finished his coffee. "What makes you think I'd help you?"

pp. 426–427

"Son of a bitch," Wrath breathed as the figure stopped twenty yards away.

The glowing man laughed. "Well, if it isn't good King Wrath and his band of merry-merry-happy-happy. I swear you boys should do kiddie shows, you're so fucking cheery."

"Great," Rhage muttered, "his sense of humor's still intact."

Vishous exhaled. "Maybe I can try and beat it out of him."

"Use his own arm to do it, if you can—"

Wrath glared at the two of them, who shot him back a pair of who-us? stares.

The king shook his head and addressed the lit figure. "Been a while. Thank God. How the hell are you?"

Before the man could answer, V cursed. "If I have to hear all that Keanu Reeves, Matrix, 'I am Neo' kind of shit, my head's going to explode."

"Don't you mean Neon?" Butch shot back. " 'Cause he reminds me of the Citgo sign."

p. 486

After a moment, Wrath turned to John. "This is Lassiter, the fallen angel. One of the last times he was here on earth, there was a plague in central Europe—"

"Okay, that was so not my fault—"

"—which wiped out two-thirds of the human population."

"I'd like to remind you that you don't like humans."

"They smell bad when they're dead."

"All you mortal types do."

p. 488

"Fuck. Me," Vishous breathed.

"I will so pass on that," Lassiter muttered.

p. 488

The stairwell fire alarm went off, its shrill cry the kind of thing that made you want to be deaf.

Phury laughed and rolled to the side, tucking her into his chest. "Five . . . four . . . three . . . two—"

"Soooooooooorrrrrrrrrrrrrrrrrryyy!" Layla called out from the foot of the stairs.

"What was it this time, Chosen?" he hollered back.

"Scrambled eggs," she yelled up.

Phury shook his head and said softly to Cormia, "See, I'd have figured it was the toast."

"Can't be that. She broke the toaster yesterday."

"She did?"

Cormia nodded. "Tried to put a piece of pizza in it. The cheese."

"Everywhere?"

"Everywhere."

Phury spoke up. "That's okay, Layla. You can always clean the pan and try again."

"I don't think the pan's going to work anymore," came the reply.

Phury's voice dropped. "I'm so not going to ask."

"Aren't they metal?"

"Should be."

pp. 526–527

The Brothers
on the Board

Brothers on the Board

When the adventure of these books being released first started, back in September of 2005, I had no idea how popular they would become. I was also incredibly clueless about the Internet. I didn't even know that Yahoo! Groups existed, or that message boards were a way authors connected with their readers, or that blogs and online reviewers were so important.

It wasn't until after *Lover Eternal* came out in March of 2006 that I started to focus on what kind of Internet presence I wanted to have. I set up a Yahoo! Group and started a message board. Now, three years later, we have thousands and thousands of readers on both, and have established a good community of folks.

Naturally, the Brothers come out every once in a while on the message board, and one of the best things about their visits, to me, is how the readers get involved. As whatever rolls goes down, the Cellies (as the enthusiastic members of the message board call themselves) join in, adding their comments (and actions!). I can't tell you the number of times I'll be rolling in hysterics, not just because of what the Brothers are doing, but because the readers are right along with them.

Here are just a few of my favorite frat-boy moments, and not surprisingly Rhage tends to be front and center in a lot of them. Bear in mind, when the Brothers come out on the board, they are in terms of their stories wherever I am in the process of writing, and I'm always at least one book ahead of where the readers are—so when V gets razzed for falling in love with Jane, the book that was out was actually *Lover Revealed*. Also, for the most part, as you follow the action, the Brothers are on their computers, but you'll see when what transpires slips into action—and you'll have to use your suspension of disbelief a little in these parts! Finally, I've edited out the Cellie comments and changed the content a little so it makes sense out of context, but you can enjoy the threads in all their glory on the BDB boards, which can be found at www.jrwardbdb.com/forum/index.php.

VISHOUS FREE TIME May 4, 2006	
RHAGE	Top Ten things Vishous does when he's not fighting 10. Stare into space wishing secretly he had someone like Mary 9. Drink Goose 8. Think to himself, Boy, if only someone like Mary would come into my life 7. Drink more Goose 6. Light hand rolled 5. Doodle on paper, *Vishous + (blank) = Happily Ever After* 4. Throw something at Butch 3. Wonder if he'll be lucky enough someday to have someone like Mary sleeping next to him 2. Trim that godforsaken goatee 1. Pray to the Scribe Virgin that she will grant him true love someday I think that's about right. Oh, except for snarl and glare a lot . . . ☺
CELLIE 1	I am so feeling the love between the Brothers . . . I don't know, Rhage, I've heard things about V's . . . um . . . habits . . . don't you think that might scare a lot of women off?
RHAGE	Frankly, I think he hypnotizes them. I mean, who in their right mind would volunteer for that shit? Especially with a guy who's got an ugly mug like V—with fuzz around his mouth. You know . . . razors are not all that expensive. If he just chilled on buying all that hardware for his desk, he could probably afford a Mach 5. Then again, maybe he needs something stronger . . . something with a little more HP. Note to self: tell Wrath to increase V's allowance so he can buy a Weedwacker for that thing on his puss.

WRATH	Good, I'm on. I didn't think this would work.
	Okay, boys, shouldn't you be crashed out? We got First Meal in three hours. Cut jerking each other off and grab some shut-eye. Long night ahead.
VISHOUS	With all due respect, my Lord . . . I don't sleep much.
	Ya know . . . Butch keeps me up.
	And I like the goatee. Grew it, like, a year ago. The females haven't complained.
RHAGE	V, my brother, you and I both know why the females don't complain. It's because of the ball gag. (Kidding.)
	And Wrath is right. I gotta go back to bed.
	Back to MARY.
	Mary..........................
	Oh, I love my Mary.
VISHOUS	Speaking of ball gags . . . you ever try one, Hollywood?
	And yeah, even though it kills me to say this . . . have fun witcha female, true? I'll see you at First Meal.
BUTCH O'NEAL	FYI, V likes to shake it at the ladi—
VISHOUS	Sorry . . . message was interrupted because I had to beat his ass.

KNITTERS ANONIMOUS	
May 8, 2006	
RHAGE (in his bedroom, posting in V's room on the board)	Hi, my name is V ("hi, V") I've been knitting for 125 years now (*gasping noises*) It's begun to impact my personal relationships: my brothers think I'm a nancy It's begun to affect my health: I'm getting a callus on my forefinger and I find bits of yarn in all my pockets and I smell like wool I can't concentrate at work: I keep picturing all these *lessers* in Irish sweaters and thick socks (*sounds of sympathy*) I've come seeking a community of people who like me are trying not to knit Can you help me? ("we're with you!") Thank you (*takes out hand-knitted hankie in pink*) (*sniffles*) ("we embrace you, V!")
VISHOUS (in the Pit)	Oh hell no . . . you did not just put that up. And nice spelling in the title. Man . . . you just have to roll up on me, don't you. I got four words for you, my brother.

RHAGE	Four words? Okay . . . lemme see . . . Rhage, you're SO sexy Hmmm . . . Rhage, you're SO smart No wait! Rhage, you're SO right! That's it, isn't it . . . g'head. You can tell me. . . .
VISHOUS	First one starts with a "P" Use your head for the other three. Bastard.
RHAGE	P? Hmmmmm . . . Please pass the yarn
VISHOUS	Payback Is A Bitch
RHAGE	Ohhhhhhhhhhhhhhhhhhhhhhhhhhhhhhhh I'm so scurrrred . . . Can you whip me up a blanket to hide under?
BUTCH O'NEAL (in the Pit)	Ummmmmmmmmmmmmmmmmm . . . Do any of you guys know why V just hightailed it out of here? With a can of shaving cream? And an expression on his face like someone pissed on his Escalade?

BELLA (in the billiards room on the lappy)	Holy shit Butch . . . V is like on fire— what did Rhage do?
BUTCH O'NEAL	Never mind . . . I found it. Knitting. Again. Man . . . V's just got to stop letting Rhage get under him like that! LOLOL My boy doesn't even knit! *races for tunnel, heading for mansion at dead run*
PHURY (in his bedroom)	Hey . . . V just came by my room. He left with a razor. . . .
BELLA	Phury! Why did you give him that!
PHURY	Well . . . he had shaving cream and said he needed to shave something. . . . I mean, how was I to know? I'll go after him. . . . *races out*
RHAGE	*looks up from computer as V bursts though the door* Shit! *lunges for the window* *doesn't make it*
MARY LUCE (in the foyer)	*running for the stairs* VISHOUS! VISHOUS! YOU TOUCH THAT *HELLREN* OF MINE AND YOUR FOUR TOYS ARE GOING TO END UP IN THE COURTYARD! AND UNDER MY CAR!
MARY LUCE	*throws open bedroom door* OMG

MARY LUCE	O.........M.........G
BUTCH O'NEAL	*bursts in to Rhage and Mary's bedroom* Man . . . First Meal is going to be SO much fun tonight. I think I'll wear chain mail. . . . *shudders* *laughing my ass off right now . . .*

	VAMPIRES WITH ONE EYEBROW ARE SEXY May 8, 2006
VISHOUS (back in the Pit, posting in Rhage's room on the board)	Hi! My name is Rhage . . . ☺ I'm starting a new trend in facial hair. Having one eyebrow is COOL. Having one eyebrow is SEXY. Having one eyebrow is very INTELLECTUAL. Come! Join me!
RHAGE (in his bedroom)	1. He immobilized me, the motherfucker. Or I would have gone to work on that goatee. AND IF HE WERE SO TOUGH HE WOULDN'T HAVE HAD TO PUT A WHAMMY ON MY ASS TO GET AT ME. 2. My hair grows back VERY fast. I should be BACK TO NORMAL in a couple of days. 3. Even if it takes me the rest of this month . . . he has SO got it coming to him.
VISHOUS	Rhage! What happened to your eyebrow! Why . . . it's gone. Did you slip while you were shaving? Hey . . . lemme ask you something. . . . . Does your head feel off-kilter? You know, heavier on one side?
RHAGE	Sure . . . yeah . . . laugh it up now that you're back at the Pit. I'm coming for you, boy. When you least expect it, I'm going to be there.

VISHOUS	You threatening me, big guy?
	You know . . . you could lose the OTHER one. . . . I mean, accidents happen. . . .
	laughing so hard it's hard to type
RHAGE	*trying hard to keep a straight face*
	loses it—starts laughing my ass off
	My brother! How could you do this to me! I mean . . . for real! I look like a freak!
MARY LUCE (in their bedroom)	There are a lot of women on this board, right? I mean . . . there are a lot of US here (as opposed to MEN who have BIZARRE ways of expressing themselves). . . .
	The only thing that saves these two knuckleheads from being total bores is that they ALWAYS end up cracking themselves up—I mean . . . you wouldn't BELIEVE how often this happens here.
	THEY ARE CRAZY!
	bats away Rhage's hand from waist Stop it . . . I'm typing.
	You want to know what they did last week?
	laughs as Rhage nuzzles her neck Stop it!
	So do you want to know—
VISHOUS	How about now, Hollywood?
	You wanna throw down? Why don't you come to the Pit, my brother, and we'll have at it.
	Cop'll time the rounds.
RHAGE	Not now, V.
	I'm with Mary and I'm going to be . . . busy for a while.
	works his way up Mary's neck to her lips

J R WARD	Do you see what I have to deal with in my head!
	LOLOL
	And yeah . . . Rhage is definitely . . . busy right now. . . .
	It's time for me to get back to Butch, too!

	PAYBACK IS A BITCH September 20, 2006
RHAGE (in his bathroom)	*peers into bathroom mirror* *looks back at Mary* You sure this is going to stay in place?
MARY LUCE	Are you *sure* you have to do this?
BUTCH O'NEAL (in mansion's kitchen)	*standing over kitchen sink* *working the faucet*
RHAGE	*to Mary* Promise me this will stay in place. *tugs at black wig*
MARY LUCE	You have enough bobby pins in there to set off the metal detectors at the airport. *shakes head*
FRITZ (outside Rhage and Mary's bedroom)	*knocks on door* Sire? I have what you requested.
RHAGE	*claps hands* Hot dayum. Let the fun begin. *kisses Mary* *draws on black silk bathrobe* *jogs to the door* *opens it* Ohhhhhhhhhhhhhhhhhhhhhhhhhhhhhhhhhhhhhhh, yeah. That's what I'm talking about!

FRITZ	*hands over Boom Box the size of Chicago*
	We are prepared to go to the Pit, sire.
	smiles Such fun!
RHAGE	*claps Fritz on the shoulder*
	Attaboy!
	heads out into hall
	two finger whistles
	hollers WE ON!
WRATH (in study)	*hears whistle*
	Hot fucking damn.
	leaps up from desk
	jogs out of study
	stops short
	OH SHIT! *busts out laughing*
PHURY (in his bedroom)	*hears whistle*
	stabs out red smoke hand-rolled
	runs out of bedroom
	stops dead
	Oh my fucking God!
	starts to laugh at sight of Rhage in black wig that looks just like V's hair
	yells Yo, Z!

ZSADIST (in billiards room)	*hears whistle*
	hears Phury call his name
	runs to the bottom of the stairs from the billiards room
	watches as Rhage, Phury, and Wrath jog down grand staircase
	fights smile
	loses
	You are fucking ugly as a brunette. S'all I'm saying.
	And that robe. What the fuck's under it?
	Rhage flashes
	OMG!
RHAGE	*yells to kitchen* # COP, YOU GOOD TO GO?
BUTCH O'NEAL	*comes out of kitchen with two Super Soakers cocked and ready to rock*
	pulls a Bruce Willis, both pump-action specials held up high
	Yippee-kayyyyyyyyyyyyyyyy-yay, motherfuuuuuuuuuuuuuuucker!
RHAGE	*glares at cop* Yeah, okay, that's my line. ## Let's move it! *sets off for hidden door under stairs, Wrath, Z, Phury, and Butch behind him*

IN THE WEIGHT ROOM
September 20, 2006

VISHOUS (in training center's weight room)	*pumping on the bench press* *Biggie Smalls in the ears* 12................................ 13................................ 14................................ *grits teeth* *pecs go rock-hard*
RHAGE	*pauses outside of weight room* *whispers* We ready?
BUTCH O'NEAL	Yeah, but do we have the basket of—
ZSADIST	Got 'em. Fritz hooked me.
RHAGE	*throws open weight room door* My brother! What up? *grins like a sick bastard*
VISHOUS	*puts weights up on the rack slowly* What the.....................................fuck—
RHAGE	Hold him, my brothers! *puts Boom Box down on weight bench* *cranks it wiiiiiiiiiiiiiiiiiiiiiiiiiiiiiiiiiiiiiiiiiiiiiiiiiiiiiiiide open* *karaoke version of sappy-ass love song plays to which Rhage adds free-floating peach-oriented verses*
VISHOUS	NOOOOOOOOOOOOOOOOOOOOOOOOOOOOO—

BUTCH O'NEAL	*tosses Super Soakers to Phury* *cranks V into a choke hold* In honor of your new situation in life—
RHAGE	*whips down robe, revealing black wife-beater that reads on front: **VISHOUS THE MIGHTY HAS FALLEN** *turns around with robe around his hips* **MY FEMALE IS THE BOSS OF ME**
VISHOUS	Oh, fuck me!!!!!!!!!!!!!!!!!!!!!!!!!!!!!!!!!!!!! *gets cut off by Zsadist, who steps up to him*
ZSADIST	This is for your own good. *pinches V's nose closed* *when V opens mouth* *shoves motherfucking peach in the piehole*
RHAGE	*singing, bouncing to the fucking beat* *shakes his moneymaker* *Cabbage Patches it, then points to back of wife-beater* # Ain't that right, V?????? Who's your mama?
VISHOUS	*bites down on MFN peach* *wishes it were Rhage's MFN arm*
BUTCH O'NEAL	# Hit him, Phury!

PHURY	*tosses one Super Soaker to Wrath*
	lets his fly
	peach juice splatters alllllllllllllllllllllllllllllllllllllllllllllll over V
WRATH	*catches other Super Soaker on the fly*
	lambastes V with peach juice
RHAGE	*still singing*
	turns around and drops robe to floor *across ass reads:*
	# PUSSY-WHIPPED
VISHOUS	*plots the deaths of all his brothers and his roommate*
	but starts to laugh his ass off
RHAGE	*working it like a flippin' idiot*
	shaking the junk in his trunk
VISHOUS	*blinks from the MFN peach juice in his eyes*
	thinks of his female
	figures, WTF, she's so worth it
RHAGE	*music fades*
	breathes deeply from the workout
	walks up to V
	Now . . . *breath* V . . . I know you like to . . . *breath* give the orders.
	But you're . . . going to tell everyone here that you love her.
	In front of all these people . . . *breath* you're going to say that you love her.
	Then we're even for the Mary shit. Mostly.

ZSADIST	*rips peach out of V's mouth* Damn, my brother . . . you smell like a frickin' peach. *smiles* Although . . . I like one peach. You ain't her thou.
VISHOUS	*swallows* *drags in breath* *sucks peach flesh from fangs* *glares at Rhage*
RHAGE	Do it.
VISHOUS	*takes deep breath*
VISHOUS	*feels lick of fear, which pisses him the fuck off*
RHAGE	DO IT!
VISHOUS	I love her.
VISHOUS	I love her.
VISHOUS	I love her.
VISHOUS	I love her!
VISHOUS	I love her!!!!!!!!!
VISHOUS	*draws in great breath* *screams until the cords in his neck stand out and his voice goes hoarse* I LOOOOOOOOOOOOOOOOOOOOOOOOOOOOOOOOVE HER!!!!!!!!!!!!!!!!!!!!!!!!!

RHAGE	Well-done, my brother. Let him go, Z. *claps hand on V's shoulder* *puts forehead on V's* Well-done and well blessed . . .
VISHOUS	This is one fight I don't mind losing . . . *clasps back of Rhage's neck* *holds on*
RHAGE	Now . . . no offense . . . but you need a fucking shower. *grins while ripping off black wig* Oh, and by the way? You can have this shirt. And the sweats.
VISHOUS	*shakes head as his brothers and roommate file out* *wipes his face on arm* *licks arm* *thinks . . . I MFN love peaches* *heads for the Pit*

	WALKIN' INTO THE PIT September 20, 2006
VISHOUS (in the Pit)	*opens door from underground tunnel* *sniffs . . .* WTF? Smells like . . .
VISHOUS	*frowns* *walks down the hall to his bedroom*
VISHOUS	*reaches past doorjamb to bedroom and flips on light* ## OHHHHHHHHH GOD—
VISHOUS	*jaw falls open* *entire room is painted peach* *bed linens are peach* *rug is peach* *drapes are peach* *lamp shade is peach*
VISHOUS	*walks over to closet* *whips open doors* Oh sweet Mary mother of GOD . . . *peach shirts hang on hangers* *peach jacket on peg* *peach *fakakta* shitkickers on floor* *expression of horror settles on face as reaches for gun closet*

VISHOUS	*opens up gun closet* # NOOOOOOOOOOOOOO! Not the GLOOOOOOOOOOOOOOOOOOCKS!
RHAGE (in the Pit)	*pokes head through bedroom doorway* Hey, this looks great! And . . . V . . . that "I love my female" shit? Nice, very nice . . . but I did tell you it only got you mostly forgiven. *grins*
VISHOUS	*levels diamond stare at Rhage* The Glocks, too . . . ?
RHAGE	Just water-based, buddy. Don't get your peach knickers in a wad. *grins even wider*
VISHOUS	You realize this can't go unavenged? That this just raises the bar?
RHAGE	Not only do I know that . . . I'm motherfucking counting on it. *laughs* Ball's in your court, my brother. Or not, as the case may be. *heads out the door laughing* *pauses and leans back in* You know I am happy for you, right? Very happy . . . yeah, this has been a long time in coming. *shakes head*

RHAGE	Funny . . . I'm not like you, I don't see into the future and shit.
	But somehow . . . now . . . I know for sure yours is a good one.
	Later, my brother.
	*********************FINIS*********************

	VALENTINE'S DAY WITH THE BDB February 19, 2007
J R WARD	Wellllllllllllllllllllllllllllllll . . . As usual, I was wrong. V is going to be bigger than Butch. At this point, I would bet the finished MS will come in at about 600 pages. Butch was 582 or something. *sigh*
VISHOUS (in the Pit's living room)	Smoke that cop.
BUTCH O'NEAL (in his bedroom at the Pit)	Bigger ain't better, roomie.
VISHOUS	Said the pencil to the baseball bat.
BUTCH O'NEAL	Maybe you're just fat. I mean, now that you're all in love and shit, you prolly just sissy around daydreaming and eating bonbons. Hey, didn't I see a bunch of Lindt wrappers around your bed?
VISHOUS	Speaking of bonbons, why don't you fess up what you did for Marissa for Valentine's Day.
BUTCH O'NEAL	Don't change the subject. Why front? Look, there's nothing wrong with lying around, staring at the ceiling, sucking back truffles, and pining for your female to come home. Of course, that's if you're a dog, I suppose.

BUTCH O'NEAL	Hey, do I need to hit Pets.com and score you some flea spray and a new leash? I could get you a pink one to match that nail polish you're wearing.
VISHOUS	Two words, ya bastard. CONSTRUCTION. PAPER. Tell me something, did you use the safety scissors like I asked you to?
BUTCH O'NEAL	Two words for you: CYNDI. LAUPER.
VISHOUS	Clearly, the paste you ate has gone to your head. Did Marissa like all that lace you glued on? Oh . . . and I'm talking to your body, not that ridiculous card you made her.
BUTCH O'NEAL	*tilts head to the side* How does that song go? Mememememememememememe . . . *sings song about true colors* *badly*
VISHOUS	I have no idea what you are talking about.
BUTCH O'NEAL	Oh. Really. So you deny that shit was playing in the weight room yesterday?
VISHOUS	Please. Like I listen to crap like that?
BUTCH O'NEAL	So you deny that song was also playing in the Escalade last night?

VISHOUS	Don't act the fool.
BUTCH O'NEAL	So you deny that song was ALSO coming out of your shower early this morning.
VISHOUS	You're imagining shit—
RHAGE (in his bedroom on the laptop)	You know . . . I saw him doodling the other day while he was doing the *NYT* crossword puzzle. Guess what he was writing?
VISHOUS	Rhage is a gum-flapping moron. There. Mystery solved.
RHAGE	Well, there was that part that went: Rhage is so beautiful, I wish I weren't an ugly-ass wanker and could be half as hot as him. But I digress. Guess what the two words were?
BUTCH O'NEAL	I SUCK. No, wait! WHERE'S JANE? Oh, even better. MORE TISSUES. 'Cause he cries like a bitch when she ain't around. ☺
RHAGE	"TRUE COLORS." I swear, boy's got a Lauper fixation. You know what's next? He's going to toss his Jay-Z and his Pac and load up on Manilow and the Bee Gees. No more G-Unit for him. From now on? Easy listening, disco drool.
VISHOUS	Lauper is NOT disco!

RHAGE	Oh . . . no . . . Oh, hell no. You didn't just go there. You didn't just defend CYNDI LAUPER. LOLOLOLOLOLOLOLOLOLOLOLOLOLOLOLOLOL OLOLOLOL—
BUTCH O'NEAL	*starts to weep* I can't deal. I can't fuckin' deal. How the mighty have fallen— V? Where are you going? Hey! V—shit—
VISHOUS (in Butch's bedroom)	*holds up red heart made of construction paper with paper lace carefully glued all around the edges* *reads cursive lettering of the sort that suggests maker of card spent hours getting the words to look right* *My dearest Marissa,* *No commercial card could do justice* *To how I feel for you,* *No Hallmark whimsy or e-card flimsy* *could count as even half as true.* *I made this card and labored hard,* *to make it worthy of this day . . .* *and here is what my heart has to say:* *I love you. I need you. I want you.* *I am always yours.* *Love, Butch*

VISHOUS (in Butch's bedroom)	*eyes roommate* And you want to smack my ass about Lauper? Please, next thing you know you're going to be writing jingles for Lifetime and Oxygen.
RHAGE	You wrote that, cop? You fuckin wrote that? LOLOLOLOLOLOLOLOLOLOLOLOLOLOLOLOL—
MARY LUCE (from their bathroom)	Rhage . . . you better stop giving them a hard time or I'll tell them what you did for me for V Day.
RHAGE	*clams up* *coughs* The Board's PG-13, Mary. So you couldn't—
VISHOUS	Mary, you have excellent timing. Do tell.
BUTCH O'NEAL	Yeah, this is FANTASTIC. *glares at V* Now give me my fuckin' card back.
VISHOUS	*holds up overhead* *runs down hall* *circles around Foosball table* Not until you admit that that is the WORST piece of sappy-ass writing in the world. I swear, this thing is dripping with sugar. I'm about to go into a diabetic coma. Now, Mary, fill us in— OW! Fuck you, cop. *rubs shoulder*

BUTCH O'NEAL	*takes card back* *carefully makes sure lace is still properly attached*
	I'd rather write my own sap than cop the shit from Cyndi mothafuckin' LAUPER.
	Now, Mary, spill, if you will.
RHAGE	Oh . . . God . . . someone shoot me.
VISHOUS	My pleasure.
BUTCH O'NEAL	Me first!
VISHOUS	Let me handle it, cop. You've got to hold your precious little card there, Casanova.
	My aim'll be better.
	Mary?
MARY LUCE	Well, you know those tubes of cake icing you can get at the store?
RHAGE	Mary, please—
WRATH (from laptop in study)	Can it, Hollywood.
	I wanna hear this.
	In fact, I'm making a kingly resolution. You don't open your mouth again till she's finished or I'll hang you.
BETH RANDALL (behind him in the study)	Wrath.
	You sure you want to go there?
WRATH	*mutters* Shit.
	Leelan, listen, just because Mary—

BETH RANDALL	Uh-huh. Riiiiiiiiight. Mary, you first. Then it's my turn.
MARY LUCE	LOL Fabulous! Anyway, he asked Fritz to get him one of those tubes of decorating icing, then laid himself out naked on our bed and wrote: MARY'S LOVE BUG across his chest. Then he asked me to lick it off.
VISHOUS	Oh, that's masculine. Yeah. Totally.
RHAGE	Listen, GIRLS JUST WANT TO HAVE FUN, you're not exactly poppin' the testosterone either.
VISHOUS	But I didn't LOVE BUG my own ass.
BUTCH O'NEAL	OH MY GOD OHMYGOD OHMYGOD OHMYGOD . . . I can't fuckin' stop laughing! *braces hands on knees* *roars with laughter*
RHAGE	I swear, I'm going to take that card and shove it up your—
MARY LUCE	Rhage, don't be rude. So, Beth—what did Wrath do?
WRATH	Nothing. It was a night just like any—

BETH RANDALL	A night like any other?
	So what have I been missing?
	As near as I can recall, you've never before done the rose-petal-on-the-bed thing.
VISHOUS	*busts out laughing*
	Oh, shit . . . you didn't rose-petal the bed, my lord.
	Tell me you didn't go like that?
RHAGE	He petaled the bed?
	Fuuuuuuuuuuuuuuuuuuuuuuuuuuuuuuuuuuuuuuuuuuuuuuuuuuuuuuuuuck!
	LOLOLOLOLOLOL
	Then what happened?
WRATH	Just so all of you are aware . . . the use of drawing and quartering has fallen out of favor.
	But I'm thinking of reviving the practice.
	I'm REALLY thinking of bringing that shit back.
BETH RANDALL	He lit a bunch of candles—
BUTCH O'NEAL	Were they pretty pink ones?
	Scented with something sweet like lavender—
WRATH	Watch it, cop. Or you'll find yourself in pieces.
	And they were black.
VISHOUS	I SO approve.
WRATH	They were used for light only, V. Not your kind of shit.
BETH RANDALL	Anyway, he laid me out on the rose petals, got on his knees beside the bed, and took out a little red box.

ᴠISHOUS	Inside of which was a . . . REALLY BADLY WORDED HANDMADE CARD WITH LACE AROUND IT?
ʙUTCH ᴅ'NEAL	Fuck you. It was a *Cyndi Lauper's Greatest Hits* CD.
ᴊ ʀ ᴡARD	Can I go back to work now?
ᴠISHOUS	Stuff it, Challa. NO.
ʀHAGE	NO.
ʙUTCH ᴅ'NEAL	NO.
ᴡRATH	YES. That's an order.
ʙETH ʀANDALL	ANYWAY! So he's on his knees with the little red box, which has Cartier written on it. He opens it and—
ᴡRATH	Pair of ruby earrings. No BFD. Told her I loved her and blah blah blah. Okay, back to—
ʙETH ʀANDALL	AND he said to me that they were very rare and perfectly matched. Just like our hearts.
ᴠISHOUS	No offense, my lord . . . but I'm going to hurl. Right after I stop laughing my ass off! LOL
ʙUTCH ᴅ'NEAL	OMG! That is just so SWEET! Did you get the two of you matching robes with hearts on them, too? Matching socks with hearts? Matching long johns with hearts? Matching—

WRATH	You know what also matches? Two black eyes.
J R WARD	Okay, that's IT! I have to go back to V. ENOUGH!
VISHOUS	Yeah, sure, now that the deets are out you decide to get hard ass. Fine . . . finish me already. God knows, it's taken you long enough, Challa. *********************FINIS********************
WRATH	Can't let V have the last word. Sorry, I'm the king, that's my zip code. Don't listen to V bitching about his book getting done. He's just got a dime between his cheeks about his story getting out. You know him, he's about as well adjusted as a broken wheelbarrow. LATER.

So, yeah, the Brothers definitely are just the way they are in the books when they come out on the boards—there's a lot of fooling around. But it's not all fun and games.

Lassiter, the fallen angel who is introduced in *Lover Enshrined*, actually made his first appearance on the boards. It was so odd. As is typical of the Brothers, I can be doing something totally unrelated to them when all of a sudden it's WHAM!—download time. Lassiter was like that. I had him in the back of my mind for a long time, knowing only bits and pieces of what he was. And then one night I was just answering questions. . . .

I'll let you see for yourself. Again, the Cellie comments have been largely edited out, and some changes have been so the content makes sense, but here's Lassiter's grand entrance:

HELLO, OLD FRIEND May 13, 2006	
LASSITER (from laptop, located God only knows where)	Well, well, well . . . looks like you finally man'd up, vampire. Remember me?
WRATH (in study at the Brotherhood's mansion)	I thought you were dead.
LASSITER	That all you got to say to me?
WRATH	Gee . . . your hair is SO different.
LASSITER	You can't see me, so how do you know what it looks like, Blind King?
WRATH	Two things about your kind will always be true. And the second is your hair never changes. So where are you?
LASSITER	Shit, you've found a sense of humor. How lucky for your Brothers. I hear you have a queen now, vampire.
WRATH	You didn't answer my question. Where are you?
LASSITER	Worried, Blind King?
WRATH	Scared to tell me?
LASSITER	Touché. Let's just say I'm around. And wanted to make sure you knew it.

WRATH	I've got SUCH a case of the warm and fuzzies right now, you can't believe it.
VISHOUS (in the Pit)	My lord, I'm about two inches away from blocking his sorry ass.
	You just say the word.
LASSITER	OMG. Look who's here. How are those tats of yours?
VISHOUS	Fuck you. Right now. Right here.
	Do yourself a favor and get gone.
WRATH	Easy, V. You know what they say about enemies.
VISHOUS	Yeah, they're best hung by their necks.
LASSITER	Vishous, such passion from you, the cold one.
	Guess you haven't forgotten me. I'm touched.
VISHOUS	You want to get touched . . . I'll touch you, all right—
WRATH	ENOUGH. V, back the fuck off.
	And, Lassiter, I want to know why you're rolling up in my house. Now of all times.
LASSITER	Just wanted to say hello. And congratulate you on your ascendance.
WRATH	So dial up FTD and send my ass some flowers. But cut the shit and get off my board.
LASSITER	Why would I do that? You wouldn't be able to see them.
WRATH	That's too petty for you.
	Which makes me realize something . . .
VISHOUS	Let me hunt him, my Lord. PLEASE let me hunt him.

RHAGE (in his bedroom)	OMG, he's alive.
LASSITER	Yeah. Go figure. How goes it, big warrior? Oh—wait, I know how it is with you. How many females have you done this week, Rhage?
RHAGE	One. Only one. And fuck you, BTW. Shit . . . this is too weird.
WRATH	LOL So, Lassiter, I can only assume by your charming conversation that you want something from us. Unless it's a stab wound or a broken femur, I don't know if we're much in the mood to indulge you.
PHURY (in his bedroom)	God . . . I can't stand it.
LASSITER	Which is why you're celibate, right? And Wrath, hell, vampire . . . we always throw down. It's always been oil and water.
PHURY	How's that female of yours. Still missing?
LASSITER	YOU DO NOT SPEAK OF HER.
PHURY	You want respect? Trying throwing some of it first.
LASSITER	YOU DO NOT SPEAK OF HER!
WRATH	Enough! I'm bored with the drama. Phury, V . . . Rhage. Off the Board. NOW. You know where I want you, so get your asses up here. As for you, Lassiter—

LASSITER	Look . . . shit, vampire, I didn't come here to stir shit.
	Well, maybe a little.
	And you're right. I may need something.
VISHOUS	Like a hole right in your head.
	FYI I got something that can take care of that. It's called a Glock nine—
WRATH	Vishous, log the fuck out! You are NOT helping.
LASSITER	Yeah, run along, you glow-in-the-dark fr—
	Shit. I'm doing it again.
	Look . . . I just wanted to . . .
	Maybe later. This just isn't the time. Or the place.
WRATH	True.
	On both accounts. Now if you'll excuse me, I have business with the Brothers.
	And just a little word of advice. Having V pissed off at you is like strapping a bull's-eye to your chest and walkin' onto a pistol range. You might consider moving from wherever you are. Because even if you scramble your IP and play hide-and-go-seek with the Internet shit, he will find where you were based on this happy little session. When he does, I seriously doubt I'll be able to talk him down.
	Probably won't try too hard at it, either.
LASSITER	Fair enough, vampire. Fair enough.
	But I'll be back. If the Fates allow. Later, Blind King.

	# I KNOW WHERE LASSITER IS May 13, 2006
VISHOUS (in the Pit)	You game?
RHAGE (in his bedroom)	Abso-fucking-lutely. When?
VISHOUS	It's going to take some time to get there—
WRATH (in the study)	Do you think I don't know you're still gum-flapping? Asses up here, now. I'm in a pissed-off mood to begin with, and if I have to wait more than a minute and a half for you two, I'm going to put my fist through the wall.
VISHOUS	Coming.
RHAGE	Me, too, my Lord.

Clearly, they didn't listen to Wrath, however. . . .

BOOK ORDER June 20, 2006	
CELLIE 1	hi! I'm fairly new to the board and i usually lurk. i was curious what is the book order for the guys? who comes after butch etc? i wasn't able to find the link so if it's already been discussed, my bad!
J R WARD	I would LOVE LOVE LOVE LOVE to write Blay's and also Qhuinn's books. YUUUUUUUUUUUUUUUUUUUUUUUUUUUUUUM
LASSITER (from his laptop, God only knows where)	WHAT ABOUT MINE
VISHOUS (in the Pit)	Sorry, she doesn't bother with your kind.
LASSITER	You sure about that? Maybe you're just worried she'll forget about you.
VISHOUS	Yeah, right. Because you're so fucking distracting. How's your car? Ooops . . . I mean your pile of metal flakes.
LASSITER	Cheap shot, vampire. But then, I'd expect it from you. Sneaking in. Ashing a male's place. Yeah, that's some scary shit, right there.
VISHOUS	You had to know I was coming. Guess you just raaaaaaaaaaaaaaaaaaaaaaaaan away.
LASSITER	Hey, Vishous . . . when you look in the mirror, do you ever wonder what your daddy would think of you now?
RHAGE (in his bedroom)	Whooooooooooooooooooooooooooooooa, okay. Time to chill this out. Lassiter, get the fuck off the Boards—

VISHOUS	When you look in the mirror, do you wonder where that female of yours is?
LASSITER	Just for that, I'm sending you a little present in the mail, vampire.
WRATH (in the study)	Vishous, Rhage, off the Boards. NOW.
	Lassiter, got a little news flash for you, buddy. You're not making friends, asshole. And a guy like you . . . man, shit, you got plenty of people who want your head on a stake.
	We're more than happy to hop on that train.
	You want a six-pack of enemies? You just keep this shit up.
LASSITER	Just looking for airtime, Blind King. Just looking for airtime.
	And tell your boy V that he needs to run home to Daddy—
	Oh! I'm sorry. Daddy's dead, isn't he.
VISHOUS	I will kill you. I swear to fucking God, I will—
LASSITER	Funny thing about my kind . . . we're hard to see, hard to find.
	You ever consider that maybe I'm right behind you?
VISHOUS	I'm out of here.
	Kiss your sister for me, cocksucker.
LASSITER	Jesus Christ . . .
	Check your mail, vampire.
	Later.
WRATH	Vishous, you get your ass up to the main house.
BUTCH O'NEAL (in the Pit)	What the hell is going on? V's shut himself in his room and—
	FUCK!

WRATH	Cop . . .
	Cop?
RHAGE	I'm going over there!
WRATH	*alarms going off like crazy*
	Wrath runs out of study
ZSADIST (in main house)	*tears off in the direction of the Pit*
PHURY	*runs for underground tunnel with the rest of the Brothers*
BUTCH O'NEAL	*grabs fire extinguisher*
	kicks open V's bedroom door
	lets fly with the spray
RHAGE	*burst into Pit*
	races for V's bedroom
	grabs first thing that he sees—a comforter
	pulls a flying tackle, taking V down to the floor
WRATH	*skids into doorway of V's bedroom*
	looks at scene
	sees huge scorched pattern on walls, ceiling, and floor, as if explosion went off
	sees Rhage get thrown off Vishous
	V wheels around, a savage expression on his face
	V . . . V, just chill—
BUTCH O'NEAL	*turns off fire extinguisher*
	listens to dripping sounds
	smells smoke
	Holy . . . shit.

VISHOUS	*scrubs face with glowing hand*
	looks at brothers
	becomes instantly composed, so calm he's robotlike
	glances at Rhage
	You okay? I tossed you hard.
RHAGE	Yeah, I'm good. I'm . . . ah, yeah.
	reaches out
VISHOUS	Don't touch me. Don't anybody fucking touch me.
	I'm going to the gym.
	I'm . . . going to the gym and then I'll come back and clean this shit up.
	walks out, heading for tunnel
ZSADIST	*watches V leave*
	without making a sound, disappears into tunnel
VISHOUS	*stops in tunnel*
	For shit's sake, Z, I don't need a babysitter.
ZSADIST	DO I LOOK LIKE A FUCKING BABYSITTER TO YOU
	I'M WORKING OUT NOW
	GOT NOTHING TO DO WITH YOU OR YOUR FRYIN' ASS
VISHOUS	I want to be alone.
ZSADIST	WITH ME YOU ARE ALONE
VISHOUS	*throws up hands*
	keeps walking
	is very aware that Z is right behind him. All the way to the gym.

WRITING SPEED & OTHER QUESTIONS July 10, 2006	
CELLIE 1	WARDen, I am amazed and in awe of your skill and talent. I hope the Brothers never stop talking. Enough said.
J R WARD	Me frickin' too . . . I have great hope for the new ones . . . John and Blaylock and Qhuinn and, yeah . . . . the new ones.
CELLIE 2	And your hope gives us hope too, WARDen. . . . But not a sodding time machine in sight here . . . Bugger!
J R WARD	LOLOL!
CELLIE 3	And dare I add, Lassiter too!
J R WARD	Mmmmmmmmmmmmmmmmmmmmmmmmmm LASSITER
LASSITER (from his laptop, God only knows where)	You rang?
J R WARD	Oh, hell, no . . . we are not doing this righ—
LEEBRA725 Site Admin	Oh, this is gonna be goooooooooooooooooooooooooooooooooooooooood............. *grabs the popcorn*
VISHOUS (in the Pit)	Sorry asshole . . . she's busy. LATER.
LASSITER	Busy, huh. With you?

VISHOUS	She is permanently busy when it comes to you. How about that?
LASSITER	I'm going to make a liar out of you.
VISHOUS	Good luck. LATER.
LASSITER	Oh, I think Ima stay right here. Why don't you run along. Run, run away—
J R WARD	Like I said, we're not doing this right now. My eyelids are drooping and I have to—
VISHOUS	No offense, Challa, but you don't get a vote. Lassiter, do you remember the grave?
LASSITER	Yeah. What about it.
VISHOUS	Meet me there.
WRATH (in the study)	Hi, V. Remember me? I'm your Brother. Your king. The motherfucker who can put you on hiatus? Okay . . . good. I've got your attention. Now get the fuck off the Boards. And come to my study. NOW.
LASSITER	Vishous. I'll be there. Hour before dawn. You got any balls, you'll show. It's your fucking idea.
WRATH	Lassiter, you just don't know when to quit, do you?
LASSITER	I have something you want, vampire. Something you're missing. Be nice, asshole. And what? You afraid your precious little Magic 8 Ball, that whacked-out FREAK, might get hurt?

J R WARD	I'm tired . . . can I go to be—
WRATH	I will be there. Hour before dawn. Don't fuck around. I am perfectly capable of killing you just because you bore the shit out of me.
LASSITER	Well, well, well . . . an audience with the king . . . wonder what I should wear?
WRATH	With the mood I'm in? Body armor. And do yourself a favor. Come armed. You might live longer.
LASSITER	You know my kind. Our weapons are always concealed and always with us. Hour before dawn. I'll be there, vampire.
LASSITER	Oh, PS leave the FREAK at home. He and I don't get along. LATER.
VISHOUS	I'm going with you, my Lord.
WRATH	Fuck you, V. He's a shithead, but you are part of the problem.
VISHOUS	Then take Rhage. But you need backup.
WRATH	EXCUSE ME?
VISHOUS	You know what he's capable of.

WRATH	GET THE FUCK UP HERE. NOW.
BETH RANDALL (from laptop in their bedroom)	Wrath?
WRATH	Not now.
BETH RANDALL	Yes, now.
WRATH	What.
BETH RANDALL	I know what he is. And the only way you are meeting him an hour before dawn without any support is over my dead body. Period.
WRATH	Jesus Christ, *leelan*, what the—
J R WARD	Can I go to bed now? I have to get up at six—
BETH RANDALL	My. Dead. Body. So who will you take with you?
VISHOUS	Thank you for talking some sense into—
BETH RANDALL	Vishous, stay out of this. And don't go into the study. Wrath? You were about to answer me.
ZSADIST	I'M GOING WITH HIM
WRATH	Shit. Is Z acceptable, *leelan*?
BETH RANDALL	Perfectly acceptable, as long as he is fully armed.

ZSADIST	WHAT THE FUCK
	LIKE I'D GO IN BALLET SLIPPERS
WRATH	*starts to laugh*
	pushes wraparounds up on forehead and rubs eyes
	Fine. Fuck it.
	Now, Beth . . . I gave you something you wanted.
	How 'bout you come on down to my study and give me something I want.
BETH RANDALL	How about you make peace with Vishous and then come find me.
WRATH	V?
	Quick, hook a Brother up.
	We cool?
VISHOUS	Welllllllllllllllllllllllllllllllllllllllllllllllllllllllllllllllllllllllll . . .
WRATH	You are a CRUEL motherfucker.
	Come on!
VISHOUS	Beg me.
BETH RANDALL	Vishous, that's just mean.
	And that's my line, not yours.
	Never mind, Wrath. I'm on my way.
WRATH	*rises from desk, eyes trained on double doors of the study*
	peels off black T-shirt
	kicks off shitkickers
	undoes button on fly of leathers

BETH RANDALL	*pushes open doors to study* I tell you, Vishous can be such a— # HELLO.
WRATH	Hi. *dangles leathers from his hand* *tosses them to the floor* So, *leelan* . . . how about you close that door. And lock it.
J R WARD	CAN I PLEASE GO TO SLEEP NOW? I'M FRICKIN' EXHAUSTED.
J R WARD	Good night, Cellies!

	LASSITER July 11, 2006
WRATH (in the study, posting in Lassiter's room on the board)	Hit me up when you get this.

	LASSITER? July 11, 2006
WRATH (in the study, posting in the WARDen's room on the board)	Come on, man. Hit me up.

	ᴅᴏɴ'ᴛ ꜰʀᴏɴᴛ July 11, 2006
ᴡʀᴀᴛʜ (in the study, posting again in the WARDen's room)	After what happened last night, I owe you, Lassiter. Are you alive? Come on, man . . .
ᴠɪsʜᴏᴜs (in the study)	Maybe he's just fucking with us.
ᴡʀᴀᴛʜ	He was shot in the chest. Thanks to taking a bullet for me. I don't think he's got playing high on his list of priorities. I think breathing is probably first and foremost.
ᴠɪsʜᴏᴜs	I can find him tonight if I have to.
ᴡʀᴀᴛʜ	Oh, there's a great fucking plan.
ᴠɪsʜᴏᴜs	I'm the best medic we've got.
ᴡʀᴀᴛʜ	(After long pause.) You go, you treat him if he's alive. You incinerate him if he's dead. The last thing we need is a body like his hanging around. And you know what? My best little buddy Zsadist is going to go with you just to make sure you don't get a hard-on and off the fucker.
ᴢsᴀᴅɪsᴛ	I'M THERE
ᴠɪsʜᴏᴜs	Done. We leave at nightfall.

	# OUT IN THE MIDDLE OF FUCKING NOWHERE July 12, 2006
VISHOUS	*materializes in front of run-down farmhouse* How the fuck does he get an Internet connection here?
ZSADIST	*narrows eyes* *listens* SILENCE IS MAKING ME TWITCHY AS SHIT, MY BROTHER
J R WARD	The farmhouse is a single-story structure from the turn of the century. Overgrown with weeds and trees and brambles, it is bearded with greenery, but not a happy place. Its vines are the kind that choke out the sunlight during the day and filter the moon in frightening ways at night. There is a front door, two windows, and a shallow porch. No cars. The garage is falling down. The walkway up to the house from the dirt lane is strewn with branches from the storms that passed through during the day.
VISHOUS	Let's go in. You got your heat out?
ZSADIST	NO THAT'S MY DICK IN MY HAND WHAT THE FUCK DO YOU THINK?
VISHOUS	I'd use the *mhis*, but he'd know we're here immediately. Let's do this. *V approaches the house, moving silently over grass that is still wet from the rains. The air smells like pine and earth and . . . something else.*

ƷSADIST	*shakes his head as the door squeaks open* *keeps SIG Sauer muzzle pointed forward* WAIT WHAT THE HELL IS THAT—
VISHOUS	No, it's cool. They smell like that when they bleed. *calls out* Lassiter? Yo, cocksucker, you breathing?
ƷSADIST	IT SMELLS LIKE— WHAT THE FUCK IS THAT ON THE FLOOR?
VISHOUS	They bleed silver . . . don't touch it. Lassiter? *heads farther into the house. There is no furniture, and it's cold even though the night outside is warm. No food, either.*
ƷSADIST	HE USES MY DECORATOR APPARENTLY
VISHOUS	*pauses* *looks over shoulder* Since when did you grow a sense of humor?
ƷSADIST	I'D SAY GET OFF MY DICK BUT I ALREADY USED THAT LINE SO I'LL GO WITH A CLASSIC
VISHOUS	Fuck you?
ƷSADIST	BITE ME. AND HOW ABOUT WE GET BACK IN THE GAME— OH.

VISHOUS	Oh . . . wow.
	eyes high-tech laptop *next to which is a pool of silver blood*
	V looks around the barren room, then turns back to laptop
	Z goes over to the window and scans the grounds
FEMALE	*Have you come to finish the job? Or save him?*
VISHOUS	*wheels around, ready to fire*
	blinks, stunned
ZSADIST	*falls into firing position*
	curses
	OH SHIT
VISHOUS	*without lowering the gun, even though he knows it won't do a damn thing against what they're looking at*
	Save him. Where is he?
FEMALE	*I don't know. I came because . . . well, I knew he must be hurt.*
VISHOUS	Lassiter has friends in unexpected places, it appears.
FEMALE	*I would say the same of you, vampire.*
	How was he hurt?
VISHOUS	For some completely unknown reason, he took a bullet for our king. *Lessers.*
FEMALE	*He is not without a certain code of honor. And he is compelled to save the righteous.*
VISHOUS	Oh, yeah. Right. I'll add him to my Christmas list.
	You must know where he might go.

FEMALE	*I don't. Going by the blood loss . . . and the fact that it was cloudy today? Not far. He needs the sun to survive, especially if he's injured.*
SADIST	THE ONLY REASON SOMEONE INJURED LIKE THAT MOVES IS BECAUSE HE HAS TO SOMEONE ELSE IS HUNTING HIM AND HE'S SMART ENOUGH TO COVER HIS TRACKS WE WON'T FIND HIM
VISHOUS	Yeah, he'll mask himself. *lowers gun and addresses female* You find him, you tell him we came. I can't stand the guy . . . but we honor our debts. *rolls eyes* As much as it's really fucking painful sometimes.
FEMALE	*Pray for clear skies tomorrow. And I don't know if I'll see him again. If I do, I will.*
VISHOUS	*watches it leave* *takes deep breath* Grab the laptop, my brother. I'm almost at my limit, between the weapons and the MedPack.
SADIST	*picks up laptop* *in process, hits mouse pad, which kicks off screen saver* HOLD UP WHAT DOES THIS SAY *turns to face V*

VISHOUS	*frowns* *leans into screen* # HOLY FUCKING SHIT! # DROP IT AND RUN!
ZSADIST	*throws computer* *pounds out of farmhouse at full tilt behind V—*

	I'M WAITING. . . . V? Z? July 12, 2006
WRATH (in the study)	What up? What happened?
WRATH	Vishous? Z?
PHURY (in the study)	I'm calling both of them on the cells right now. Neither are answering.
PHURY	Pick up. . . . Fucking pick up.
RHAGE (in the study)	Let's go to the coordinates. Fuck this. *heads for door of study*
VISHOUS (out in front of ruins of farmhouse)	*answers phone* *hears Phury's voice* WHAT? I CAN'T HEAR A THING? *glances up as Rhage materializes in front of him* Oh, don't look at me like that. I landed in mud. SUE ME Hollywood— NO DON'T HUG ME!
PHURY	*prays silently to Scribe Virgin with thanks* Z, you okay?
ZSADIST (on V's phone)	FINE WHOLE FUCKING PLACE BLEW TO HIGH HEAVEN I FEEL LIKE I'VE BEEN PUNCHED IN THE HEAD
WRATH	Were you two the targets?

VISHOUS	Who the fuck knows.
	We must have just missed him. Maybe he knew we'd come at dark. He'd had computer access, so he could have read it on the damn Boards.
	Maybe he thought I was coming to kill him.
ZSADIST	OR HE HAS OTHER ENEMIES WHO COME AFTER DARK
	WHY THE FUCK WOULD HE THINK WE'D KILL HIM AFTER WHAT HE DID LAST NIGHT THOUGH
VISHOUS	He and I ain't exactly pen pals, feel me?
	Look, I don't know where he is. But he's not going back to that place.
WRATH	Great. Wonderful. Fucking fantastic.
	We sit. We wait. We see if he contacts us.
	narrows eyes
	V . . . what aren't you telling me?
VISHOUS	We ran into a buddy of his.
	A ***************Edited by Admin***************
WRATH	Really?
	Surprise, surprise.
	Odd combination there. Well, like I said.
	We sit. We wait.
	And in the meantime, get out into the night, boys. You have work to do.

WRATH	*leans back in pansy chair and puts shitkickers on little froufrou desk*
	crosses arms
	mutters Shit. Now I know how I'm spending the rest of tonight.
	gets up *stalks out of study in a bad mood*
	********************FINIS*********************

	WHAT ARE YOU DOING? July 18, 2006
BUTCH O'NEAL (in the Pit)	Yo, V. What the hell are you doing?
VISHOUS (in the Pit)	Nothing.
BUTCH O'NEAL	Then why are you packing up all that shit? And what's with the—
VISHOUS	NOTHING. Shut up, cop before you—
WRATH (in the study)	What's up, boys? I don't like the sound of this.
VISHOUS	It's all good. Nothing—
BUTCH O'NEAL	He's packing up a MedPack. And—shit, like a pound of sugar?
WRATH	Jesus Christ. When did Lassiter get in touch with you? And why the fuck didn't you talk to me about this?
VISHOUS	Just today. And I was going to tell you before I left.
WRATH	I can't post right now. I really fucking can't post right now. *signs off*
VISHOUS	Wrath? Come on, Wrath. . . . Shit. Cop, hold it down at the Pit. I'll be back. . . .

V IN DEEP SHIT WITH THE KING July 18, 2006	
VISHOUS (at the mansion)	*runs up stairs* *knocks on closed doors of study* Wrath? My brother?
WRATH (in the study)	*rubs eyes underneath glasses* *curses and fights down the childish urge to pick his mofo desk up and hurl it at the fireplace* *yells out* V, you come in here it's at your own risk. I'm on my last fucking nerve with you.
VISHOUS	*opens door* *sees Wrath sitting at that little desk, dressed in a black T-shirt and leathers. Wrath's hair, which is so very long now, is down over his shoulders* Hey, man, seriously, I wasn't going to—
WRATH	The fuck you weren't going in alone—
VISHOUS	WHOA. Back the hell up. You don't call me a liar.
WRATH	*slowly gets up from desk* Then you don't play me like a fool. You talk to Z? Phury? Who were you taking with you as backup? I'll bet you your balls on a plate none of them knew what you were doing. Did they? *Did they, Vishous?*

VISHOUS	*measures Wrath's stance and realizes that the two of them are about an inch and a half away from going at it*
	turns away
	walks around
	takes out hand-rolled *lights up and inhales*
WRATH	Were you going to kill him? All nice and quiet?
	And try being honest. You might get off on it for a change.
VISHOUS	*stretches arm out straight from the shoulder* *points at Wrath with the cigarette*
	Fuck you.
VISHOUS	*realizes he's just told the king to fuck off*
	I'm sorry.
WRATH	Screw the apology, I could care.
	Answer me.
VISHOUS	If I were going to off him, why would I bring first aid?
WRATH	You know, I really feel like popping you already. And the attitude is REALLY helping here.
	Who's your backup?
VISHOUS	*inhales on hand-rolled* *opens up leather jacket, flashing butt of Glock*
	Captain Nine Millimeter—
WRATH	*slams fist on desk*
	You think this is a joke?

VISHOUS	*stares at Wrath, frustrated, angry*
	inhales on cigarette
	brings gloved hand up to his mouth and bites through the clasp, then strips it off with his fangs
	in slow motion brings lit tip of hand-rolled to his bare, glowing palm
	light flares and the butt is ashed immediately
	I can handle myself. I didn't want anyone else to get hurt, and we've got a lot of fucking heroes around here.
	He's hurt. He's dying. And he's hunted. I was going to go and clean him up and then get the hell away from him.
	That is all.
WRATH	*slowly sits back down*
	silence
VISHOUS	Come on, my Lord. Give me a fucking break here.
WRATH	Trust, V. It's about trust.
	You should have told me. If you get cracked tonight, how would we have known what happened?
	I get the motives. But don't do us any favors, dig?
VISHOUS	*bends down and picks up glove* *slips it back on his hand*
	So I can go, right.
WRATH	*has to smile*
	You know, that would work a hell of a lot better if it were phrased as a question, asshole.
	Yes. Go. At nightfall . . . which is in, what?
VISHOUS	Fifteen minutes. I'll head out in fifteen minutes.

	LITTLE TRIP INTO THE FUCKING WOODS July 18, 2006
VISHOUS	*steps out of mansion* *eyes sky* *winces and blinks* *checks Glock* *dematerializes to the north*
VISHOUS	*takes form at the side of the southbound exit 13 on the Northway, I-87, in Saratoga Springs* *standing on the shoulder of the road, he hears an occasional car go by and watches their headlights flare and fade* *eyes shallow woods to the right* *walks through the short grass into the trees* *smells the fragrance of wet earth and a hot summer night*
VISHOUS	*sees thin-trunked trees, the leaves of which block the sight of the sky* *says quietly* Cocksucker, the ambulance has arrived. *extends glowing hand* *finds the center of his chest and feels his heartbeat* *pulses emerge from his hand to the rhythm inside his rib cage, spreading outward across the landscape* Come on, cocksucker . . . let up on your *mhis* there, big guy. Let me find you.

VISHOUS	*landscape suddenly becomes flat plane of whiteness, the trees, the grass all disappearing*
	Lassiter is revealed, lying on the ground about fifty yards away
VISHOUS	*starts to jog over as landscape re-forms*
	slows down
	Oh, shit.
	Enemy mine . . .
J R WARD	Lassiter lies curled on his side on the earth, silver blood saturating the ground like a mercury puddle. His black-and-blond hair is matted. Golden skin is now the color of a dove.
	The woods smell like a fresh bouquet of flowers. The scent is Lassiter's death, the sweet saturation of the soul that wandered off from the broken body.
	The sun didn't save him. And trapped the help he needed in a cold stone house far away.
VISHOUS	*kneels down*
	strips MedPack off
	You know something, cocksucker?
	Death really fucking annoys me.
VISHOUS	*pushes Lassiter over onto his back and examines wounds*
	Yeah, that *lesser* got you right good.
	But it's *Good Morning, Vietnam* for you, asshole.
	takes hand and holds it right over the center of Lassiter's chest
	Wakey-wakey.

VISHOUS	*BRILLIANT EXPLOSION OF LIGHT*
LASSITER	*HAULS IN BREATH* *CHEST JACKS UP OFF THE GROUND*
VISHOUS	*falls back onto ass* How's that for an alarm clock?
LASSITER	*gasps for breath* *gasps* *gasps* *gasps* *gasps*
VISHOUS	*reaches for MedPack* Okay, you with me? I'm going to go in and see what's doing with that chest wound. Nod if you can hear me and you understand.
LASSITER	*gasps* *gasps* *nods*
VISHOUS	*under breath* Shit, golden boy, you smell like a sissy when you die, you know that? *night vision reveals unhealed gunshot wound penetrating left lung*

LASSITER	*gasps*
	slowly lifts hand
	extends middle finger
	gasps
VISHOUS	*barks laughter*
	Okay, Goldilocks, I can see the bullet. I'm going to remove it, and then you're going to have to zone out and do yourself a little heal bit. Then I'll close.
	Fucking bullet probably had nickel mixed in with the lead, which was what cooked you, right?
LASSITER	*gasps*
	hoarsely Couldn't get it out
VISHOUS	Yeah, hard to operate on yourself. *reaches down with calipers*
	This is going to hurt like a—
LASSITER	**FUCK**
VISHOUS	*continuing to work*
	Lassiter is writhing on the ground
VISHOUS	Got it.
	Okay, do your thing.
LASSITER	*****************EDITED by Admin.******************
VISHOUS	*leaning far away, arm up to eyes*
	creates shield to block force

VISHOUS	*drops arm*
	sees before him a golden glow
	You know, all things considered, it's a wonder we don't get along better.
LASSITER	*takes a deep breath and looks at chest*
	glances at Vishous
	How fucking ironic is this?
VISHOUS	Yeah . . .
	Anyway, you want me to close you up? Or are you planning on walking around with that big, gaping, nasty-ass hole in your chest?
	No offense, but you look like a Rick Baker special here. All *Werewolf of London* and shit.
LASSITER	Close me.
VISHOUS	*smiles* Never been so glad to be on the business end of a needle before.
	Even when I'm tatting.
	closes wound in a series of precise stitches—black thread on golden skin
	Lassiter doesn't even flinch now—just watches V
VISHOUS	*bites off thread* *pitches needle into MedPack*
	sits back on heels
	silence
LASSITER	*puts hand out*

VISHOUS	*looks at it*
	accepts invitation and their palms meet briefly
	V stands up *puts on MedPack*
	You don't have to say it.
LASSITER	Honor's going to make me.
	Circle will be closed. Sometime.
VISHOUS	*inclines head*
	looks at the sky
	Yeah, well, in the words of my roommate, we ain't datin'.
	I'll tell the others you're alive.
	LATER—
LASSITER	You know the future.
	So you know the when and the where and the why.
VISHOUS	That program isn't working so well right now.
	Guess it's on your word.
	looks down at Lassiter
	Yeah, ironic as fuck. That's what this is.
	You know where to find me.
	LATER.
	*********************FINIS*********************

Lassiter and V definitely share history, and the fallen angel has a lot of enemies. But he does return Tohrment to the fold after having taken a bullet for Wrath, so there are a lot of ties that bind him and the Brotherhood. Watching him with the Brothers over the next couple of books (and on the boards, if he chooses to appear) is going to be a wild ride, I promise you!

For the most part, when the Brothers show up on the boards, it's totally unexpected. I'm the only one who goes on as them, and I usually have no idea who will come out or what will happen or when they'll demand to be heard. In a few cases, though, I have known what was doing. The rollout of V going after Lassiter and saving him, for example, was one that I knew about, and accordingly, I gave notice to the Cellies that something was going to go down that night.

The below is another occasion when I was aware of the whole thing. I put out an invitation and said that the Brothers were going to be on the board, but what I didn't tell folks was that it was going to be for Phury and Cormia's mating ceremony. I had just finished their book and gotten it off to my editor, and I was feeling like I wanted to involve everyone in their joy.

What transpired, though, was absolutely incredible. There were so many people posting and so many refreshes to the board within every given moment that we killed the server. Which is traumatic, but kind of cool. Fortunately, everyone stayed with us and we fixed the problem, and the result . . . is my single favorite thing on the message board. To date, the Ceremony, which is located in the Brother Interaction Thread Forum, has well over two hundred fifty thousand views. When we closed the thread, there were over seventy pages of posts, and as you can see, the Cell was having a ball, toasting to the mating of a male and a female of worth.

Yeah, this is my favorite thing out of the over fifty-five hundred different threads we've made. I love the community of readers that make up the BDB board, and if you read the unedited version of the Ceremony, you'll see how great they all are.

And now, without further ado, I give you Phury and Cormia. . . .

	# THE FOYER January 20, 2008
FRITZ	*brings in sterling silver bowl of salt and pitcher of water* *places both on low-slung table* *lights black candles* *departs*
WRATH	*looks around* *nods* *takes crown* *settles on head*
RHAGE	Takes a brother back . . . Don't it? *double-checks daggers on chest*

	IN PHURY'S BEDROOM January 20, 2008
ZSADIST	*knocks* Yo, my brother?
PHURY	*straightens white satin robing* *clears throat* Yeah . . . I'm . . . Come on in.
ZSADIST	*opens door* Aw, shit. Check you out. You're ready. So fucking ready.
PHURY	*laughs* You know, I think I am. *brushes out hair*
ZSADIST	I feel like I should give you advice or some shit. But I'm coming up with a whole lot of nothing.
PHURY	You're here. That's all that matters. Hey . . . did you think about them? You know, when you and Bella . . .
ZSADIST	You mean the parents? I thought about them more after Nalla's birth. I mean, for this kind of thing, the most important thing was having you and the brothers with me. Family is where you find them. And listen, if you want a blunt, it's cool to want one.

PHURY	Yeah . . . not going to light up, though.
	takes one last look in the mirror above his bureau *meets Z's eyes*
	smiles
	Who'da thought it, eh?
ZSADIST	Until I met Bella, not I.
	Come on, brother mine, let's get your ass good and mated.
	opens door Oh, and ps, if your stomach feels like a lead balloon, that's totally fine, too.
PHURY	*steps out in hallway*
	picks up Boo
	Actually, I'm tight. I feel good.
	Let's do this.
	heads down the hall and pauses at the head of the grand staircase
	*sees the Brotherhood assembled down below with the *shellans* in gowns of red and blue and silver and peach and midnight*
	Shit, I lied about the stomach.

THE PARTY
January 20, 2008

FRITZ (in the foyer)	*Arranges *doggen* with serving trays* *tops up vodka luge* *adds garnish to spinach crepes* *turns on chocolate fountain* *prepares to meet guests*
WRATH	NIIIIIIIIIIIIIIIIIIIIIIIIIIIIIIIIIIIICE. Foyer is tight. *reaches for Beth* Come on, *leelan*, give us a kiss.
FRITZ	*to Cellies* Hello Mistresses, please help yourself to refreshments—eat, drink, and be merry!
BETH RANDALL	*steps into his arms* You remember ours?
WRATH	Always. *kisses her*
FRITZ	*ensures *doggen* are handing out refreshments* *worries that everything will be perfect*

THE CEREMONY January 20, 2008	
WRATH	*looks up and sees Phury at the head of the mansion's grand stairwell* Finally. *winks* *calls out* Shall we begin? *looks to library* *extends hand* Cormia?
CORMIA	*comes out of library in a high-waisted golden gown with an overlay of pearls* *her hair is loose down her back in waves of blond* *feet are bare* *looks up the grand stairwell and sees Phury standing at the top, the flames of a hundred black candles lighting his proud face and his brilliant citrine eyes* *puts hand to mouth* *blinks quickly as Zsadist begins to sing Puccini's "Che Gelida Manina" from *La Bohème** *mouths to Phury* I LOVE YOU.
FRITZ	*holds out to Cellies platter of linen handkerchiefs embroidered with Phury's and Cormia's initials and the date*

PHURY	*sees Cormia come around to stand by Wrath*
	hears his twin's tenor filling the Brotherhood's mansion
	thinks that for this moment, life is like a crystal before the candle flame, reflecting an endless spectrum of beautiful light into the eyes and hearts of them all
	watches her mouth, I LOVE YOU
	mouths back, I LOVE YOU MORE
	dematerializes down to the foyer because he can't wait one moment longer to be by her side
THE SCRIBE VIRGIN	*comes forward in black robes*
	addresses Cormia
	This male asks that you accept him as your *hellren*, my daughter. Would you have him as your own if he is worthy?
CORMIA	*looks into Phury's eyes*
	bows to the Scribe Virgin
	Yes, yes, I will have him for my own.
FRITZ	*hands out more platters of handkerchiefs to *doggen*, and bottles of smelling salts in case of fainters*
	dabs own eyes
	is so happy
THE SCRIBE VIRGIN	*nods to Cormia*
	addresses Phury
	Warrior, this female will consider you. Will you prove yourself for her? Will you sacrifice yourself for her? Will you defend her against those who would seek to harm her?
PHURY	*nods gravely at Scribe Virgin*
	*wishes he could kiss his *shellan* Cormia already*
	I will.

THE SCRIBE VIRGIN	*addresses Phury and Cormia*
	Give me your hands, children.
	accepts both hands as they are offered
	smiles under her robing
	A very good mating. I pronounce the presentation to me acceptable.
	*cheers rise up out of the Brothers and their *shellans**
	Nalla claps her hands in her mother's arms
FRITZ	*takes the sterling-silver bowl of salt and pitcher of water forward to the King*
	bows and proffers bowl and pitcher
WRATH	Thank you, Fritz.
	And now if the Brothers will join me?
PHURY	*kisses Cormia*
	lingers for a moment, just looking in her eyes
	steps back and removes his white robe so that he stands in his silk pants
	goes forward to his brothers and his king
	kneels before Wrath, moving his hair to the side so his back is exposed
FRITZ	*picks up black-lacquered box*
	takes forward to the King and proffers with a bow
	teardrop hits highly polished shoes
WRATH	*accepts box*
	pours water from pitcher into salt bowl
	stands over Phury
	My brother, what is the name of your *shellan*?

PHURY	She is called Cormia.
WRATH	*unsheathes black dagger* *bends over Phury's bare back* *carves in the Old Language* C
ZSADIST	*unsheathes dagger* *steps forward* What is the name of your *shellan*, twin of mine?
PHURY	She is called Cormia. *braces self again* *bears pain with strength and fortitude, feeling his love throughout his whole body*
ZSADIST	*bends over Phury's back* *carves in the Old Language* O *looks over at Bella and Nalla, feeling love for his females* *watches as Bella waves Nalla's hand at him* *winks*
VISHOUS	*steps forward, unsheathing dagger* What is the name of your *shellan*, brother? *looks over at Jane and rolls his shoulders, feeling the remnants of what she did to him during the day* *returns her secret smile*

PHURY	She is called Cormia.
	feels blood trickle down his side
	glances at Cormia and is glad that Beth and Mary and Marissa are there beside her holding her hands, as she looks a little woozy
	ducks head and prepares for fresh cut
FRITZ	*dabs eyes with handkerchief*
	chest swells with pride
	is humbled by awe
VISHOUS	*bends down with blade he made*
	thinks he is so glad that things worked out for Phury
	carves in the Old Language the letter
	R
BUTCH O'NEAL	*steps forward, unsheathing dagger*
	remembers Marissa's name getting carved in his back
	looks at her and smiles
	What is the name of your *shellan*?
PHURY	She is called Cormia.
BUTCH O'NEAL	*bends over Phury's back*
	next to V's perfect R carves in the Old Language
	M
RHAGE	*steps forward*
	blows kiss to Mary
	addresses Phury
	What is the name of your *shellan*, brother?

PHURY	*swallows hard*
	bears down into mosaic floor
	Her name is Cormia.
RHAGE	*bends down over Phury's back*
	carves in the Old Language the letter
	I
WRATH	*looks to the right, as everyone in the foyer does*
JOHN MATTHEW	*starts to walk forward*
	holds on to the forearm that is linked through his, providing steadying strength
TOHRMENT	*shuffles forward, leaning on John Matthew's arm*
	hair is long and shaggy, with white streak at the front
	approaches Phury while biting the inside of his lip until it bleeds
	asks in a hoarse, quiet voice
	What is the name of your *shellan*, brother?
PHURY	*keeps head down, as tears have come to his eyes while he pictures what he is gaining and what Tohr has lost*
	clears throat
	shoots glance at Cormia
	clears throat
	roughly . . . Cormia. She is called . . . Cormia.
TOHRMENT	*unsheathes dagger with shaking hand*
JOHN MATTHEW	*shifts weight*
	steadies Tohr's body as he leans down

TOHRMENT	*takes deep breath*
	calls on strength
	executes in one stroke a single perfectly composed letter in the Old Language
	A
LASSITER	*watches John Matthew lead Tohr back over to a chair*
	looks up to the ceiling
	sees image of Wellsie and their unborn son in the clouds within the warrior painting—both are overseeing the ceremony and Tohr
	makes eye contact with Wellsie
	inclines head to Wellsie, who takes one last look at Tohr and disappears back unto the Fade
WRATH	*waits until Tohr is seated*
	takes a moment to compose self
	needs to look at Beth for a second
	picks up bowl of salty brine
	pours it over Phury's back
PHURY	HSSSSSSSSSSSSSSSSSSSSSSSSSSSSSSSSSSSSSSSSSSSSSSSSSSSSSSSSSS
WRATH	*takes white cloth out of black-lacquered box*
	carefully blots his brother's back
	folds the white cloth back up and returns it to box
	addresses Phury
	Rise my brother.
PHURY	*stands up with pride, eyes glowing*

WRATH	*addressing Phury while presenting him with the lacquered box*
	Take this to your *shellan* as a symbol of your strength, so she will know that you are worthy of her and that your body, your heart, and your soul are now hers to command.
	smiles at Phury
PHURY	*turns to Cormia*
	worries for a moment at how white her face is, but then she smiles
	steps forward with a straight spine, all pain forgotten
	drops to his knees before her, bows his head, holds up the box
	Will you take me for your own, my love?
CORMIA	*heart is so full can barely breathe*
	reaches forward and places her hands on the box, making sure that her forefingers brush his
	Yes, yes, I will . . . oh, yes, a thousand yeses . . .
	cradles box to heart
PHURY	*throws arms around Cormia, not even feeling the burn in his shoulders*
	embraces her as Brotherhood begins to chant
	whispers I can't wait to be alone with you. . . .
	kisses her neck, nipping her with his fangs
	bonding scent roars
THE SCRIBE VIRGIN	*comes forward*
	*releases from thin air twelve perfect white doves, which soar above the assembled family as the Brotherhood and their *shellans* embrace one another and clap and chant*

FRITZ	* arranges ten *doggen* dressed in full livery into a queue*
	ensures that each has a silver tray of Dom Pérignon '98 in crystal long-stemmed glasses
	*arranges second row of ten *doggen* with silver trays of assorted fruit juices and sparkling waters in crystal tumblers*
	* leads *doggen* into foyer*
	*supervises as *doggen* offer drinks to all the gathered Cellie guests*
WRATH	*takes glass and pulls Beth close to his side*
	whispers in her ear I can't wait to be alone with you . . .
	more loudly
	May the assembled please raise their glasses?
WRATH	*addresses Phury and Cormia, the Brotherhood, and assembled Cell*
	A toast to the mated couple.
	in the Old Language
	May their burdens be light,
	and their joys overflowing,
	may destiny smile upon their joined paths,
	and carry these two souls forth into countless peaceful nights and passionate days.
	raises voice, bellowing
	TO THE MATED! TO THE MATED! TO THE MATED!
FRITZ	TO THE MATED!

PHURY	*draws Cormia close*
	*bows to Brothers and *shellans*, Fritz and *doggen,* and the wonderful Cellies*
	And now . . . if you'll excuse us?
	laughs gently as Cormia blushes
	the two wave and bow, then turn to the grand staircase and go up arm in arm, Cormia's long golden gown trailing behind, Phury's back bearing the letters CORMIA in the Old Language
	they retire to his bedroom
	Opera swells as the party continues on and their lives together truly begin
	*********************FINIS*********************

	AFTER THE CEREMONY
FRITZ	The sires and their good ladies have retired for the evening, but they asked me to inform you that you are welcome to stay as long as you wish. However, the bedrooms are out-of-bounds. ☺

Have a superb evening, and thank you all for your attendance, and please keep the handkerchiefs, I insist.

Fritz ~~~ |

Slices of Life from the Board

Slices of Life

Slices of Life are little vignettes of the Brothers that I've posted on my message board. If you're a member there, you'll recognize them! If you aren't, here they are reproduced. Again, the Board may be found at www.jrwardbdb.com/forum/index.php.

Movie Night

posted May 17, 2006

This first one was posted after Lover Awakened *was written, just as I was starting to work on* Lover Revealed:

So the question was asked on the loop what free time is like for the Brothers. And what the girls did at the mansion. And I figured I'd share this little Slice of Life with folks. . . .

The Brotherhood did movie night the other night and it was hysterical! Well, movie day, as it were. The bunch of them ended up piling into the Pit— which, I'd like to point out, only has two leather couches and not a lot of floor space. Picture this: Wrath and Beth in one corner of a couch. Rhage and Mary on the opposite side. Z on the floor with Bella in his lap. Butch and Phury on the other couch. V behind the Four Toys on his chair. The place was like a frat house, and they watched the first two *Die Hards* back-to-back. Between Phury's red smoke and V's hand-rolls the place smelled delicious. Butch was drinking a lot of Scotch (well . . . duh). V was into the Grey Goose. Mary and Bella were drinking chardonnay. Rhage was into the Perrier—busy rehydrating from a hard night on the streets with the *lessers*.

Halfway through the first movie, someone fell asleep. And can you believe it? It was Wrath! He's usually so incredibly focused but he's been working too hard. The thing was, he had his Brothers and his *shellan*—his family—all around him, and they were safe. He literally passed out, head flopping back on the top of the sofa, his long, long hair all over his chest (he's grown it out superlong because Beth loves it that way). Beth slid his sunglasses off and tucked a blanket around him—which was a nice thing to do, except . . . unfortunately the movements woke him a little, and he ended up repositioning himself all over her—he fell back asleep, mashing her up against Rhage. She just laughed. She was so relieved he was relaxing a little. She has to see him get up during the day and pace and pace and pace around their bedroom. It just about kills her, because he's almost stopped sleeping at all and he's losing weight. Straight up? This king stuff is killing him.

Anyway . . . Fritz kept bringing over hors d'oeuvres—you remember the spinach crepes Rhage loves? The group of them went through trays of those and other things. Fritz was so happy, running back and forth in the tunnel between the main house and the Pit.

Rhage, naturally, insisted on yelling out lines. You know what his favorite one is, of course: "Yippee-ki-yay, motherfucker." But 'bout halfway through the second movie, he started nuzzling the back of Mary's neck. And then his hands started traveling. She tried to get him to cut it out—but not too hard. When his eyes flashed white, the two of them disappeared for a little while. Um . . . Er . . .

ANYWAY, Phury was really quiet. He's gotten terribly quiet. Sadly quiet. He keeps to himself mostly, and was really there more because he felt he had to be than because he wanted to be.

Z watched both movies for the first time. He was ABSORBED by them. Imagine the surprises in store—when Mr. Takagi gets shot by Alan Rickman? When the body shows up in the elevator with HO HO HO on the shirt? When McClane is in the ventilator shaft? Then later when McClane's wife Tasers that idiot reporter? Z LOVED the movies. . . . He jumped in the right places and cursed at the screen and snarled and yelled. He was all involved and had a death grip on Bella through the whole thing. The only time he looked away from the TV was to make sure she had something to drink. Or to eat. Or to ask if she was comfortable. "Too cold? You need another fleece, maybe?"

I will say—even though I shouldn't—that Bella had a huge bite mark on her neck. He'd fed from her about an hour before they started to watch the movies. He'd gotten home from a night of fighting and he felt this . . . urge . . . to feed. He ended up sidling up to her in the bathroom. She was just out of the shower and was talking to him about this writing class she's taking online. Anyway . . . he was staring at her in the mirror, and she was chatting away and toweling off her hair and . . . she stopped and asked him what was wrong. When she got the picture, she turned and smiled at him. Um . . . dropped the towel she had wrapped around herself. At first he was apologetic about it. Like embarrassed, almost, because he hadn't come to her before. But then she was in his arms and he lowered his mouth to her throat and.....................well, they really got into the swing of things. *clears throat* Boy, did they ever . . . *blushes* Er . . . ANYWAY . . .

V stayed out of the movie thing, for the most part. He was doing searches on the Internet, although what he was looking for I have no clue. Every once in a while someone would yell at him to get off the computer. He ignored them until Butch fired an empty beer can at him. (And who was drinking the beer? Beth . . . she likes Sam Adams, remember.) V ended up sitting with Phury and Butch. The bachelors, as the others call them.

Soooooooooooooo, that was movie night (day). Next one is going to be an *Aliens* marathon. And yeah, Rhage is going to insist on acting out the alien-out-of-the-stomach routine on the floor in front of the TV. *sigh* Hollywood's just like that, you know?

Wrath and the Letter Opener

posted July 23, 2006

This one is done properly, and it's long—but man, what a scene with Beth and Wrath at the end, huh?

Whoever said it couldn't snow in July had their fucking head wedged.

Wrath sat back in his throne and looked at the piles of white before him: Requests to him as king for intervention on civil matters. Powers of attorney to Fritz for banking transactions. The *glymera's* constant stream of "helpful suggestions," all of which served only them.

It was a wonder the pansy desk could hold it all up.

From behind him he heard a series of metallic clicks, and then the shutters rose for the night with a whirring noise. Along with the lifting of steel came a rolling bass rumble, advance warning that one of Caldwell's summer thunderstorms was getting its groove on.

Wrath sat forward and picked up his magnifying glass. The damn thing was getting to be an extension of his arm, and he hated it. First, the piece of shit didn't really work: He couldn't see much better when he used it. And second, it reminded him that for all intents and purposes his life had been reduced to a desk job.

A desk job with purpose and honor and nobility, sure. But still.

Idly, he picked up an envelope opener that bore his royal seal, and he balanced the tip of it on the end of his forefinger, suspending the knife-shaped slice of silver in midair. To make the game harder on himself, he closed his eyes and moved his hand around, creating instability, testing himself, using senses other than his weak eyes.

With a curse he cracked his lids back open. Christ, why was he wasting time here? He had about ten thousand things he needed to do. All of which were urgent—

From the open double doors across the study he heard voices—and, riding his uncharacteristic wave of procrastination, he tossed the opener onto the snowbank of shit he had to do and walked out. At the balcony he planted his hands on the gold-leafed balustrade and looked down.

In the foyer below, Vishous, Rhage, and Phury were getting ready to go out, yakking it up while they double-checked their weapons. And off to the side Zsadist was leaning back against a malachite column, one shitkicker crossed over the other. He had a black dagger in his hand, and he was tossing it up into the air and catching it over and over again. On each trip the blade caught the light in flashes of navy blue.

Damn, those daggers V made were fantastic. Sharpened to a razor edge, weighted perfectly, the handle contoured with precision for Z's grip alone, the weapon was not state-of-the-art, it was a state of grace: a simple configuration of steel that meant survival for the race.

And fuck-you, have-a-nice-trip-back-to-the-Omega for the *lessers*.

"Rock on," Rhage said as he went for the door. Heading over the mosaic tiles of the foyer, he moved with his typical swagger and impatience, clearly craving the fight he was damn well going to find, his beast no doubt as ready for some hand-to-hand as he was.

Vishous was right behind him, all cool strides and lethal calm. Phury was likewise collected, his limp not noticeable in the slightest, thanks to the new prosthesis he was using.

In their wake, Zsadist stood from the column and sheathed his dagger. The slide of metal on metal reverberated up to Wrath like a sigh of satisfaction.

Z's vicious black eyes followed the sound as it lifted. In the light from overhead his scar was very noticeable, that distorted upper lip more pronounced than ever. "Evening, my lord."

Wrath nodded down at his brother, thinking that the Lessening Society was facing a demon in the male who stood down there. Even though Bella was in Z's life, whenever he left to go fighting, his hatred came back. With a nasty aura, the burn weaved through his bones and muscles, becoming indistinguishable from his body, making him as he had always been: a savage capable of anything.

Though, considering what the guy's *shellan* had been put through, Wrath didn't fault him for the killing rage. Not in the slightest.

Z walked to the door and then paused. Over his shoulder he said, "You look tight tonight. And not in a good way."

"It'll pass."

The smile that flashed was a slash of aggression, nothing happy. "I can't count to ten for very long. Can you?"

Wrath frowned, but the brother was already out the door. Out into the night.

Left by himself, Wrath headed back for his study. He sat down behind the frilly desk, and his hand found the envelope opener, his forefinger running up and down the dull edge. As he looked at the thing, he knew someone could kill with it. Just not with any finesse.

Cranking his fist tight, as if the silver opener actually were a weapon, he pointed the thing out in front of him, leveling it over his paper mountain. As he moved, the tattoos running up his forearm stretched out, his crystal-clean lineage all loud and clear in black ink. Not that he could read the purebred stamp of approval.

Jesus, what the fuck was he doing here ass-rotting on this throne?

How had this happened? His brothers out working the war. Him sitting here with a goddamned letter opener.

"Wrath?"

He looked up. Beth was in the doorway, wearing a pair of old cutoffs and a muscle shirt. Her long dark hair was down past her shoulders, and she smelled like night-blooming roses . . . night-blooming roses and his bonding scent.

As he stared at her, for some reason he thought about the workouts he put himself through in the gym . . . those hard-core, hamster-wheel, full-body masturbations that got him exactly nowhere.

God . . . there were edges you just couldn't work off on a treadmill. There were things that were missing even if you burned yourself out until the sweat ran as fast as the blood in your veins.

Yeah . . . before you knew it, you lost your edge. You went from being a dagger to a desk ornament. Castrated.

"Wrath? Are you okay?"

He nodded. "Yeah. I'm steady."

Her dark blue eyes narrowed, and the color struck him as being the same as Z's dagger blade catching the light: midnight blue. Beautiful.

And the intelligence in them was just as sharp as that weapon.

"Wrath, talk to me."

Downtown on Tenth Street, Zsadist jogged over the pavement quick as a breeze, quiet as a ghost, a leathered-up wraith tracking his prey. He had found his first kills for the night, but at the moment he had his body on Master Lock, holding himself back, waiting until there was a little privacy.

No fighting in public for the Brotherhood. Unless you absolutely had to.

And this little impending shindig was going to create some noise. The three *lessers* ahead of him were primes, all paled-out, looking to go at it, moving with the deadly rhythm of heavy bodies on solid ground.

For fuck's sake, he needed to get them in an alley.

As the four of them went along, the storm overhead stretched out its arms and started to pound on the night, its lightning flashing, its thunder cursing. Wind sprinted down the streets, then tripped and fell, forming gusts that pushed and then relented at Z's back.

He told himself, *Patience*, but holding back felt like a punishment.

Except then, like a gift from the Scribe Virgin, the trio ahead turned into an alley. And wheeled around to face him.

Ah, so it wasn't a gift or luck. They knew he'd been in their trunks and had been looking for some darkened corner to do business in.

Yeah, well, time to waltz, motherfuckers.

Z unsheathed his dagger and fell into a jog, triggering the starter gun on the fight. As he came forward the *lessers* backed up, disappearing further into the long alley, finding the shadows necessary to keep what was about to happen from human eyes.

Zsadist targeted the slayer on the right because the bastard was the biggest and had the largest knife, so disarming him was a tactical priority. It was also something Z was just plain jonesing to do.

His momentum carried him faster and faster until he was skimming the ground, shitkickers barely touching the pavement. As he moved in, he was the wind, carrying along, rushing forward, sweeping down on what was ahead of him.

The *lessers* got ready, switching positions, crouching for conflict, so that the big guy was up in front and the other two flanked him.

At the last moment Z tucked into a ball and rolled on the asphalt. Then he sprang up and led with his dagger, catching the linebacker *lesser* in the gut, opening the bastard up like a pillow. Man, abdominal cavities were always a messy affair, even if you didn't eat, and the slayer went down on a waterfall of black blood.

Unfortunately, on the way to his dirt nap, he managed to clip Z right in the neck with his switchblade.

Z felt his skin split open and his vein start leaking, but there wasn't time to get thought up about the injury. He focused on the other two slayers, popping free his second dagger so he was a two-fisted slashing machine. The fight went into hard-core territory fast, and as a second wound broke open on his shoulder, he thought he might even need a pickup at the end of it.

Especially as a length of steel chain snaked around his neck and went tight as a tire rim. With a yank he was whipped off his feet, and he back-landed it so hard he felt like he'd been body-punched: All the air left his lungs on that eviction notice, and it stayed away, his rib cage refusing to reexpand no matter how much he worked his mouth.

Right before he blacked out he thought of Bella, and the panic of leaving her gave him the crash-cart shock he needed. His sternum heaved for the heavens, drawing in breath so hard the shit went all the way down to his balls. And just in time.

As the two *lessers* fell on him, he twisted to the side and somehow popped off the pavement and found footing. Going on instinct and experience, he lick-splitted a classic two-knife lock and cross on the first of the slayers, all but decapitating the thing. Then he stabbed the other one in the ear, shorting him out cold.

Except then four more showed up: backups called in, all nice and fresh, ready to work.

Z was now in goat-fuck territory.

He sheathed a dagger and palmed one of his SIGs, even though the gun would make noise when it went off. And the thing took a bite out of his pride. He was just flipping the safety off when he saw a pair of pale green lights at the back of the alley.

As the *lessers* went all standstill, clearly they noticed, too.

Z cursed. Dollars to dickheads that was some new kind of xenon headlight, and they were about to get a visit by a carload of kibitzers.

Except then the air temperature dropped twenty degrees. Just like that. As if someone had unloaded two tons of dry ice over there and hit the shit with an industrial blower.

Zsadist threw his head back and laughed loud and long, the power coming back into his body even with his slit throat and his dripping shoulder. As rain started to fall, he positively sizzled with aggression.

The *lessers* clearly thought he was nuts. But then lightning snapped out and turned the alley daylight bright.

Wrath was revealed at the far end, his massive legs set like oak trunks in the ground, his arms stretched out like I beams, the storm's wind whipping his waist-length hair around. His glowing eyes were a roaring call of death in the night, his fangs white and sharp and visible from yards and yards away. In his hands were his trademark throwing stars, on his hips were his Berettas . . . and across his chest, crisscrossed with handles down, were the daggers, the black daggers of the Brotherhood, the weapons that he had not used since his ascension.

The king had come out to kill.

Zsadist glanced at the *lessers,* one of whom was dialing for more backup.

Man, Z thought, he was so ready to get back in the game.

He and Wrath had never fought together before, but they would tonight. And they were going to win.

* * *

Much later, back at the mansion, Beth paced around the billiards room. Over the course of the night she'd turned the pool table into the center of her universe: The green felt square with its pockets and its rainbow balls was the sun to her solar system, and around and around she went. . . .

God. She didn't know how Mary and Bella handled this . . . knowing that their *hellrens* were out there in that evil night fighting an endless enemy, an enemy with weapons that didn't just maim, but killed.

When Wrath had told her what he wanted to do, what he needed to do, she'd had to force herself not to scream at him. But, Christ, she'd already seen him lying in a hospital bed, hooked up to wires and machines and tubes, injured, dying, lurching back and forth between life and nothingness.

She had zero interest in reliving that nightmare.

Sure, he'd done his best to reassure her. And told her he'd be careful. And reminded her that he'd fought for some three hundred years and been trained and honed and bred for this. And said it was only for tonight.

Except like that all mattered? She wasn't thinking about the three centuries he'd come home at the crack of dawn safely. She was worried about this specific night, when he might not make it back. After all, he was flesh and blood, and there was a timer on his life, a timer that could zero out in the work of a moment. All it would take was a bullet in the chest or the head or—

She looked down and realized she wasn't moving anymore. Which kind of made sense. Evidently, her feet had just superglued themselves to the floor.

Forcing them to start walking again, she told herself that he was what he was: a warrior. She hadn't married a goddamned nancy. That fighting blood was in him, and he'd been chained to the house for the past year, so it was inevitable he'd crack.

But, oh, God, did he have to go out there and—

The grandfather clock started chiming. Five o'clock.

Why weren't they back—

The door to the vestibule opened, and she heard Zsadist and Phury and Vishous and Rhage come in. Their deep voices were hopping, their words fast with power and life. They were juiced about something, invigorated.

Surely if Wrath were injured they wouldn't behave like that. Right? *Right?*

Beth went to the doorway . . . and had to grab onto the jamb. Z was bleeding, his skintight turtleneck soaked with a red rush, his daggers wet and glossy as well. Except it wasn't as if he noticed. His face was shining, a sparkle lighting up those eyes of his. Hell, he carried himself as if he had a couple of bug bites instead of two gaping wounds.

Feeling light-headed, because she felt like someone should on his behalf, she watched the four head for the hidden door under the staircase. She knew they were making a beeline for the first-aid station in the training center and she wondered how Bella would feel if she saw Z like that. Then again, knowing the Brothers, the female wouldn't get a chance to. The mated males in the house were always careful to get stitched and cleaned before they found their *shellans*.

Before the Brothers disappeared down in the tunnel, Beth stepped into the foyer, unable to stand it any longer. "Where is he?" she said loudly.

The bunch of them stopped and their faces masked up tight, as if they didn't want to offend her by how pumped they were.

"He'll be right here," Phury said, his yellow eyes kind, his smile even kinder. "He's just fine."

Vishous smiled darkly. "He's more than fine. He's alive tonight."

And then she was left alone.

Just as she was about to get pissed off, the vestibule's door swung open, and a cold rush unfurled across the foyer like a rug rolling out.

Wrath stepped into the mansion, and her eyes popped wide. She hadn't seen him leave earlier, hadn't been able to watch, but she saw him now.

Holy Christ, did she see him now.

Her *hellren* was as she had first known him that night he had come into her old apartment: a killing menace dressed in black leather, the weapons strapped on his body as fundamental as his skin or his muscles. And in his war dress he radiated power, the kind that broke bones and slit throats and bloodied faces. In this his fighting dress, he was a horror, a nightmare . . . who was nonetheless the male she loved and had mated and always slept beside, who fed her from his hand, who held her during the day, who gave himself to her, body and soul.

Wrath's head twisted on his thick neck until he stared at her and he spoke in a distorted voice, one so low that she barely recognized it as his. "I need to fuck you right now. I love you, but I need to fuck you tonight."

She had one and only one thought: *Run. Run, because he wants you to. Run, because he wants to come after you. Run, because you're just a little scared of him and it makes you hot as hell.*

Knowing that she smelled of her arousal, Beth took off in her bare feet, flashing toward the stairs, taking them fast, her legs a blur. Within seconds she heard him behind her, his shitkickers pounding like thunder. The erotic threat of him bore down on her, enticing her until she couldn't breathe, not because of exertion, but because she knew what was coming as soon as he got his hands on her.

When she reached the second floor, she randomly tore down a hallway, not knowing where she was headed, not caring. With every yard she covered, Wrath was closing in on her. . . . She could feel him tight on her heels, a wave about to break all over her, crash down on her, sweep her up and hold her down.

She burst into the second floor sitting room and—

He caught her by the hair and the arm, pulling her around, tripping her up, sending her to the floor.

Just before she made impact, he twisted so his body absorbed their fall and cushioned her. As she fought to get up, she had the dim thought that she was faceup on him, his chest under her shoulders, his erection right where it needed to be.

And then she didn't think anymore.

Wrath's legs shot up and linked around her shins, spreading her legs wide, trapping her. With rough authority his hand shot between her thighs, and she arched with a cry as he found out exactly how turned-on she was. As she stopped fighting the double doors in front of her slammed shut, and then he rolled her, laying her out facedown on the floor. He mounted her, holding her in place by the back of the neck and the way he straddled her legs. Up close he smelled like clean sweat and the bonding scent and the leather of his clothes and the death of their enemies.

She nearly came.

Wrath was breathing hard, and so was she as he hauled back and split her old cutoffs right up the crotch, the worn fabric letting go as if it didn't dare disobey him.

Jesus, she knew how that felt.

Cool air hit her ass as his fangs bit through one side of her panties, and then there was the sound of a zipper. His hands angled her hips, and the head of him bumped down to what was waiting for him, what was his for the taking.

He slammed into her, shoving in hard as a board, wide as a fist.

Beth splayed her hands out on the marble as he locked into her body and started pumping with a fierce pace, two hundred and eighty pounds of sex all over the top of her, stretching the inside of her. Her palms squeaked against the marble as the first of the orgasms jumped into her.

She was still climaxing as he clamped his hand on her chin and pulled her mouth around. His rhythm was so hard he couldn't kiss her. . . .

So he hissed and bit her right in the jugular.

He froze in midstroke as he started to feed, sucking hard, pulling at her vein with a wild supremacy. The pain swirled and tingled, mixed with the tail end of the orgasm, kicked off another rush of pleasure. And then he was riding her again, his lower belly rubbing on her ass, his hips slapping against her, his growl that of a lover. . . .

And an animal.

He roared loud as a beast as he started to come, his erection kicking in her like a living thing with its own mind. The bonding scent rose even stronger as he filled her up, his pulses hot as embers, thick as honey.

The instant he was finished, he flipped her over and loomed between her legs, his sex glistening and proud and completely erect. He wasn't done with her yet. Linking his tattooed forearm behind one of her knees, he pulled her leg up high and entered her from the front, his huge arms knotting as he held himself above her body. As he stared down at her his hair came forward, great falls of black that tumbled from his widow's peak and got tangled in the weapons on his body.

His fangs were so long he couldn't close his mouth, and as his jaw unhinged and he got ready to bite into her again, she shivered. But not from fear.

This was the raw edge, the reality of him under the clothes he wore and the daily life he led. This was her mate at his purest, distilled essence: Power.

And God, she loved him.

Especially like this.

Wrath was taking Beth with furious action, his cock hard as a bone, his fangs like ivory nails driven deep in her neck. She was everything he needed and would ever want: the soft landing for his aggression, the female sex squeezing him, the love that captivated and captured him.

He was the storm bearing down on her; she was the land with the strength to take what he had to let out.

As she sang again from her body splintering apart with pleasure, he pitched himself off the ledge and went flying with her. His balls clenched up hard and his orgasm pistoled out of him . . . *bang, bang, bang, bang* . . .

Releasing her vein, he collapsed into her hair as he shuddered and bucked.

And then there was only their desperate breathing.

Dizzy, out of it, satiated, he lifted his head. Then his arm.

He bit into his own wrist and brought it to her lips. As she nursed quietly, he stroked her hair with a gentle hand and felt a stupid fucking weak-ass urge to tear up.

When her blue-black eyes lifted to his, everything disappeared. Their bodies dematerialized. The room they were in ceased to exist. Time became nothing.

And in the void, in the wormhole, Wrath's chest opened up sure as if he'd been shot, a piercing pain licking over his nerve endings.

He knew then that there are many ways for a heart to break. Sometimes it's from the crowding of life, the compression of responsibility and birthright and burden that just squeezed you until you couldn't breathe anymore. Even though your lungs were working just fine.

And sometimes it's from the casual cruelty of a fate that took you far from where you had thought you would end up.

And sometimes it's age in the face of youth. Or sickness in the face of health.

But sometimes it's just because you're looking into the eyes of your lover, and your gratitude for having them in your life overflows . . . because you showed them what was on the inside and they didn't run scared or turn away; they accepted you and loved you and held you in the midst of your passion or your fear . . . or your combination of both.

Wrath closed his eyes and focused on the soft pulls at his wrist. God, they were just like the beat of his heart. Which made sense.

Because she was the center of his chest. And the center of his world.

He opened his eyes and let himself fall into all that midnight blue.

"I love you, *leelan*."

In the Nature of Phury

posted August 15, 2006

This one was written after Lover Awakened *as well, when Phury's yearnings for Bella were at their strongest:*

Over this past weekend I found myself alone in the house, pacing around. I was skipping over the surface of everything around me . . . not really tracking, roaming. Restless. I do this a lot, because I'm a high-strung nutcase and my head just chews on things practical and impractical until I think I'll go mad.

In a Hail Mary move, I got into the car and opened the windows and the sunroof and cranked the bass: Sometimes our escape hatches have four wheels and righteous beats. And bless these chariots of relief.

When I took off, the sun was starting to set and I drove far, far from home. . . . I drove to the Ohio River and took the road that coasts along its bank. I've been doing this lately . . . just getting away, nothing but me and the car and the summer air and the music. The trees were black green overhead, a tunnel I followed with desperate hope that it could take me somewhere other than where I was.

It worked.

As I went along, to the left the sun was a big fat disk drifting down, like someone had hooked it and was trying to pull it out of the sky, but its inherent buoyancy was fighting the draw. Around me the air was so damned wet, thick as a cloud, smelling like . . . summer, really. And that sweet humidity coated my skin, and I liked what I was wearing when it was there.

Out there on the road life was sweet. Life was a precious gift, not the burden it can be sometimes. Life was the vivid mystery it should be.

And I found myself thinking of Phury.

Driving along, driving alone, driving out far from home . . . he followed me. Like he was in the car with me, elbow on the open window sash, the air moving all that hair of his around. I pictured his yellow eyes as the color of the setting sun, glowing like that, warm like that, beautiful like that.

Now, of course, he wasn't with me. Would have been up in flames had he been. But he was in my head and looking out of my eyes and listening to what was around me. And he slid into my chest like a ghost and took up the space in my marrow and he assumed the wheel and the gearshift and the gas pedal.

And while he was with me, he spoke to me of the nature of the Do Not Have. The Cannot Have. The Never Possible.

The Unfulfilled.

I saw him sitting at the dining room table. Bella was across the way, across the china and the silver and the crystal, across the divide of the mahogany . . . across a million miles that would never be walked. He was watching her hands. Watching her cut her meat and switch the fork and knife back and spear the lamb and bring it to her lips. He watched her hands because it was the only remotely, socially acceptable option he had.

It is a special hell to want what you cannot have. Because his mind wanders. Takes him in directions he doesn't want. Teases him with tastes he will never have on his tongue, curves he will never learn, feelings he can never, ever express.

He is trapped in his honor and his love for his twin, trapped also by his respect for Bella . . . a slave to his moral nature.

I think what makes it hardest for him is that she is always around him. He sees her every day. He knows each dawn when he returns she is where he lives.

What does he do? He lies in his big bed and smokes the blunts that keep him calm and he prays that it will all fade soon. What makes it even worse is his honest-to-God happiness for Z: There is tremendous relief in Phury's special hell because he knows that Z has a future now.

Relief . . . yes, relief. But there are times that that pales. Phury looks down at his missing leg and feels unwhole and unworthy and weak and lame, and it's not really all about the amputation, because he has no regrets there. What stings during the days when the house is quiet and Bella and Z are sleeping entwined in their mated bed . . . what stings Phury is the fact that he is sexually clueless and inept, and there is no way out of that desert. Even if he gave up the celibacy, even if he found a female and put her on her back and rode her out, what would that cure exactly? A graceless, uncaring sex act wouldn't make him feel any better. If anything, that would cut him deeper . . . because he knows that isn't what's doing between Z and Bella.

No . . . Phury's on the far side of the riverbank, watching a sunset. Unable to touch. Only able to look. And Never Have.

So in his ineptness and his pathetic yearning, in his despicable weakness, in his deplorable swill of emotion . . . he watches Bella's hands as she eats. Because that's all he can do.

He waits for some relief. Knowing it's not coming anytime soon.

And he hates himself.

The descent he is on seems bottomless, and he has no rope to cast out for purchase, no net to fall into, nothing to break his fall. All he can do is anticipate a hard impact, a shattering body blow whenever the bottom finds him.

For Phury, the nature of the Do Not Have, the Cannot Have, the Never Possible, the Unfulfilled, is taking him into darker places than he could have predicted. I think he assumed that if Z ever healed a little, that his own suffering would be over.

Wrong. Because the flavor of Z's healing is a taste Phury would kill to have.

Anyway . . . that was what I found out by the Ohio River the other night in the summer air . . . in the bass-ridden solitude . . . where all there was was myself and the headlights of oncoming cars and the wet breeze of the air.

Some distances will never ever be closed.

The Interview That Never Happened

posted October 6, 2007

This was done right after Lover Unbound *was released:*

Last night I showed up at the Brotherhood's compound for a scheduled interview with Butch and Vishous. They kept me waiting—which shouldn't have been a surprise and wasn't. And the interview didn't happen, either. Also not a surprise . . .

Fritz is the one who lets me into the Pit, and he fusses over me as he usually does. I swear, nothing makes a *doggen* more agitated than if they can't do anything for you. He's getting so worked up, I actually hand him my purse—a move marked with the kind of desperation usually associated with folks who perform the Heimlich on a choking person.

Now, I'm not in the habit of turning over my day bag to other people—even a butler who's suffering from a terminal case of the need-to-pleases. But here's the thing: My purse has a lot of pale-ish leather detailing, and the strap that runs over the top and down the front has a streak of blue pen ink on it. No one notices this relatively tiny mess-up except me, but it's bugged me since I did it, and I've wanted to get rid of the imperfection like you read about. (Hell, I even went back to LV and asked them if they could take it out. They said no, they couldn't, because the leather is porous and has absorbed the ink into its fibers. I assuaged my depression with sundry purchases, needless to say.)

As I hand the bag over to Fritz and ask him if there's any way he could get the pen ink out, he glows like I've given him a birthday present and beats feet out the front door. Just as the Pit's huge eight-paneled, fortress-worthy, portal-from-a-dungeon-movie slams shut, I realize my only pen, the one that made the mark, is in the damn bag.

Fortunately, V and Butch tend to be memorable, so I figure I'll just take mental notes.

The Pit is empty except for me. Jane is out, doing physical exams at Safe Place. Marissa is there as well, running things. It's three a.m., and Butch and V are supposed to be coming home from fighting soon. The plan is for them to talk to me and for me to move along smartly when they're done. Interviews aren't high on the Brotherhood's list, and I understand. They get precious little free time, and they're under constant stress.

I check my watch and find it hard not to worry. Man, I don't know how their *shellans* stand waiting for them to get home. The what-ifs must be a killer.

I look around. The Foosball table is hale and hearty-looking, fresh as a fricking daisy. This, of course, is the new new one, though. The old new one gave up the ghost during some kind of showdown involving a can of Silly String, twelve feet of duct tape, two paintball guns, and a Rubbermaid container the size of a small car. At least, that's what I heard from Rhage. Who has a big mouth, but never lies.

Across the room, on V's desk, the Four Toys are humming away, the computers looking like a bunch of gossips all huddled together, trading stories about who is where doing what within the Brotherhood's compound. The stereo system stacked behind them looks just as high-tech—like you could use it to do a brain scan on someone if you had to. Rap is on, but not as loudly as it's been in the past. 50 Cent's *Curtis*. Yeah, I kind of figured, for V, it wouldn't be Kanye.

What I can see of the kitchen is kind of a shock. It's neat as a pin, the countertops free of glasses, the cupboards all shut tight, the clutter down to a minimum. I'm willing to bet there's something else in the fridge other than Taco Bell leftovers and packets of soy sauce. Damn, there's even a bowl of fruit. Peaches. Natch.

Change, I think. Things have changed here. And you can tell, not just because there's a pair of black stillies next to the couch and copies of the *New England Journal of Medicine* in the midst of all those SIs.

Looking around, I get to thinking about the two guys who live here now with their mates. And I remember back to the good old *Dark Lover* days, when V and Butch spent the night in that guest room upstairs at Darius's. Butch asked about V's hand. V ID'd Hard-ass's death wish. The two of them clicked. My favorite part was when Wrath came in the next evening and gave them a "Well, isn't this cozy." I think you remember what their response was, right?

Here we are, two years later, and they're still together.

Then again, we members of the Red Sox Nation are a loyal lot.

But everything is different, isn't—

The door in from the underground tunnel flips open and Butch comes in. He smells like *lesser*, all sweet baby powder. I put my hand up to my nose to keep from gagging.

"Interview's off," he says hoarsely.

"Ah . . . that's okay, I don't have a pen," I murmur, measuring how grim he looks and how he weaves in his boots.

Butch trips over his own feet and bangs off the walls as he goes to his bedroom.

Great. Now what do I do?

I wait for a minute. Then I go down the hallway because . . . well, in a situation like this, you want to help, don't you? When I get to the door of his room, I catch a shot of his naked back and quickly look away.

"You need anything?" I ask, feeling like an idiot. I may write about the Brothers, but let's face it, I'm a ghost in their world, an observer, not a participant.

"V. But he's coming—"

The front door bangs open and my head whips around like it's on a pull cord.

Oh . . . shit . . .

Now, see, here's the thing about V. He doesn't like me. Never has. And considering he's nearly three hundred pounds of vampire and he's got that hand of death thing happening, every time I get around him I am reminded of all the panic attacks I've ever had in the course of my life. They come back to me. Each one of them. At the same time.

I swallow hard. V is dressed in black leather and bleeding from a shoulder wound and in a bad fucking mood. One look at me and he bares his fangs.

"You have got to be kidding me." He all but rips off his leather jacket and throws it across the Pit. He's more careful as he removes his daggers. "Man, this night just keeps getting worse."

I kept my piehole shut. I mean, like there's any response to that kind of welcome? Short of hanging myself in the bathroom, I'm pretty confident there's nothing I can do to cheer him up.

Vishous stomps by me to get to Butch and I make like a wall hanging, trying to get as flat as I can. Which is easy. I'm built like a plank to begin with, long and curveless.

I'd like to point out that V is huge, by the way. HUGE. As he passes by my head barely reaches the top of his shoulder, and the size of his body makes me feel like I'm five years old and in a sea of grown-ups.

As he pauses in Butch's bedroom doorway, I find myself unable to leave, even though I know I should go. I just can't, though. Fortunately, V focuses on the cop.

Poor Butch.

"What the fuck were you doing?" V barks.

The cop's voice is rough, but not weak. "Can we shelve this for about ten minutes? I'm going to throw up—"

"Did you think those slayers weren't armed?"

"You know, this shrewish wife thing is so not helping—"

"If you'd used your brain for once—"

As the two start in on each other, I think, *Okay, I am ready to leave.* Too much testosterone in the air like this and I get woozy. And not in a good way.

I back down the hall, wondering what the hell I'm going to do about the interview I was supposed to have with them, when I realize . . . bloody footprints. V has left bloody footprints. And he must have been injured quite badly, given the amount of glossy crimson on the floorboards.

Stupid male. Stupid, arrogant, miserable, reclusive SOB. Stupid, reckless, pigheaded, nasty-tempered, bullhorned, I-am-an-island, close-lipped bastard—

Have I mentioned that after the horrid process of writing V's book, I have a couple of issues with him, too? He's not the only hater in our relationship.

As Butch and V continue to growl at each other like a pair of Dobermans, I get pissed. I march over to V's leather jacket and grunt as I pick it up off the floor. The thing weighs almost as much as I do, and to be honest, I really don't want to know what's in it.

But I find out, because I go through his pockets.

Ammo for his Glock. Hunting knife with *lesser* blood on it. Solid-gold lighter. A little black book I don't flip through (because, hey, that is SUCH an invasion of privacy). Wrigley's spearmint gum. Swiss Army knife (probably because his hunting one doesn't have that nifty scissors attachment).

Cell phone.

I flip the RAZR open and hit *J. Two seconds later, Jane answers the ring.

"Hey, you. How's my puppy?"

Yeah, she calls him *puppy*. I've never asked for deets. V would just bite my head off, and it seems too intrusive to ask Jane herself. Although Rhage would know . . . hmm . . .

"Hi, Jane," I say.

"Oh, it's you!" She laughs. Jane has a warm laugh, the kind that makes you take a deep breath and release it nice and slow, because you know everything's going to be all right if she's involved. "How's the interview going?"

"It isn't. Your man's injured, Butch is down for the count, and I get the sense that if I don't leave ASAP, I'm going to be shown the door by your mate. Headfirst."

"Oh, for God's sake, V can be such an ass."

"Which is why I dedicated *Lover Unbound* to you."

"I'm coming right now. Let me just tell Marissa."

As I hang up, I realize the Pit is much quieter now . . . and that there's a glow coming from the hallway. I tiptoe down and freeze when I get to the doorway of Butch's room.

They're on the bed. Together. Vishous has lain down and wrapped his arms around Butch, and his whole body is glowing softly. Butch is flush against the Brother, breathing slowly. V's healing power is working. You can tell because the smell of *lesser* is going away.

V's ice-white eyes flip open and nail me with the unblinking stare of a predator. My hand goes to my throat.

In this moment between us, I wonder why he hates me so much. It hurts.

The response I get is his voice in my head: *You know why. You know exactly why.*

Yeah, I kind of do, don't I. And strike the *kind of*.

"I'm sorry," I whisper.

He closes his eyes. And that's when Jane materializes right next to me.

Jane is only a little different as a ghost than she was as a human. She takes up space the same and sounds the same and looks the same . . . and as she gives me a hug, she feels as warm and solid to me as she did before what happened to her happened.

"Baby . . ." V drawls from the bed.

Damn, that's an erotic sound.

Jane looks into the bedroom, and the smile that lights her up is breathtaking. Jane's not supergorgeous. But she's got an intelligent-looking face to match her enormous brain, and as I like smart people, I really like her.

"Hey, pup," she says to Vishous.

V smiles at Jane. Have I mentioned that before? When he sees her, he truly smiles. With everybody else he just smirks. If he feels like it.

"Heard you're hurt," Jane says, putting her hands on her hips. She's wearing a white doctor's coat and has a stethoscope around her neck, both of which are solid to the eye. The rest of her is a little hazy, unless she wants to pick something up or hug someone, in which case she becomes fully present.

"I'm fine," he shoots back.

"He's hurt," Butch and I say at the same time. V glares at me. Then soothes the cop by running his hand down the male's spine.

"Meet me in our room when you're finished," Jane says to her *hellren*. "I'm going to check you out."

"Now, that's what I'm talking about," V replies on a husky purr.

I follow Jane down the hall because it's starting to feel a little voyeuristic staring at V and Butch together. (I'd like to put in here, by the way, that Jane isn't bothered at all by how close the two males are, and neither is Marissa. Which shows you how secure those two females are. How secure and how well loved.)

"So Safe Place is really coming along," Jane says as we go into the book-filled bedroom she shares with her male. The place could be a library if not for the king-sizer in the center, and the two of them are happy with it that way. They are both big readers.

"Yeah, I've heard." I pick up the title on the bureau. It's a biochemistry textbook. Grad school level. Could be either of theirs. "You have how many females now?"

"Nine mothers, fifteen children."

Jane starts to talk, and her enthusiasm and commitment are obvious in her animation. I let her go on, but I'm only half listening. I'm thinking back to a conversation she and I had about three months ago, in June.

It was about death. Hers. I asked her whether she was disappointed with where she'd ended up. As a ghost. Her answering smile held a lot of well-duh in it, and she said to me something I haven't been able to get out of my mind since: "Forty years as a human versus four hundred with him?" she'd murmured, shaking her head. "Yeah, I have a real hard time doing that math. Right. I mean, the tragedy gave me life with the man I love. Where's the disappointment?"

I guess I can see her point. Yes, there are some things they don't have. But Jane was very well into her thirties when the two of them met. Which means she'd have been lucky to get another two to three decades with him before the aging process really sank its teeth into her. And that's assuming she didn't get cancer or heart disease or something else god-awful that either killed her or crippled her. Also, she's already lost her sister and both her parents and, jeez . . . countless trauma patients. After all the death she's seen, I think it's kind of nice that she gets a pass on that from now on. And she doesn't have to worry about V's dance with the Reaper. She can go back and forth to the Fade. They will always be together. Always.

So she's living eternity. With the male she loves. Not a bad deal.

Plus . . . erhm, from what I understand the sex is still out of this world.

"Off with your clothes," she says.

I look down at the black outfit I have on and wonder if I spilled anything on myself. But no, it's Vishous. He's finished with Butch.

I get out of his way as he comes in, and yeah, I look down at the floor as I hear the rustle of clothes getting removed. V laughs in a throaty way, and I smell his bonding scent. I'm willing to bet the second I leave they're going to . . .

Erhm . . . yeah.

Great, now I'm blushing.

Jane curses, and I hear a box getting flipped open. I look up. It's a first-aid kit, and after she finishes cleaning what seems like an enormous gash in Vishous's thigh, she takes out a needle and black surgical thread and a syringe I'm thinking is full of lidocaine.

Okay, I'm so looking down again for this part. I love to watch medical shows on TV, but I always have to avoid the gory sections—and as this is happening right in front of me, it seems twelve times more vivid. Or maybe twelve hundred times more so.

I hear V hiss and Jane murmur something.

Crap. I have to watch. I glance up. Jane's hands are very much solid, and she's stitching up her man with quick precision, like she's done this a million times. Vishous is staring at her, a dippy little smile on his face—

"It's not dippy," he cuts in. "I do not have a dippy little smile on my face."

Funny, now that he's in Jane's presence, he's softer all the way around. He's not exactly nice to me, but I don't wish I were wearing body armor anymore.

"It's kind of dippy," I say as Jane laughs. "But I mean, sure, it's dippy in a very I'm-a-warrior-vampire-I-eat-*lessers*-for-lunch sort of way. You're straight-up gang-sta. No one's going to mistake you for a lightweight."

"Wise of them," he says as he reaches up to Jane's hair with his glowing hand. It's kind of cool what happens. The instant the light of him hits any part of her she becomes solid, and the longer he touches her the greater the area becomes. If the two of them are cuddling on the couch—and yes, he does cuddle with her—she'll become wholly solid and stay that way for a time afterward. His energy pulls her form together.

Which is kind of romantic.

Out in the hall I hear a door open and shut and footsteps coming toward us all. I know it's Marissa because I can smell the ocean . . . and because I hear Butch start to growl with an erotic kind of welcome. Marissa pauses and pokes her head into V and Jane's room. Her hair is cut now so it's just down to her shoulder blades, and she's wearing a very nice black Chanel suit that I wish were in my closet.

The four of us talk a little, but then Butch gets impatient and calls out for his female, and Marissa smiles and leaves. She's taking off her jacket as she turns away. Probably because she knows her clothes aren't going to be on for long.

"There," Jane says as she snips the thread. "All better."

"I have something else that needs attention, true?"

"Oh, really? Would that be the graze on your shoulder?"

"Nope."

As V reaches for her hand, I clear my throat and make for the door. "Glad everyone's okay. Maybe we can reschedule the interview. Yeah . . . um, take care. I'll see you later. Have a good—"

I'm saying all these things because I'm feeling awkward. Like the intruder I am. Jane replies with some nice words as V starts to pull her down to him. I shut their door.

I walk down the hall and take a last look around the Pit's living room. Change is good, I think. And not just because in this case there is less Frat and more Home to this place now. I like the change that's happened, because those two guys are settled and happy and their lives are better because of who they ended up with. And Butch and Vishous are still together.

I step out into the September night and have to wrap my arms around myself. It's cold in Caldwell; I've forgotten how upstate New York gets cold so early. I find myself hoping my rental car has heated seats.

I'm getting behind the wheel when the front door to the mansion opens and Fritz comes rushing out. He's like Tattoo from *Fantasy Island,* holding my bag up while he runs, calling through the dark, "The purse! The purse!"

I get out of the sedan. "Thanks, Fritz, I would have forgotten."

The *doggen* bows low and says in a heartbroken tone, "I'm so sorry. So very sorry. I couldn't get the pen mark out."

I take my bag and look at the strap. Yup, the little blue streak is still there. "It's okay, Fritz. I really appreciate your trying. Thank you. Thank you very much."

After a little bit more soothing, and my declining the offer of a picnic basket of food, he goes back into the house. As I hear the door *thunch* shut, I stare down at my bag's defect.

The moment I first noticed the pen streak, I wanted to get a new purse. Totally. I kind of like things perfect, and I was so frustrated I'd messed up my own bag . . . its imperfection made it less in my eyes.

Now I measure the thing in the moonlight, looking at all its little dings and faults. Man . . . it's been with me for almost two years now. I've taken it to New York City to meet with my editors and my agent. On vacation to see my two best friends in Florida. It's been to signings with me in Atlanta and Chicago and Dallas. It's held my two cell phones: the one I use for my friends in the States and the one for my friends overseas. I've put in it receipts from car tows and bank deposits and dinners out with my husband and movies with my mother and my mother-in-law. It's held pictures of people I love and change I didn't want and the business cards of folks I needed to keep in touch with. It's been locked in my car during walks with my mentor and quick trips into shops for bottled water and . . .

I smile a little and toss the thing onto the front seat of the Toyota Prius I rented from Enterprise. I get in and close the door and reach for the key I'd left in the ignition.

A knock on the Prius's windshield scares the shit out of me, and I nearly dislocate my neck to look toward the sound. It's Vishous with a towel around his hips and a bandage on his shoulder. He points down like he wants me to disappear the window.

I do. A cold breeze comes in, and I hope it's just the night and not him.

V gets down on his haunches and puts his massive forearms on the side of the car. He's not making a lot of eye contact. Which gives me a chance to study the tattoos on his temple.

"She made you come out here, didn't she," I say. "To apologize for being a prick."

His silence means *yes*.

I run my hand up and over the wheel. "It's okay that you and I don't get along. I mean . . . you know. You shouldn't feel bad."

"I don't." There's a pause. "At least, not usually."

Which means he actually does feel bad.

Jeez. Now I don't know what to say.

Yeah, this is awkward. Very awkward. And frankly, I'm surprised he's staying out here with me and the car. I expect him to go back to the Pit and to the two people he feels comfortable with. See, V doesn't do relating. He's a thinker, not a feeler.

As time passes, I kind of decide that his presence with me now proves that yeah, in his own way, he really does care that it's been rough between the two of us. And he wants to make amends. So do I.

"Nice bag," he says, nodding to my purse.

I clear my throat. "It has pen on it."

"You can't really see the mark."

"I know it's there, though."

"Then you need to stop thinking so much. It's a really nice bag."

V bounces his fist against the car's panel, as a little good-bye kind of thing, and gets to his feet.

I watch him go into the Pit. Across his shoulders, cut into his skin, are the Old English letters: JANE.

I glance at my purse and think of everything it's held and everywhere it's been. And I start to see it for what it does for me, instead of what it lacks because of that imperfection.

I start the car and turn it around, being careful not to hit Rhage's purple GTO or that giant black Escalade or Phury's sleek M5 or Z's Carrera 4S. As I leave the compound's courtyard, I reach into my bag and take out my cell phone and call home. My husband doesn't pick up because he's asleep. The dog doesn't answer because he doesn't have opposable thumbs (so operating the handheld is difficult for him).

"Hi, Boat, I didn't get the interview, but I got something to write about, anyway. I'm wired, so I'm just going to drive until I get to the other side of Manhattan. Probably end up crashing in the middle of the day in Pennsylvania. Call me when you're up."

I tell my husband I love him; then I hang up. Phone goes back in my bag. I focus on the road ahead, thinking of the Brothers. . . .

There's nothing new in that. I'm always thinking about them. I start to get stressed about Phury.

On a whim, praying to get my head to shut up, I lean forward and turn on the stereo. I start to laugh. "Dream Weaver" is on.

Cranking the music as loud as the Prius can bear, I turn the heater on full bore, put the windows down, and floor the accelerator. The Prius does what it can. It's no GTO, but the effect for me is just as good. Suddenly I'm enjoying the night, just like Mary did when she needed to get away from herself.

Racing through the darkness, hugging the curves of Route 22, I am the bird that fly, fly, flies away. And I hope this stretch between Caldwell and real life lasts forever.

Question and Answer with J.R.

Q and A with the WARDEN

If you come to one of my signings, the Q and As are the best part. I get pelted with questions about the Brothers, the books, what's coming, what's happened, Boo, the coffins, whether the *shellans* have girls' night out, how in the hell Jane works. . . . The lawyer in me loves it, and man, the readers are SMART. They don't miss a thing, and I have mad respect for them. When it comes to stuff that has already occurred in the books, I'm straightforward with my responses. When it pertains to the future of the series, though, lawyer that I am, I am careful with my words. Undoubtedly the "leaf," as they say, slips and I'll reveal a secret or two. But most of the time I give a KEEEEEEEEEEP READDDDING, or I answer exactly what they asked—and not one word more.

They know when I'm being a little shifty.

For this insider's guide, I had to keep the Q and A tradition going, so I posted on my message board and my Yahoo! Group that I was looking for questions. I received over three thousand of them! After reading each one, I chose the following:

Have you ever had a character in the middle of the writing process commit mutiny and say, "Nope, we're not going to do it that way"? Who was it and how did you get them back on track?   —Jillian

I have to admit that when I saw this question I had to laugh a little—I WISH! Jillian, you give me far too much credit. As I said in the dossier section, the way it works with the Brothers is . . . I have no control over them. They do what they do in my head, and the job for me is just trying to faithfully record what I see. I don't know where they came from or why they picked me, but I know one thing for sure: If they leave, I got nothing. So I'm the one who needs to stay on track, not them, if that makes any sense!?

Where did your inspiration come from for the names of the Brothers? Most vampire romances I have read seem to borrow old-fashioned or elegant names, while yours are hard-hitting, to the point, and leave no room for confusion with regard to the types of males these are.   —Amber

The Brothers named themselves, actually—and I was a little confused at the beginning. When Wrath came into my head and I started outlining *Dark Lover*, I kept hearing him referred to by others as Roth. Roth? I thought. What kind of name is that? Roth . . . Roth . . .

The Brothers and their stories are always on my mind, but there are two situations in which they really take over: when I run and when I'm falling asleep at night. So there I was, pounding out the miles, staring at the ceiling in the dark . . . and this Roth name was banging around in my head, along with a hundred other things that happened in *Dark Lover*. . . . Suddenly, I realized I'd gotten it wrong. It wasn't Roth—it was *Wrath*. Wrath . . . As soon as I got it right, the rest of the Brothers' names fell into place, and so did the spellings.

The story behind the names, as I've said before, is that they are traditional names of the Brotherhood and can be given only to descendants of the Brother lines. Over time the names were bastardized in the English language and came to be associated with strong or aggressive emotions. I think they suit the Brothers perfectly because, as you say, they leave no room for confusion when it comes to what kind of males you're dealing with!

If you were given the opportunity to go back and rewrite any part of the books published of the Brothers, would you make any changes? Is there anything that was edited that you wish could be added back in? Is there a depth to one of the characters in the BDB that you wish you had explored more? Are there any regrets?   —Flowerlady

Well, I never think the books are as good as they should be. I always feel I could do a better job. But that's my personal makeup. I'm never satisfied with myself or anything I do—so that reaction isn't specific to the writing.

When it comes to editing the books, I am the only one who takes anything out of them or puts anything in them. My editor and I touch base and she'll give me her opinion and we'll discuss this and that, but nothing changes unless I want it to and unless I do it. Control freak much? Er . . . you bet! (Also a lifelong characteristic of mine.) Any regrets? Not on that front. Any choices I've made I've done deliberately and with a lot of forethought.

For the depth issue, I'd have to say no—but only because I try to wring every single ounce of emotion and drama and pathos out of each of the stories. But I do have a regret on this front. As I said, I wish I'd put another couple pages at the end of *Lover Unbound* so readers saw more of what was in my head with respect to V and Jane's happiness with how things worked for them.

I was wondering, where did you come up with some of your terms, like *leelan*, *hellren*, *shellan*? Are those terms you came up with? Or are they part of some ancient language you researched?   —Beth

Believe it or not, they just came with the stories—and still do. I'll hear one of the Brothers or the *shellans* say a word and I use it accordingly. I didn't expect, while I was writing *Dark Lover*, to end up with as many as I did! The glossary, by the way, was my editor's idea. After she read the final on Wrath, she was like, you know . . . you should do one. And she was right.

I was actually wondering how you keep your writing styles separate? I think I heard that you write under a pseudonym and I['ve] read a couple of other authors who do that as well. I guess I'm wondering how you make sure that your different characters don't cross into the wrong genre or are written by the "wrong" person?   —Rebekah

It's true, I write contemporary romance under Jessica Bird and urban paranormal romance under the Ward name. And you know, I've never had that crossover problem—probably because of the way the stories come to me in my head. The lines are just incredibly clear when the scenes hit, and the worlds are so completely different that confusing them is impossible. I will say that the voice when I draft on the page is not that dissimilar—although in the Brotherhood series the tempo is different and the writing more raw, because the Brothers are more raw.

I like writing in two vastly different veins. It refreshes me as I go from one to the other. The way I look at it, it's two separate tracks that never cross, and I can only follow one at a time. I'm really lucky that I get a chance to do both.

You mentioned some coffins in the garage. What are the coffins about, and who is in charge of taking care of them?   —Meryl

I love this question! It's something that I get asked a lot in one form or another. If it's not the coffins, people want to know what the deal with Boo is, or the deets on other things that are shown but not explained.

As I said, I don't always know what everything means when I see it. When it comes to the coffins, while I was writing *Lover Revealed*, I saw Marissa walk into the garage with Fritz . . . and there they were. I have absolutely no idea what's in them, where they came from, or what role they're going to play, but because it's happened before, I know that if I see something as clearly as I did them, it's going to be material. So really? I can't wait to find out what their deal is!

What is the significance of the *lessers'* jars? I know the heart is removed and placed into that ceramic jar, but why? Why isn't it just destroyed? Why do they keep it? Why do the Brothers always want to retrieve the jars and put them in the Tomb (if there is another reason other than just as trophies), and if it IS just for trophy value, why is it so important to the other *lessers* to go to the dead *lessers'* homes and pick up their jars before the Brothers do, and what do they do with them if they beat the Brothers to them?   —Murrrmaiyd

I'm glad you brought this up, Murrrmaiyd, as it's something I've wondered about myself. It has always struck me as odd that the *lessers* keep those jars after their induction ceremony—I mean, the Omega pretty much demands everything of them that is human, you know? Their blood is gone, their heart is taken out, they can't eat, they're impotent . . . so why keep something like that? And after they join the Society, they have no possessions of their own (they don't even retain their own names!). The only thing that seems logical to me is that the jars serve as a tangible reminder of the power of the Omega. After all, someone who can replace your blood with his, then take your heart out can come back and get your ass if he doesn't like the way you're behaving. Plus the Omega is subversive—he deliberately creates situations that burden his *lessers*. By forcing them to keep their heart with them, it gives him one more thing to punish them for if they don't do it. To this end, I think that the other slayers go after the jars because they know they're going to have to tell the Omega if one is lost—and that's a conversation that no one wants to have. As a side note, there is a central Society crypt that is used to store certain artifacts, but if a jar is recovered by another slayer before the Brothers get it, the heart is presented to the Omega. We won't go into what the Evil does with it. Ew.

In the history of the Brotherhood, has there ever been a Brother who has (for lack of a better word) gone rogue?   —Tee1025

If you mean left or been kicked out of the Brotherhood, as a matter of fact there has been: Muhrder. I don't know a ton about him at this point—but he's in the wings, so to speak. He gets mentioned in the books for the first time in *Lover Enshrined*, but he's had a space on my message board for nearly two years.

Each current Brother seems to have a loss of faculty/curse. Is this relevant to just this group or was it a common thing amongst the BDB (like a Scribe Virgin thing—give and take)?   —lacewing

As far as I'm aware, not all Brothers have had issues—though the current members of the Brotherhood certainly do: Wrath didn't want to lead because of his past. Rhage had (has) his beast. Zsadist was a sociopath. Butch didn't know where he fit in. Vishous had (has) his hand and his visions. Phury had his addiction. In the case of these "faults," each is part of the individual makeup of the Brother, often rooted in his past—so it's not a group curse or group burden, as it were—and Rhage's beast is the only one directly brought about by the Scribe Virgin. The others are happenstance.

Out of professional interest, I would love to know if the Brothers only get tattooed for reasons involving ritual. Or if they would get tattoos just for aesthetic reasons? —Cynclair

Hey, Cyn! The Brothers for the most part only have tattoos for specific reasons: Wrath has his on his forearms to represent his lineage; Rhage has his dragon on his back; Z unfortunately has his slave bands on his wrists and neck; Vishous has the warnings on his temple, hand, groin, and thighs. As for the other males, Rehv has his two red stars on his chest and his others, all of which are ritualistic. That being said, Qhuinn has his teardrop on his face, which is ritualistic, and the date on the back of his neck, which is not. I think you're going to see Qhuinn adding to his collection, and John and Blay getting their first ones—although I'll keep to myself whether they're ritualistic or not!

WARDen, it is understood that in the ceremonies there is a skull present, and this skull is the first original Brother. If I may ask . . . who is this Brother, and how did he become the first Brother? —Court2130

Okay, so this is a great question. I won't answer it—except to say that I know some of the details. Ideally, what I'd love to do someday is write the history of the Brotherhood—I'm not talking about time line stuff, but the stories of the early players. Maybe it's a series of Slices of Life or maybe a full novel—it would be very cool, though. From what I've seen, it was a tough life in the beginning. Picture what it would be like for the first vampire warrior to run into a *lesser*, or what happened during the first meeting of the Brotherhood, or what it was like to be a part of the breeding program. I think that's all fascinating stuff. So hopefully I'll get to do it at some point!

Oh, but I will say this . . . Wrath is a direct descendant of the first Brother!

How does one get nominated for the Brotherhood? What is the protocol? Has anyone ever declined? —Danielle

From what I've seen, it's exactly what happened to Butch. The Brothers who are currently members are the ones who make the decision. There is a sponsor, usually the guy closest to the candidate, who advances his name for consideration at a meeting in the Tomb. It's a blackball situation. If even one of the Brothers has a problem with the candidate, the guy's out—no questions asked, no chance for reconsideration, ever. The king, who has, since Wrath's great-grandfather, been a member of the Brotherhood, then takes the name of the nominee to the Scribe Virgin—so there are no surprises at the ceremony.

I have seen only one decline thus far. More on that at some point, hopefully. But, as Wrath says to Butch, you are only asked the once. Never again.

What is the background to the things in the museum case in the Chosen's Temple (e.g., the fan and cigarette holder)?   **—Lysander**

From what I've seen so far, it's a case of those objects having been left behind by visitors to previous Primales or having been taken by Chosen who have visited this side. A few (like the gun that was used to shoot V in the beginning of *LU*) were dropped in the process of that raid seventy-five years ago.

We know that Fritz is a whiz in the kitchen, but what does he consider his specialty?   **—Mary**

Lamb! He's been cooking it for generations of the royal family. And, wait, I can guess the next question! How did he end up with Darius, then? Ah, now, that's a story . . . but it's wonderful that he's back with Wrath (and that he's still with Darius in a way).

Of all the things to have your enemy smell like . . . why baby powder?   **—Haytrid**

LOL! Haytrid, I know, right? But when I saw the first *lesser* . . . that's what it smelled like. It's so incongruous—and strangely perfect.

Time Line
of the
Brotherhood

Black Dagger Brotherhood Time Line

from 1600 to present

1618	Darius is born
1641	Darius transitions
1643	Darius is sent to war camp
1644	Tohrment is born
	Darius leaves war camp
1665	Wrath is born
1669	Tohrment goes through transition and is promised to the firstborn female of the Princeps Relix
1671	Darius meets Tohrment; nine months later Tohrment is inducted into the Brotherhood
1690	Wrath goes through transition
1704	Vishous and Payne are born
1707	Vishous goes into war camp
1729	Vishous goes through transition and leaves camp (drifts, then functions as merchant heavy)
1739	Vishous meets Darius and Wrath
1778	Phury and Zsadist are born
	Zsadist is abducted
1780	Zsadist sold into slavery
1784	Wellesandra is born
1802	Phury and Zsadist transition
1809	Wellesandra goes through transition

1814	Tohrment and Wellsie are mated
1843	Rhage is born
1868	Rhage goes through transition
1898	Phury rescues Zsadist from the Mistress
	Rhage joins Brotherhood, kills owl and is cursed by Scribe Virgin with the beast
1917	Zsadist and Phury meet Wrath
1932	Phury on his deathbed—Z gets Darius, who contacts Wrath for last rites (Phury survives)
	Phury and Zsadist inducted into Brotherhood
1960	Butch O'Neal is born
1969	Jane Whitcomb is born
1975	Mary Madonna Luce is born
1980	Beth Randall is born
1983	John Matthew is born in bus station
2005	Wrath and Beth are mated
2006	Rhage and Mary are mated
	Zsadist and Bella are mated
	Wellesandra is killed
2007	Butch inducted into Brotherhood
	Butch and Marissa are mated
	Blay goes through transition
	Qhuinn goes through transition
	Lash goes through transition
	John Matthew goes through transition
	Vishous and Jane are mated
	Nalla is born

Table of
Abbreviations

ABBREVIATIONS/ACRONYMS USED IN THE BOOKS/ ON THE BOARDS

AARP	American Association of Retired Persons
BFD	Big Fucking Deal
BMOC	Big Man on Campus
BTW	By the Way
BVD	Men's full briefs that Wrath hates
DL	Down-low
FNG	Fucking New Guy
FUBAR	Fucked up Beyond All Recognition
FYI	For Your Information
GW	God Willing
HEA	Happily Ever After
IIRC	If I Recall Correctly
IMHO	In My Honest/Humble Opinion
IMO	In My Opinion
ITA	I Totally Agree
MFN	Motherfucking
MYOB	Mind Your Own Business
OD	Overdose

ABBREVIATIONS/ACRONYMS USED IN THE BOOKS/ ON THE BOARDS

OMG	Oh My God
OPP	Other Person's/People's Property
PNG	Persona Non Grata
POS	Piece of Shit
POV	Point of View
PTSD	Post-traumatic Stress Disorder
RTFM	Read the Freaking/Fucking Manual
SOL (1)	Slice of Life
SOL (2)	Shit outta Luck
SOP	Standard Operating Procedure
TBH	To Be Honest
TLC	Tender Loving Care
TO	Time-out
WASP	White Anglo-Saxon Protestant
WTF	What the Fuck

The Old Language

The Brothers
Interview J.R.

The Brotherhood's Interview

My husband and I are moving into a new house. Which is great. Actually, it's almost a hundred years old, but it's new to us and our dog. My mother and her business partner and their crew have been working on it for a couple of months, and they're just about finished. I figure we'll be settling in a few weeks from now—and going through that wonderful process of figuring out where in the hell to put everything.

It's about ten thirty at night and I'm pacing through the house, going from empty room to room, dodging spray machines and cans of paint and the occasional sawhorse. The place is heavily perfumed in *eau de latex* and I have to be careful not to brush against any of the walls because most of them are barely dry. There is plastic matting over all the wood floors, and the windowpanes are smeared with goo so their frames can be painted.

Being here all alone is creepy. Shadows are created, thanks to the streetlights down below, and every dark corner looks like a place someone could jump out at me from.

And then someone does.

I'm in the dining room when Wrath condenses out of thin air right in front of me. I yelp and pull a Chaplin, arms pinwheeling as I tap-dance backward. Rhage catches me from falling as Butch and V materialize behind the king. Z comes in last, sauntering in from the living room as if he's been there all along.

Rhage:	(to me) You okay there?
Butch:	We could lay her down on a pair of sawhorses.
J.R.:	Don't you guys knock—
V:	Oh, please.
Butch:	How about the kitchen countertop?
J.R.:	I'm fine!
Rhage:	There's carpeting on the third floor.
J.R.:	You mean you've been here already?
Butch:	No. Not at all. Us? Trespass? I vote for the third floor.
V:	Or we could hang her ass up in a closet.
J.R.:	Excuse me?
V:	(shrugging) Goal is to keep you from knocking your shit out from the vapors. Come on. Work with me.
J.R.:	I don't have the—
Butch:	Third floor.
Rhage:	Third floor.
J.R.:	(looking to Wrath for help) Really, I'm—
Wrath:	Third floor.

Chaos reigns during the trip up the stairs in the form of deep male voices arguing with one another. As far as I can tell, the topic is treatment for fainting, and I hope to Christ the remedies aren't inflicted on me. Somehow I don't think cold showers, stink bombs, old episodes of *Barney* (evidently the annoyance factor is supposed to be restorative), shots of Lagavulin (which would serve only to knock me out entirely), or laps around the neighborhood naked fall under the accepted standard of care for light-headed humans. Although the trip to Saks doesn't sound so bad.

The third floor of the new house is a big, open space—basically a finished attic. Total square feet is only a little less than the first apartment I had with my husband, and the Brothers reduce the place to the size of a doghouse. Their bodies are huge, and unless they're standing right in the middle of the room, which has a cathedral ceiling, they have to stoop to fit under the sloping roof.

Wrath is the first to sit down, and he picks the spot against the far wall that is the head of the room. The rest circle around. I end up doing an Indian-style across from the king. Z is to my right. They are all dressed as they would for a meal at the mansion: Wrath in a muscle shirt and leathers; Phury and Butch wearing elegantly tailored designer casuals; V and Zsadist in nylon sweats and tight T-shirts; Rhage in a black button-down and dark blue jeans.

Wrath: What the hell are we supposed to ask you?

J.R.:   Whatever you—

Rhage: I know! (takes cherry Tootsie Pop out of his pocket) Who do
           you like most? It's me, right. Come on, you know it is. (un-
           wraps the thing, pops it into mouth) Come onnnnnnn—

Butch: If it's you, I will kill myself.

V: No, that just means she's blind.

Butch: (shakes head in my direction) Poor dear.

Rhage: It has to be me.

V: She said she didn't like you at first.

Rhage: (making point with Tootsie Pop) Ah, but I won her over,
           which is more than anyone can say about you, hot stuff.

J.R.:   I don't like anyone best.

Wrath: Right answer.

Rhage: She's just sparing all of your feelings. (grins, becoming impos-
           sibly handsome) She's so polite.

J.R.:   (prayerfully) Next question?

Rhage: (wags eyebrows) Why do you like me best?

Wrath: Enough with the ego trip, Hollywood.

V: That's his personality. So it's a permanent vacation to la-la
           land, not a trip.

Butch: Which means it's actually a surprise he won't wear that Ha-
           waiian shirt Mary got him.

Rhage: (under breath) I'd burn that eyesore, but it's a lot of fun to take
           off her.

Phury: Amen to that.

Butch: You have a Hawaiian shirt? You're fucking kidding me.

Phury: No. But I like taking Cormia out of my clothes.

Butch: Respect. (pounds knuckles with Phury)

Wrath: Fine, I'll ask a question. (The Brothers all quiet down.)
           Why the hell do you still jump when I turn up in front of you?
           It's fucking annoying. Like I'm going to hurt you or some
           shit?

Rhage: She's afraid you've left me behind and she's not going to get to
           see me.

Wrath: Don't make me stab another wall.

Rhage: (grins again) At least her contractors are still around, and she
           could get it fixed easy enough. (Bites down on Tootsie Pop.)

Butch: Wait, I know the answer. She's afraid you're going to tell her
           V's got a brother she's going to have to write about.

V: Whatever, cop. I'm an only.

Butch: Lucky her, considering you almost killed her—

Z: I know why.

All heads, including mine, turn to Zsadist. As usual, when he's in a meeting, he's sitting perfectly still, but his yellow stare is shrewd as an animal's, tracking the people around him. Under the lights that are mounted along the ceiling, his scar is standing out with special depth.

Wrath: (to Z) So why does she jump?

Z: Because when you're around she's not quite sure where reality is. (glances at me) Isn't that right.

J.R.:   Yes.

At this moment, I recall that Z's had the same problem a number of times—and it must have shown in my eyes, because he looks away quickly.

Wrath: (nodding with a kind of huh-that-makes-sense) Okay, cool.

Butch: I got a question. (grows serious . . . then channels that ass from *Inside the Actors Studio*) If you were a tree, what kind would you be?

Rhage: (amid laughter from the Brothers) I know, a crab apple. She bears fruit, but she's cranky.

V: Nah, she'd be a telephone pole, not a tree. Trees have too much body.

Butch: (glaring at his roommate) Chill, V.

V: What? It's true.

J.R.:   I like the crab apple.

Rhage: (nodding at me with approval) I knew you'd agree with me over these steakheads.

Phury: How about a Dutch elm? They're long and willowy.

V: And a dead species. At least I only insulted her figure. You gave her a disease that's going to mottle her leaves.

J.R.:   Thank you, Phury, that's lovely.

Wrath: I vote for oak.

V: Please, that's a total arboreal projection. You're an oak and you assume everyone else is.

Wrath: Untrue. The rest of you asses are saplings.

Rhage: Personally, I'm a shaaaaaaaaaaaaaaaaaaaaaag bark hickory. For obvious reasons.

Butch: (laughs in Hollywood's direction, then turns to me) I think she's a Christmas tree. 'Cuz she's into the bling. (pounds my knuckles)

Wrath: Z? You got a tree?

Z: Poplar.

Rhage: Oh, I like those. Their leaves make a cool clapping sound when the wind goes through them.

Butch: Nice. I remember those from when I was a kid.

Phury: Those are friendly trees. Not snotty. I like that.

Wrath: Poplar is up for a vote. All in agreement say aye. (The Brothers all "aye.") Any dissent? (silence) Motion is carried. (looks at me) You are a poplar.

I'd like to point out that this is precisely how things go with the Brothers. They decide. I follow. And incidentally, the common, lowly poplar is probably one of my favorite trees of all time.

Wrath: Next question. Favorite color?

Rhage: (raises hand) I know! Rhaging red.

Butch: Rhaging . . . (Busts out laughing.) You are such an assaholic, you know that? A real assaholic.

Rhage: (nodding gravely) Thank you. I try to excel at everything I do.

V: We need to get him into Asses Anonymous.

Rhage: I'm not so sure about that . . . that Knitters Anonymous program didn't do jack shit for you.

V: That's because I don't knit!

Rhage: (reaches over and grabs Butch's shoulder) God, denial is sad, isn't it.

V: Listen—

Wrath: Black's my favorite color.

Phury: I'm not sure black's a color, my lord. Technically it's the sum of all colors, so—

Wrath: Black's a color. End of.

Butch: Phury, that ass-burning sensation you feel is because you just got booted with a royal decree.

Phury: (wincing) I believe you are right.

V: I like blue.

Rhage: Of course you do. It's the color of my eyes.

V: Or a good facial bruise.

Butch: I'm all about gold. At least when it comes to metals.

V: And it suits you.

Rhage: I like blue, because V does. I want to be just like him when I grow up.

V: Then you're going to need to go on a diet and stop wearing lifts.

Rhage: Bet you say that to all the girls you date. (Shakes head.) You make them shave, too, don't you?

V: Better than having to back them out of their stalls, like you do.

J.R.: I like black.

Wrath: Score! Now, next question—

V: How about making this more interesting.

Wrath: (cocks eyebrow up from behind his wraparounds) In what way?

V: (staring over at me) Truth or dare.

They all get quiet at this point, and I do not feel comfortable—although not because they are silent. I don't trust V to play nice—and going by the tension in the room, neither do the Brothers.

V: Well? What's it going to be?

If I go for truth, he's going to hit me with something that's either impossible to answer or way too revealing. If I go for dare . . . well, he can't kill me with whatever he makes me do. I'm pretty sure the others would make sure I live through it.

J.R.: Dare.

V: Fine. I dare you to answer my question.

Butch: (frowning) That's not the way it works.

V: It's truth or dare. I gave her the choice. She picked the dare.

Wrath: Technically, he's right. Although he's fucking around.

V: Oh, I'm quite serious, true?

J.R.: Okay, what's your question.

V: Why did you lie?

The question doesn't surprise me, and it's a private thing between him and me. And he already knows the answer, but he's asking it here to cause problems. Which it will.

Wrath: (cutting in before I respond) Next question. Favorite food?

Rhage: A Rhage and Butch sandwich.

J.R.: (turning beet red) Oh, no, I—

Rhage: What? Like you're going to want any V in there?

J.R.:   No, I don't think of you like—

Rhage: Look . . . (pats my knee, all that's-okay-dear) fantasies are good. They're healthy. It's why Butch's skin glows like it does and his right palm is hairy—he wants me, too. So, really, I'm used to it.

J.R.:   I don't—

Butch: (laughing) Rhage, buddy, I hate to slow your roll, but I so don't feel you like that.

Rhage: (wags brows) Now who needs a truth-or-dare?

V: You know, Hollywood, in the DSM-IV there's a picture of your ugly mug next to "Narcissistic Disorder."

Rhage: I know! I sat and posed for it. It was so sweet of them to call.

V: (barks out laughing) You are such a freak.

Wrath: Food, *challa*?

J.R.:   I'm not a big foodie.

V: You don't say.

Rhage: I like almost everything.

V: And again, you don't say.

Rhage: Except olives. I just . . . meh. Meh on the olives. Olive oil is fine to cook with, though.

V: What a relief. The whole country of Italy was worried about their national economy.

Butch: I don't like seafood.

Wrath: God, neither do I.

Phury: I can't stomach anything with fish in it.

Z: No way.

V: I don't even like the smell of the shit.

Rhage: Come to think of it . . . yeah, big meh on anything that had a fin on it or comes with a shell. Well, excluding nuts. I like nuts.

V: Go. Fig.

Butch: I love me a good steak.

Wrath: Lamb.

Phury: Lamb is fabulous.

Butch: Oh, yeah. With rosemary. Done on a grill. (rubs stomach) Anyone hungry?

Rhage: Yes, starved. (Everyone roles their eyes at this point.) Well, I'm a growing boy.

Butch: Which, considering how big your head already is—

V: Strains the bounds of credulity.

Rhage: I like all kinds of meat.

V: (laughs) Okay, I'm so not touching that.

Rhage: Which is kind of a surprise. (Grins.)

Wrath: Can we please get back on track? *Challa*? Food?

The truth is, I'm loath to say anything and am disappointed to have the focus on me again. I love just watching the Brothers take the piss out of one another. Really, this vibe right here is what my days are like. I am among them, but not with them, if that makes any sense, and I'm always fascinated, wondering what they're going to say and do next.

J.R.:   It depends.

Rhage: Okay, build your own sundae for us, then. What's on it? Oh . . . and don't be embarrassed. I know you're going to picture me serving it to you wearing nothing but a loincloth.

V: And your elf shoes. 'Cuz you're mad hot with your little bells on.

Rhage: See? You totally love me. (Turns back in my direction.) *Challa*?

J.R.:   I . . . er, I don't eat ice cream. I mean, I love it, but I can't eat it.

Rhage: (looks as if I have a horn growing out of my forehead) Why?

J.R.:   Teeth problems. Too cold.

Rhage: Oh, God. That sucks . . . I mean, I love me some coffee ice cream with hot fudge on it.

V: That's one thing I'll agree with you on. No whipped cream shit or cherries for me.

Rhage: Yup. I'm a purist as well.

Phury: I love a good raspberry sherbet. On a hot summer night.

Wrath: Rocky Road. (Shakes head.) Although I'm probably just thinking of life as king with that one.

Butch: Me? Ben & Jerry's Mint Chocolate Chunk.

Rhage: Okay, that's another good one. Anything they make with Oreos, also very good.

Z: We just tried Nalla out with some vanilla. (Laughs quietly.) Loved it.

At this point the Brothers . . . they actually "Awwwwwww." Then cover it up with a lot of scowling, as if they have to reestablish their masculinity.

Rhage: (looking at me) For real? Have you *seen* that kid? She's like . . . spank gorgeous.

V: Yeah, 'cuz that's the way you say, "My, that young is beautiful" in his language.

Rhage: Come on, V, you totally feel me on this one.

V: (ruefully) Yeah, I do. Man . . . my niece is the most perfect young on the planet. (Pounds knuckles with Rhage, then turns to Butch.) Isn't she?

Butch: Beyond perfect. Into a whole 'nother category. She's . . .

Wrath: Magic.

Phury: Total magic.

J.R.:   She's got you guys wrapped around her finger, doesn't she.

Rhage: Absolutely—

Phury: Totally—

Butch: Wrapped tighter—

V: Than a drum.

Wrath: Completely.

Z: (looking over at me and positively glowing with pride) See? For a bunch of violent, antisocial nut jobs, they're okay.

Wrath: Hey . . . did *Challa* ever answer the damn food question? (Resounding *no* echoes in the room.)

Butch: She passed on the ice cream. (glances at me) Why don't you build us a sandwich. You can use me, by the way, in any fashion. (grins) No probs with that.

Phury: (smoothing over Butch's comment) Or a meal. What kind of meal do you like?

J.R.:   I don't know. Well, anything my mother cooks. Roasted chicken. Lasagna—

Rhage: I love lasagna.

Phury: Me, too.

V: I like mine with sausage in it.

Rhage: Of course you do.

Wrath: (whistling through his teeth) Shut it, ladies. *Challa?*

J.R.:   Roasted chicken with corn-bread stuffing made by my mother.

Wrath: Excellent choice—and wise of you. I was getting ready to make them vote again.

Rhage: (leaning over conspiratorially) We wouldn't have given you fish, though. So you don't need to worry.

J.R.:   Thank you.

The Brothers keep talking, and I don't really get asked much more, which is fine. I'm struck as they banter by how much they care about one another. The razzing never cuts to the bone; even V, who's perfectly capable of cleaving someone in half verbally, sheathes his bladed tongue. As their voices bounce around the empty room, I close my eyes, thinking that I don't ever want them to go.

When I open my lids again, the Brothers are gone. I am alone in my new old house, sitting cross-legged, staring at the blank wall where seconds before I saw Wrath so very clearly. The silence is a stark, sad contrast.

I stand up and my legs are stiff as I go over to the stairs and put my hand on the rail. I have no idea how long I've been up here, and when I look back to where we all sat, I see nothing but a stretch of wall-to-wall carpet under a row of ceiling lights.

I turn off those lights as I go down the stairs, and I pause at the second-story landing. I still don't know where I'm going to write after we move in—which is causing agitation. There's a bedroom that has a great view, but it's small. . . .

I reach the first floor and turn off more lights, making a circle around all the rooms. Before I leave the dark house, I pause in the den and look through the foyer and the living room out to the sunporch—which is the other candidate for my writing place.

I'm staring across the way when a car makes the corner down below on the street. As its headlights flash up through the banks of windows on the porch, I see Zsadist standing on the tile. He points downward with his finger a couple of times.

Right. I will write out there. I lift my hand and nod my head, so he'll know the message has been received. With a flash of his yellow eyes he's gone . . . but I'm not feeling so alone, even though the house is empty.

The sunporch is going to be a great place to work, I think to myself as I walk out to my car. Just perfect.

In Memoriam

In Memoriam

What follows below is the last interview of Tohr and Wellsie together, which I conducted during the short time span between Lover Eternal *and* Lover Awakened. *I'm reproducing it below in Wellsie's memory and in memory of their unborn son.*

ecember in Caldwell, New York, is a hunker-down kind of time. The days get dark at four in the afternoon, the snow begins to pile up as if it's in training for January's onslaughts, and the cold seeps into the very foundations and load-bearing walls of the houses.

It is in days after Thanksgiving that I come into town for more interviews with the Brothers. As usual, Fritz picks me up in Albany and drives me around in circles for two hours before taking me to the Brotherhood's mansion. Tonight's trip is even longer, but not because he's obscuring the path more: To my discredit, I pick the first storm of the season to travel through. As the butler and I go along, the snow lashes against the Mercedes' front windshield, but the *doggen* isn't worried, and neither am I. For one thing, the car is built like a tank. For another, as stated by Fritz, Vishous has put chains on all four tires. We chow through the thickening blanket on the roads, the sole sedan out amidst municipal plows, trucks, and SUVs.

Eventually we pull into the Brotherhood's compound and come to a stop in front of the massive stone castle they live in. As I get out of the car, snowflakes tickle my nose and land on my eyelashes, and I love it, but I'm chilled instantly. This doesn't last long, though: Fritz and I go in through the vestibule together, and the outrageously beautiful foyer warms me just by its very sight. *Doggen* rush over to me as if I'm in danger of hypothermia, bringing slippers to replace my boots, tea for my belly, and a cashmere wrap. I'm stripped of my outdoor clothes like a child, wrapped up and Earl Grey'd and marched toward the stairs.

Wrath is waiting for me in his study. . . .

(edited out)

. . . At this point, I leave Wrath's study and head down to the foyer, where Fritz is waiting for me with my parka and my snow boots. Tohr is my next interview, and the butler is going to take me to the Brother's house, as evidently he's off rotation tonight.

I'm rebundled in my nor'easter clothes and get back in the Mercedes. The partition goes up, and Fritz and I chat using the intercom that links the front and the rear of the car. The trip is about twenty minutes, and man, the Merc holds steady in all the snow.

When we stop and stay that way, I figure we're at Tohr's and I unlatch my seat belt. Fritz opens my door and I see the low-slung modern house the Brother and Wellsie and John Matthew live in. The place looks incredibly welcoming in the snow. On its roof two chimneys are gently smoking, and in front of each of the windows pools of yellow light condense on top of the thick white ground cover. On their travels from cloud to earth, flakes hit these patches of illumination and are spotlit for a brief time before they join legions of their accumulated brethren.

Wellsie opens the back door, motions me in, and Fritz escorts me over. After bowing to Wellsie, he heads back to the Mercedes, and as the car turns around in the driveway, my hostess shuts the house's door against the wind.

J.R.: What a storm, huh?

Wellsie: God, yes. Here, off with the coat. Come on.

I'm unwrapped again, but this time I'm so distracted by the smell coming from the kitchen that I barely notice my parka disappearing.

J.R.: What is that? (inhaling) Mmm . . .

Wellsie: (hanging up my coat and dropping a pair of L.L. Bean moccasins at my feet) Boots, off.

J.R.: (kicking the boots free and putting my feet into—ahh, bliss— soft lamb's wool) It smells like ginger?

Wellsie:	You warm enough in just that sweater? You need another? No? All right. Just holler if you change your mind, though. (Heading into the kitchen and over to the stove.) This is for John.
J.R.:	(following) He's home? Were classes canceled tonight for the storm?
Wellsie:	(lifting lid off a pot) Yes, but he wouldn't have been able to go anyway. Let me finish this real quick and then we'll go get Tohr.
J.R.:	Is John okay?
Wellsie:	He will be. Have a seat. You want tea?
J.R.:	I'm fine, thank you.

The kitchen is all cherry and granite, with two gleaming ovens, a six-burner cooktop, and a Sub-Zero refrigerator done up to match the cabinets. Over in the windowed alcove there's a glass-and-iron table set, and I sit down in the chair closest to the stove.

Wellsie has her hair up tonight, and as she stirs the rice in the pot she looks like a supermodel in a magazine ad for luxury kitchens. Beneath the loose black turtleneck she wears her belly is a little bigger than when I saw her last, and her hand keeps going to it, rubbing slowly. She's glowing with health. Absolutely radiant.

Wellsie:	See, here's the thing with vampires. We don't get human viruses, but we have our own. And this time of year, as with human schools, the trainees trade off bugs. John came down with the aches and a sore throat last night and woke up with a fever this afternoon. Poor thing. (Shakes her head.) John is . . . a special kid. Truly special. And I love having him home with me—I just wish, tonight, it was for a different reason. (Looks up at me.) You know, it's so weird. I've been doing my own thing for a long time . . . you can't be mated to a Brother and not be really independent. But since John's started living here, the house is empty when he's not around. I can't wait to see him by the time he gets home from the training center.
J.R.:	I can understand that.
Wellsie:	(rubbing belly again) John says he's all excited for when the little one gets here—he wants to help out. I guess at the orphanage he was in, he liked to watch after the young.
J.R.:	You know, I have to say you look great.
Wellsie:	(rolls eyes) You're kind, but I'm, like, big as a house already. I have no idea what size I'm going to be right before the young

comes. Still . . . it's all good. The young is moving all the time, and I feel strong. My mother . . . she did well with her children. She had three, can you believe it? *Three.* And that was before modern medicine for my sister and my brother. So I think I'm going to be like her. My sister did just fine. (looks back down at the pot) This is what I remind Tohr of when he wakes up in the middle of the day. (turns off stove and gets serving spoon out of drawer) Let's hope John will eat this time. He's been off his food.

J.R.: Hey, what do you think of Rhage's getting mated?

Wellsie: (spooning rice into bowl) Oh, my God, I love Mary. I think it's great. The whole thing. Although Tohr was getting ready to kill Hollywood. Rhage . . . doesn't take direction well. Hell, none of them do. The Brothers . . . they're like six lions. You can't really herd them all that well. Tohr's job is to try to keep them together, but it's tough . . . especially with Zsadist being the way he is.

J.R.: Wrath said he's on a rampage.

Wellsie: (shaking head and going to refrigerator) Bella . . . I pray for her. I pray every day. You realize it's been six weeks now? Six weeks. (comes back with a plastic container that she puts into the microwave) I can't imagine what those *lessers* . . . (clears throat, then hits buttons, little beeping sounds rising up, followed by a whirring) Well, anyway. Tohr's not even trying to talk sense into Z. No one is. It's like . . . something snapped in him with that abduction. In a way—and I know this is going to come out wrong—I wish Z'd find her body. Otherwise there's no closure, and he'll be completely insane by New Year's. And more dangerous than he already is. (microwave stops and beeps)

J.R.: Do you think it's . . . I'm not sure what the word is . . . maybe astonishing that he cares as much as he does?

Wellsie: (pours ginger sauce on the rice, puts the container in the dishwasher, then takes out napkin and spoon) Totally astonishing. At first it gave me hope . . . you know, that he cared about someone, something. Now? I'm even more worried. I can't see this sitch ending well. At all. Come on, let's go to John's room.

I follow Wellsie out of the kitchen and through a long living room that is done in a great mix of modern architectural details and antique furniture and art. At the far end we head into the wing of bedrooms. John's is the last one before the master suite that anchors the left side of the house. As we get closer, I hear . . .

J.R.:   Is that—
Wellsie: Yup. Godzilla marathon. (pushes open door and says quietly) Hey. How are we doing?

John's bedroom is navy blue, and the bureau, headboard, and desk have a Frank Lloyd Wright feel to them, all sleek wood. In the electric glow of the television I see John in the bed on his side, his skin as pale as his white sheets, his cheeks flaming red from fever. His eyes are squeezed shut, and he's breathing through his open mouth with a slight wheeze. Tohr is right next to him, propped up against the headboard, the Brother's huge body making John look like a two-year-old. Tohr's arm is outstretched, and John is wrapped around it.

Tohr: (nodding at me and blowing a kiss to his *shellan*) Not good. I think the fever is higher. (As he says this, across the way on the TV, Godzilla lets out a roar and starts trampling buildings . . . kind of like what the virus is doing inside of John.)
Wellsie: (putting bowl down and leaning over Tohr) John?

John's eyes flutter open and he tries to sit up, but Wellsie puts her hands on his cheeks and murmurs to him to stay down. As she talks to John softly, Tohr leans forward and puts his head on her shoulder. He's exhausted, I realize, no doubt from staying up and worrying about John.

Looking at the three of them together, I am so happy for John, but also a little shaken. It's hard not to picture him in his decrepit studio apartment in that rat-infested building, sick and alone. The what-if's are just too disturbing. To keep my head from rattling, I focus on Tohr and Wellsie and the fact that they've made him part of a family now.

After a moment Wellsie sits down next to Tohr, who makes room for her by drawing up his legs. His free hand, the one John is not holding, goes to her belly.

Wellsie: (shaking her head) I'm calling Havers.
Tohr: Should we take him in?
Wellsie: That'll be up to the clinic.

Tohr: Range Rover's got the chains on. You pull the trigger, I'm behind the wheel.
Wellsie: (patting his leg, then standing up) Which is exactly why I mated you.

Wellsie leaves and I hang in the doorway, feeling useless. God, there were all kinds of questions I had to ask Tohr, but now none of them matter.

J.R.:   I should go.
Tohr: (rubbing his eyes) Yeah, probably. Sorry about all this.
J.R.:   Please . . . not at all. You have to take care of him.
Tohr: (looking down at John) Yes, we do.

Wellsie returns, and the verdict from the doctor is that John has to go in. Fritz is called to come pick me up, but it's going to take him time to get back, so I'm told how to lock the house after I leave. I follow as Tohr carries John in his arms down the hall, through the living room, and out to the kitchen. Instead of making the boy put on a jacket, John is wrapped in a duvet, and he has slippers on his feet that are like the L.L. Bean moccasins I've been lent—only smaller.

Wellsie gets into the back of the Range Rover, seat-belts herself in, and when Tohr settles John in her lap, she cradles the boy to her. As the door is shut, she looks up at me through the window's glass, her face and red hair obscured by the reflection of the wall of the garage behind me. Our eyes meet and she lifts up her hand. I lift up mine.

Tohr: (to me) You all right here? You know how to reach me.
J.R.:   Oh, I'm fine.
Tohr: Help yourself to anything in the fridge. Remotes for the TV in the den are right by my chair.
J.R.:   Okay. Drive safely, and let me know how he is?
Tohr: We will.

Tohr puts his huge palm on my shoulder for a brief moment before he gets behind the wheel, puts the SUV in reverse, and backs out into the storm. The chains rattle on the concrete floor of the garage until they reach the lip of the snow; then all I hear is the deep growl of the engine and the crunch of millions of tiny flakes compacting under the tires.

Tohr K-turns and heads out, triggering the garage door. As the panels trundle shut, I have a last image of the Range Rover, its taillights flaring red through the billowing snow.

I go back into the house. Shut the door behind me. Listen.

The silence is scary. Not because I think there's someone else in the house. But because the people who should be here are gone.

I go into the living room, sit down on one of the silk couches, and wait by the windows, as if maybe being able to see where Fritz is going to pull up will mean he comes a little faster. My parka's in my lap and my boots are back on.

It seems like years until the Mercedes turns into the drive. I get to my feet, go to the front door as instructed, and step out. As I pivot around to lock up, I look way down the hall, to the stove where Wellsie had been cooking about a half hour ago. The pot that had John's rice in it is where she left the thing, and so is the spoon she used.

I'm willing to bet that on a normal night, those things would never be left out like that. Wellsie keeps a tight ship.

I signal to Fritz that I need a sec; then I race back to the kitchen, clean the pot and the spoon, and put them to dry next to the sink because I don't know where they belong. This time when I go out the front door, I lock it behind me. After a quick test to make sure I did it right, I piff through the snow toward the sedan. Fritz comes around and holds my door open for me, and just before I slide into all that leather, I look at the house. The glow from the windows doesn't seem welcoming anymore . . . it strikes me now as if the light is plaintive. The house is waiting for them all to come back, so that its roof shelters more than just inanimate objects. Without its people? It's merely a museum full of artifacts.

I get into the back of the sedan, and the butler takes us out into the storm. He drives carefully, just as I know Tohr did.

Excerpt from Lover Avenged

From the # 1 *New York Times* bestselling author of the **BLACK DAGGER BROTHERHOOD** series comes a sneak preview of her hardcover debut

Lover Avenged

On sale May 2009

REHVENGE, AS A HALF-BREED SYMPHATH, is used to living in the shadows and hiding his true identity. As a club owner and a dealer on the black market, he's also used to handling the roughest nightwalkers around—including the members of the Black Dagger Brotherhood. He's kept his distance from the Brotherhood, since his dark secret could make things complicated on both sides—but now, as head of the vampire aristocracy, he's an ally that Wrath, the Blind King, desperately needs. Rehv's secret is about to get out, though, which will land him in the hands of his deadly enemies—and test the mettle of his female, turning her from a civilian into a vigilante. . . .

As bad ones went, her father's paranoia attack hadn't been that bad.

Ehlena was only a half hour late to work, dematerializing to the clinic as soon as she was able to calm herself enough to pull the travel trick off. By some miracle, the visiting nurse had been free and able to come early. Thank the Scribe Virgin.

Going through the various checkpoints to get down into the facility, Ehlena felt the weight of her bag in her hand. She'd been prepared to cancel her date and leave the change of clothes at home, but the visiting nurse had talked her out of it. The question the female had asked struck deep: *When was the last time you were out of this house for anything except work?*

Caregivers had to take care of themselves—and part of that was having a life outside of whatever illness had put them in their role. God knew, Ehlena told this to the family members of her chronically sick patients all the time, and the advice was both sound and practical.

At least when she gave it to others. Turned on herself, it felt selfish.

So she was waffling on the date. With her shift ending close to dawn, it wasn't as if she had time to go home and check on her father first. As it was, she and the male who'd asked her out would be lucky to get an hour in before the encroaching sunlight put an end to things.

She had no idea what to do. Conscience was pulling her one way, loneliness another.

After she went through the last security checkpoint, she walked into the reception area and beelined for the nursing supervisor, who was at a computer by the registration desk. "I'm so sorry I'm late—"

Catya dropped whatever she was doing and reached out. "How is he?"

For a split second, all Ehlena could do was blink. On some level, she hated that they all knew about her father's problems, that a few had even seen him at his worst. Though the illness had stripped him of his pride, she still had some on his behalf. "He's calmed down, and his nurse is with him now. Fortunately I'd just given him his meds when it hit."

"Do you need a minute?"

"Nope. Where are we?"

Catya smiled in a sad fashion, like she was biting her tongue. Again. "You don't have to be this strong."

"Yes. I do." Ehlena gave the female's hand a squeeze in hopes of closing down the conversation. "Where do you need me?"

By this time several of the other nurses were coming over and expressing sympathy. Ehlena's throat closed up, not because she was overcome with gratitude that they were thoughtful, but because she got claustrophobic. Compassion choked her like a dog chain even on a good evening. After a start like she'd had tonight? She wanted to bolt.

"I'm fine, everyone, thanks—"

"Okay, *he's* back in the room," the last nurse to arrive said. "Should I get out a quarter?"

Everybody groaned. There was only one *he* out of the legions of male patients they treated, and flipping a quarter was how the staff decided who had to deal with *him*. Furthest from the date lost.

Generally speaking, all of the nurses kept a professional distance from their patients. You had to, or you'd burn out. With some, though, you couldn't help but get emotionally involved. With *him*, you stayed separate for reasons other than professional ones. There was just something about the male that made them all nervous, an underlying threat that was as hard to diagnose as it was evident.

Ehlena cut through the various years being chosen for the toss. "I'll do it. It'll make up for my being late."

"Are you sure?" someone asked. "Seems like you've already paid your dues tonight."

"Just let me get some coffee. What room?"

"I parked him in three," the nurse said.

Amid a chorus of *atta girls*, Ehlena went to the nurses' locker room, put her things in her locker, and poured herself a mug of hot, steaming perk-your-ass-up. The coffee was strong enough to be considered an accelerant and did the job nicely, wiping her mental state clean.

Well, mostly clean.

As she sipped, she glanced around the staff area. The banks of buff-colored lockers had names over them, and there were pairs of street shoes here and there under pine benches. In the lunch area, folks had their favorite mugs on the counter and snacks on the shelves, and sitting on the round table there was a bowl full of . . . what was it tonight? Little packs of Skittles. Above the table was a bulletin board covered with flyers for events and coupons and stupid comic-strip jokes and pictures of hot guys. The shift roster was next to it, the white board marked with a grid of the next two weeks, which was filled in with names.

It was the detritus of normal life, none of which seemed significant in the slightest until you thought about all those folks on the planet who couldn't keep jobs or enjoy an independent existence or have the mental energy to spare on little distractions. Looking at it all, she was reminded yet again that going out into the real world was a privilege, not a right, and it bothered her to think of her father holed up in that shitty little house, wrestling with demons that existed only in his mind. He'd once had a life, a big life. Now he had delusions that tortured him, and though they were only perception, never reality, the voices were completely terrifying nonetheless.

As Ehlena rinsed out her mug, she couldn't help thinking of the unfairness of it all.

Before she left the locker room, she did a quick check in the full-length mirror next to the door. Her white uniform was perfectly pressed and clean as sterile gauze. Her stockings were without runs. Her crepe-soled shoes were smudge- and scuff-free.

Her hair was as frazzled as she felt.

She did a quick pull-free, retwist, and scrunchie-again, then headed out for exam room three.

The patient's chart was in the clear plastic holder mounted on the wall by the door, and she took a deep breath as she picked it out of its nest. The thing was curiously thin, considering how often they saw the male. His last visit had been . . . only two weeks ago.

After she knocked, she walked into the room with confidence she didn't feel, her head up, her spine straight, her unease camo'd by a combo of posture and purpose.

"How are you this evening?" she said as she forced herself to look the patient in the eye.

The instant his amethyst stare met hers, she had no idea what had come out of her mouth.

Rehvenge son of Dragor sucked the thought right out of her head until nothing mattered except for those flashing purple eyes of his.

He was a cobra, this male, mesmerizing because he was deadly and because he was beautiful. With his cropped dark mohawk and his hard, smart face and his huge body, he was sex and power and unpredictability all wrapped up in . . . well, a black pinstriped suit that clearly had been made for him.

"I'm tight, thank you," he said, his voice much deeper than the average male's. Much deeper than most oceans, it seemed. "And you?"

He smiled a little, because he was fully aware that none of the nurses liked being in the same enclosed space with him, and evidently he enjoyed the fact that he made them all uncomfortable.

At least that was how she read his expression.

She put his chart down on the desk and took her stethoscope out of her pocket. "I'm very well."

"You sure about that?"

"Yes." She turned toward him. "I'm going to take your blood pressure and your heart rate."

"My temperature, too."

"Yes."

"Do you want me to open my mouth now?"

Ehlena's skin flushed, and she told herself it was not because that drawl of his made the question sexual. "Er— No."

"Pity."

Rehvenge's shoulders rolled as he removed his suit jacket, and, with a lazy flick of the hand, he tossed the thing onto the sable coat that was carefully draped over a chair. He always had a coat like that with him no matter the season. Usually he wore them, but not always.

They were worth more than the house Ehlena rented. Apiece.

His long fingers went to the diamond cufflink on his right wrist.

"Could you please do that on the other side?" She nodded toward the wall she would have to squeeze against. "More space for me on your left."

He hesitated, then went to work on his opposite sleeve. Rolling the black silk up past his elbow and onto his thick bicep, he kept his arm turned in.

Ehlena took the blood pressure equipment from a drawer and ripped it open as she approached him. Touching him was always an experience, and she rubbed her hand on her hip to get ready.

When she clasped his wrist, the current that licked up her arm landed in her heart, making her think of that coffee she'd just downed. It was as if the male carried an electrical charge in his body, and considering that those eyes of his alone were enough to distract the hell out of her, the voltage routine didn't help.

Damn it, where was her usual detachment. . . . Even with him, she was typically able to keep straight and do her job.

Kicking herself into professional gear, she moved his arm into position, brought the cuff up and— "Good . . . Lord."

The veins running through the crook of his elbow were decimated from overuse, swollen, black and blue, as ragged as if he'd been using nails, not tiny needles, on himself.

Her eyes shot to his. "You must be in such pain."

"Doesn't bother me."

Tough guy. Like she was surprised? "Well, I can understand why you wanted to come in tonight." She gently prodded at a red line that was traveling up his arm, heading in the direction of his heart. "There are signs of infection."

"I'll be fine."

All she could do was raise her eyebrows. Given how calm he was, clearly he was clueless as to the implications of sepsis.

Death would not look good on him, she thought for no particular reason.

Elhena shook her head. "Let's take your reading on the other arm. And I'm going to have to ask you to take your shirt off. The doctor's going to want to see how far up your arm that infection goes."

His mouth lifted in a smile as he reached for his top button. "My pleasure."

Ehlena looked away fast.

"I'm not shy," he said in that low voice of his. "You can watch if you like."

"No, thank you."

"Pity." In a darker tone, he added, "I wouldn't mind you watching."

As the sound of silk moving against flesh rose up from the exam table, Ehlena made busywork going through his chart, double-checking things that were absolutely correct.

From what she'd heard, he didn't do this stuff with the other nurses. He barely talked to her colleagues, and that was part of the reason they were nervous around him. Her, though? He talked too much and always about things that made her think . . . very unprofessional thoughts.

"I'm ready," he said.

Ehlena turned around and kept her eyes pinned on the wall next to his head. His chest was magnificent, a warm golden brown, the muscles defined even though his body was relaxed. Each of his pecs had a five-pointed red star tattooed on it, and she knew he had more ink. Because there had been a couple of occasions when she'd looked.

Stared was more like it.

"Are you going to examine my arm?" he said softly.

"No, that's for the doctor." She waited for him to say, "Pity," again.

"I think I've used that word enough around you," he murmured dryly.

Now her eyes shifted to his. It was the rare vampire who could read his own species' minds, but somehow it didn't surprise her that he was among that small group.

"Don't be rude," she said.

"Sorry." But he wasn't, given the way his lip curled up on one side.

God, his fangs were sharp. Nice and white, too.

Ehlena slipped the cuff around his bicep, plugged her stethoscope into her ears, and took his blood pressure, the little piff-piff-piff of the balloon followed by a long, slow hiss.

The patient was staring at her. He always stared at her.

Ehlena took a step back from him.

"Don't be frightened of me," he whispered.

"I'm not."

"Liar."

This was the nurse he liked, the one Rehv hoped he would get each time he came in. He didn't know her name, so in his mind he called her *luhls* because she was lovely all the way around, serious and pretty, smart.

With a good deal of "fuck off" radiating out of her. And how hot was that.

In response to his "liar," her toffee-colored eyes narrowed and she opened her mouth like she was going to snap his chain. But then she gathered herself, her professional veneer returning.

Pity, indeed.

"One sixty-eight over ninety-five. That's high." She ripped the cuff's lip free with a quick jerk, no doubt wishing it were a strip of his flesh. "I think your body's trying to fight off the infection in your arm."

Oh, his body was fighting something off all right—but it had fuck-all to do with whatever was cooking in his injection sites. With his *symphath* side overpowering the dopamine, the impotent state in which he usually existed had been knocked right out of the park.

His cock was stiff as a bat in his slacks.

Shit, maybe it would have been better to have another nurse in here. It was hard enough to be around her when he was "normal."

Tonight he was anything but.

Also Available from J.R. Ward

The Black Dagger Brotherhood Series

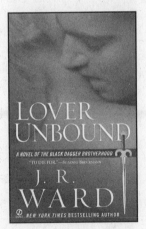
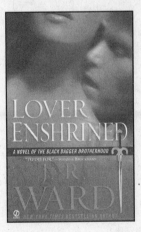

"The hottest collection of studs in romance."
—Angela Knight, *USA Today* bestseller

"Tautly written, wickedly sexy, and just plain fun."
—Lisa Gardner, *New York Times* bestselling author

"To die for." —*Publishers Weekly*

jrward.com   penguin.com

Signet
A member of Penguin Group (USA)